the
RAVEN'S
BRIDE

the RAVEN'S BRIDE

ELIZABETH CROOK

Doubleday

New York · London · Toronto · Sydney · Auckland

PUBLISHED BY DOUBLEDAY
*a division of Bantam Doubleday Dell Publishing
Group, Inc.
666 Fifth Avenue, New York, New York 10103*

DOUBLEDAY *and the portrayal of an anchor
with a dolphin are trademarks of Doubleday,
a division of Bantam Doubleday Dell
Publishing Group, Inc.*

Book design by Guenet Abraham

Library of Congress Cataloging-in-Publication Data

Crook, Elizabeth, 1959–
The raven's bride / Elizabeth Crook. — 1st ed.
p.   cm.
I. Title.
PS3553.R545R38   1991
813'.54—dc20   90-44222
CIP

ISBN 0-385-41775-6

Printed in the United States of America

February 1991

3   5   7   9   10   8   6   4

For my mother and my father

There is a dreadfull stir . . . about our governer
he was married two months ago and is now parted
from his wife there is a thouseand diferent tails a
float he has resined, and poor fellow is miserable
anough. I never can believe he has acted ungentle-
manly . . . he was a man so popular I know it
must be some thing dreadfull or he never would
have left her.

—citizen of Tennessee, 1829

It is stated that my treatment induced her to return to her Father's house for protection. This is
utterly false. . . . I never was unkind to her, & I
refer to her to bear witness. I have sacrificed everything that was Glorious.

—Sam Houston

I have this moment heard a rumor of poor Houston's disgrace. My God, is the man *mad.*

—President Andrew Jackson

She was cold to me, and I thought did not love me.

—Sam Houston

A biographical novel is a hybrid creature of fact
and fabrication, in which authenticity becomes
a dubious virtue. At every juncture the author
must choose between adhering to the most
probable story and altering slightly to tell a better one. That dilemma was muted in the case of
The Raven's Bride, because there is not a single
most probable story. What transpired between
Sam Houston and Eliza Allen is, emphatically, a
mystery. "I am sorry for him," the Reverend
Mr. Hume wrote of Houston after the governor's resignation and departure for Indian territory, "and more sorry for the young lady he has
left. . . . I know nothing that can be relied
upon as true. Tales in abundance . . . but
which of the two is the blame I know not."
They nurtured their secret.

Therefore, not only did I attribute motive
to my characters' actions, I also contrived many
of those actions and, to some extent, forged the
characters. Sam Houston is portrayed as I know
him from his own copious writings, with his egotism and eccentricities, his great wit, and his
fears. Andrew Jackson is also a personality of his
own making.

But Eliza left no such record of herself; the
only clues into her nature are mere scraps—a
few statements made about her, long after her
separation from Sam Houston, touching mostly
on her demeanor and appearance, and a few
words attributed to her on the subject of her

marriage to Houston. Most of what has been written about her is speculation, and none of it is very enlightening. The composite provides only a glimpse of a private woman whose one abiding expression of desire was that she did not want her story told.

I honor that woman, but I disclaim her. The woman in these pages is not that Eliza—is perhaps not even a semblance of that Eliza—but is a character in her own right. This Eliza is my own creation. Her place in family and the statistics of her life are derived from the historical Eliza Allen, but the personalities within her family and the emotional chaos embedded in their relationships are fictional. Perhaps her father was not fascinated with power, nor adept at mental manipulation. Perhaps her mother was not weak in spirit. Perhaps Eliza herself was not a woman of remarkable intelligence or intensity, though the record suggests she was. An inventory from John Allen's estate and other documents give insight into the family's public lifestyle, but no sources reveal their private lives.

Will Tyree, also, is largely an invented personality. Yet he did exist, and fable names him as Eliza's lover—if in fact she had a lover. That, also, can be questioned.

I do not claim to have written the true account of Sam Houston and Eliza Allen, but I believe I have come close to the truth. Still, there is no touchstone for validation; therefore, as a historian I am uneasy with my characters and their maneuverings. But as a novelist I am devoted to them, which is redemption enough, for this narrative is, in every respect, a novel. I ask the reader to accept it as such, with an integrity of its own, separate from the historical antecedent.

Elizabeth Crook
Austin, Texas, 1990

the
RAVEN'S
BRIDE

CHAPTER

I

April 1824

If the chestnut mare won, this was the place to be standing. Congressman Houston was adept at drawing attention to himself; he could easily create his own audience, but on this occasion it was more practical to make use of John Allen's. Allen owned the chestnut mare, and she was firmly in the lead. Houston did not particularly like the tidy man, whose eyes in constant motion under heavy lids betrayed an uneasiness at odds with his demeanor of singular indifference. He did not know him well, and did not wish to. But this was the place to be standing.

The congressman had just arrived at the Gallatin track, though it was late in the afternoon. He was not an avid gambler, and had come simply to make an appearance—a memorable one, as always. His peculiar attire displayed a perversity which constituents found either annoying or endearing: a calico Indian hunting-shirt and a woven belt with tassels hanging to his knees where his trousers were tucked inside cowhide boots. A traveling hat shadowed his high, heavy brow and broad nose, but the sun was sloping low enough to light the cleft of his chin and shine full on the colored beads he wore around his neck.

At once he had seen that Colonel John Allen's chestnut was leading, had tied his mount at the rails and sought Allen out. The colonel was standing apart from the crowd, at the gate to the track, one delicate hand resting on the top plank of the fence. "She's going to take it, Congressman," he said placidly. Hearing was difficult over the shouting crowd, and Houston bent his head closer. "I've wagered a bundle on her," Allen added.

The mare was in perfect form and increasing her lead with every stride. A black jockey leaned low against her; behind, other horses struggled for space on the crowded track, their riders flogging them. Houston admired her speed; he knew her strength. He had heard romantic horsemen speak of such movement as "effortless," as if that were the beauty of it. For him, it was the effort that was beautiful—and the power.

She passed in an instant of dust and pounding hooves, and then stumbled, and went down. The jockey was tossed forward and lay facedown, shielding his head with his arms as the other horses came on. As dust settled the mare rose up out of it, fell back again, lifted onto her knees and pulled herself forward, the jockey lunging after her with a cry. Houston witnessed her labor with a squint of his eyes. Both of her forelegs were broken. He had seen too many animals wounded in battle to grieve for this single, frenzied mare, but her forbearance gripped him. She crawled, her hind legs pushing her body forward, her head thrown back and groaning up through dust into a blue sky.

John Allen stood watching but did not move; he tightened his hold on the fence plank. A woman cried out for someone to shoot the mare. Balie Peyton raised the smoothbore pistol which had fired off the race and cursed that he had only blanks. He called out for pistol balls and yelled for someone to stop the horse; the jockey was having no effect. She sank again, lifted herself and crawled forward, the reins dragging.

And then there was the girl. She came from behind Sam Houston; he heard her panic before he saw her; she cried, "Papa, stop her. *Stop* her—" and Sam Houston turned to see a girl—a woman, possibly—with the face of a frightened child, pleading with her father. A yellow braid hung over one shoulder; in a wild and frantic gesture she tossed it back and appealed to the colonel with her eyes, the sunlight full on her face. John Allen stood looking at her and said, in his detached fashion, "Eliza, calm yourself." Turning casually to the spectators behind him, he added, "Will someone please kill the mare."

But Eliza did not wait; she pushed open the gate and ran onto the track toward the struggling horse. The jockey had hold of the reins but could not gain control. Eliza reached her and stopped. Sam Houston, following, saw the girl's anguish, her hands knotted together at her chest, her childish body bent slightly forward in a dress of blue domestic. He saw her speak to the jockey, then reach for the reins and take them. As the mare lurched forward, Eliza moved with her, repeating her name, "Chessy," pulling back in an attempt to bring her down. Houston approached, wrapped one arm around the animal's neck, and stroked her once.

"Miss Allen," he said in a voice solid and clear despite his effort to restrain the mare, "please leave."

She looked at him, and at the gun he held. Her expression lost its urgency; she reached for the gun. Astonished, he pulled it from her reach. She said, "Then shoot her now. Please shoot her now." Her eyes held him; for a lifetime he would wonder at the intensity of that moment, looking into this child's gaze and firing a ball into the animal's head. The complicity shocked him. The mare fell and lay sprawled, grotesque and unnatural, one broken foreleg splayed outward, her neck twisted against the earth in such a way that blood coursed from the wound into her open eyes and over the whiskers of her chin. Her bottom lip spilled its foam into the dirt.

A quiet settled. No one spoke; no one approached. The jockey crouched over the animal and embraced her, a wail like a child's cry pressing from his lungs. Balie Peyton fired a warning blank, and the other riders reined their mounts three quarters around the track. Houston turned his face toward the fields, then back to Eliza, the pistol hanging downward from his hand. She was staring at the mare. He wanted to comfort her, but sensed a resistance and composure that stopped him. She glanced once around the track, a lopsided circle of loose dirt like a wounded beetle would make on a dry summer day; then turned and made her way to the stable.

She knew the races would resume after Chessy's body was dragged away. Doren, her father's second most prized, was to race next, but they had not yet come to get him. No one was in the stable. Smells of leather and damp hay were a familiar solace. Thin lines of late sun pressed through cracks between the boards, and spots of light shone down from holes in the rusted tin roof. The spring wind whistled outside. She wanted to cry, but had learned the futility of it. She needed to make some statement of her grief. Taking a bit from Doren's rack, Eliza went to him, easing up to slip it in. He pulled back and shifted his eyes to the doorway; the girl turned to see someone entering and recognized him as the man who had shot her mare.

He was large, wearing Indian garb, and stooped to enter, his form blocking the light. He walked the length of the stable toward Doren's stall, his boots quiet on the dirt, then passed, not looking to either side. In the back doorway he stopped, resting one hand against the frame, his face in sunlight, his body casting a long shadow inward. He took off his hat; his auburn hair, thin at his temples but cut long over his ears, lifted in the air blowing from the mountains. Then he turned and set his eyes directly on her. He had known she was watching him. He had followed her there. "Are you all right?" he asked, his voice hushed and forceful like a rumble of thunder far off across the Cumberland Mountains, a voice that could make quite a storm. "That was not a pretty sight," he added, nodding in the direction of the track, "not for anyone." He paused, then asked again, "Are you all right?"

"I should have done it myself," she said. "She's my horse."

"If you mean you should have shot her, I couldn't allow that. I'm sorry."

His patronizing offended her. "That track was too crowded," she said, as if the fault were his.

Doren pawed fretfully and Houston remarked, "That's a beautiful animal," and then, seeing the bit in his mouth, "Does he race next?"

"Not today."

"No?" With a downward smile, knowing, he added, "Ah, you're taking him out of the race." He paused. "And what will your father say?"

Papa. Always Papa. It was he who had insisted Chessy was ready for the track, though her knee was still swollen from an earlier stumble on a practice run. Picking a tangle from Doren's mane, the girl asked, "Do you know my father?"

"I have met him. I'm a friend of your Uncle Robert—Sam Houston."

She lifted her eyes. He still had a slight smile, as if he had expected the name to affect her. Congressman Sam Houston, General Andrew Jackson's protégé. Her father often spoke of him. She had felt his authority even before she heard the name, and was inclined to resist it. "My father will be angry." She shrugged as if she did not care. "He has a lot of money on this race. And it doesn't matter."

"He might say different."

She declined to answer, wanting him to leave.

His voice hardened. "Miss Allen, may I make a suggestion? I think you should reconsider. What you saw happen out there is not a common thing—you know that. It isn't likely to happen again today."

His logic, in the face of her loss, was worse than ineffectual; it was offensive and seemed a sanction of the wrong done. "Did it move you?" she asked in a manner he could not read.

He had indeed been moved, less by the incident than by this

girl. His interest in her seemed to him inappropriate: she was a child. He addressed her as such. "I've seen worse."

In answer she led Doren from his stall into the sunlit aisle and began saddling him for the ride home. Her movements were orderly and gentle, performing, Houston thought, a lovely act of defiance. The only saddle available was the jockey's. She took it from the rack, and before she could object, Sam Houston took it from her and slung it onto Doren's back. The horse lunged forward, and Houston reined him in. Tightening the girth, he said, "You're acting hastily. This horse wants to race. It was a sad thing that happened out there, but it shows the commitment these animals have." The mare's blood was on his shirt, a small spattering against his heart. Looking at it, Eliza felt that his kind of thinking was to blame for it all, was in some way responsible for the brutalities.

"Commitment?" she said. "It was instinct, that's all."

Placing one elbow on the jockey saddle, he flexed his hand into a fist and rested his chin on it, looking at Eliza: her smallness, the tilt of her face, the gray eyes meeting his. Idly he stooped and ran his hands down one of Doren's forelegs from body to hoof, his fingers probing, moving downward in search of tender places, seeming, to Eliza, to mold flesh and bone as they moved over and down. "You're acting hastily," he said again, cutting his eyes at her. "I understand why you're upset: it's ugly, a fine animal going down. But these horses are born to race. It's in their blood. You're doing him a disservice by taking him out. You're cheating him." He lifted and looked at her.

"I'm taking him home," she answered flatly.

"I see."

Tossing the reins over the horse's neck, she led him through the doorway into the wind.

Sam Houston followed and said, "You can't ride that animal sidesaddle." She looked back at him. He stood with his arms crossed at his chest. "It's too dangerous, with that saddle."

She did not intend to. She could ride straddle as well as any jockey; she herself had trained Chessy for the track, often riding with no saddle at all. With ease she mounted Doren. He pitched his head, grinding the bit in his teeth.

"That horse wants to race," Sam Houston repeated. "Be careful." Then suddenly he laughed, throwing his face up toward the sunlight.

Leaning forward, Eliza pressed her knees into the horse's ribs.

She took the short way home, more path than road, narrow between dogwood trees and larkspur and honeysuckle in fresh bud. She tried to fill her senses with spring and shut out the tortured mare and the congressman, laughing, pictures that mingled into one image—that of obstinancy—taking what happens and laughing in the face of it, struggling on against odds.

At the end of the path the woods opened into fields. The sun was red and low but not yet touching the horizon. Ahead was a grove of poplar trees beside the main road, and beyond them the stables and servants' cabins and the frame house on the river bend. She knew the field hands were sowing wheat in fields over the rise, out of sight. There was no one on the road. The only life visible was in the horse paddock and the far pasture stretching beyond the grain barn, where sheep grazed, yet the landscape was alive with sound, the fracas of birds and the wind passing through.

Doren fought against the bit and sidestepped, trying to break free. Feeling his muscles tighten, Eliza allowed him to sprint from the trees into the open, pushing forward with full force, scattering yellow field larks from the grass sprouts. His speed seduced her, made her careless and forgetful of the mare, the bullet wound, oblivious to all but the sun and pounding stride and the slap of the braid against her back. She leaned into his neck, loving his strength and rhythmic movement, and tried to rein him more directly toward the road. But she had no effect; he was heading for the stables. Needing to control him, she lifted, pulling back, but the effort was futile. Before her was the poplar grove against the evening sun, and she braced herself, thinking he would charge through the trees or veer suddenly around them, perhaps in an attempt to be rid of her. But when he reached them he stopped without warning, of his own accord, throwing her forward into his neck. Shaken, she dismounted and stood gripping the reins as he tossed his head and sucked in air. His mouth was bleeding. He had mocked her. She had thought herself equal to his power and found she was only a victim of it, carried along as far as it would take her and then spurned. A mare would not have done it, she thought. A mare would not have done it in that way. She glanced toward the house, the servants' log quarters, the hill before the wheat and corn fields, hoping no one had seen. As if carried on the wind, she heard the congressman's voice: "That horse wants to race."

The poplar leaves rustled derisively in the April air.

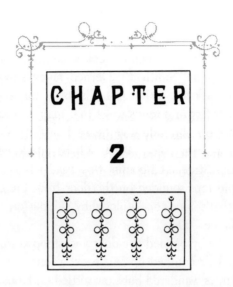

CHAPTER

2

September 1826

"**C**ocky son of a bitch, ain't he, Sam?"

"Damn it, Jack, get back from that door."

"Never lost a duel, they say, and he's fought seven of 'em. Myself, I wouldn't mess with him."

Houston declined to answer. He was sitting on the edge of the bed in a third-story room at the Nashville Inn, his legs stretched out to the floor and crossed at the ankles, his hands busy whittling a dog the size of his thumb from a chunk of ash wood.

Colonel Jack McGregor stood in a rectangle of morning sunlight that stretched across the pegs of the oak flooring from the balcony doors that opened over the public square. He was a spare, peppery man.

"He's crazy, Sam. I hear after he kills a man he walks up to see if he shot him through the eye. He wears a coat of mail, too, and goes around aggravatin' men just to make 'em draw, and if they do he slices their throat. He's crazy. Look what the cockeyed bastard calls himself: 'Colonel Smith T.' Derned fancy name for a hired gunfighter if you ask me. What in hell's the *T* for, anyway? I'd bet my bottom dollar Erwin intends to let that man do the shootin'. No way Erwin will do it himself. I've heard Smith T—" He stopped, then added in a lower voice, "Well, I'll be godderned if he ain't turnin' on Cedar Street and comin' this way."

Three rapid taps sounded on the door from the hall.

"I hope that's Doc, or Willoughby," Houston said, meeting McGregor's glance. "Doc?"

Dr. John Shelby opened the door and stepped in, tall, skeletal, with sleek gray hair combed up and back, a long nose, and a blind eye that sometimes wandered but now settled on Houston. The congressman stood. "I guess you've heard," Doc said.

"Yeah, we've heard," McGregor cut in, shifting his focus back to the street and picking at his teeth with a sliver of pine. "That snake John Erwin has gone and hired Smith T to deliver his challenge for him. I guess everybody else was too shit-scared to do it. Erwin's got plenty of friends but I don't see none of 'em steppin' up."

"We don't know exactly if Smith T's hired, Jack," Shelby corrected him. "What matters is—"

"What matters is he's just come in downstairs," Jack said, chewing the pine, pulling his greasy slouch hat low over his forehead and leaning far out of the balcony doors, looking down. The hat dwarfed his wiry body, exaggerating his meager size and intensifying Houston's irritation. "Have you heard, Doc, after he shoots a man he walks up to see if he got him in the eyeball. They say—"

"Back off, Jack. Get in here and close that door," Houston said. "You'd think you were watching a goddamned parade."

"Well, he do make quite a show," McGregor retorted amiably, backing in and closing out the sunlight, "with that getup he's in. Brass-toed boots as pointed as Doc here's nose, beaver hat bigger'n your head, Sam—"

"Think he's on his way up?" Houston asked Shelby, ignoring McGregor. "Where's Willoughby anyway?"

"I haven't seen our deputy all day, Sam. Wish I had. Maybe he could talk you out of this."

Houston lifted a hand in warning. "I won't be blamed, Doc. I'm not the one sending the challenge over."

"You would be if Erwin had said about you what you said about him."

"I don't set myself up for accusations like that. That man is a liar and a thief. Low as bloody hell."

"That's right, Doc," McGregor said, crossing his arms over his chest. "Erwin's a pure Federalist. Everything Sam accused him of is dead true." He pulled on his long mustache, twirling the pine toothpick with his tongue.

"What, a want of integrity?" Shelby queried, lifting his brows, his voice heavy with sarcasm. "No character? Lack of support from citizens of Nashville? Eavesdropping? Stealing a single newspaper? For God's sake, you know that's bombast. Sam does it well and that's fine, as long as that's as far as it goes. But when killing gets involved . . ."

Houston sat on the bed again and began carving out the dog's ears.

"I ain't believin' this, from you, Doctor," McGregor said, his small eyes squinting under the dirty brim of his hat, "of all people. Everything Sam said about John Erwin is true. That cockeyed President Adams gave Erwin that appointment as our postmaster for no other reason than 'cause Erwin's brother's married to Henry Clay's daughter and Clay got Adams elected. That's what I call spoils, and it ain't right. Erwin don't deserve the job just 'cause of who he's married to. Like Sam says, Erwin don't pay his debts; he's gone insolvent before and now lives high on the hog—and everybody knows he's got the money to pay up if he had a mind to do it. Nobody around here wants him for postmaster. The postmaster general don't recommend him, Nashville don't want him, General Jackson don't want him—"

"You've hit the nail there, haven't you," Shelby interrupted. "This thing has nothing to do with the postmastership of Nashville. It's a feud between Andrew Jackson and John Erwin. You know as well as I do that Erwin's biggest faults in Jackson's and Sam's eyes are a Federalist mind and a Federalist newspaper that fights everything Jackson stands for, right here in his hometown."

"Well, I'm sure that do have somethin' to do with it, but I wouldn't go so far as to say it's the whole thing. Problem is, Erwin's a damned scoundrel. That's the problem. And Sam's constituents don't want him for our postmaster. Me included."

"So Sam shoots him? Is that the answer, Jack? I don't think so. If Jackson and Erwin want to duel it out, then let them. But for Sam Houston, a man with as much promise as any I know"—his voice rose—"a lawyer, a major general, a congressman, to kill a total stranger over this, or get killed by him, is darn near pure ignorant. I think, Sam," he said, turning his full voice on Houston, who crossed his legs leisurely in front of him and glanced up from his whittling, "I think the General is using you. He's a great general, would have made a great President if he'd been elected. But in this he's gone too far. I know he's fought duels himself, and won, and I assume you'd win too. But son, what if you don't?" His voice trailed off; his blind eye shifted. He had kept Houston from dying before, when Sam was a boy fighting Creek Indians at the battle of Tohopeka, the Horseshoe, and he intended to do so again, to talk him out of this.

Houston blew the shavings away and looked sidelong at Shelby. It was true Jackson was using him. And he, Houston, was also using Jackson, to further his own aims. But there was more to their relationship than that—a firm bond, at times antagonistic, yet always sincere. It did involve power, because the Old Hero had so much of it, and Sam Houston wanted power too. But still, in an odd give-and-take way, there was caring such as a father might have for his son, and a son for his father, an affection that would endure if both men were stripped of power and the ambition for it. The old memory came again, vivid as the cowhide trunk at the foot of the bed and the pegs in the floor: the General, mounted, his white hair like a cock's plume on top, the long white face, skin pitted, scar from forehead to cheekbone, voice shrill above the noise of battle, "Lie still, boy, you've done your part today—lay out now."

"Well, I been tellin' him—ain't I, Sam?—that he ought not mess with that son of a bitch Smith T," McGregor was saying. "But sometimes a man's just got to go ahead with things, Doc. And if Erwin challenges, Sam here can't just say he ain't in a mood to fight. They'd post him as a coward quick as you can spit. If Sam's gonna run for governor like Jackson's sayin', he can't go around dodgin' duels. Guts and honor, that's what counts."

"More than lawfulness?" Shelby turned to Houston. "It's going to be difficult campaigning while you're dodging the law. If you live to dodge it."

McGregor said, "Nobody pays no attention to that law about duelin'. Anyway he can ride over to Kentucky where it's legal."

"You're way off, Jack," Shelby retorted. "This isn't a political question. It's a question of living or dying."

"Cut the dramatic shit, Doc. It's a question of—"

"It's a question of what to do now," Houston said, setting aside the whittling knife and the half-finished dog. "Smith T may be on his way up. Where in the hell is Willoughby?"

"Who knows," McGregor answered, lifting his hands, palms up, with mock exasperation. He spat the toothpick on the floor. "God, it's hot in here with them cockeyed doors closed."

"Willoughby's the law, Sam," Shelby said. "He probably knows he can't talk you out of going ahead with this and figures the best thing is for him to stay out of it himself."

"Did he tell you that?"

"No. I said I haven't seen him."

"He'll show up," Houston said. "He always shows up."

The room smelled stale. A cart rumbled in the street below, and down Market Street a dog was barking. Houston looked at McGregor. "You meant it when you said you'd second me?"

"Damn right I meant it."

"Good. Now. Where is this Smith T from?" Houston spoke to

McGregor but glanced at Shelby, knowing the doctor would dislike what he was about to say.

"I don't know where he's from, Sam; not here. What's it matter anyway? Missouri or somewhere."

"That's what I thought," Houston said. "Jack, what would you say about a congressman taking a challenge from this sort of a hired bravo who was driven from his own state for God knows what or brought here on Erwin's personal pocketbook that should have been used to pay debts owed to my constituents."

"Sam, we don't know if he's hired," Shelby corrected, stepping toward him with a surprised look, "and we don't know why he left Missouri, if he was driven out or just left. We don't know anything about him!"

"Neither does anyone else," Houston said.

The doctor shook his head. "That is real shabby. And it's arrogant."

Houston stood and crossed his arms. "You yourself said this is a matter of living or dying. I'm doing my best to maneuver out of it. But I won't come away from it looking yellow."

Their eyes confronted, then McGregor broke in, pounding one fist in the palm of the other, "It's good, Sam; it's dern near ingenious! So I don't take any message brought by the hired scum, Smith T!"

Shelby spoke in a hoarse whisper. "You're just buying time, Sam, and getting in deeper. Erwin isn't going to back off that easy."

"Then neither am I," Sam answered, turning to McGregor. "Jack, let him come to me first. I'll send him to find you."

McGregor grinned, saluting against his slouch hat.

"Let him find you where somebody can hear," Houston continued. "I don't want anyone saying I ducked him because I didn't want to fight. Make sure someone hears our reasons—that this is a home affair, a local and political matter, and as he's not a resident of this state, we won't recognize his involvement." While Houston spoke he watched from the edge of his sight Shelby turning, leaving, closing the door firmly behind him, but the congressman's voice never faltered. "If it gets nasty, allude to his reputation. Tell him Sam Houston doesn't fight downhill. And make sure you're heard—by as many people as possible."

A few minutes later, Colonel Smith T knocked at room 308. Sam Houston was alone, sitting on his bed with congressional correspondence scattered over the rumpled spread. The balcony doors were wide open, the room bright and airy. He carried a few pages with him to answer the knock.

"Colonel Smith, I believe? Sam Houston." His smile was friendly, his handshake firm, but he did not invite the man into his room.

Smith T took an envelope from his black vest and presented it with a flourish. He was older than Houston, short with a sagging belly and a bulbous nose. His brass-toed boots seemed too big for him. He had not removed his hat and observed Houston with bloodshot eyes and a benign smile. He did not look like a killer. "General Houston," he said, "I have a conveyance for you from Colonel John Erwin."

Houston answered, "Then I must refer you to my friend Colonel Jack McGregor. You can find him downstairs, or nearby; he was here not long ago."

"You can be sure I will find him." He turned and without further provocation walked off down the hall.

Houston closed the hallway door, went to the balcony, and standing back so not to be seen, watched below. The sun was centered. A crowd had gathered. Disgusting, the way news spread: a flogging, a hanging, a duel or the prospect of it—if blood was involved, the crowd would come to watch. At least this bunch wasn't rowdy. No one seemed sure what they were waiting to see. He couldn't hear the remarks clearly without moving closer to the balcony, and that he wouldn't do. Well, he could use the publicity, work it to his advantage. If Jack just did things right—so much depended on that. And Jack was enjoying this affair far too much.

A few of Houston's friends were across the street by the court-house hitching posts, slightly apart from the crowd, waiting. Doc Shelby, Philip Campbell, John Anderson, Jesse Wharton and his nephew William. McGregor was not in sight.

Smith T walked out of the shadowed doorway into the street and mingled with the crowd, searching faces. A buckboard toiled along Water Street on the other side of the square. A woman stepped out of the post office at the corner. In front of the hardware store a sleek, half-broken bay with the temper of a Texas mustang spooked and fought the hitching post. "Come on, Jack," Houston grumbled. "Where in hell are you?"

As if on cue, McGregor rounded the corner from Market Street, seeming oblivious to the crowd, his step brisk and purposeful, heading toward his tannery business down the street, the grimy hat pushed back from his forehead. Houston watched Smith T speak to an old man, who nodded toward McGregor. He moved closer to the balcony as Smith T called out in a friendly voice, "Are you Colonel McGregor, friend of General Sam Houston?"

McGregor looked toward him. "Yes, I'm Colonel Jack Mc-Gregor."

In a rocking walk that suggested a leg injury he had learned to favor over the years, Smith T approached with the envelope flashing in his hand. "I have here a communication from Colonel Erwin to General Houston, which I now hand to you, sir."

McGregor shoved his hat further back, crossed his arms over his spare chest and looked at the offering hand. Then his eyes locked with the steady gaze of Smith T. "I ain't got any quarrel with you, sir," he said loudly, "and don't wish to court your enmity. But as you ain't a legal resident of Tennessee I can't receive no communication from Colonel Erwin through your hands." Houston flinched at the sloppy grammar but thanked God that McGregor hadn't sense enough to be intimidated. Smith T lowered the hand with the enve-lope to his side. "I ain't challengin' your honor, sir," McGregor added, clearly wanting to prolong his moment, "as you're a gen-tleman of some reputation. But I do happen to question your authority in this here local matter." He uttered the word "gentleman" with a sneer.

Houston wished Jack would ease up. For a full moment the two men in the street stood confronting each other in noon sunlight, McGregor with his arms still crossed and hat shoved back, Smith T with the envelope at his side, one pointed boot poised slightly in front of the other. The crowd was still and attentive. A tall woman in gray homespun shifted a baby in her arms, and the child laughed, catching at her hair. Then, shoving the envelope back in his vest for the second time that day, Smith T said, "I will consider your objection and return within the hour," and took his leave.

Aware of the moment's drama and the eye of the crowd, McGregor turned in a near military about-face and headed toward the inn.

Back in the room, Houston informed McGregor that he would take over himself when Smith T returned.

"You can't do that, it's against the code," McGregor said.

"It won't be my doing. He will break the code, not I. Just wait up here like you're expecting him, and I'll go down."

"No way in hell I'm gonna do that, Sam! I risked my goddern life for you talkin' to Smith T like that, and now you're tellin' me to stay in this hell furnace of a room when everybody else is down there? They'd all think I was chicken scared. It ain't gonna be that way, it just ain't." They were standing in the center of the room. Houston stared at him. "Don't ask me to, 'cause I won't," McGregor added.

"Jack," Houston said softly, "Don't let me down." McGregor lowered his head as if to dodge a blow, then yanked his hat off and threw it on the floor. His bald spot shone white and sweaty. He lifted his eyes to Houston, who said nothing.

"All right," McGregor said at last, spitting the words out. "But if there's fightin', I won't sit here on my ass and twirl my thumbs. Goddernit."

CHAPTER 3

Eliza and her father stepped out of J. Decker's Confectionery on the corner of Cedar and College. She was wearing green, her favorite color. Her bonnet was green. The large package under her arm was wrapped with a blue ribbon; blue was her mother's favorite color and the candies were for her. "What do you think it's about?" she asked, looking over at the crowd.

"Nothing you should be involved in," he said. A thousand times she had heard that. "There's Doc Shelby. I'll go ask him. You wait here."

Eliza watched him walk away, his tailored suit fitting close around. Sunlight glistened on his top hat. When he reached Dr. Shelby and fell to conversation, Eliza moved nearer, to the far side of the street, across from the Nashville Inn, and stood apart from the crowd between a roan and a placid bay at one of the hitchrails that surrounded the courthouse block. If her father chanced to look in her direction he would see the top of her bonnet, so she took it off to be completely hidden. She had a clear view of the inn. Two men approached from the direction of Hick's block and faced each other in the center of the street; the crowd noted them and watched. The older of the two was broad and gray-haired with spectacles resting heavily on his nose. The other was shorter, round-bellied, and attired in fancy boots and a beaver hat.

A young man, without noticing her, stepped in front of Eliza and blocked her view. She waited, thinking he would move on, but he crossed his arms over his chest and settled in. The horses shifted in on her, and she was surrounded by the sweat-stained saddles on either side, the hitchrail behind, and the man's back in front of her. He was of medium height, his hair dusty brown and longer than fashionable, a little dirty, worn in a queue down the back of his neck. He was not wearing a hat. Eliza pressed a hand in a stirrup and tried to see over his shoulder. Sensing the movement, he turned, and smiled.

"Pardon me," he said in a Tennessee drawl. His face had an easy look. The features were not handsome. His nose was crooked—apparently it had once been broken—and a pale birthmark patched his right cheek down to his chin. His eyes were blue. "Don't you want in front of me here?"

She said she did and moved in front of him.

"My name's Will Tyree," he said over her shoulder.

"Tell me," she answered without turning, "who are those men?"

He explained: Congressman Sam Houston was to be challenged to a duel; the challenge had been offered once by Smith T—he pointed him out—but Houston's second refused it on grounds that Smith T was from another state and the matter was local. "But," he added, "my guess is he refused it because Smith T has the reputation of a marksman. That other man is General William White. He's a Jackson man but a friend of John Erwin. Erwin's the one sending the challenge. White is probably accompanying Smith T to persuade

McGregor to accept the challenge this time." He laughed in a low chuckle and said, "What foolishness." The confidence pleased her.

Eliza tried to see her father but could not. At last Sam Houston stepped, with an easy stride, out of the shadowed doorway of the Nashville Inn. The gathering quieted. He moved casually, showing some surprise at the number of people, as if wondering why they were there. His clothes were immaculate: the collar of his ruffled shirt stood from beneath a bright Indian hunting-jacket, a beaded red sash draped his shoulders, the silver buckles of his shoes were polished. He was clearly a man who dressed for occasions, for appearances. He seemed mystified by the crowd.

"Where is Jack McGregor?" Eliza asked.

"I wonder" was Tyree's answer. Eliza waited for him to speculate where McGregor might be, as her father would have done, but he said nothing. She felt an intimacy with him and tested it. "What if he doesn't show up?"

"He has to. Houston can't take that challenge himself; that's against the dueling code. One man's second can only talk with the other man's second. There can't be direct communicating between Houston and Smith T about the challenge or the particulars."

"Mr. Houston looks like he wasn't expecting this crowd," Eliza said. There was the smell of horse sweat, and dung at their feet. "If Smith T breaks the code by approaching Houston directly, is the duel off?" She glanced back at Will. Her hair was falling loose and that annoyed her. Brushing it from her forehead with the back of her hand, she almost dropped the package and her bonnet.

"Let me hold that," he said, taking the package. "He'll probably still have to fight sooner or later, but he'll buy time first."

"So he has to fight him, no matter what?"

Houston touched his hat to a woman and crossed the street toward the courthouse, stopping to converse with a group of men. He did not look at Smith T.

"He'll have to fight somebody," Will said. "Erwin or Smith T. The code's lax about who does the actual shooting. When somebody sends a challenge, then he or the second or anybody else can do the fighting, and by the code, his honor's defended. As long as somebody gets shot." He smiled.

As they spoke, Smith T eyed Houston, then ambled toward him. General White followed.

"General Houston," Smith T called out amiably, "would you step aside and have a word with me?"

Sam Houston turned to look at him. "Certainly . . . Mister Smith T."

They walked together a few steps, Sam Houston with an apparently indifferent stroll, Smith T with his odd, rocking movement. Again William White followed. The three stopped within a dozen feet of Will Tyree and Eliza. Sam Houston and Smith T turned toward each other, and Eliza had a clear profile view.

Across the street Dr. Shelby signaled the crowd to be still and keep quiet, his long fingers raised and spread high above his head.

Smith T tipped his head back to meet Sam Houston's eyes and said, "Colonel McGregor refused to accept the message from me on grounds that I was not a resident of Tennessee."

"He was so advised by me," Houston answered.

"He made insinuations about my reputation." This was uttered with a pleasant smile.

"Did he now."

They were standing close together. The Indian summer sun drew sweat in patches through the congressman's bright jacket. His eyes flickered downward; Eliza followed his glance and saw what he was looking at. Smith T had come armed. The piece was partially concealed beneath his suit coat.

"He's armed," she whispered to Will Tyree.

"I know."

Casually, with his left hand, Colonel Smith T thrust the envelope forward. But his right hand was tense, the fingers poised less than an inch from his gun. Sam Houston accepted the envelope with grace, with extravagant poise, and turned to go.

"Well," Tyree said, his voice mingling with the murmur of the crowd. "I'll be damned if Sam Houston isn't afraid of that man's gun."

Old General White called out with a sneer, "Colonel Smith, I reckon General Houston will not now deny having received it!"

But he was fooled. Eliza knew it by Sam Houston's expression, slow and triumphant; he had seen an out and would take it. She could not guess what the out would be, but there was victory in his eyes and in the slow, deliberate rotation of his head as he turned back to focus on White.

No one in the crowd that day could have known that General William White was about to fall prey to a stratagem that years later would cost General Santa Anna an empire. Sam Houston knew how to choose his enemy, draw him into his web, and destroy him by surprise. If he had to fight a duel, then he would rather fight an older man gone to fat, with poor eyesight and an unsteady hand, than Smith T, who had left seven opponents dead on the dueling field. Sam Houston turned on White and with calm, dramatic cadence, loud enough for all to hear but giving the impression that more of his power was concealed than displayed, replied, "I have not received it. I do not know its contents. I will not open it. I will refer it to Colonel McGregor, who is the only one with authority to receive it."

Had William White accepted Houston's statement without retort, he might have saved himself. But Congressman Houston knew the man. He knew White could not take an insult; he knew he could not withstand silent confrontation. White licked his lips. His eyes moved vaguely over the crowd. Suddenly he turned full face to Houston and embraced Smith T's cause with indignation. "I do not think, sir, that you have extended the proper courtesy to Colonel Smith."

Houston replied, "If you, sir, have any grievances, I will give you any satisfaction you demand."

It was too late. General White realized what was happening; his sudden panic was obvious. But he was in deep. "I have nothing to do with your difficulty, General Houston, and prefer to stay neutral." Sam Houston did not respond, did not even move his eyes. White spoke again, "But I do presume to know what courtesy is due from one gentleman to another."

He started to turn, but the web had him. Sam Houston's voice was like judgment day; everyone heard. "I also presume to know what is due from one gentleman to another, and I say to you, sir, that you may give me any conveyance you please, and I will accept it. With pleasure."

There was no way out for a proud man, and General White was a proud man. Eliza saw him try to steady himself like a man who has lost his balance. He knew the congressman's methods, his way of backing men into small corners. Yet he had walked directly into it, like an old bull to slaughter. "And I will receive one from you, General Houston," he said, his chin lifted, his voice faint, so obviously hoping for a miracle, for the man to back down.

But Sam Houston did not back down. Neither did he charge forward. It was part of his genius; he knew when to move, and how quickly. He coaxed his opponent into the offensive position so that when he, Congressman Sam Houston, fought the duel, it would be because General White was an aggressive, high-tempered man who left him no choice but to retaliate. Eliza understood what he was doing; how slyly he did it. He took possession of White, and the crowd. "The saddle is on the other horse, General," Houston said, watching White's eyes behind the spectacles. "And that is enough to be understood between gentlemen."

It was as if at that very moment General White saw the butchering knife at his throat. "You have tried to draw me into this business," he gasped. "You have tried to draw me into it—"

Sam Houston replied quietly, but distinctly enough for the crowd to hear, "Sir, you have forced yourself into it." As he said this, a man came toward them from the inn.

"It's McGregor," Will Tyree said to Eliza. Dr. Shelby broke from a group of men, joined McGregor, and the two went directly to Houston. Shelby touched Houston's elbow in a warning to ease up.

General White, a small tremor in the folds of his face and neck, crossed both arms over his chest. "If I call on you there will be no shuffling, I suppose?" His tone hinted he was hoping that perhaps there would be shuffling—somehow—and he would not have to pursue this affair.

If that hope existed, Sam Houston destroyed it with two words. His jaw muscle tensed in the sunlight. "Try me."

The confrontation was ended, for now. General White would have to challenge. Sam Houston would accept. They would meet on the field. The congressman had proven he could outmaneuver; certainly he could outshoot. Colonel Smith T was dismissed completely.

The men turned simultaneously, as if on signal. As they did so, Eliza said to Will, though she was watching Sam Houston as she said it, "So this is a thing of honor? It seems more like trickery to me."

White and Smith T retreated through the crowd. Sam Houston, huge between Doc Shelby and Jack McGregor, set his pace toward the inn. Just before he passed through the doorway, the congressman glanced back at Eliza with a furtive movement of his head and eyes. His lips moved slightly as he disappeared into the Nashville Inn, and she knew he had heard her.

She turned to see Will's smile open to a grin. "Trickery," he said. "You pick words well, Miss—?"

"Eliza Allen."

And then her father was beside her, saying, "For God's sake, why aren't you where I left you? And what . . ." His voice fell away, and he stood staring at Will.

She looked to Will. "Are you his daughter?" he asked her, his eyes set on John Allen.

"She is," the colonel answered. "And you are to keep your distance."

"I have not forgotten you, Colonel Allen."

"Stay away from her, Tyree."

With a drawn smile Will answered, "I'll save you the humiliation of exposing you in front of her." He lowered his eyes to Eliza with an intense, puzzled look, handed her the package, then without another glance at her father moved off into the crowd.

It was a step toward womanhood, taken not hesitantly but impetuously, almost instinctively. It moved Eliza into a position where she was not only seen and noticed but seen and recognized—a girl reaching for some small sign of preference, and finally someone turns. Will Tyree's open smile, Sam Houston's eyes on her and no longer laughing, an instant in which she won them both. And then her father's voice, setting her back. "For God's sake, why aren't you where I left you?" So easily he cheapened her victory, made it petty and small, and her a mere shadow in its wake.

She sat as far as she could from him on the wooden seat of the buckboard as they jerked along the road following the Cumberland River northeast to Gallatin, and said nothing at all, her head turned to the fields. His posture was rigid, his eyes averted. He set a killing pace; the mule suffered most.

The stretch was twenty-five miles and they would not reach home until after dark. She endured the heat, the dust, the angry man —and across the fields and clearings now and then caught sight of oak trees and cool Cumberland waters. She, too, had her anger.

At Mansker's Creek they watered the mule. The creek marked halfway between Gallatin and Nashville and set the boundary of Davidson and Sumner counties. It was ferried and merged into Jones' Bend of the Cumberland, a wide curve of water and trees extending almost to the road. Oak and ash trees grew tall around Mansker's Creek. Thirty years had passed since the last Indian massacre of white settlers in Sumner County, but the stockade at the creek was still standing. While the mule drank, Eliza waited at the edge of the water, looking at the old fort downstream, the brush grown around it, long timbers upright with portholes just big enough for a rifle barrel. Silas Dinsmuke came from his hut on the opposite bank to ferry them across, hailing them with a lifted hand. During the crossing he spoke of the weather: they needed rain and the river was low. Eliza kept her silence, a hand on the mule's neck. Then she and her father took their seats in the buckboard without comment and continued northeast.

They were ten miles from home with the sun low and hot on their backs when John Allen finally spoke. All afternoon he had been thinking what to say, until finally it did not seem to matter what logic or words he used as long as the girl understood she had been wrong.

"Trickery," he said at last, controlling his voice. "For God's sake. To Sam Houston."

So he, too, had heard. He would cut loose at whatever she answered. His anger pleased her in a way. She needed to affect him, for he was her father, and she was still more daughter than anything else. It was partly that she could never please him that she resorted to these tactics. She made no answer to his admonition.

"Damn it, child!" he shouted so loudly that the mule faltered and swiveled his ears back. "The point isn't what you meant, it's what you said. Don't you know who the man is? Or haven't you sense enough to care? There is no saying how far he will go if Jackson continues to . . . Damn it, Eliza!"

"I'm sorry."

"Robert will be humiliated; he's got to finish out the session with Houston." She watched the fields, felt the rise of an afternoon breeze, and tried to detach herself from his fury. "A girl your age cannot understand a man's actions, especially his political actions. And she cannot judge his motives." His voice fell to an incredulous whisper, spit forward with more force even than his shouting. "Trickery? Trickery, for God's sake? What, Eliza, in the name of—"

"I don't know," she said, holding back, still looking out toward the fields, the rows of cotton and tobacco awaiting harvest in the yellow light of late afternoon. She wondered why he did not mention Will Tyree. "Perhaps he didn't hear me," she said. "It could be he just looked back at us by chance and didn't recognize us, and anyway if he did, I doubt he cares much what a woman says."

He turned his face to her and she looked directly at him for the first time since Nashville.

"What a woman says? Woman?" he repeated, meaning to put sarcasm in his tone, but sounding unsettled. "Do you say 'woman' in reference to yourself?"

She knew by his voice that at that instant, her eyes set on his, she was womanish.

"You have a lot to learn before you're a woman," he said.

The sun was gone, the moon a yellow sliver low against the evening sky in front of them. The mule's pace quickened; he could smell stables. They passed between limestone walls bordering a narrow lane and were almost home, dark woods on either side.

Eliza took off her bonnet. Anxious to be away from him, she said, "I'd like to walk the rest of the way."

He did not answer. They moved along, two silent figures surrounded by trees and the sounds of frogs and crickets and the mule's step and Cumberland waters washing against soil and twisted exposed roots of oaks that would one day fall and sweep downstream.

Then the trees ended and the path opened and she saw the poplars, their leaves moving just below the yellow moon. When the buckboard reached them and Eliza could hear the breeze in them, her father, without warning, reined the mule to a stop, jolting her. She clutched the seat with both hands to steady herself. "All right," he said. "If you want to walk, walk. You do have a lot to think about."

She glanced at him. He was holding the reins in both hands, his face, like the animal's, looking ahead toward home. His straight nose and chin were sharp and dark against the blue-black sky and she saw his throat move as he swallowed once.

"If Mama waited supper on us, have her go ahead without me," she said, and he squinted slightly, as if offended by the idea that her mother would wait on her. "Are you going to tell her about today?"

He swallowed again. The mule pawed impatiently, snorting, and the man turned to his daughter. "No. For the same reason I never told her what you did at the races that day. She would have despised it. She would have been humiliated."

"You were the one who despised it," she said, and then, with renewed anger, "Chessy was bred in our stables; an Allen should have put her down. I wanted to do it myself."

He thrust the back of his hand toward her as if to hit her, but did not touch her, and shouted, "That was as apparent as it was appalling!"

She answered, "At least there was an Allen on the track."

They fell silent, staring at each other, each wanting to be left alone. He did not know what to think of her; he did not want to think of her. He wanted to dismiss her accusations. In his practiced voice, feigning less belligerence, he said, "It makes no difference who shot her. Certainly Sam Houston did a cleaner job of it than you would have. What matters is that you achieve some sense of propriety. But no, I will not tell your mother. She has enough to deal with. . . . She is . . ." He paused; he intended to say she was too ill, but his hesitation touched Eliza's fears, and her own mind finished the sentence thus: "She is with child."

Eliza said, "Papa, she can't be—not again so soon." Images of her mother, swollen, in the pain of childbirth, weak and nursing and confined to her room like a brood mare in the stables, cradling baby Harriet's lifeless body in her arms—these visions came to Eliza with terrible privity. "She's still sick from Benjamin's birth. She cannot be again with child. I can't believe you would—"

"She is not," he said, staring at her, his eyes catching the moonlight. She was pushing his limits, pushing her own, and both were confounded by it. But their tempers goaded them. "And you've no right to talk to me in that way."

Her expression was as hard as his and as angry, but without the surprise. She knew what she was up against; she knew his methods. But he—caught off guard by her defiance and what he saw as a crude intrusion into his relations with his wife—he was confronting an adversary he did not know. His daughter had challenged him before, but never like this. "I have no right?" she said, willing her voice to be calm, full-grown. "I suppose that's what you've told Mama all these years. She has no right to do anything but have babies. Until she dies having babies. Like Aunt Rebecca. And then you'll marry someone else, like Uncle Robert did and—"

"Stop it, Eliza."

"—then you can have more children to tell what their duties and their rights are, and mostly what their rights are not!"

Her hostility came at him like a she-cat with her claws out. It was not his nature to take her seriously, but he found himself in a defensive position. He tried to put her in perspective: an impudent child. But her sincerity was disturbing; she believed what she said, believed he had wronged his wife, her mother. And her belief unsettled him and kept him mentally backing away, afraid of her. His fear frustrated his thinking so he could not respond except to repeat, "I said your mother is not with child," and to add, looking to the house and jerking his head sideways at her, "Now get out."

She stood beside the road and watched him shake the reins forward. He seemed a tiny figure against the house as he entered the circular drive. His servant Beek greeted him with a brass lamp, yellow light flashing in the deep recess of the door. When he was inside, Beek took the mule and the buckboard around the house to the stables. Eliza was alone near the poplar grove with the light of the moon and the steady throb of cicadas closing in around her. She stood looking up through leaves at the moon, only a quarter lit.

CHAPTER

4

That night Houston was drunk to the point where his voice slurred, and he was irritated about it. The old wound was a constant bother. "Just tie it up," he said. "Goddamn it."

"It hurts, Sam, I know," Shelby answered, setting the lancet aside.

The streets below Houston's room at the inn had been quiet for almost two hours, since the Louisville stagecoach passed through, later than usual. The balcony doors were cracked open, letting in bugs and the night. Houston stood surrounded by tapers, his hands knotted in fists around the heavy bedpost, his trousers crumpled at his feet. He was naked but for the ruffled shirt that hung to his thighs just below the wound, which Dr. Shelby had lanced.

Sam had received the injury when he was twenty, in the battle against the Creek Indians at the Horseshoe, a bend in the Tallapoosa

River. The first time Doc Shelby saw the young ensign he lay wounded from a barbed arrow that had pierced his thigh as he lunged, the second one over the Creeks' massive breastwork of tiered pine logs. The boy, frantic with pain, had threatened to kill a nearby lieutenant if he did not get the arrow out. He knew if he lay still for a while his blood would loosen the thongs that fixed the point to the shaft, but he could not wait. He wanted the thing out. And so he threatened the lieutenant, and after the man twisted and pulled, the point at last broke free, tearing muscle in a gush of blood. Shelby had plugged the wound with cloth, and the next time he saw Sam Houston was later in the afternoon. The stubborn boy had again charged into battle, down into a brushy ravine roofed over by breastworks, where the last Creek warriors waited behind portholes. A misty rain was falling. Not one man followed him as he flung himself down the slope of soggy undergrowth like a raging animal. He was leveling his awkward musket at the portholes, not five yards distant, when a ball shattered the upper part of his right arm, and another entered his shoulder. Shelby watched him drag himself up the ravine, alone, struggling for a foothold and clutching at the undergrowth, and was compelled to risk his own life to help him. Houston won Doc Shelby's heart that day with his stoic fortitude under the surgeon's knife, cutting at the ball in his shoulder—and won, also, General Jackson's respect.

Shelby, now kneeling on the pegged floor, soused the lanced wound with cheap corn whiskey. The liquor mingled with blood and pus and coursed in rivulets down Houston's leg to the floor. Sam grunted, gutturally, as whiskey seared the open wound, and the doctor tied cotton cloth around the upper thigh and groin. "For God's sake, Doc, not so damn tight."

Shelby looked up at Houston. "Would you prefer I send for one of your Cherokee shamans?"

"Just untie it," Houston responded, and started to do so himself.

"You're so inebriated I'm surprised you feel it, feel anything. I'm going home."

They had been through this before; Doc Shelby knew Sam disliked being alone when he was drunk and hurting, and Sam knew he knew it. He wrapped the cloth looser and started to pull on his trousers, then tossed them aside and slumped onto the bed. Doc went to the washbasin where he poured water and dipped his lancet, drying it carefully in the dim light with cloth and then placing it back in his leather bag.

"A hell of a day," Houston said, to keep the talk going.

Doc carried his bag back across the room and set it on the small table beside the bed, then leaned and blew out the tapers on the floor, except one, which he carried to the table. He seated himself, and using the cloth with which he had cleaned his lancet began rubbing on the leather, moving in on the hinges and working over them. "Where's Deputy Williams?" he asked. "What does he think about today?"

"Willoughby's the law; he has to stay out of this. Isn't that what you said this afternoon?"

"Of course." Shelby paused. "And you said he would show up." Houston was sullen and quiet. Bearlike, he swiped at a mosquito buzzing near his ear. "As the law," Shelby continued, "why doesn't he convince you to get out of it?"

"Because it's my business," Houston answered, glaring. He grimaced with pain as he pulled his legs up, then relaxed and lay with one long arm hanging off to the floor groping for the whiskey bottle, the other grabbing at the mosquito.

Shelby turned to face Houston, his long nose catching the candlelight. "Why is it, Sam, that you antagonize people who care for you?" Houston did not answer. "I know you don't want to fight that duel. I know you're questioning your motives. But that's no reason to drink yourself insipid and take it out on me."

Houston sat up, angry. "I know my motives in this duel, and they're valid. You're reading me wrong, Doctor."

Shelby resumed his polishing and spoke in a monotone. "I wouldn't presume to read you, Sam. But I do question. I question why you quit law, and why you quit your family when you were a boy and went to live with the Cherokees, and then quit them to open a school, and then quit teaching, and quit your position as Indian subagent, and then as county attorney general, and then Tennessee militia general, and why you've quit your mother all these years and never speak of her." A june bug buzzed in the corner. "And while we're speaking of quitting things, Sam, I have to ask why you don't quit that bottle, and some of those Cherokee women too. Whatever happened to the lady you talked about marrying last year? The one in South Carolina?" He expected an eruption and gave Houston a glance.

"God knows," Houston said slowly. He leaned back, shook his head drunkenly at the ceiling and belched twice. "God knows what happened to her. God knows I don't know what happened to her." He lay still on his back, looking up, his jaw hard in the candlelight and a deep shadow drifting through his mind; for a moment nothing was clear. "Goddamn mosquito." Again he sat up, bending to look on the floor for the whiskey, and with a synchronized movement he swung it to his mouth with one hand and wiped the bottom half of his face with the other. Then he turned to Shelby. "Providence," he said. "The Conducting Providence." He paused and belched, but his eyes didn't waver. "When I first came to this place, to Nashville, I came without more than ordinary education, without friends, without cash, almost without acquaintances and consequently without credit. People, friends, have lifted me up, and I've done some lifting of myself too. But behind it all there's the Conducting Providence. It makes a future for us; it makes plans. Maybe it doesn't set the outcome, but it makes the plans." He tapped his chest with one finger. "And it's got plans for Houston. Today I did what I did because Houston has a destiny, not because he's afraid of dying." He was moving into his Cherokee speech pattern, referring to himself as a separate being, Houston, his voice low and rhythmic, his eyes strange.

"Whoever accused you of that, Sam, of being afraid of death? My God, son, that wound I just tended to—well I know the difference between fear of dying and just God-given desire to keep on living. You're more cautious now, that's all; you've learned the price of recklessness. Don't explain yourself with some Indian philosophy about destiny."

"It isn't Indian; it has nothing to do with Indian. It's what I believe."

"Oh? You've turned Presbyterian? Predestination, is it?"

Suddenly Houston was riled, and loud. He pushed his face close to the doctor, his feet planted on the floor as if ready to spring forward. "What Houston did today has nothing to do with timidity toward death, or even with instinct to survive; it's more than either of those things, more powerful, something a woman could never understand."

The inflection, the stress on the word "woman," told his friend that he had reached it, that this was what he was leading into, that "a woman" was the essence of it. "A woman?" Shelby repeated, remembering Eliza Allen in the crowd and Houston's expression when he turned and saw her.

"Any woman," Houston answered. Having come to the core of his frustration, and knowing Shelby understood and would pick up on it, he backed away from it. "Any woman," he stressed again, finally, and there was silence between them.

At last the doctor spoke. "No, Sam, not any woman. Eliza Allen?"

Sam leaned back on the bed again. "She called me a coward."

Shelby smiled to himself. You had to love a man like that. He could come on as fierce as a Tennessee black bear, but if you knew him well enough and confronted him when he felt vulnerable, which was usually when he was acting onerous, then he'd back down or nuzzle up warm as a huge dog.

"A coward?" Shelby queried.

"Not in so many words. But it's what she meant. She called it trickery."

"Wasn't it?"

"That's not the point."

"So. What is the point?"

"The point is, damn it, she didn't have to declare it out loud."

"Um. For the whole crowd to hear. I see. Since you're planning to run for governor and all. But you said a minute ago that you weren't questioning your motives, that you did what you did because you have some sort of a calling—"

"Not my motives, it's my methods she assaulted. She had no right to judge me like that, out loud."

"Are you mad because she said it out loud or because she saw through you?"

"Don't try to figure me, Doc."

"You've met her before, I take it."

"She's presumptuous." He slurred the word. But it was not what he was thinking; he was thinking of Eliza on the horse, how she commanded it, leaning low in a tenderly childish yet somehow sexual way. He pulled his muscled legs up on the bed and sat cross-legged, rubbing gently where the bandage bulged beneath the tail of his shirt. "Do you know her?"

"I delivered her."

Houston stretched his arms up as if he were bored, their enlarged shadows from the taper's light passing over the wall behind him like searching spirits. "How long ago?"

"If you're asking how old she is, I'd say fifteen, or sixteen. She's the oldest of seven. No, six. One of her sisters died." He paused, watching Houston's face. "Her mother's dying of consumption."

Houston flashed his eyes at him. "Tell me about John Allen."

"I thought you knew him."

"I've met him a time or two at the races. Of course, I know his brother well."

"John's a strange fellow. He owns most of Sumner County, puts all his money in land. And he's a founder of the Gallatin Bank. I think he was a director until a year or so ago when he got into some controversy with the Tyrees of Tyree Springs. After that, he withdrew from everything. I don't know the particulars, except that it happened around the time his wife took ill with consumption." Doc rubbed at his blind eye, took up his rag and resumed polishing.

"When did you meet Eliza?" The june bug hurled itself across the room and thumped near the taper on the table. Shelby brushed it to the floor.

"Two years ago at the Gallatin races. She was taking her father's horse out of the race because a mare went down." Houston paused, then added in a softer voice, "There's something about her that hangs on me." When he continued his tone quickened. "People can say all they want about my ambitions. Or vanity. But I have never been a coward. The girl is damned impudent."

"And," Shelby added, "quite charmingly so."

They looked at each other. "Unfortunately," Houston said, recalling her gray eyes wounded by sight of the mare, the low voice saying, "Did it move you?" And he had answered, "I've seen worse." A pompous mistake, so small and instinctive, and yet . . .

Shelby's blind eye was wandering, a sign he was tired.

"You need your sleep, Doc," Houston said, rising. "But before you go . . . I've written a letter for the newspapers explaining my actions today. I'd like to know what you think."

"I don't want in on it."

Sam accepted that. "Well, tell me at least if you think the *Banner* will publish it."

"They claim to be nonpartisan. But even though Erwin's resigned, he still runs that paper. I don't know. My guess is they will. For appearances."

"I'm thinking if I throw this thing into the papers maybe I can avoid shedding blood." He looked at the floor, then back at Shelby. "White is a Jackson man, and it was a little shabby the way I pulled him into this."

They looked at each other, and Sam broke a sudden grin.

"Sam, if you won't be contrite, at least be presentably humble. If for no other reason than your public image."

The congressman took a deep, mocking breath. "Never. I regard humility with a cold eye."

Doc Shelby turned away, then turned back, his good eye shining. "Do you? You were quick enough to call Eliza Allen presumptuous, and—what was the other word, Sam—impudent? Would you not have preferred her to act more humble?"

Houston responded with a dry smile, one finger up, a tap on the air, "Touché, Doc."

"You see, Sam, White isn't alone. Even you can get snared by your own words."

Sam left a silence, then said, "The fact is, I do not prefer humble women. Serenity bores me."

Shelby noted the green eyes, naked legs, huge bare feet on the floorboards. Perhaps it does bore you, he thought but did not say, eyeing, with a sympathetic expression, this beautiful, half-naked, imperious, giant genius of a man. But there may come a day . . .

CHAPTER

5

Laetitia Allen seemed an old woman in her four-poster bed. Easter had finished bathing her and had gone, and Laetitia slowly pulled the red checkered quilt up over herself.

"Supper's almost ready, Mama," Eliza said from the doorway.

The woman's eyes lifted as if even such small movement was painful; she made a drama of her pain. "Eliza, come sit down by me, please." Her speech was languid; she gave a slight movement of her head.

Eliza went to the foot of the bed and stood with one hand circling the bedpost. "What is it, Mama?"

"Will you apologize to your father?"

"He—told you?"

"No. He hasn't told me anything. But I've known something was between you since you went to Nashville together."

"If you don't know what happened, how can you ask me to apologize?"

"Eliza. He needs you."

"He has George."

"He needs you."

"No, Mama, he doesn't."

"Why? What is it between you?"

"It's just who he is. Who he thinks he is."

"Tell me what happened."

She was asking without really wanting to know, and Eliza understood. The arthritis, the consumption, had sapped her like suckling creatures. And with each birth she weakened and her joints swelled, and then at last there was the cough and flecks of blood. Since then she had closed herself in her room and was carried down only for supper. Sometimes the boys played in her room, their wooden toys cluttering the floor, their wooden pecking chickens bobbing as the string was pulled, the beaks hitting hard, wood on wood, with a hollow sound. And when their games were over, the boys were taken away, and Martha Ann and Eliza would sit with their mother and read Pope, or Milton, and the Bible. She loved Scott's "Lady of the Lake."

George, the oldest next to Eliza, seldom came to his mother's room. Laetitia would say, "He's becoming a man. He shouldn't have to sit here with an old woman." And Eliza would answer, "But you're not old, and you're his mother." At which she would reply complacently, "I am old. I've borne seven children and lost one. Losing just one can make a woman old." She was thirty-four.

Standing witness to her mother's burden, her asthenic voice, Eliza was agitated. Her malice toward the pain had grown into resentment of the woman who suffered it. Often she would go alone for long rides toward town or along the Cumberland where paths were cleared through the canebrake, trying to escape Laetitia's placid demeanor. It seemed to Eliza that her mother coveted the helplessness. She hated Laetitia's submission when her joints ached less on dry nights and John Allen crept to her room, as if ashamed and afraid to be caught. He knew he was wrong. But Laetitia would have him—and have his babies. And Martha Ann and Eliza were taken from school to be with her. Eliza asked why and was shamed for asking and told, "Because you've learned enough for any girl to get by with. And," the colonel said, "your mother needs you." This was to justify it all. Her mother's debility became the curse of Eliza's world.

John Allen had been out in the fields early, then in town at Sheriff Douglass's public auction of lands, where he purchased six hundred and forty acres on the middle fork of Red River for three hundred dollars. Now he sat at his walnut desk in the library, evening sun shining in through the window and resting bright across one shoulder, his eyes keen on the map spread before him—here, just so far east of Clarksville, just so far northwest of his properties on Desha's Creek, here the thin, awkward line of Red River moving southwest spills into Elk Fork and Sulphur Fork, and here the six hundred and forty acres, now his. It was farther west than he had ever bought, farther north, and he, so disinclined to risk, had bought it at auction without even sight of it. It was good land, at a good price; he knew it. He was thinking that his brother Robert would know it too and would wish he had not been in Washington City when Sheriff Douglass's auction came around.

He looked up and saw Eliza. If she had spoken, he could have waved her away, too busy, but her silence invaded his thoughts, and he set the map aside and leaned so far back it was as if he had stood and walked away from her.

"Sit down," he said, and she did. "What is it?"

"Just—I'm sorry for what I did that day. And for what I said. I want you to forgive me." There was no feeling in her voice, no remorse. She had not come for pardon; she had come only to request it, so she could tell her mother she had done so. Even John Allen, who could never perceive her emotions, now sensed their absence.

"You've been a long time coming to it," he answered, dissatisfied.

"I'm sorry," Eliza repeated, facing him straight on, feeling his equal. On the ride home from Nashville, two weeks before, she had experienced a role outside of daughter, and now there was no going back. She was hurt that he would not accept her on any other terms than daughter. But she was not surprised. She had always loathed his control, his iron hand (as he so proudly termed it), but it was the sudden discovery of the weakness behind that iron hand that unleashed her anger. She had, on the road from Nashville, seen him as a person in awe of powerful men like Congressman Houston and one who catered to power. She saw that he lacked control of himself—he who controlled so many others. He could not even keep himself from hurting the woman he loved. That night, in her sudden fear that he had gotten her mother with child again, she saw him as a willful boy, spoiled. His deceit was so huge. With the discovery of it, her resentments were suddenly legitimized and intensified. If he had admitted his vulnerability she could have loved him better; if he had said he was sorry too, for losing his temper, and asked forgiveness, then she could have excused him for so much. But he did not know this. Had he known it he could not have done it, for he had too much at stake. And so he held to the belief that she had been wrong in her accusation of the congressman, held to this excuse for his anger, when in truth his real frustration grew from her accusations of him, of his relationship to Laetitia, charges he had already made against himself. Before the moment under the quarter moon, when she came at him so fiercely, he had been a father reprimanding his daughter for impertinence. Since then he had become a man defending himself against a charge he had always feared, a charge he had made against himself a long time ago. He had wronged his wife; another birth might kill her. Dr. Shelby had said so. But since he could not reverse the wrong and would not stop it, neither would he admit it.

"I knew you would be," he said. "I knew you'd be sorry sooner or later."

He seemed so sure. That illusion of certainty was the confusing thing. A person could fall into it, be carried off by it and never ask where to. One second of thought, not questioning but aggressive, the kind of thought that gets results, one snap movement of his eyes and his direction was determined, opinion set, decision made, the die cast. And there would be no turning back. He was so easy to trust if you had no convictions of your own.

And what was there for her to say? She had made her pilgrimage and confessed her guilt, though she did not believe in it. She had asked his forgiveness and received only a confirmation of her sin. He was so sure, he almost convinced her of that sin; but she had seen too much for that.

"Eliza. How can a man keep his family living in style and prominence when his daughter goes around insulting men like Sam Houston? Do you have any idea just how much power Sam Houston has? He will be our next governor; there isn't any doubt about that. General Jackson is supporting him for it. Do you know what that means? Or don't you care?" She met his look but declined to answer. "Let me assure you, Eliza, the day Houston becomes governor and Jackson becomes President, it will matter to you." He seemed eager for that day, and she despised him for it. "Do you think your Uncle Robert would be where he is, a congressman, if his children behaved as you did yesterday?"

His attitude of superiority invited her to shock him. "Who is Will Tyree?"

Their gaze held. "You are never to mention that name again."

Her eyes were as cool as his, her voice as steady. "Who is Will Tyree? You know I can find out."

The two of them sat motionless, so solemn in the room together, with the sun sinking over the poplar grove far off outside the dusty window, each with their own fears and frustrations, their own adamant beliefs, their own ignorance of the many shades of truth that drift like dark shadows, gradually, imperceptibly, into something so far from the original that the difference is that of bright morning and a moonless night. For a long moment they confronted each other across the desk, a walnut expanse as far as the longest distance

between man and woman, adult and child. Eliza stood and left the
room.

Autumn came creeping in, not in a gusty front but steadily. Each day
dropped a few degrees. The night was cool and still. Servants lit fires
in the bedrooms upstairs, and Easter filled the warming pan with
coals and warmed the sheets. When the fire in the girls' room
burned low, Martha Ann moved closer to Eliza, her plump, flannel-
clad body pressed against her. There were no flames, only red embers
glowing, popping occasionally, throwing red light on the candlewick-
ing of the bedspread, tiny shadows leaning from each cotton knot of
the spread. The clock at the foot of the stairs chimed midnight,
muffled, an old friend calling from a distance. Eliza was pulling the
down quilt up over them, over the white spread, when the door
opened slowly and Dilsey came in, two logs resting in the crook of
her thin arms out in front of her, her narrow hip leaning against the
door to close it. She was young, with aquiline features and hair
cropped short. A brown knitted shawl over her shoulders hung to the
floor. Her feet shuffled to keep the slippers on as she crossed to the
fire and shoved the logs in. Then she turned and saw Eliza sitting up,
watching her, the quilt pulled close around her chin.

"What you doin' awake?" she whispered across the small room.
Eliza shrugged.

"Well, I come to warm my feet. That old cabin's cold."

"Papa told me he plans to put Lucky in charge of building
fireplaces in the cabins."

"Hm," Dilsey grunted. "He done told me that too. About three
years back."

So. Again he deceived. Every deception further justified her
anger.

A log caught with a tiny lick of flame, and Dilsey's face shone
smooth and brown in the light. She pulled a chair over the rag rug to
the hearth, sat and reached her feet toward the flames. No permis-
sion was asked or given. She had raised Eliza, had carried her on her

hip when she was a baby and Dilsey herself but a child. The intimacy held, but with a strain. Eliza no longer needed Dilsey, and dependency had been the foundation of their relationship. What remained was a bond fraught with resentment, for Dilsey was not prone to submission, and Eliza was no longer a child.

When her feet were warm, Dilsey moved back in her chair and tucked one leg up against her. "Mr. Will Tyree come here today," she said, staring at the fire.

Eliza responded in a whispered breath, "Here?"

For a moment Dilsey held on to her secret. Eliza pushed the covers aside and went to stand in front of her.

"Lucky was pickin' in the fields real early," Dilsey said, "and up comes this gentleman, says his name's Will Tyree and he'll give him a dollar if he'll get somethin' to you without Colonel Allen knowin' it. An' he holds the dollar out. Lucky, he don't like it, but a dollar's a lot. So he says sure and takes the dollar and takes this." She pulled from her breast an envelope, dirty and creased from the afternoon inside Lucky's shirt. Eliza took it from her. Dilsey lifted her shoulders and her hands, the palms up and brown in the firelight, a gesture claiming her innocence in anything that came of this. Then she moved her feet into her slippers and stood and went from the room, the tail end of the shawl dragging behind her.

There were only two lines, in a loose, casual hand:

*I would like to see you tonight. In
the grain barn? After midnight—W.*

Again she played the scene in her mind: Congressman Houston turning, Dr. Shelby and Colonel McGregor on either side, moving together with the precision of an Austrian clock, turning away from her and starting toward the inn. Will Tyree's smile, so close, a touch of his finger, then Sam Houston's eyes turning on her like a buck's eyes on the pursuing hounds, his pace never slackening. He had heard the words, and he had known her. Her father could cheapen the victory, but it remained a victory. What Sam Houston had thought, she could not tell; it was enough that he had heard her and been, for at least one fleeting instant, moved in some way.

Cold slipped in through the window lights. She recalled Will Tyree's eyes, open as the blue sky, then Sam Houston's, murky green, shadowed, deep as the Cumberland in rainy season, dangerous, magnificent. She imagined herself alone with Will in the grain barn, fantasized how he might touch her. The fantasy was compelling.

The barn was of sawed lumber with cedar shakes for a roof. In the center was a threshing floor where oxen circled in the winter months, treading wheat from the chaff.

Eliza met him there, and the seduction, from the beginning, was mutual. There was nothing courtly in his demeanor and nothing coy in hers, only a shared drive toward physical intimacy. Will greeted her near the door, but they retreated in back of the grain bins and sat in darkness on the ground littered with fodder and dusty wheat that had spilled from between the slats.

"I've thought about you," he said. "I don't suppose I can call on you, publicly."

"No. What happened between you and my father?"

"I thought he might have told you."

"He won't even speak your name."

"It's over, anyway."

"But I'd like to know."

He hesitated, then answered simply, "I prefer not to talk of it."

She accepted that. She respected it. And, beyond curiosity, she did not care much about knowing. The fact that her father and this man had encountered each other with some unpleasantness did not surprise her. "Your name," she said. "Tyree. Is it the same as Tyree Springs Resort?"

"Yes. We sold after my father died, a few years ago."

She told him she had been there with her parents when she was a child, but he shunned the topic, asking if her father had heard what she said about Sam Houston that day; he was sure that Houston had heard.

"Yes."

"Angry?"

She nodded. "Yes. Did they fight the duel?"

"White hasn't challenged yet, but he will. Houston didn't leave him a choice. If he's got any pride at all. Houston's written a slew of letters to the newspapers and has the public on his side. He's about ruined Erwin, and White too. They've both published their own accounts, which have fallen by the wayside. All of Jackson's people are siding with Houston, and Erwin's happy to let White fight the duel for him. Smith T has left town. You were right about the trickery."

She smelled sweet fodder in the stillness and wanted him to touch her. Her eyes were adjusting to the dark, and she could see his shape clearly, but his voice was what moved her. They let a silence settle in, and then she reached for him, moving her hand, without timidity, from his neck across his chest and down against his groin. She had never touched a man in such a way; she cupped her hand and felt him harden into it. He did not guide her, but unfastened the buttons of his pants, exposing himself and allowing her to stroke him. She wondered if her father's body felt like this, and rejected the thought.

She thought how angry her father would be if he knew what she was doing, and she said, "I love this." The freedom enchanted her, as did her power to entice him. Here was a man who was not inclined to resist her. On the contrary, he wanted her. She felt that anything was permissible. He encouraged her mouth on his, moving his tongue inside. He allowed her to help undress him and to examine the hair on his chest and belly and to taste him. Instinctively, he made no attempt to master this woman, but withheld his urgency, permitting her to pace herself, undress herself. She had seen animals but did not know how people were to do it. She had thought a lot about it. Will let her create her own way; she felt his body more than she allowed him to touch hers. After a while, when she was naked on top of him, he pushed up into her gently, and she welcomed him. But when he became hurried and was about to release inside of her, she slowed her breathing and stopped moving and said in a voice so certain and deliberate that it startled him, "We can't. I don't want to have a baby."

He pressed in farther. "Just once."

"No." She was unequivocal.

He disliked her timing, imposing such a restriction now; she could have said something earlier. But he was also surprised she had given so much, so easily, and he was, in a boyish way, grateful. So he honored the stipulation and withdrew and satisfied himself against the small, hard protrusion of her hip. She herself was not satisfied and did not want to be. She was afraid to be. It would mean an abandonment of self-consciousness and of composure.

In parting before daylight, Eliza was not contrite over her loss of innocence; in a way, she exulted in it. The heat of his body inside her, within her control, was the dearest sensation of her life. They planned another meeting. He kissed her again before starting toward the trees where his horse was tethered, and she said, "If it weren't for my mother, I'd see you in public in spite of Papa. But she's ill and I can't worry her. She has consumption."

He had been reaching for her again but stopped and lowered his hand. There was a flicker of lightning far to the north. He looked away from her, toward it. She felt a sudden severance of the intimacy.

"How long has she had it?" he asked.

"About a year. Why?"

His eyes were fixed on the horizon, as if watching for another flash of light. He said, "I'm sorry about it," and then, without touching her, "I have to go. Good-bye."

His sudden detachment disturbed her. She felt he was falling away from her. "But you'll be coming back," she said, "when we planned?" And suddenly she regretted making love with him. She felt frightened.

He looked at her but did not answer. It was as if the lightning had distracted him. She wanted to reach out but felt he would not respond, and so without waiting she turned and started toward the house. Once she looked back and saw, in an instant of white light, Will lift his arm, the hand spread. It was only a parting wave, but oddly resembled a gesture she had seen as a child when the stables caught fire one summer night—a man shielding his face from severe heat, his silhouette black against flames in a gaping door.

CHAPTER

6

Houston was in bed snoring, his Indian blanket thrown over him, the bedspread in a heap on the floor beside him. He had been up most of the night with a bottle of Madeira wine and *Gulliver's Travels*. A firm knock woke him and he sat up. "Who is it?"

"Willoughby."

Houston said angrily, "Come on in."

The door opened, a glow from the hallway lantern lighting a large man with red hair and curling sideburns that grew into a short beard. He stepped in and closed the door.

"Am I dreaming or is it really the long-lost deputy?"

The man crossed his arms over his chest.

"Where in the hell have you been?" Houston demanded, scrutinizing the dark shape of this friend from boyhood who had been with him the day he joined the army and had met him outside Kingston when he was carried home on a litter, near dead from wounds and measles. "You used to be around when I needed you. God knows I've been there when you needed me." He cleared the mucus from his throat and spat on the floor.

"I didn't used to be the law," Williams said in a stentorian drawl. "And you didn't used to break it."

"I had no choice. Keep your voice down." Houston looked toward the balcony doors, the pale light of a still dawn creeping in, then stared back at his friend. "He challenged me."

"You can fool others with that stuff in the papers, Sam. But this is me."

"So, you've been keeping abreast through the papers. Jack Mc-Gregor risks his life getting involved, and you won't even risk your job."

"You're asking a lot, Sam."

"I've given a lot, too, damn it. Who do you think put your name out for deputy?"

Even Sam Houston was hard put to get Willoughby Williams on the defensive. His patience was boundless. "Jack McGregor gets into it wherever there's trouble," the deputy said. "He weren't risking his life, Sam: trouble is his life."

"He was risking his life, Willoughby, while you were sitting home reading the goddamn papers. Well, so what are you here for?"

"I've got news. But you're close to talking me out of telling it."

"Cut the dramatics. Tell me."

The deputy had a penchant for relaying news. "Everybody in town's taking your side, saying you've backed down Erwin and White too. That's what made White finally go ahead and send his challenge yesterday. The man's got his pride on the line. Anyway, Sheriff Horton's heard about it, and he's out to arrest the both of you. I was with him earlier. He's so happy he can hardly sit. He's been wanting to pin something on you for years. He's probably at White's now, and I'm supposed to be with him. We was to come here next."

"So," Houston mumbled, getting out of bed and pulling on his trousers. "Deputy Sheriff Willoughby Williams comes through in the end." He buttoned his pants and looked at his friend. He could see the red hair clearly now, with dawn sliding in around the balcony doors, and could just make out the tidy jacket. Nancy Williams kept her man well ironed. In a different, softer voice, Houston asked, "What do you think I should do?"

"Leave town. Go to the Hermitage. Nobody'd arrest you there."

"No. I won't leave. I may stretch the law, but I won't run from it."

"*Walk* your horse out of town if you want to."

Houston reflected a moment, scratching his leg through the trousers. The wound was scabbed and itched. "Suppose I did leave town. The law would come after me, wouldn't it?"

"I'm half the law around here, Sam."

"The other half would come after me."

"Not if you're at the Hermitage."

"I can't stay there forever. Sooner or later they would come for me. And nobody would vote for a man the law was hunting."

"You think they wouldn't be after you if you shot somebody?"

"I would do it in Kentucky."

They were quiet, then Willoughby continued, "What I figure is, if White's arrested and you disappear, it might all blow on over. You can let it blow on over. They'll let White go after a day or two, and you'll come out looking better than if you kill him. Best of all, you'll come out alive."

"I'll come out alive regardless. Your plan is enticing, friend, but I can't ignore a challenge. White wouldn't let it go even if I did. If we're both arrested we'll get off soon enough and then we'll go through with it. There's no other way."

Willoughby stroked his beard. "You're wrong," he said.

"All of my friends are so goddamn opinionated," Houston answered forcefully.

"If it's appearance that matters," Willoughby drawled, "I think we can get around that. Just move around today, go visit Doc, Mc-Gregor, Campbell, anyone. Have plenty of witnesses that you was here today and in no hurry. But don't stay anywhere too long, and don't get seen in the streets. Have McGregor look out for Sheriff Horton, 'cause with or without me, he'll try to sniff you out, and he's got him a nose like a hound dog." He eyed Houston, adding, "But I'll do my best to keep him off your tail. I'll send him on a goose chase, make him think I'm looking for you too. Meanwhile, you ride on to the General's this evening. Nobody's gonna say you're running. I'll do my best to see White's released. Then, if you two have got to fight, fight and get done with it. All I ask is that you stick to that idea of going over to Kentucky. I don't want to have to hang you for murdering him here in Tennessee." He added with more fervor, "For goodness' sake, Sam, I wish you'd just give it time to blow over."

Houston moved, stretching, to the balcony and cracked the door open. Cool air rushed in. He stood looking out, scratching his chest and fingering the hairs. "Is that lightning?" he asked.

"It's a while off," Willoughby answered.

Houston watched for another flicker in the growing light, then closed the door, turned suddenly and crossed the room to his friend. "I knew I could count on you," he said. "If you'll keep Horton out of my way today, I'll do it. I'll leave after dark." Their eyes were level. "Now get out of here before someone sees you. I don't really want you to risk your job." He left a silence. "I just needed you. Doc's not with me on this, and I needed you."

"So you're gonna fight it?"

"I'll talk it over with the General. But I don't see a way out. Not one with any dignity in it."

"I don't like it, Sam."

"But you know why I'm doing it. And you can't completely fault me on it. Old Hickory has been good to both of us for a long time. Like a father. To both of us." Houston smiled, then added softly, "I guess that makes us almost brothers."

"I guess so," Willoughby answered hoarsely, uncomfortable

with the closeness. "Sam, I can't be with you on this, but I am behind you. And Doc is too. We'll be there if you need us. Meanwhile, I'll keep Horton out of your way so you can get on to the Hermitage. Do you understand?"

"I understand," Houston said. "Do you understand?"

"No," Willoughby answered.

That evening Congressman Sam Houston left through the back door of the Nashville Inn just after dark, his Indian blanket around him and pulled high over his ears, saddlebags draped over his shoulders. Ten minutes later he crossed out of the city limits on his gray mount, riding northeast. The rain had passed through, and autumn hung in the clear sky; a waxing moon topped the horizon.

He kept to the main road, listening, moving off into the trees when he heard or saw a rider approach, waiting and then moving on, at times pushing the horse for speed, then allowing it to slow— stopping, listening, and moving on again.

The Hermitage was near the east line of Davidson County, twelve miles northeast of Nashville on the Lebanon Road, between the Stones and Cumberland rivers. When the brick edifice was in sight, Houston pulled his pocket watch from beneath his blanket, bending close to the face and tipping it toward the moon's light. It was just before ten o'clock. Most of the windows were dark or dim with dying fires, but yellow light flickered from the ground-floor window of Jackson's library. Houston debated whether he should see the General tonight; he was not sure how the old man would receive him. Jackson had sent no word since publication of the newspaper letters, no encouragement or advice. Just like the old bastard, Houston thought, to set him on Erwin like a fighting cock and then stand back and enjoy the blood.

He contemplated going around back to Alfred's cabin, or old Sam's—a Negro the General had freed a decade before but could not induce to leave. He could rouse one of them to show him to an empty guest cabin, if one was empty. The Jacksons welcomed the dregs of society into their home, and often the dregs came and stayed. Sam Houston never complained about that (as did some of the Jacksons' more scrupulous guests), in light of his own appearance some years back at the Hermitage—very nearly a dreg himself, though one on his way up.

He could take a cabin and talk to the General in the morning. But then, there was that light in the library, its flicker like an invitation, a beckoning hand. He dismounted in the driveway, pulled off his leather gloves, rubbed his thigh and bent to look at it—no dampness, no smell of pus or blood. The wound had not broken open on the ride. He had a dread of being killed in the duel and buried with the thing all pussed up. The thought was purely academic, for he did not intend to die, but still he was relieved the scab had held. He draped the reins over a low tree limb near the front porch, smoothing his hands down the horse's neck into the damp creases between the front legs, warming his fingers and thinking of Jackson's whiskey decanter in the firelight.

The latchstring was out. He knocked, the brass knocker sounding louder than he intended. In a moment he heard a woman's soft voice inside, "Here, Hannah, you hold the lamp." Then the door opened to two dark female faces, one black and the other a mottled brown, almost Indian in color, both as high as Sam Houston's chest. Rachel Jackson stood slightly in front, the lace of her cap falling to rounded shoulders.

"Sam," she said, her pleasure lit by the whale-oil lamp Hannah held up. "He'll be so glad. He's been expecting you for days. Come on in—Hannah, wake Alfred to take the horse—Sam, you must be cold. Riding after dark."

She reached toward him like a child wanting to be held, and he folded over and around her, pressing her into his chest and smiling over at Hannah, saying, "Aunt Rachel, I've missed you. I would have come sooner but . . ." and here he left off, their bodies moving apart but still joined by the arms, her eyes searching his face.

"Don't beg pardon, Sam, you would have come. But for . . . the trouble. The General couldn't keep it from me." She smiled, focusing her eyes on the knotted cravat at the base of his neck. "I've seen them papers." Her mouth tensed in the lamplight held high by Hannah, the glow lighting dark hairs above her mouth.

Houston looked back to Hannah as she turned, the light thrown from wall to wall, huge and rocking. She lit four beeswax tapers in the silver candelabra on the table near the staircase, one at a time like a silent ritual, and went up the stairs, her broad hips swaying with the light.

Rachel Jackson was a kind, uneducated frontierswoman in her sixtieth year, her lusty beauty turned corpulent and sagging, as if she carried with her every sorrow and disgrace of sixty years. "He's fell asleep by the fire in the study," she said. "We had the family here yesterday. It was A.J. and Emily's second anniversary." They walked toward the library, her hand in the crook of his arm, feeling the Indian blanket. "So"—she smiled up at him—"this keeps you warm?" and without waiting for an answer, "Because of the storm, most everybody stayed the night. You know how the General loves having his namesake with him."

Mention of Andrew Jackson Donelson—A.J.—Rachel's nephew, always stirred up something Houston disliked in himself: envy, to put a name to it. The man was a few years younger than Sam Houston. His father, Rachel's brother, had died when he was a boy, and the Jacksons took him in, as they did so many children. They gave him and his brother Daniel the best of everything. They sent him to college, then to West Point, then to law school at Transylvania University in Lexington. He excelled in his classes, became Jackson's aide-de-camp in Florida, and had been the General's personal secretary ever since. Now he lived near the Hermitage in a house provided by Andrew Jackson.

And here was the thing Houston despised in himself (though with a certain enjoyment): any mention of A. J. Donelson, any glimpse of him, even thought of him, brought on this pervasive sensation of envy, not of the young man himself but of what he had been given. Houston did, in fact, feel entirely preeminent to the man, which only intensified the resentment because it led Houston to thinking what he himself could have accomplished with such education and advantages. The idea that he, Houston, was inherently superior but was, by virtue of the circumstances of his life— namely, poverty—set at a disadvantage, imparted a not entirely unpleasant feeling, by dint of the fact that Houston had pulled himself up to Congress, while A.J. was still a secretary. It was a savory thing to think on, though Houston could only deem envy of a lesser man as an immaturity in his own character.

"The General gets so tired, Sam," Rachel was saying in her hesitant voice. "I love the house full of friends. But he gets so tired and won't rest. Even this morning after they was gone, he would not sleep. John Overton was here too. He left this afternoon. They was awake talking till morning."

They had come to the library door. She took her hand from his arm, clutched her lace gown and turned to face him with a puzzled look. "I wish I could do more for him, or he wouldn't try to do so much. But . . ." She made a small, supplicating movement with her hands, almost hidden in the lace folds, meaning, Who can stop him? Houston understood the futility in the movement; if anyone could stop Andrew Jackson from anything, Rachel was the one. And she had tried.

He had pulled one of the twin mahogany sofas, covered in black horsehair, near to the fire, and Sam Houston could see only his thin slippered feet sagging over the scrolled arm. He was snoring. Newspapers littered the floor around him. Houston waited a few seconds, and Rachel whispered, "I didn't know he was so asleep." She did not want to wake him. But then the snoring ended in a rattling choke and the General sat up, facing the fire and thumping his chest as he coughed, muttering "Blast it" and "Goddamn lungs" between the fluid bouts of coughing. His white hair stood out with firelight shining through it but was flat on the crown where he had been lying. He kept one arm immobile, crooked at the elbow and pressed close to his side; it had a lead ball lodged in it and was of little use to him.

"General," Rachel said, almost inaudibly. He jerked his face around with a flash of his eyes, his long profile sharp against the fire and lengthened by the hair standing up. "Sam!" he said, rising, an old man on a sofa made from the hair of a dead horse, suddenly unfolding, lanky, energetic as a yearling colt. "By God it's good to see you!" They met halfway around the sofa, their handshake moving into an embrace, the tall elderly man instantly dwarfed in Sam Houston's arms. "Your old law partner Overton and I were up talking about you most of the night—Rachel, don't leave, come sit with us."

"Thank you, General, but no." She meant that already the conversation was moving in a direction she did not like; she knew what her husband and the judge had discussed the previous night, and the topic of challenges and duels made her afraid. But this she did not articulate; she had never had cause to express her feelings in words, since they were evident in her face, uncomplicated and naked, reduced to a smile, a tremor of her lips, a lift of the eyebrows. She apologized and excused herself, her stout figure in firelight, turning and closing the door behind her as gently as one closes in a sleeping child.

"She has never gotten over it," Jackson said quietly when she was gone, watching the door through which she had moved away, and Houston felt himself an intruder in this house. No matter how many people, visitors and servants, came and went through these rooms and about the grounds, the place belonged to the General and Rachel Jackson, the bond between them so strong that others, no matter how welcome, were, inevitably, shut out. "She still blames herself for my killing Dickenson in that blasted duel. She just won't accept he had it coming. Profaning her name like that. Anyone who would talk about a woman like he talked, with his false, filthy lies—" He was interrupted by coughing and sat back on the sofa, thumping his chest. "Take a chair, Sam, please, and excuse this damnable cough. Well, is there to be a duel?"

"I don't know," Houston replied, pulling a wide wing chair in closer and sitting. "I've come for counsel."

"Has White challenged yet?" Jackson squinted as a spasm of dysentery gripped his bowels.

"Yes sir, he has. And I have accepted."

The old man arched his brows, his eyes scrutinizing, the scar from his forehead to his sharp cheekbone and the pits in his skin vivid in the moving yellow light. "And you don't know if there is to be a duel?"

"I was told a warrant had been issued for his arrest and mine. I don't know what has been done with him. I have reason to believe he's been arrested."

"Willoughby informed you?"

Houston nodded.

"Willoughby's a good man." Jackson leaned back and moved his gaze to the settling logs, his long body slumped in the sofa, his knees close to the fire. "You've handled things well so far, Sam, with enthusiasm I admire. Erwin is a tough fox to take on. No matter how many chickens he's stole, he doesn't leave tracks behind, doesn't leave even a scent though he stinks to high heaven. You've done well, but I hoped it wouldn't go so far." He stopped. Houston said nothing, knowing the situation had, in fact, gone exactly as far as Andrew Jackson intended. "General White was a fool to get involved," Jackson continued, "and it's shocking how Erwin's left him holding the whole bag. Erwin is really a disreputable old bastard." He quirked one side of his mouth and paused, as if it took deep concentration to think on Erwin's infamy. "But White's in now, and unless I'm missing something, if the challenge has been made and accepted, then the duel has to be fought." His eyes shifted to Houston. "Sam. You must never, my son, outlive your honor. If you fight the duel and live, you live with honor. If you're killed, you die with it. If you weasel your way out, your honor's defunct and you're good for nothing. I've read all your letters in the papers, of course; you put forth a damned admirable effort to reduce this thing to print. But if the hand's been called, the cards have got to come out."

"That's what I've thought, sir, and what I said to Willoughby.

But I have to admit the situation's been muddled. It's not as clear to me as it was. White's one of your best supporters."

"I suppose you'd rather fight Erwin? Or that Smith T character?"

Houston managed a smile. "Hardly."

"So I thought. It has been muddled, my boy, but two things stand obvious. General White has challenged you to fight. You have accepted that challenge. He challenged you; don't forget that. Your choice is between running and fighting. Is there any chance you'll run?"

"Of course not. Sir."

"Then. You can't question so much, Sam. When you're into something follow it through; when you've made a decision stick to it and go ahead, or you'll never accomplish a damn thing."

"I can't help but hope it doesn't come to blood."

"There's no hope of that now, son; the blood's good as spilt. It's a matter of honor, they say, and I happen to be one who agrees. You've handled this thing like a gentleman. You'll fight it like one." Houston stared at the fire. "Let me tell you something about honor, Sam, as one who's seen both sides of it. When I got the most votes in that election but lacked the majority, it never occurred to me Congress would make Adams President over me. I was so goddamn naive." Naive—Houston repressed a smile. "Everyone kept telling me—you among them—that Henry Clay was up to dirty work, that if I wanted the presidency I would have to cut a deal with him to get it, or Adams would. I'd known Clay from way back; he used to be the lawyer for my Kentucky trading firm. I didn't believe he could be so wicked as to do a deal like that, but I laid the matter to rest, regardless. And stood firm. I said he could go to bloody hell before I'd bribe myself into a position rightfully mine to start with. And I played by the rules. Fair. And Clay cut his deal with Adams, went against his own constituents and spoke out for Adams, and Adams won the election by a single crooked representative's vote. And do you know, I still didn't believe Adams or Clay either one had played foul. Until, of course, Clay was appointed Secretary of State. Then"

—he lifted a finger—"but not until then—I knew. And here's the point, Sam: if I had to do it again, I would still stick to the rules. Because honor is all a man has that's worth anything in the end. Cheating, corruption, bribery, manipulation—when the chips are in, they'll all damn you." He took a pillow from the sofa and positioned it behind his head. "Sometimes things are muddled, son, but that's just all the more reason to go by the rules. Don't think I haven't asked myself if it wouldn't have been better for my constituents if I'd cut the deal. Just as you're asking yourself if it wouldn't be better for everyone if you could settle with White off the field. The answer to both is no. That kind of question will tire your brain, Sam, make you old. The rules are: if you accept the challenge, you fight the duel. Stick to them."

Houston was not taken in. The old bird had broken every rule in the books at one time or another when it suited his purpose. He had refused to cut a deal with Clay—if indeed Clay had actually proposed one—because of image, not honor. Jackson only talked honor when he wanted to fight, or have a traitor shot.

Jackson stood, crossed the room to the walnut secretary near the window and opened the top drawer, its brass pulls dropping back against the wood as the fire whined gases from the logs. He turned back around, blued metal flashing in his hand, a slender barrel pointing up. "This is the gun I used to shoot Mr. Dickenson," he said, admiring it. "I think I have just the right set for you and White, if you're interested. You've chosen pistols, of course?"

"Yes sir." There was a sarcasm in his tone that always crept out when Jackson, or anyone besides himself, called the shots.

"No dirty business or hair triggers, I hope?"

"No."

"Good. Tomorrow we'll take up practice in the far field. I can't afford to lose you, Sam."

So this was all. How easily the man could pronounce judgment and give sentence. Houston resented him for it but knew it was what he had come for—assurance, conviction. He also knew Jackson would make the same judgment if he himself were to fight the duel.

Houston sat a few seconds without answering, then slapped his hands down on his knees, pressing down, a close to the topic. He forced a smile. "Well. Tell me about Overton."

"The man's a genius," Jackson said, putting the gun away and returning to the sofa. "That town of ours grows by the day. We were discussing it last night. Thirty-two years ago Memphis was just five thousand acres on a desolate bluff over the Mississippi River. Infested with savages. And John Overton said, 'Picture a boat landing here, Andrew, think of the potential for trade.'" He paused, then added in a lower voice, "Sam, there's a whole half of a continent farther west to be got and settled." He set his eyes on Houston, who felt a lifting, a rush of blood, and the instinctive caution to hide his emotional, even physical reaction to talk of the West. "But it takes men of vision to see it, Sam. And men of courage to do it." The General fell silent, his words heavy in the air; there was always weight in his voice when he spoke of the West to Sam Houston. Sam heard the tone; he himself was clever enough with voice to recognize insinuations, but what it was the General was thinking or suggesting remained a mystery. As always. Settling the West was a common theme with Old Hickory, most common when the General was speaking with Houston. But the particulars—when the West should be taken, by what means, and how far it extended—were not discussed. Once Houston had asked him directly what he thought should be done with the West. "That's for younger men to worry with" was the answer, and Houston had not been deceived; he knew the General worried the idea constantly. Of course the old man had to be mysterious—Aaron Burr was tried as a traitor for scheming to take the West and make himself emperor of it. Jackson had been, in some remote way that was a buried secret to all but himself and Burr, connected with Burr during the time of his western maneuverings. Jackson escaped indictment and Burr hanging, but both were censured. It had never been officially proven that Jackson was involved in or even aware of Burr's plan to conquer western territories and institute an empire. Most believed it was just Jackson's readiness to fight the Spanish—or any other foreign power with a foothold in

North America—that had led him into a hasty and deluded relationship with a foxy scamp like Aaron Burr. Whatever the truth, Jackson had learned his lesson well: now he set all talk of conquering in a vague, subjunctive and somewhat whimsical vein—a cautious, private mind scheming behind the facade of a rambling backwoods idealist. "I was so naive," he had said earlier—a born liar, though one with an almost boyish decency about him, springing from his unshakable belief that whatever he did was right. Though scores of lies would be told and blood spilt along the way, in the end, Houston guessed, through fair means or foul, Andrew Jackson would get the West, but he would get it—and here was the redeeming thing—for the Union. Whatever he had meditated as a young man, Jackson was now too much of a Unionist to dream of personal empires.

"We bought Memphis, Sam, but the West cannot be bought now. The Mexicans have made it clear they are not amenable to selling even one foothill to the United States. But it can be got."

A second of hesitation, then a leap. "Fighting, sir?"

The General frowned, too staged a frown and contradicted by the shine in his eyes. If there was anything he loved as much as battle, it was the prospect of it; God blast old age to bloody hell. Houston saw him lean forward eagerly, then check himself. "Overton and I were not even thirty when we bought that land," he said.

He was toying with Houston. Houston was irritated and responded likewise, antagonizing the General. "And the Chickasaws," he said, "began their long march westward."

Jackson turned his head to Sam, and his voice was hard, "You miss my point, son. I'm talking about ingenuity, initiative, risk. Not your godforsaken savages."

"Your point is well taken, sir, though not fully understood."

"Good." His eyes went back to the fire and he continued his talk of Memphis: the city had finally been approved, but the smallpox epidemic was killing off citizens. The mayor, Marcus Winchester, was married to a Negress, and the couple had taken in a Scotswoman named Fanny Wright, who was buying and freeing slaves and giving them land to farm.

Houston made little response. The General was no longer talking West, he was talking trivia, and Houston was suddenly very tired. To him slavery was a damnable thing at best, but, he thought, at least the Negroes weren't being methodically shoved westward and killed off. Jackson's voice came to him as out of a dream—the warmth, the steady ticking of the mantel clock and maundering of the fire—"It's passing strange, Sam, how a radical thinker like Marcus Winchester could befriend an ignorant backwoodsman like David Crockett. I suppose they identify with each other's rascality. I can't figure how Crockett ever got elected to the state legislature. He's got no policies, only personality and tall tales and the orneriness to oppose every policy I've got on land and Indians." The General paused, and Houston stared at the fire, his lids drooping. He had the vague feeling he should respond. Then Jackson's voice came at him charging full tilt, "But I guess you're not the one to talk to about Indians, right, Sam? Wake up, boy—damn you, wake up!"

A command. The General wanted to argue, and had chosen an arousing topic. "You know my feelings on removal policy, sir," Houston answered forcefully.

"Yes. A boy's feelings. Soft."

"No sir."

"No?"

"There's nothing soft about it. By moving the Cherokees west we have pushed them into Osage land, and the Osage are killing them. What is it you called it, General, the Land of Promise?"

"It is the Land of Promise."

"The land of ten thousand promises," Houston responded, "all broken by our greed and the corruption of U.S. officials." He checked his acid tone and continued in a lower voice, "Yes, I do find removal a foul policy, though I fear it's inevitable. But if we would just live up to our promises and pay the Indians for their land, provide new, fertile land that is safe, and return to them their rights and their native dignity, the policy would not be so irksome. The policy itself is unjust, but it's the corruption in implementation that causes so much suffering. As you well know."

The General yawned, a revenge for Houston's earlier lapse.

"We have violated every treaty we ever made with them," Houston pressed. "Twenty-eight to be exact—"

"They also have broken the treaties, Congressman."

"Until a few years ago they couldn't even read the treaties they signed without white men interpreting for them. We took advantage from the very first of negotiations."

"The missionaries teach them to read," Jackson replied. "Sam, my boy, don't rack yourself over them. The Cherokees have been known to burn white men alive. To scalp them and make them dance until they bleed to death."

"And we have been known to—"

"Spare me your obsessions, Sam. You're talking to a man who took a Creek child into his home and raised him as his own."

"That's true, sir. As a white. You raised Lincoya as a white after we killed his parents."

"Yes. We. You killed more Creeks than I did. And with enthusiasm, I must say."

"Creeks. You know the difference there. The Cherokees fought with us against them."

"So they did. And in their own interest. It wasn't a favor, Sam. And anyway, even if I was inclined to help your Cherokees, I'm in no position to do it; I was defeated for President, in case you don't recall. You're arguing with the wrong man. I happen to be a mere farmer, and the Adams administration isn't in the habit of listening to farmers' opinions on national policies. Your Indians are at the mercy of the President."

How the old scoundrel could gall. Now that Houston was fully awake, Jackson went back to his original topic, as if nothing had been said in between. As if the diversion had been good sport, but now back to what mattered. Houston had a mind to cut him off but resisted.

"Anyway," Jackson said, resuming his previous genial note, "Crockett was taking a cargo of staves to New Orleans a few weeks ago. He hit a snag a couple of miles upriver from Memphis."

Houston deduced that the conversation must be going somewhere after all, must all along have had a purpose to it, or the General would not be so doggedly pressing on with it. In his exhaustion, Sam had let himself believe the man was rambling—a mistake —for the General was never without purpose, never lost or even temporarily sidetracked; every topic Jackson pulled up, every word he uttered led along a path in a steady direction. It might be years before his meaning and purpose were clear, before the path got anywhere at all, but you could count on it not being a dead end or a dry run. "He lost all his cargo and some men. Marcus took him in. He was traveling south but talking West. Talking Texas. Do you want a drink?"

Texas. Again the rush of blood, of anticipation; Jackson had tantalized him with nebulous talk of the enigmatic West and was now getting down to a place, a determined area with a name and known features and known obstacles and possibilities for fame and fortune, getting down to it, finally, sending Houston's mind racing west past Memphis into regions radiant in his imagination, a blur of green and April breezes and desert farther on. He saw it as a huge, fertile territory ripening for conquest, waiting for men like him, waiting for a specific word, or even a nod, from a man like Andrew Jackson. For an instant Houston thought the General might give that word of direction, lay out the scheme, tell Houston to visit Texas and see how the ground lay, how the settlers were getting on with the Mexican government, and assess the nature of local Indian sentiments. But it seemed the only word Jackson would give was the one that elicited rather than directed Sam Houston's wild visions and ambitions—a great mass of potential like an eager horse, hobbled—*Texas;* and then no other word, for the General was moving on, talking on, pouring Pennsylvania red whiskey from a decanter on a table in the far corner. He took up his Turkish pipe, stuffing tobacco in with knobby, crooked fingers, saying with his back to Houston, "Anyway, so much for that. Overton has lots of news. You'll have to see him yourself. He's excited about a new contraption of a lamp he has in his dining room, invented by some foreigner. It gets more oxygen to the flame so it burns better. Of course it uses more oil because it burns it so fast, and with whale oil at two dollars and fifty cents a gallon . . ." He shook his head and crossed the room, his countenance pondering with a staged expression, and presented the drink to Houston. Houston took a swallow. The General turned to the fire, and taking up slender tongs from the hearth reached and lifted an ember with which he lit his pipe. "He wants me to come see it. You and I should go together."

And suddenly the future, the West, vanished, leaving the quiet room with the clock on the mantel and Jackson's pipe glowing red— a moment outwardly calm, as calculated and predictable as the ticking clock, but for Sam, suddenly shattered. He might die in the duel. The pipe trailed smoke like a pistol after firing, reminding Houston of lines from Lord Byron's *Childe Harold*, whole cantos of which he knew by heart:

> *Love, fame, ambition, avarice—'t is the same,*
> *Each idle, and all ill, and none the worst—*
> *For all are meteors with a different name,*
> *And Death the sable smoke where vanishes the flame.*

He might never go to Judge Overton's home and see the new invention. He might never see Overton again. No matter how old and blind White was . . . freakish things could happen. . . . Fate had two people to look after. It occurred to Houston he had never really believed he was as mortal as the next man. He had come close to death at the Horseshoe and during the operation afterward, in New Orleans, when they dug the musket ball from his shoulder. But he had not died. Perhaps he had gained too much confidence in his own stamina. Now, in this instant, death seemed possible, and very near. And the man who had always looked after his best interests, the man to whom he looked for advice, was planning trips and concerned with the cost of whale oil. The old, bigoted bastard. Sam felt alone, victimized, a mere pawn in the General's game, to be sacrificed for the sport of a move and the small purpose of ridding the board of one Federalist pawn in an obscure position. And then through his angry solitude came Jackson's voice, firm, quiet, believable. "Sam," he said, his pipe idle in his hand, the voice falling to a whisper, "you will not lose. I promise you that. You have my word of honor that you'll come back alive and whole. You have to. I have plans for you." His eyes took on a fiery glow like that in the bowl of his pipe, as he took a long draw.

Houston met his look, his body tense and still. "What plans?" he said.

Jackson kept the stem in his mouth, puffing out, saying, "You're always ready, aren't you, Sam? Good. You'll see—after the duel. Come back from that as eager as you are now, and we'll talk about plans."

And Houston believed him, believed he would live, that his Conducting Providence was alive and well in this very room, in the eyes of Andrew Jackson. He was Houston, and he had a great future awaiting him, with plans. The General's plans, whatever they were, coupled with his own superior nature, could not fail.

The two men set eyes on each other in a silent communication. "Of course," Jackson said harshly, "I've had plans before, that were thwarted by corrupt men who have twisted the American system in order to implement their own bloody plans."

He was a tired man with a thin, bitter line of a mouth, all his charismatic power still intact, but the fulcrum of power, the presidency, stolen from him by two men who manipulated the American Congress into disregarding the will of the people. He had a right to his acerbity. He leaned and took up a newspaper from the floor; the room was always littered with papers, for he subscribed to over twenty. Squinting down at it, he walked to the fire, tossed it in to see it flame, and sat again on the sofa. "So," he said. "We know you are to fight and win a duel. We suppose also that you will then be elected governor." He waited for the younger man to disagree or question, but Houston said nothing. "Governor Carroll's a good man; he fought well for me in the Creek wars and New Orleans. But you're better." He paused again. "In fact, you only lack one thing to make you a great man." A spasm of coughing interrupted; he thumped his chest with an open palm. "Bloody cough."

"May I get you some water?"

Jackson shook his head. "You need a wife, Sam," he said during a gap in his hacking. "A woman would bring out the very best in you." He smiled, showing ghoulish gray teeth. "Like Mrs. Jackson does for me."

It was the old argument with a new tack. "Sir, marriage is your prescription for everyone."

"You most especially. I know how you are, Sam, with women. But you can change. And you should change. Having so many different women implies disloyalty in a man's nature. A man does need variety in his life—in horses, interests, friends, and so forth. But not women. Not at your age. People just don't respect it in a man your age." He gave a final cough and cleared his throat, then took a draw on his pipe. "It's high time, Sam."

Houston said nothing. The "variety" passed through his mind in a parade of flesh—pale skin against white sheets in a plush Washington hotel, dark nipples on small breasts in the forest undergrowth of Cherokee territory. He saw the angles of one mix-breed's face: Diana Rogers, named for the Greek goddess of the moon and hunt, called Tiana by the Cherokees. He saw the red hair of Peggy O'Neal, the round white thighs of the prostitute he had had at the inn two nights ago, thighs wrapped tight around him, his own body sunk into the warmth of Female—not *a* female, never a single female, but the essence of femininity, Eve in a thousand guises.

And then Eliza Allen, a small embodiment of the best characteristics of her sex, Eve in a single guise of complex womanhood: the defiance, the air of striving, of wanting, the yellow braid flying back the day she rode so wildly, her body low, her legs clinging close around the animal, her skirt catching the wind and coming up. . . . "General, I'm thirty-three years old. And I do get lonely. Not for women, of course. For a woman. But a wife would alter everything."

"Bah." He brushed his hand through the air. "Change. Change is the only constant."

"I spend most of my time on the road between Washington and Tennessee. I never know what I'll be doing the next year or where I'll be doing it, and when I do decide, I'm free for it. But with a wife . . ."

"Sam, one good thing about a wife is you can leave her at home."

"Then what is the point?" Houston asked, imagining chastity for long months of separation. Marriage under such conditions seemed of little advantage, something destined to reduce a man to lunacy or lies, for who could go for months without sex and stay sane? But this he did not say, for Andrew Jackson had done it, and, as far as anyone knew, without a single indiscretion.

"A wife would give you a foundation, stability, respectability. To be precise, Sam, and honest, a wife—if you chose the right one— would give you exactly what you lack."

"Stability? Respectability?"

"Yes."

The old bastard. Houston leaned back in his chair and looked at the fire. "I gained those on my own. Sir."

The General left a silence that denied it. Then, "You're not a coward, Sam, so why are you afraid to make a commitment?"

It was a calculated challenge, and Sam decided not to take it seriously. He responded quietly, as if addressing himself. "I am not afraid to make a commitment. I am not set against it. I simply haven't gotten around to doing it."

"Your old excuse—you haven't found the right girl?" He was pressing, and Sam was annoyed.

"That was Overton's defense, not mine; I own up to the fact I'm not looking for the right girl. The variety you mentioned is more my style."

"An outmoded one, at your age. What you mean is it's more to your liking."

"Do I need to respond to that?"

Jackson's voice was close and intimate, "I'm not going to badger you about this, Sam. But I want you to think about it. I'll be honest with you: you have more potential than any young man I know. But you need a restraining influence. You're drinking too much, and your language, I've been told, is even more vile than mine. Your attire is excessive and your demeanor is pompous. God knows why everyone likes you so much. But they do. Your charm with women and command with men is impressive. I can only guess what it would be if you were respectable."

Houston forced a smile. "If these are the plans you were talking about, sir, you'd better change them. Marriage is something I intend to do, when I do it, on my own."

Jackson laughed, high and rasping, and stretched his agile arm in the air. "No, Sam. Marriage was only part of the plan. You'll like the rest better. Now. Tell me about Washington. What are our President and Secretary of State saying these days? Anything I would not have heard?"

"Silent as a tomb."

"Ah." The Old Hero leaned back with an air of confidence. "The very liberties of this country are in danger. As I see it, it's a contest between the aristocracy and the democracy of America, and as long as that bargaining dog Adams is in the White House he'll keep democracy buried like a dirty bone. The goddamn puritanical mongrel." Houston made no comment, and the General leaned over the rounded horsehair arm toward him, his breath close and foul. "And Clay, I think that poor devil is frightened of his own corruption. He's digging for something against me to dwarf his own cheating. The best he's done so far is call me an ignorant military chieftain. I take it as a compliment. He finds fault with me because I've risked myself for my country, when by disobeying the desire of United States citizens, he's risked his country for himself. This is the kind of man we're up against, Sam, a man keen enough to know his own treachery and wretched enough not to let it bother him. A man manipulative enough to get away with it. For a while." He paused, the two men leaning toward each other, Sam with his elbows on his knees, the knees spread wide, whiskey in one hand, Jackson leaning into and over the horsehair arm. "He's trying to ruin me, Sam. He's bent on it. And that man could make the Angel Gabriel look black. His methods are foul. There's no knowing what he'll come up with." He flashed a grim smile. "I'm afraid my name will be easier to ruin than the Angel Gabriel's. Prepare yourself for a bloody, vicious battle before we drive Adams out of the White House, because Henry Clay put him in and is determined to keep him in. And Henry Clay is the meanest bastard that ever disgraced the image of his God." He leaned back and added with a side glance at Houston, "Even the Vice President is on our side."

Houston answered harshly, "We don't want him."

Jackson raised his brows. "We?"

"He's no friend to you, sir."

"Just because he reprimanded you for dressing like a savage. Are you still holding that old grudge?"

"No. But Calhoun is without honor. He's a liar. He refused me the army commission I rightfully earned. He accused me falsely of complicity with slave smugglers, and when I proved my innocence and resigned from his service as subagent—a job, I might add, that I excelled in because I could get on with the Cherokees, dress their way and speak their language—when I proved my innocence he made no apology." Houston drained his glass and sat looking down at it, turning it in the firelight.

"That's over and done with," Jackson said.

Houston met his look. "I'll fight your battles, General, and your duels, and I'll refrain from vocally opposing your Indian policies. But Houston will not support John Calhoun—not even for you."

Jackson's eyes burned. His long chin moved gradually forward and up, and his words came slow and emphatic, "No one, Congressman, fights my duels for me. I fight my own battles. And I win them. This duel is yours—you got yourself into it. I asked you to handle a small matter for me, and you created a national affair. I did not ask you to take it so far. And as for my Indian removal policies, the reason you don't speak out against them is because you know you can best serve your Cherokee friends by remaining my ally. I need

Calhoun's support, just as you need mine. Do you understand my position?"

"Fully, sir. And I believe it is a compromised one."

"You're overstepping, Sam."

Neither man could afford to back down. Houston would not support Calhoun and would not release Jackson from his responsibility in the affair with Erwin. What Sam had done in the situation with Erwin was exactly what Jackson had wanted him to do; both men, in this moment of confrontation, knew it. But Houston also knew how far he could push the General, and he had reached the limit. Still glaring, he managed a smile.

Jackson, without hesitation, spread his meager lips into a grin, the fire in his eyes instantly gone as if soused by water. "Let's call it a night, Sam. We've got a long day of pistol practice ahead of us, son. We'll start at daybreak." Houston set his glass down beside the dying fire. The two men stood. "And you might sleep on the marriage idea. Mull it over in your dreams. When the fire burns out and the cold creeps in."

Morning sunlight stretched Houston's shadow out before him. Extending his arm full length, he turned sideways and squinted his left eye, marked the stump with his right, and squeezed off the trigger. The ball hit dead center, splitting the stump in two, the jagged core splintering.

"Better!" Jackson hollered, punching the crisp air with his fist, "Damn fine! Use that very pistol, Sam; it's never hung fire yet. I guarantee the dispart is no more than a half inch for fifteen yards. Just make sure the powder's dry and the touchhole ain't foul, aim a tad left and you've won yourself a duel!"

Houston measured in more powder, dropped in another ball, a wad, and tamped it all down. "Careful on the powder, son, it's easy to overload that set. A.J. damn near blew himself up toying with that one you're using. Now, you'll have your back to him like this. Say you've already paced it off, and you're standing like this. You've got to the count of four to turn, take aim, and fire. Now if you position your feet like this, spread about this much and turned just so, just slightly, then you can make a quarter turn of your body without taking a step. It'll save you a fraction of time. Try it from there. That stump is William White. That's right. Good. Perfect. The feet about an inch closer together—well, whatever's comfortable. Now when you draw, try biting down on a bullet—put your force into it— it'll steady your aim. Ready? Fire. One . . .

Sam clenched down, turned, and fired, the ball lodging in one side of the split stump. He lowered his arm and heard a horse approaching from behind.

"Well, speak of the devil!" Jackson called out. "A.J., my boy, I was just telling Sam about when you almost blew yourself up with that pistol he's using."

A.J. reined in his bay gelding and lifted his hat. "Morning, Uncle. Morning, Congressman." His lean face split into a grin. "I hear we're to have a duel."

Houston despised the man's jovial greeting, but answered lightly, "So we are, Mr. Donelson."

Jackson beamed in the sunlight, crow's-feet around his eyes. "And he's a damn good shot," he said with a nod. "Better than you, A.J. In fact, let's add some spice to this thing, some competition. Do you both good. Come shoot that stump from this distance, A.J. Sam's just hit it twice." Donelson's smile lapsed. "Come on down, boy," Jackson urged. "What are you—afraid? With that West Point training I paid for, you should be able to outshoot a country boy like Sam."

How he could demean. Sam felt ridiculed for his lack of education: a boy living with the Indians and a copy of Pope's *Iliad;* he was sure A.J. felt put down for his fancy schooling. The two men avoided each other's eyes.

Leaning to stroke the bay's neck, A.J. said, "No thank you, sir; at West Point they cuff a man up if he's caught anywhere near a duel."

"My God, but the world is sinking. How can they train men to be honorable soldiers if they won't let them fight for their honor? Get on down off that horse, son. I want to see you shoot."

It was an order. Donelson glanced at the stump and dismounted. "I'm rusty," he said.

"Nonsense. You were practicing last week. Here, come take Sam's place right here. Sam, get that pistol ready for my nephew."

Houston loaded with the air of a professional duelist, his movements steady and graceful. A.J. talked casually—When was the duel to come off? Had Erwin backed out completely? Well, White wouldn't be much of a match; an old woman could shoot down General White.

Sam handed him the pistol.

Old Hickory moved over beside him and nodded toward the target. "Now shoot it," he said.

The young man positioned himself, sighted down the barrel, glanced over at Houston, who was watching the stump, and then back at his target. He pulled the trigger and the ball raised dirt a foot in front of the stump. "Rusty," he said, shaking his head.

"Well try again," Jackson answered.

A.J. loaded, aimed and fired, again hitting just short.

"You're supposed to learn from your mistakes, Andrew," the old General goaded. "If you aim low the first time, aim higher the next." He looked at Sam, turned down the corners of his mouth and shook his head. "I'll swear, a West Point education don't amount to a damn thing if they don't teach you that." Then, to A.J., "Try again."

This time it was too high. "Here, give that to Sam, let him show you how it's done."

Houston reloaded. He had already proved himself, already hit the stump. He was embarrassed for Andrew, but his keen sense of competition, his pervasive desire to excel and beat even his own records, made his blood rise. He held the ball between his thumb and forefinger and dropped it in. Part of the victory was imparting the subtle message that the game was more important to the other man, that defeat of such a man as your opponent was insignificant, all in a day's work. He put a ball in his mouth and bit down, tasting the acrid lead, and said with his teeth closed, "How many paces do you men think I should call for with White?"

"Make it, say, twelve," Jackson answered.

"So, twelve each," Houston repeated, still biting down.

"No. Twelve. Six each." Houston spat the ball from his mouth and stared at the General. "In deference to White's poor marksmanship," Jackson added. "Give him a chance."

"Six paces, sir—that's murder!"

"Or suicide," Donelson observed with a lift of his brows and a boyish, pleased expression.

"It's only thirty-six feet!"

"I'm tolerable with numbers, Sam," Jackson said.

"We'll kill each other."

"No, not a chance." He shook his head and lifted a finger. "General White's done plenty shooting under my command, and I've never seen him kill a man yet. Never seen him even hit one, come to think of it."

"But six paces each—twelve paces . . ."

"Twelve paces is a good solid distance. Walk it off, A.J. Start here where Sam is and walk it off. Let's have a look."

The young man approached Houston, came close, then turned and began stepping off the distance, each plant of his foot coming down with force—even, in Houston's eyes, with blatant glee.

Jackson stretched a long finger toward the mutilated stump. "If you can hit that stump at twenty yards, you can certainly hit a man at twelve. You could hit him at thirty, Sam, between his eyes if it weren't for the dispart." He lowered his hand and leveled his gaze on Houston. "You're going to shoot him no matter what distance you set. So do him a favor; at least let him think he's got a chance to hit you too." He winked, his eyes glassy in the sunlight. "It'd be good politics, Congressman. Taking his bad eyesight into account." Houston did not smile and the General became serious, his voice lower. "And he won't hit you; I promise you that. With your speed and steady aim there's no way in hell he'll even pull the trigger before he's down."

His damned imperiousness, as if he could know. God himself. "But I'd kill him at that distance."

"Son. What do you think a duel is? Recreation?" Frowning, Jackson turned his face to Donelson, who was standing in the crisp morning light with a pleased expression, one knee cocked and a hand on his hip. "See there. That's not too close." He gave a stiff shrug, the dry hands slightly lifted. "But do as you please."

Houston stared at the Old Hero. A.J. called over, his voice clear and happy as the birds singing from the skirt of timber near the water, "Like my uncle says, it'd be mighty noble of you, Congressman. Or, if you wanted to be especially fair, you could blindfold yourself!"

Houston cut his eyes at him, then back at the stump, and in a swift movement lifted his arm, taking quick and careless aim, and fired past Donelson toward the stump. The ball lodged dead center of the left half.

Silence followed; it seemed not even the birds were singing. Houston turned to look at the General. "That's good," Jackson said in a hoarse whisper, his eyes steady. "You get angry. And then you remember that William White sent the challenge over. Not me, not A.J., and not you. In the end it is William White who forced you into this. Believe that. Remember his arrogance. And when you sight him down that pistol barrel don't you dare see a nearsighted old man with a family—you look at him, and you see an arrogant fool who intends to kill you. And you shoot him down." He paused, then added, "Aside from all my jesting about his marksmanship, he will do his damnedest to hit you, and if you hesitate for one instant, if you pity him for a single godless second, he might get lucky and do it. If that happens, and you haven't fired yet, you remain standing until you do—and then you hit him. I had Dickenson's bullet in my chest when I took aim and fired; I would have killed that devil even had he shot me through the brain first. You set any distance you want, and you set it to your advantage." Then he smiled, slow and wicked, "Of course I wasn't serious about six. Just testing you, my boy, to see how you obey orders."

A flight of doves passed overhead, moving south. Andrew Donelson began to walk toward the General and Sam Houston. "I failed your test, sir," Houston said with a lift of his chin. "I would not have done it."

"Good." Again the smile. "I would not have done it either."

CHAPTER 7

Two days after her meeting in the grain barn with Will Tyree, Eliza went to stay with her step-grandmother, MaryAnn Mitchie Smith Donelson Saunders, or Polly. She was the only person Eliza loved without intimidation, or guilt, or some provocation. Balie Peyton, her other confidant, a friend since childhood, had been too involved with his law practice to spend time with her the past two years, and so a distance fell between them. And Dilsey also had her barriers. She aroused Eliza to self-accusation. There were times when Eliza believed that Dilsey was wiser than she, and felt uneasy with authority she could not justify. So Polly was her only innocent love; with Polly she had nothing to apologize for, nothing to live up to, and nothing to be angry about.

Polly took Eliza into her home, an extended cabin of hewn logs. They shared a fire and a cozy evening. After Dry Saunders and the children had gone to bed, Polly talked awhile about her sons from her first marriage, A.J. and Daniel Donelson—how well they were doing, Andrew as secretary to General Jackson, Daniel at West Point. She recounted again how General Jackson had helped her climb from her window and elope with Rachel Jackson's brother Samuel when she was fifteen. It was a story that pleased Eliza, especially this time, for it told of a girl who defied her father's command and married the man of her choice, without trepidation. She did not tell Polly about Will.

The next morning Eliza helped Polly with the laundry (they kept no slaves) and took a walk. The home was on Saunders Ferry Road, originally a buffalo path and Indian trail running north from the Cumberland River to the Gallatin Pike. Just down a way, on the east side of the road in a grove of oak trees near a spring, was the church Grandfather Dry and his first wife, Eliza's blood grandmother, had started. She was buried there, with two of her children. Now the place was abandoned; a new church stood at the Gallatin and Walton Ferry crossroads.

Dry kept the old churchyard cemetery in perfect order, often weeding it in moonlight. Eliza could recall once as a child hearing him leave through the side door of the house late at night; she had gone to the window and watched him move off down the road between the tall timber on either side, toward the old meetinghouse, his body slight, his huge head of gray hair tilted to one side, like a fugitive child in the moonlight with an odd sadness in his walk.

The day was bright and cool. She wore one of Polly's dresses, a blue gingham, because hers were hung to dry. The bodice was too large, so she wore a shawl around it. She walked off down to the old meetinghouse and stood awhile at her grandmother's grave, listening to the creek. *Hannah Dyer Saunders*—the stone was covered in yellow lichen. She had never known her.

On this day Eliza was melancholy with the sort of heightened feelings one has when in love, a desire to feel, be it sadness or joy— the sort of probing, fearless venturing into emotion that a person can manage only when there is something very right in her life, like a new love. And Will Tyree, despite the confusion he left her in and the strangeness of that last moment together, was a new love, a first love, and right for her. With him in mind, the whole world, even her deceased grandmother, held a mystery, a pleasurable uncertainty and a thousand possibilities.

She stood for a long time, listening to the water and watching oak leaves fall through the grapevines. She thought of Will Tyree touching her, eliciting the sensations.

And she played other scenarios in her mind. One was not sensual, but provocative in a disturbing way: It was spring, sunny; she was riding along the Cumberland and heard a horse coming full speed from behind. She turned; it was Will. There had been an accident. Her father was hurt—he had been kicked by a horse. Together they rode back, full speed. The colonel was lying in the aisle of the stable, badly injured. Perhaps he was dying. George was with him, and the field hands were watching in silence. Will took her in his arms. And this was the emotion of the dream—not the pain, but the tenderness. It was a terrible nightmare of a dream, and yet she conjured it up like a fantasy. Perhaps death played a part because she was standing over a grave, or perhaps she was looking at some distorted perception of the future. Whatever, she was suddenly uncomfortable with the wickedness of her vision, and out of a need for sanity and forgiveness—though she was already, at sixteen, beginning to doubt that either existed—she went into the old church.

Sam Houston started out from the Hermitage and rode due north toward Kentucky, crossing the Cumberland on the ferry just below Jones' Bend. He arrived near the headwaters of Drake's Creek, less than a mile from the old meetinghouse.

The benches had been moved to the new meeting place. Eliza sat on the floor in a square of sunlight that shone in through one of two window frames. The floor was dusty and warm; dust drifted in the light. The shadow of a tree limb dipped down into the square of light when a breeze blew; sun was tepid on her back. She imagined

Will Tyree walking in through the door. She touched her face where he had touched her, her neck, and slid her fingers down into the loose bodice of the dress, feeling what he had felt when he touched her—what she had felt when he touched her.

The enchanting memory was not without complexity, for he had left her with an odd dismissal. She changed her fantasy: they were Sam Houston's hands. She heard the sound of a horse approaching on dry leaves, the creak of a saddle; she watched the door and listened to be sure. Few travelers passed through this way, off the main road; for a moment she thought perhaps it was Will, that he had come to find her. The horse stopped outside and the rider dismounted. After a moment a man dipped his head to enter, and at first the wide-brimmed hat hid his face. He wore a red flannel shirt and brown trousers with Indian leggings. Then he raised his eyes and saw her.

For an instant his face was haggard, then surprised, as a sleeping boy who wakes to a room he does not know. He blinked once, slow and curious, and stopped in the doorway. Eliza stood in an instinctive bid to get herself on equal terms.

"Miss Allen," he said. "Fate seems to bring us together at odd moments." He took off his hat. "I didn't mean to startle you," he added and then was silent, his eyes demanding something of her.

She was aware of the sagging bodice, how childish she must look in Polly's dress, and pulled the shawl around her. "You didn't startle me," she said.

He gave his slow, dry smile with a hundred meanings—she amused him, she pleased him, she aroused him, some or all, she didn't know.

His eagle spurs tapped on the puncheon floor as he came toward her, but he did not remove them. He stood over her, holding his hat, his great height and his silence taking over the empty church, taking over completely. The top of her head was level with his lower chest. She looked at the floor, at his huge cowhide boots. He placed his finger under her chin and lifted her face. "I'm on my way to Kentucky," he said. "It seems General White is determined to go through with the duel. Tomorrow."

She thought of the old man's face, his voice, so pitiful, "You have drawn me into this business. You have tried to draw me into it—" and Sam Houston, now so close with his finger still lifting her chin, had said, "You have forced yourself into it." She did not realize, with him touching her so lightly, lifting her face to his, that she too had forced herself into it. And that there was no way out of it. She lowered her eyes from his face and watched the steady pulse throbbing hard in his neck; she had never seen a pulse so evident and near. Seeing life this close, firm and strong and yet a day away from facing death, impressed her. She could smell his sweat. She lowered her gaze still further, to his chest, and saw from the bottom edge of her sight that the bodice of Polly's dress had puckered out, exposing her. A moment she hesitated, then corrected it and looked up to see if he had noticed.

"It's all right," he said. "I'm charmed." As she had known he would be. He could have pretended he had not seen; his honesty created intimacy. They shared a secret. He took his hand away and stood looking over her head, out the window. "I stop here sometimes," he said, "on my way to see your grandfather."

"It's the emptiness," she answered, meaning the church, the quiet. "I come here too, when I'm visiting." She did not need to resist him as she had before; she felt she was his equal now, neither child nor virgin.

"The emptiness," he mused as if to himself. "Yes, I know."

"I meant, the church."

Again he looked at her. "Empty," he said, his voice mysterious and full of implication, "except for you and me, and ghosts, and memories. What are you thinking, Eliza? Do you think I'll die tomorrow?"

The power of it, as if she could determine his fate. The idea was alluring. She did not realize he was not talking to her at all, but to himself, not the easy, direct speech of a man like Will Tyree, but the dreamy tones of a mystic—a man too complex to be understood, too paradoxical ever to understand himself—a man who has spent his life searching, believing that someday he will find and understand, now suddenly living what could be his last day, and it is all still a puzzle. The wonder of life. "No," she answered.

"I feel I have so much to live for." He said it very simply, as Will might have said it, but behind the words were a myriad of meanings, and also apprehension and a great amount of regret. It occurred to her there were two Sam Houstons, the public and the private—a man split in two. "I came with a letter for Polly, from her son A.J.," he said, taking a folded paper from his shirt pocket, "Would you give it to her?"

She accepted it.

"Tell her I intended to stop. But had to press on." With a direct look at her, he added, "Will you be here if I come back this way?"

For only an instant, as she looked up at his hard face, she thought again of Will, his backwoods voice and gentle hands; she felt nostalgia, as for a favorite piece of clothing, warm and comfortable. He had given her courage. Yet he had also, in that parting moment, confused her. Had he not done so, had his final demeanor been consistent with their tender lovemaking, she might have answered Sam Houston differently. Or so she tried to believe. "Yes," she said, "I will."

It was not a promise to a dying man, but a commitment to the future, his future; this she knew, and in knowing sacrificed her innocence in a fuller way than she had done with Will Tyree. There was a small, lingering part of her still a child, swept up by his strength, coaxed into trusting him. There was another part of her, a girl reaching out to a person facing death. But she was also, suddenly, a woman who saw the power of this man and was no longer opposed to it, but instead—in a way that sealed her guilt in all that later came of that moment, that promise—in love with it.

"Tomorrow," he said, "in the evening." Reaching slowly, he moved his hand under her chin, around the back of her neck, his eyes on hers. He felt her hair and fingered the blue satin ribbon that tied it. "May I?" he asked but was already pulling it free. "For luck. For destiny and all that." He paused, his green eyes searching. Then he turned and crossed to the doorway, the ribbon dangling, so small, from his hand. Just outside he turned and looked back at her and replaced his hat; it was an honest, questioning look, half-fearful—a look that won her heart.

CHAPTER 8

Fog. He could smell it. It was three-forty in the morning; a hound pup yapping outside had awakened him. Morning crept dark and chill into the living area of Sanford Duncan's double-level log home. Houston rose, and pulling his blanket around him went to the shuttered window, careful not to wake the other men. He flipped the latch and pushed the shutters outward.

Duncan had two pups, gangly mottled mutts, part bulldog, the only survivors from a large litter. The bitch had died before they were five weeks. Duncan, an old political ally of General Jackson, had named the pups Andrew Jackson and Thomas Benton because they fought so viciously, often drawing blood but making peace in the end. It was Andrew Jackson who now sat yapping in the fog outside the window. He caught Houston's movement, cocked his head, lifted his ears and bounced to the window, his tail cutting through the fog in rhythmic sweeps. Looking Houston in the eye, he barked joyfully and jumped at the window. Houston saw it as a voice from God, Andrew Jackson himself encouraging him on. He leaned out and stroked the dog's head.

Behind him, the men were snoring. Doc Shelby had shown up after all, around midnight, quiet, disapproving, but supportive just by being there. Another friend, Captain John G. Anderson, a grocer merchant from Nashville, had learned of the duel; he informed Shelby and the two rode out together. Anderson's mild, relaxed manner was a salve to Houston, who was caught between McGregor's readiness and Shelby's silent reprehension. Anderson, McGregor and Houston drank late into the night around the kitchen table at Duncan's home—Houston's face deadly serious, his jaw muscles flexing continuously, McGregor chewing a sliver of pine and trying to make light of it all, Anderson just letting time pass and filling his belly with Duncan's good whiskey.

McGregor had arrived at Sanford Duncan's almost simultaneously with Houston, had explained the situation to his host and solicited him to serve as unbiased officiator. If there was killing, McGregor said, he wanted it to look fair. This was supposing, of course, that White was released from custody and he and his second, Dr. Boyd McNairy, showed up. McGregor, with his natural enthusiasm, made the affair seem a picnic and participation a privilege. "This isn't a goddamn ball," Houston had said, but by then Duncan was avid for it.

The fog outside was as thick as cotton. "Any sign of day?" a husky voice whispered. Houston turned and saw Anderson's shape lifted on his elbow, his broad, weathered face turned up from a pallet on the floor.

"There's fog," Houston answered.

"It'll lift," Anderson replied, clearing his throat. "Want company?"

McGregor's vigorous snoring sounded from beneath the slouch hat over his face; Shelby's slender body rose and fell quietly under his blanket.

"No thanks," Houston said. "Get some sleep." Anderson leaned back.

Sam closed the shutters, pulled on his trousers and went through the doorway into the kitchen. He poured a drink from last night's bottle and swished it in his mouth, then spit it into the glowing embers of the fire. The liquid hissed as it hit hot ashes; only two hours ago the men had left the fire in full flame and stumbled off to bed.

His head ached and he fought a creeping nausea. He stirred the embers, took a small iron crucible from the plank table where he had left it earlier, and heated it in the coals. In this he melted bits of lead to a smooth, thick liquid and ladled it into the sprue of a bullet mold, the mold's two halves clenched like halves of a walnut shell. When the mold cooled, he opened its jaws; a ball perfectly round but for the rat's tail left by the sprue dropped out on the table. A gamecock crowed—another sign of morning and light and life. Two good signs already, even before dawn, but the fog was bad. He filed away the rat's tail and etched a small mark resembling the swing of the dog's tail on one side of the ball, another mark on the opposite side, two slashes like a cock's beak open and screaming in the day. He would use this for his first shot; hopefully, both parties would be satisfied with the first round of fire, and there would not be a second. Yet he had to be prepared. He made more bullets before he was joined by Shelby, McGregor, Anderson, and Sanford Duncan. Mrs. Duncan did not come down; Sanford made the coffee and biscuits himself. The men drank and ate quietly, a hollow, solemn look in their eyes. Doc Shelby did not speak at all. Even Jack McGregor was subdued.

The designated field was a mile ride down a narrow lane between stands of red hickory and beech and September elm turning autumn colors. The five men moved through the fog on their mounts like reticent fugitives, their senses honed, nerves on edge. There was a chill in the air.

"It don't seem to be breaking," McGregor said about the fog.

"It will," Anderson answered after a pause. "Ever seen a fog not break?"

Shelby and Houston fell behind; even their horses seemed wary. "I hope you'll have the sense to postpone until this fog lifts," Shelby said, his first words of the morning.

"I'm not a fool."

"You might step out of character for one day, Sam, and have a little humility," the doctor responded flatly. "You could prove more fool than you think. Has it occurred to you, you might lose?" Houston said nothing. "I've watched a lot of men die, Sam. A lot of good men. Some are afraid, some aren't, but they're every one surprised it's happening to them."

Houston's voice was set but not angry. "If you have to talk like that, I'd just as soon you take your leave. I don't need it this morning."

Shelby said, "I guess Dr. McNairy would tend to you if you were hit."

"Like hell he would. Not if I had life enough to stop him."

"He's a good doctor, Sam. We used to be partners, you know."

"He's a Federalist and dead set against the General."

"That's true. But he did a fine job of patching up the General after his shoot-out with the Bentons. Jackson was taken to McNairy's house, you know."

"Yeah, I know. And McNairy tried to take his arm off. He had the saw out, and the General had to fight him off—"

"That's enough, Sam. A doctor does what he has to. Life is life to a doctor. Anyway, I'm not leaving you."

"I know," Houston answered.

The lane opened into a field. Duncan, McGregor and Anderson slowed to wait, and the five riders moved out into the open. The stout figures of Dr. Boyd McNairy and General William White appeared through the mist like apparitions, posed under the only tree in the field, motionless, their mounts grazing. Houston's party advanced on them slowly, then stopped about twenty yards away.

"Morning," Duncan called nervously.

"Morning," McNairy answered. His voice was hoarse and fierce.

The riders dismounted, each loosely holding his horse's reins. The dueling code spelled out so many rules—who chooses the type of weapon, how the distance is determined, where the seconds and physicians and observers are to stand. But no code can tell a man how to greet another man he intends to kill, a man who might within minutes kill him. No code can tell a man how not to be afraid, how to look at death down a pistol barrel and aim his own pistol calmly, and pull the trigger without qualms. General White and General Houston looked at each other, each squinting as if in pain, and then looked away.

Sanford Duncan was a short man with a winking eye. He was wearing a tall beaver hat. Handing his reins to Anderson, he stepped forward. "It's a somber occasion, gentlemen," he said. "I've been requested to officiate. Are there any objections?"

McNairy consulted White in a low monotone, then announced, "No objections."

"All right then," Duncan continued, turning to one party and then the other. "Is there any possibility we can settle this matter amicably and avoid bloodshed?"

"We done tried that already," McGregor said, "and it ain't gonna work."

Duncan took off his hat, revealing a bald head, and turned to White. "General White," he said with his unfortunate wink, pulling himself up to full height, his voice becoming loud and full, "I give you three minutes to reconsider and withdraw your challenge." He took a watch from his pocket and fixed his eyes on it. White stood without any movement and looked directly at him, as if counting down the seconds in his own mind. A hawk screamed shrilly somewhere off in the fog. "Ten seconds remain, sir. Does the challenge stand?"

White shifted his glance to Dr. McNairy, who had been watching him and waiting for this signal. "The challenge stands, sir. Proceed," McNairy called.

"General Houston, I give you three minutes to withdraw your acceptance of the challenge. Your time now begins counting." Again he lowered his face to the watch in his hand. McGregor pulled out his own watch and focused down on it.

"I will not withdraw, sir," Houston cut in. "You may proceed now."

Duncan jerked his head toward Houston. "I remind the principals to communicate only through their seconds. If we are to have a duel here, we will stay within the rules and make it as civilized as possible. Is that understood, gentlemen?"

Houston was piqued. The man was playacting, taking on the lead role, exulting in it. He started to say so, but Doc Shelby, standing slightly in front of him, turned and caught his eye with a warning look. The fog seemed to be getting worse. Houston looked to McGregor and said, "All right," low, between his teeth, and McGregor called in a loud, excited pitch, "General Houston don't want to withdraw. He wants to get on with it."

"Then," Duncan said, "I ask you, Colonel McGregor, what distance General Houston wishes to suggest."

Houston had instructed McGregor to let White call the distance—the courtesy of a gentleman, but with other reasons behind it, such as letting destiny or William White, anyone but himself, call the shots here. In most situations Houston craved control, but when it came to killing, or dying, for a nebulous matter of honor that he did not, in fact, fully believe in, he wished to forfeit responsibility.

"General Houston wants to know what distance Dr. McNairy's man suggests."

Duncan turned to McNairy, relaying the message though it was easily heard by all.

"My man's name is General White, and Colonel McGregor will show enough courtesy to refer to him as such," McNairy answered in a raspy voice. He could not abide McGregor, and thought Houston too cocky for his own good. Four years ago, when Houston was elected major general of the Tennessee militia, McNairy had served as his aide-de-camp. The thought of being subordinate to such a man still rankled him.

There was a slight pause. McNairy and Shelby exchanged a look that neither could read. "All right. What pace does General White call for?" McGregor said with blatant sarcasm.

McNairy looked to White, who said, "Ten."

McNairy turned to Duncan. "Ten paces each from the center mark."

White gestured for McNairy's attention, and they consulted quietly. Duncan watched the discussion and held off pronouncing the distance. McNairy's face took on an ugly expression. At last he turned to Duncan and said, "Pardon, there has been a mistake. General White calls for ten paces, total. Five from the center mark."

Houston took in a breath.

"Isn't that a little short?" Duncan asked, his winking eye active.

"It is indeed," Dr. McNairy replied. "But General White suffers from a severe case of myopia. He cannot see farther than ten paces." He paused, adding, "General Houston forfeited the call, sir. The choice belongs to General White. Ten paces. Total."

A sinking, a deep, deep sinking, and yet not even a blink of his eyes. He would have done better to go with six from the center, as Jackson had goadingly suggested. "I would not have done it," he had said, and Jackson had answered, "Good. I would not have done it either." But now there was no choice: ten paces, thirty feet. Jackson had been right about one thing—the man's arrogance. Well, if White wanted to die, so be it. "Ten," Houston said, nodding; he saw Shelby stiffen but did not look at his face.

"Sam—" Shelby said.

"I gave him the call," Houston responded harshly.

Even Jack McGregor was appalled. But Houston had set his mind. "Ten it will be!" McGregor yelled. "But it's barbarous!"

"This whole thing is barbarous," McNairy retorted, his finger jabbing at the air. "And if it weren't for Mr. Houston, we wouldn't be here—"

McGregor lunged forward. "I beg your pardon; it was your man who made the challenge!"

"And it was your man who drew him into it, and—"

"Gentlemen, gentlemen!" Duncan interceded. "If the principals agree on ten paces, then so be it. Ten paces, gentlemen—five from the center mark—are you ready to walk it off?"

"Ready!" White said, followed by McNairy's dry voice, "General White is ready!"

Shelby turned full face to Houston, the message clear in his eyes. Houston hesitated, then said to McGregor, "Request a thirty-minute delay on account of the fog."

"It ain't gonna lift in thirty minutes, Sam; waiting will make you crazy. You can see a man that big around at ten paces even in this—"

"He said request a thirty-minute delay," Shelby growled.

McGregor scowled and spat but called out the request. White and McNairy consulted. "Agreed," McNairy answered at last.

At first no one moved from where he stood, but after a while McGregor and Anderson sat down on the dewy grass, chewing and spitting tobacco. Shelby remained standing, shifting his weight first one way and then another, his long arms crossed at his chest. White seemed rooted beneath the oak tree like a squat weed growing there, red leaves falling silently through the fog around him and Dr. McNairy, who leaned up against the trunk smoking a pipe, blowing the smoke out into the fog, slow and hostile.

Houston mounted and rode a few paces off, dismounted, and stood with his back to the others, looking east for the sun. His thoughts were paranoid and fearful. And he was angry. Ten paces—thirty feet. He tried to boost himself, remembering Jackson's voice: "You'll come back alive and whole. . . . I've never seen him kill a man yet," and his parting words, "Staying alive, son, that's the whole thing. Besides, I've got plans for you." But the voice was far away and old, a racking cough disjointing the words.

He closed his eyes, thinking in the language of the Cherokee, sending his soul up to the treetops so it would not be harmed if his body was wounded, and he would not die. But the fog was heavy on him, and it seemed his soul could not lift through it, and he was not sure he believed it would have lifted anyway. Even if the Indian gods existed, they might be indisposed to answer his call for protection, for Sam Houston was a white man. He had red friends, he called them red brothers, but he was a white man. And God? The Christian God? He also might be disinclined to spare Sam Houston's life, for reasons just as obvious—the women, the drinking, the bold defiance of restrictions and conventions. The Conducting Providence, be it gods or God or only a man meeting his future with some degree of faith in a perceived master scheme, remained a hope, but at this moment a silent and remote one.

After twenty minutes the fog was still heavy, clinging low to the ground but clearing higher up. Yellow rays shone from the east. Houston heard a whistle from behind him, turned and saw through the fog the vague shape of McGregor waving one arm high in the air. He rode back over and McGregor said, "White says he wants to proceed. Now."

Anderson spat a wad of tobacco saliva into the grass and looked up at Houston. "He's got nothin' to lose anyhow, Congressman; I guess he just figured that out. He can't see a thing, fog or no fog. Even at ten paces. I'd insist on the ten minutes."

Houston looked to Shelby, who nodded and said, "Ten minutes."

The men's nerves were hair-triggered. Houston knew he could not take much more waiting. "Five minutes," he said aloud, and "Five minutes!" McGregor yelled over to McNairy.

"I heard him, Jack—" McNairy hollered back and Duncan interceded, "Gentlemen, let's keep this thing civil."

"Go to hell, Duncan," McGregor said. "I asked you to officiate, not play the godderned schoolteacher."

The minutes ticked by and the fog was lifting rapidly. "Time's up," Duncan said. "Seconds, you may now load the pistols."

McGregor lifted the case of nine-inch smoothbore pistols from his saddlebag, eager now to have it done with. As Houston had instructed, he went to White and held the case open, offering him the choice of weapons. White, as a gentleman, waived the choice, and McGregor returned to Houston, who took the pistol Jackson had suggested—marked with a small scratch on the barrel—and handed it to McGregor. Then he removed his greatcoat and gave it to Shelby.

"I see you came dressed to kill," McGregor said with a smile, noting Houston's fine black trousers and linen shirt. Houston frowned at him, said, "Crass, Jack," then glanced at Shelby, whose blind eye was shifting.

"You'll wing him, Congressman," Anderson remarked calmly. "That man's as big one way as he is the other so it don't matter which way he turns. He's a sittin' duck."

Houston tried to smile.

"Shit," McGregor said, "at ten paces you'll blast him over with powder burn."

Duncan called the seconds to him and watched as they measured out the powder, checked flints, and tamped in the balls and wads. He chose a center mark that both seconds agreed to. The pasture timberline ran east and west, parallel to the Kentucky border; the distance would be paced off at right angles to the line so when the men made a half-turn to fire, neither would be looking into the sun. Only small drifting clouds of fog remained. Duncan motioned to the principals. Houston and White approached without speaking. Duncan answered, "General White called the distance; therefore, General Houston chooses position."

"South," Houston replied. There was no advantage in it, but while waiting to turn and fire, he would be looking past the timberline and over the hills toward Tennessee. Home. And also . . . something more. He would turn westward to fire.

"Fine. You will stand back to back. I will count off five paces, at which time you will reach your mark and remain standing with your backs to each other, the pistol in your awkward hand. When I give the word for you to cock your pistols, you may change them to your shooting hand. Hold them muzzle downward until I say the word 'fire.' I will then count from one to four. At any time during the count, you may turn and discharge the pistols. If you have not fired by the count of four, then it is too late to do so. If you shoot before the word is given or after the count is over, Colonel McGregor and Dr. McNairy have the duty to shoot you down. Are you ready?"

"Ready." Houston nodded with a glance at White, who stood stout and awkward, the thick glasses distorting his eyes to the size of a rodent's.

"Ready," White said, stepping to his mark, face to face with Houston.

They turned their backs; accidentally, their elbows touched. McGregor handed Sam his pistol. McNairy presented the other to White, and then the seconds retired to designated places eight yards from the line of fire, each holding his own pistol cocked and ready to shoot should his man fire too soon. Duncan stepped back between them, with Shelby and Anderson two feet behind.

"Gentlemen," Duncan called out, "Pace . . . one . . . two . . . three . . . four . . . five. Now you may cock your pistols."

Houston positioned his feet as Jackson had instructed, shifted the pistol to his right hand and pulled the hammer back with his thumb. This was worse than war.

There was a moment of silence. For God's sake, go ahead, Houston wanted to say. . . . "I've got plans for you—" Plans, destiny; he thought of the ribbon tucked deep inside his front pocket. "For luck. For destiny and all that." And she had said . . .

"Fire!" Duncan shouted. Houston turned, lifted the pistol and took aim, sighting White's chest down the barrel, biting hard on the lead ball in his mouth. Dear God, he thought with a sudden pulse of fear, he had forgotten to tell McGregor to go easy on the powder.

"One!" Duncan called out. The myopic eyes, squinting—Jackson's voice, "An arrogant fool who intends to kill you," and then the girl's voice, low, truthful, "It seems more like trickery to me."

"Two!" Houston lowered the pistol slightly, purposefully aiming low, and pulled the trigger.

If White fired, Houston did not hear it. The old man fell instantly, clutching himself, pulling his knees up to his chest as he rolled over on his side.

"He's down!" McGregor yelled, throwing his hands up, his pistol pointed skyward.

Houston rushed forward with a cry. Blood poured from White's belly, and he writhed in the wet grass. The stench of bowels and blood fouled the air. Shelby and McNairy were over him, holding him down and cutting his pants away, working together with the cooperation of old partners. The intestines were mangled where the ball had entered at a downward slant.

"Is he going to die?" Houston asked. "Doc?" His voice was like a boy's.

Shelby looked up at him, his good eye piercing. "Get out of here, Sam, go—now!"

And McGregor was there pulling at his arm; Anderson brought the horses. The three men mounted and broke into a full gallop at once, Anderson cutting through the trees and heading home with the news, McGregor and Houston running west, then north, headed God knows where. They had not planned what to do after it was over.

CHAPTER 9

Eliza arrived at the church before evening, intending to wait. But he had already come and gone. A note was adhered with tree sap to the wall beside the window frame; it was folded and sealed with the same sap, making a perfect envelope with "Miss E. Allen" written on the front. The script inside was large and elaborate.

My dear Miss Allen

I am passing thru earlier than expected. I have a mind to call on you at your grandfather's but time forbids. I must return to Nashville and directly to Washington. I will keep the ribbon, please take no offense. It has served me well. I am not wounded and General White, I pray, will survive.

> *Thine,*
> *Sam Houston*

The letter did not say she would hear from him again, but the tone suggested it, and she expected he would write soon from Washington.

He did not. She went home to Allendale and waited, but no word came. Three months passed. The colts were weaned, crops harvested and winter wood logged. Two weeks were set aside for hog butchering, the pork salted down in log troughs and hung in the smokehouse. Oaks by the water dropped all their leaves; her hopes, also, began to fall, and with their falling her resentment rose like the mists off the river between the barren trees. Over and again she read the letter, and the voice behind it began to change, to sound foppish and condescending, the voice of a conceited man who placates a child with flattery—as if she was supposed to believe that he believed that ridiculous ribbon had saved his life. Most humiliating of all was that she had taken his words to heart and been deceived by his searching, fearful looks, which, as winter wore on, she began to suspect had been acted as skillfully as his performance in Nashville the day of the challenge. There was no private Sam Houston, no genuine man behind the visage—or so she convinced herself for the purpose of turning her hurt to anger.

But Will was a solace. He returned, as promised. There was no further hint of his odd behavior at their first parting; when she asked him about it, he seemed puzzled, apologized, and said he had not meant to offend her. He said he did not recall feeling detached from her that night, at all.

As often as possible they met, usually in the grain barn at night, though a few times they arranged daylight meetings in the woods or by the river. The secrecy became burdensome, and Eliza's fear of getting with child, Will thought, was excessive. He always disciplined himself to pull from her body in time, a difficult expression of his esteem, but this did not fully appease her concern. He felt she was not receiving him. He told himself that if just once she would forsake her control and truly abandon herself to him and harbor his seed in that part of her, then his frustration would dissipate. But this she never did. He knew he never satisfied her, and felt this was not because of any failings on his part, but because she would not allow it. "You're resisting me," he said once, "or withholding yourself— some part of yourself."

She considered it. "Maybe," she answered. "I just don't want to have a baby."

"That isn't what I mean."

"I know what you mean," she said. But she refused to talk about it. Still, their bond held. She enjoyed unbraiding his short queue of hair, touching and witnessing her effect on him.

When his father died, leaving Tyree Springs and a heavy debt, Will had been studying law. Selling the resort, he told her, had not been sufficient to provide for the family, and as the oldest child, he took that responsibility to heart. He quit his studies and moved home to work the fields and do odd jobs in town for extra pay. He admittedly would have preferred a law practice and had the intelli- gence for it, but he satisfied himself with what, for the present, seemed his only option. This resignation, or acceptance, was what Eliza liked least about him; it was tediously reminiscent of her moth- er's complacency. He had an old black dog named Skunk and brought him along sometimes. When Eliza first saw Skunk, with his mangy fur and a limp, she understood better what Will's life was like: a poor family living on what they could hunt and grow.

Will took an interest in local and national politics, though not due to any aspirations of his own. He was no more a Federalist than a Jackson man and tended to favor the loser. He put more stock in a man's personal honesty than in his policies. And he found Eliza to be interested. On nights when the moon gave enough light to read, he brought a newspaper with him and they left the barn doors cracked and read in the sliver of light. These were full days in Tennessee, with Jackson so close to the presidency. He was eager for it, everyone knew it, and this was something new. In the last election, he had acted as expected of a candidate—reticent, saying if the people called him to serve, he would go; if they did not, he would be pleased to stay home and farm his land. But the suspected bargain between John Quincy Adams and Henry Clay had changed his attitude. As

Jackson, and most of Tennessee, saw it, the people had chosen him in 1824, and collusion between two greedy men had prevented him from serving.

At the time of that election, Jackson was a senator; when Adams took office, Jackson resigned and came home, not to tend his crops but to organize his people to defeat the Administration. He charged President Adams and Secretary Clay with fraud and claimed that the people's power had been stolen from them by a few wealthy aristocrats. Tyree doubted that Adams and Clay had actually made the deal they were accused of but felt it a faulty system that could put one man in office when the other had received more popular votes. In this respect Will was a democrat, though he disliked General Jackson, who he felt played the roles of farmer and wronged candidate a little too much to his advantage. Jackson was, actually, a wealthy planter, not a humble farmer—an aristocrat in his way of life, if not in his mode of thinking.

At first it seemed the Administration had no adequate retaliation for the charge of corruption, except denial. But then they happened onto it or perhaps went in search of it. Whichever, when they found it, it was a deadly thing.

Many believed that Secretary of State Henry Clay sent out spies to collect every sordid detail of Rachel Jackson's past. There was, in particular, an Englishman by the name of Day, a debt collector for merchants in the eastern cities of Baltimore and Philadelphia. He traveled in ragged clothes from Kentucky to Nashville and then on to Natchez, the places of Rachel Jackson's past. Then he took his findings to the Administration, and they assembled the pieces into a damning picture of illicit love: a first marriage to Lewis Robards in which the divorce had not been properly finalized before the second marriage, to Andrew Jackson, which, because of the first marriage, had questionable validity.

It was John Overton who told Rachel and Andrew Jackson of Mr. Day and his work. Overton had stood with them at their wedding ceremony in Natchez, had brought them the news two years later that they were not, in fact, married, had arranged the second wedding, at Rachel's request, and stood with them again. Will had more respect for Overton than for Jackson, because Overton, at least, with all his democratic philosophies, did not pretend to be other than he was—the wealthiest man in Davidson County. Like Jackson, he had made his money through toil and astute speculation and was generous with it. But unlike the General he did not go about publicly damning wealthy aristocrats and dwelling on his own unpretentious birth—though many presumed he was the one who put Jackson up to doing so about his. It was generally thought he sparked Andrew Jackson's political fires, though the General himself was the one who kept them burning.

At the same time Rachel Jackson learned of Mr. Day, his reports were being printed throughout the country. Will and Eliza read them together in the Federalist newspapers: Rachel Donelson Robards had lived for two years with Andrew Jackson before she was legally divorced from her first husband.

And this was just the beginning. Supporters of the Administration, or perhaps the Administration itself, found more evidence against the woman; where they could not find it, they created it. "Ought a convicted adulteress and her paramour husband to be placed in the highest office of this free and Christian land?" They attacked like wolves closing in on the weak and wounded animal of the herd. And Rachel—who had suffered through a first marriage to a demented, jealous man, who had endured the humiliation of what she believed was a legal divorce and found what peace she could in her second marriage, which for two full years, the happiest years of her life, had been a fiction—Rachel was very slowly and without mercy devoured.

At first it was all the General's friends could do to keep him from another duel. He had fought several in his prime. Repeatedly they implored him to be still, keep quiet. Sam Houston, in Washington, almost fought a second duel for the old warrior but managed to contrive a way out and also to dissuade Jackson from fighting it himself. This was news for a while; though no one knew the particulars, it was enough that anyone had talked the General out of anything he intended to do—and by mail, no less. The populace concluded that Sam Houston must have a persuasive way with words—something Eliza knew. She disguised her interest in him as a general regard for politics.

It was said that during this time the General wandered through the rooms of the Hermitage, sometimes morose, often raving, but never getting too far from Rachel. Some began to question if perhaps even God had turned against the old man when one night lightning struck his stables and all of his horses—many of the finest in Tennessee—died of smoke and fire.

During it all, Judge Overton and Major William B. Lewis stayed close by. Senator Eaton, Congressman James K. Polk and Congressman Houston wrote often from Washington City, urging the General to hold together, encouraging Rachel to take heart.

No one knew exactly when it was that Andrew Jackson's old friend, Judge John Overton, devised his plan. He orchestrated with such skill that few even realized there was a scheme afoot until it was effected. He created a committee of the most respected men in Nashville—men like Doc Shelby, Major Lewis, Jesse Wharton, Mayor Felix Robertson, and many more. Even General White, recovering from the wound Sam Houston had inflicted, rallied his strength to attend the committee meetings; whatever his feelings toward Houston, he was still a Jackson man.

This committee went at the task of vindicating Rachel Jackson. Major Lewis rode throughout Tennessee and Kentucky, obtaining letters from men and women who had known Rachel in her youth and were willing to bear witness to her integrity. Every attack on her honor was dealt with, consistently, thoroughly, until at last the Nashville committee emerged with a report that testified not to her complete innocence or the legality of her first two years with Andrew Jackson, but to her ignorance of any wrongdoing. Will Tyree, despite his cynicism about the General, rejoiced at this small victory in the vindication of Rachel Jackson.

Yet it was not over; the wolves had scented blood and wanted flesh. That was to come. But before it came, there was to be more success for the committee, for this group of Tennesseans dedicated to defending a woman's reputation was expanding into a network of committees throughout the United States whose purpose was to put Andrew Jackson in the Executive Mansion. Never had such a campaign been waged.

In the midst of all of this, in April 1827, Sam Houston returned from Washington to Tennessee and began electioneering for the governorship.

Eliza and Will were lying in darkness, in the corner of the grain barn where loose hay was stored, their bodies nestled close together, Will's chest pressed against her back, his arm over her shoulder. He loosened the laces of her bodice and slid his hand inside, just barely touching, the movement almost imperceptible yet having such an effect on her. She felt him push against her, his hardness against the back of her thighs, and reached to hold his hand still, cupping it around one breast, pressing it to stop its movement. Her heart beat against it; his breath was in her hair. They stayed this way until her heart slowed to normal and his hand seemed no longer an intruder but an extension of her own private self.

"Don't move at all," she said.

"Just this much? You feel so good."

"No. Not yet." She was enjoying the intimacy, without stimulation. She also wanted something else from him. It was at these moments, when he was just holding her, that she liked to think of Sam Houston. "Just talk of something else," she said.

He pressed tighter, a playful grip. "All right. We're supposed to lie here like this and talk about . . . what?"

"Texas," she said. The topic intrigued her. She had heard her Uncle Robert Allen say that Sam Houston had an avid—even excessive—interest in the place.

"I've told you all I know about Texas," Will answered. "What else?"

"Anything. The campaign." It had been a while since he had

mentioned Sam Houston, and she was eliciting it from him. She had various ways.

"This is sort of distracting for politics," he said.

"Not if you keep your hand still."

"All right." He threw the words out with a careless breath. "Politics. There's nothing new with Jackson. Eaton is acting like a horse's behind. And, oh, Sam Houston's back from Washington."

He felt it, the lurch of her heart, the quickening pace. She wanted to shove his hand away; she felt he was violating her. But she lay still.

He moved his hand and sat up.

"What is it?" she asked softly.

"I was going to ask you."

"Ask me what?"

"Why your heart jumped just then."

"It didn't."

"Don't tease me, Eliza. It was when I mentioned Houston."

She sat up and faced him in the dark. She had known it would come to this sooner or later. She had almost wanted it to. "He's as old as my mother," she said defensively.

"You know him?"

"I've met him a time or two."

"Why didn't you tell me?"

"You have your secrets too."

"But why didn't you tell me? All the times we've talked about him."

She shrugged. "It was a long time ago."

"But it means something to you. Did you know him before you met me? That day in Nashville, you acted as if—"

"I don't know him; I've met him is all."

"I don't think so."

"Yes, it is."

At last he said, "I've got this sick feeling, Eliza. Like you're a stranger. How could you not have told me?"

"I just didn't."

And into the following silence, with the casual sound of the barn doors creaking open, stepped her father; he stood in the doorway with blue moonlight behind him, holding a lantern, unlit. When he spoke, his voice was slow and scorching. "Are you going to show yourselves, or do I have to rout you out like rabbits?"

She was afraid. Despite everything, she still needed to please him, or at least not to shame him.

Will hesitated, then stood and stepped out toward the colonel, who turned his head slightly toward him with the quick movement of a blind dog who listens for a bee about his head. He did not yet see him. Will stopped a few feet from him. Eliza watched their silhouettes against the moonlight from the doorway.

"Eliza, go into the house," her father said, his voice low with fury, his face turned on Will. But she did not move.

"I think she should stay," Will answered, "if she wants to. If we've got something to say, she has a right to hear it." Even now, in spite of his hurt, he allowed her dignity.

"No doubt she has already heard it. From your point of view."

"No. I haven't seen fit. But if you'll say your piece and let me say mine, then it's fair. She can make her own judgment."

John Allen took a single step toward Will, one hand lifting with a finger up, then turned his face toward where Eliza crouched in the hay. He was still holding the unlit lantern. She could not see if his eyes had found her. "Get to the house, Eliza," he said, and lowered his hand and stood waiting. "Eliza!"

Still she did not move. The night was warm for April, misty warm, the blue moon just visible in an upper corner of the doorway. Will's roan, tied near the door, swished his tail and shifted weight. "I want to stay."

"I said no."

"She's not a child," Will said.

Allen answered, "And do you think, after she's heard it all, she'll want anything to do with you?"

"It's a chance I'll take."

Their voices were low, barely audible. "Then tell it. Leave anything out and I'll stop you. Do you understand?"

Will took an awkward step toward Eliza, turned back to the colonel, and then with the manner of a man who has labored over the game too long and at last determines to lay out his cards and lose or win all, spoke to Eliza. "A year ago my father was sick with consumption." She took in a breath but said nothing. "He'd had it awhile. We knew he was dying." The voice came to her as in a dream, distant, his eyes shadowed like blue haze around the moon. "The resort was losing money because he didn't have the strength to keep it up. And I didn't have the experience. I did the best I could and at the same time was studying law. We went to your father at the bank, and he made us a loan. It came due while my father was dying."

"He'd been dying for a year," the colonel interrupted.

Will kept his eyes on Eliza. "He'd been sick for a year. But the note came due when he was dying. I told your father that at the time." He turned his head; his eyes caught the light.

"I knew he was dying. I was sorry for that. But it was a sorry excuse for you. The truth was that you didn't want to run the place. Your heart wasn't in it. You weren't trying hard enough, or you weren't capable."

"With all respect, sir," Will's tone was acrid, and there was no movement in his body, "I was doing the best I could for my family."

"And I was doing the best I could for my bank."

"Your bank would have got by fine without that note."

"You've proved that well enough by never paying it off. Get on with your story."

Will paused, then continued in the flat voice of an actor rehearsing in the privacy of his room, not the drama but the words only. "The note came due while my father was dying. I went to the bank to ask your father for an extension. An extra month. He'd given me one extension before and so refused."

"Upon advice of the board," John Allen said. "Your record was not good. And neither was your father's."

"You know nothing of my father's record."

Here was an advantage the colonel had not foreseen: the boy was ignorant of his father's debts. "Evidently more than you know," he said. "I had loaned him money before. Personal money—which he never repaid. Finally, I forgave that debt." Will's shock was evident in the silence, a moment in which the colonel held the laurels. "If you had listened to me that day instead of causing your scene, I would have told you."

"You're lying," Will said. "I would have known."

"Obviously you didn't."

Will was putting the pieces together, and suddenly knew it was the truth. "I see," he said, speaking to the colonel but still looking toward Eliza. "Because he couldn't pay his debt you assumed I wouldn't either."

"I gave you your chance."

Will turned to face him. "One chance. A month's extension on a debt like that. And while my father was dying."

"You had no experience in managing that place; you've admitted that. I could have given you a thousand extensions and never seen your money."

"Then why did you loan it? With foreclosure and that nice profit in sight? You and your bank made a bundle on Tyree Springs, did you not, Colonel?"

"We got our money out."

"Plus how much?"

"It isn't your business."

"Go to hell."

"That's right, boy. Lose your temper like you did that day. Lose your mind and yell like a maniac. Show my daughter how you did it. Tell her what you said. She gets the picture: your father dying, your family hungry, your only property at risk; you've set it up very nicely. Now let's see if she thinks it justifies what you said to me that day."

Will did not look at her. Suddenly he crossed toward the doorway, passed the colonel without a glance, and took up the reins of his horse. He stood with his back to them, then turned and spoke in a rapid monotone. "Nothing would justify it, sir. I don't expect her to excuse it. I do hope she'll forgive it. Eliza, I told your father I hoped some day he would know my feelings, that some day he'd see the people he loved dying of consumption. His wife, his children. His grandchildren." He faltered, turned as if to go, then looked back at her. "I wished it on him," he said, as calmly and clearly as if it were still true. And it was that last added statement and his lack of remorse or any show of feeling at all, that kept her from going to him in the quiet moment before he mounted and reined his horse through the doorway and out into the night.

She stood, and avoiding her father's eyes went past him and to the door. Just before she went out, he cried, his passion bursting, "Look at you, girl! With straw in your hair!"

She turned on him; their eyes met full in the hazy light. She almost wanted to comfort him. "Don't, Papa," she said softly, and left him alone.

As Eliza saw it, Will and her father had both been wrong and wronged, though Will's sin was more natural, a loss of temper in a time of grief, while the colonel's crime was planned and crafty. He must have known the bank could sell the Springs for profit and so concluded too readily that Will would never pay the debt. Eliza knew her father was likely right about something: Will was not prone to clever business notions and without a miracle could never have paid the note in another month. But she also knew he would have paid it eventually. He would have gone without food to pay it. She believed her father must have known this too. In dismissing it, he denied Will the chance to redeem his credit and his reputation.

It appeared John Allen had kept his poise during the encounter at the bank, but to Eliza this was all the more damning: it was the calculation behind the crime. That he could now blame Will for Laetitia's illness, in whatever rational or irrational way he blamed him, was the least damning of all, the hardest transgression to condemn him for, since there was a small, persistent question in her own mind that wondered at the timing of it, why her mother had become fatigued just after Will wished it to happen, and then begun to cough blood. She could not justify him. In that way, a tendency to blame and not forgive, Eliza was like her father. Despite his basic ignorance of her, he knew this one thing and had counted on it when he allowed Will to tell his story. And so she, too, was at fault and knew it, and wanting atonement and understanding, she at last sent word to Will, by Balie Peyton, that she would meet him at the May dance at Tyree Springs. There could be no more encounters in the woods or midnight connections, for the colonel was keeping a close watch. His persistence degraded her.

She rode out with Balie. Tyree Springs Resort was fourteen miles west of Gallatin on the Nashville Road to Kentucky, a cluster of log buildings amid the trees on the Highland Rim. The dance pavilion, a netted structure with a pitched roof, was set apart. This was the first dance since autumn, and the place was crowded, the banjo's twang and fiddle's scream piercing the woods and sliding off over the Highland Rim, old Simon's tambourine keeping time: "Get out of the way, Old Dan Tucker. You've come too late to get your supper."

When they arrived, Will was not there, and Eliza danced with Balie. He was a few years older than she, a young lawyer bent on doing things with his life; it was generally believed he would. He was lively, full of motion, sturdy and strong-featured. His father had been among the first settlers in Tennessee, having come with Captain James Robertson's expedition across the mountains from the Watauga to the Cumberland. When Balie was a child, his father and grandfather were killed by Indians. He had seen his father scalped and held on to the memory. He supported Jackson's removal policies and disdained Congressman Houston's affinity with the Cherokees.

The band slowed tempo to a waltz; Eliza and Balie had learned to dance together as children and moved as easily as two legs of one body, saying nothing, lost in the shuffle of feet. They had just made a turn, during a slow moment in the music, when Eliza glanced toward the door and saw Sam Houston step in. For eight months she had wanted to see him striding through some doorway toward her, but that moment, when it happened, she was completely unprepared.

He did not see her. She felt a lifting inside, and faltered, thankful Will had not yet arrived. Perhaps he would not come. Balie looked down at her; she found her footing, smiled, then looked back toward the door as they made another turn. The congressman was with Deputy Willoughby Williams and his wife. The deputy was carrying a child, a girl with brown curls. The three adults were laughing together, the noise lost in music.

Keeping his perfect step, Balie said, "Well, if it isn't our royal congressman."

"Sam Houston?"

"That's him."

She kept her voice casual and her feet from flagging. "Papa says he'll be governor."

"He will. Which I'd rejoice in if he weren't half Indian."

"Half Indian?"

"Not literally of course. But in the way he thinks. Even in the way he moves. Watch him."

He drifted into the crowd, as fluent as the spring air. Deputy Williams placed the child in his arms and joined the dance with his wife. Sam stood apart with the little girl on his hip, both of them taking in the crowd, his eyes attentive, hers unsure, watching her parents dance away. She put two fingers in her mouth and turned to look at the side of Sam's face, his brushy sideburns, then reached up and grabbed hold of his hair. Patting her, stroking her curls, he said something softly, his look still searching the dancers, seeming to notice everyone but Eliza.

His hair was longer than she recalled, and he was not wearing his noted eccentric garb—beaded buckskins with head scarves or expensive beaver hats and claw-hammer coats—but a black cape falling past his knees, luxurious, flared, extravagant in its simplicity, with a high-winged collar and trousers of fine osnaburg.

Several men stepped up to Sam Houston, then a few women. It seemed to Eliza that the center of the room shifted from the dance floor to him. Even the children gathered around. Partly it was his height that set him apart. No one quite seemed his equal.

"He looks almost sober," Balie whispered down. "I guess because the campaign's starting."

"He drinks a lot?"

Balie grunted by way of answer.

"I didn't know."

He pressed his hand more firmly into her back, damp with warmth, and turned her in a full circle. "Then you're the only one in Tennessee who didn't," Balie said. "See how he's dressed? Like that poet Lord Byron, with that cape? He imitates Byron and wears his hair like him, down over his forehead like that. And he carries a book of Byron's poetry around with him, like he used to do the *Iliad.* They say he can spout off six pages from *Childe Harold's Pilgrimage* and never miss a word, that he never forgets a face, an insult, or a line."

"An insult?"

"He gets his share. And retribution. William White is lucky to be alive."

"Why does he drink so much?" She caught old Simon's eye. He was standing humped and idle with the other black musicians, busy at their instruments, his arms hanging with the tambourine in one hand and nothing in the other. He was known as Monkey Simon, which she thought was cruel. He cast a smile at her.

"Principle. Houston does everything to excess."

As they came around and through the crowd in the ending notes of music, she saw him at the far end of the floor, the child in his arms with her tiny legs wrapped around his waist, her hands still holding to his hair, and her head thrown back in laughter. He was dancing with her. He had removed his cape. Eliza was taken with the sight: his huge form, the child clinging to him, both as wild and happy as the melody, but somehow apart from it, as if moving in a pantomime of their own. The music ended but they kept dancing, laughing together; he dipped her down, her brown curls swinging almost to the floor, and swung her up and around. The next song started up with stomping feet, the beat of Simon's tambourine and the pounding of shoes on the floorboards becoming one beat, one rhythm, becoming the music itself; and yet Sam Houston and the child glided on together, still waltzing in a world of their own. On a turn, he looked at Eliza. She excused herself from Balie and went outside, believing Sam would follow.

The night was crisp, the sky freckled with stars. Thirty yards away among the trees hung a swing facing out through woods to the bluff. The white oak and sugar maple and shagbark hickory were sprouting, their new leaves delicate green in the careening light thrown out by whale-oil lanterns hung from rafters inside the pavilion. Eliza went through the trees to the swing. It was built for two, of wide planks nailed together, suspended between two oaks and rocking in the breeze.

For a while she sat in the swing, the ropes rasping around the limb, her feet just reaching the ground, reaching and pushing off with a thrust of anger at her confusion, and her anticipation, satin slippers scuffing in the dirt, a small satisfaction in their ruin. She watched out into the trees, down at scattered tufts of sprouting green, up through high limbs to the sky. She could not see past the trees to where the rocky slope gave way to shadows but felt the precipice there. Music drifted to her; the tambourine was high and tinny, the banjo a diminished twang amid the voices and thud of pounding feet. When she turned she could see inside through the nets, dancers lit by tiny flames of swinging lamps. Simon's voice called out the moves. She had heard he was a prince in Africa, of a tribe at the foot of a mountain, before he was brought to America and sold. Until a few years ago he had jockeyed the best horses in Tennessee and trained them without a whip, because, people said, he had felt the whip himself when first in America. When he was young. Now he was too old to race horses; he made up songs, sometimes songs about Africa. He was singing out an old backwoods tune, "Billy in the Wild Woods." A few times she saw Sam Houston circle by, the tallest man there, graceful with someone in his arms. She imagined the movement of his muscled legs and his body against her. "Our royal congressman," Balie had said with a snicker. She looked out toward the Highland Rim, her hair floating about her face, blowing forward around it as she pushed back, blowing back as the swing rushed forward, the air dry and cool. Creaking ropes joined time with the distant music, and the swing seemed to move in rhythm, faster, higher, until she was lost in a reverie of movement and stars and night air, marred only by an indefinable longing.

She was recalling Will's last words to her, cruel in their dispassion, "I wished it on him," when Sam Houston came out with his cape over his arm and stood in front of her. "I have something that belongs to you," he said, holding out the blue satin ribbon.

It was a posed gesture; the very staginess of it hinted he was less self-assured than he appeared, less in command, though she did not perceive his real uneasiness. She let the swing slow. Seeing she would not reach for the ribbon, he tucked it in his trouser pocket. "Of course, this isn't why I came out," he said. "I wanted to see you."

"I'm waiting for someone," she said.

"May I stay until he comes?"

Without commitment but with a partial surrender, she touched her feet to the ground, slowing the swing almost to a stop, but not a stop. He reached, held it still and offered his cape. "Are you cold?"

"No."

Tossing the cape over the back of the swing, he sat and stretched his legs out, pushing off again. She noticed his thighs flexing beneath the osnaburg trousers. "I'm sorry I missed you that day," he said simply, looking up at the stars.

"It's all right." Her voice was cool. "I was late anyway."

He gave her a look, as if he wondered at that, and said, "I've been gone longer than I intended."

She didn't respond.

"In Washington."

"I know."

They were not looking at each other, but off into the trees. "I came to ask for a dance."

"But I'm waiting for someone," she said.

"Mr. Peyton?"

"Someone else." She wondered, almost absently, as if it hardly mattered, what Will would think if he found her there, what he would feel.

"Would he grudge me one dance? I was watching you dance with Mr. Peyton when I first came in. You reminded me of something from my childhood, a myth the Cherokees have about pixies who live in rock caves on the mountainside and love music and dancing." His voice was low like the strains of waltz drifting out, not soft, but resonant with rhythm and modulation. He turned to look at her, his eyes reflecting miniature flames of the lanterns. "They're called *Yunwi Tsunsdi,* 'Little People.' You reminded me of them." His eyes held her. "It must have been your hair. The Little People have yellow hair." He took a few strands in his fingers, studied them, and looked at her again. "Or your size and how you move." His eyes were blue-green and steady. They spoke a thousand meanings, a thousand questions, and revealed almost nothing about Sam Houston. "Did you get my letter?" he asked. "From Washington?"

"No."

"I wrote you two months ago. That I was coming home."

"I didn't get it." She wondered if he was lying.

"Probably, it's lost in the mail," he said. "It just said I was coming home and would like to see you." He paused, letting that stand as a question, and when she did not answer, added, "Or are you promised to this mysterious person for whom you're waiting?"

"No. I wanted you to write."

Leaning back, he slipped his arm onto the back of the swing behind her. "I've thought about you. You're not the sort of woman a man forgets, Eliza. You didn't think that, did you? That I had forgotten you?"

"I thought you would write and you didn't."

He touched her shoulder. "I should have, sooner. But Washington kept me busy."

"I've been busy also," she answered, deliberately matching her egotism to his.

He sat staring at her profile. "Do you know how beautiful you are?" With one finger he felt her cheek, a smile in his voice. "Has this phantom, for whom you're waiting, told you?"

"He is coming; he's no phantom."

"I don't doubt it," he answered. "Are you engaged to him?"

"I wonder, if you thought about me so much in Washington, why it didn't occur to you then that I might get engaged. . . . I don't have any hold on you. I would never have asked you to write, but I did feel something that day—at the very least I liked you, and I did think to hear from you. Certainly a letter doesn't take so much time. In fact, no, I am not engaged, but it piques me that you pretend to care and yet did not write."

He leaned back, looking up into the branches and saying, so low she barely heard it, "You intimidate the devil out of me."

They were the last words in the world she expected from Sam Houston; she did not know if he was taunting her, or if he was at last, with a sort of total, brutal undressing, showing her his true self. "I don't know if I believe that," she answered.

"Your choice," he said, still looking up.

"I don't think you're intimidated or afraid of anything."

His tone lightened and turned amiable and teasing, but behind it was a subtle defensiveness. "Then why the comment on trickery? You might as well have called me a coward. Your insinuation was, wasn't it, that I was afraid to fight that man. Smith T."

"I only meant you were too clever to fight him."

"And you admire cleverness?"

"Not so much as honesty. I thought you should have fought him, if you were bent on fighting."

Houston let the remark stand, and Eliza thought she had gone too far. She was intensely attracted to him and yet continually found herself pitting against him. At last he said, "Who is he? The person you're waiting for. May I ask?"

"A friend. Will Tyree."

"Tyree, like this place?"

"Yes."

"And not engaged?"

"No."

"Then may I call on you?"

It was what she wanted. It was what she had been waiting to hear. She thought of Will and his familiar, endearing, sensual movements and his voice muffled in her hair. The recollections brought her down to a more guarded mood; she was more bonded to Will than she had known. "Don't ask me that tonight. Please." And then, with a need to show him she had not been gulled and would not be, she added, "You don't really believe that ribbon gave you luck."

"Of course it did."

"Are you superstitious?"

"If you're asking if I believe in powers beyond the ordinary physical powers, of course."

"Spirits?"

He slid his voice to a whisper; she could not tell if he was goading or serious. "If you listen you can hear them in the trees."

"I'm not easily fooled."

"Listen."

They were quiet; the swing slowed. "I hear the wind, and the music," she said, her voice lower but not a whisper, for she was not yet sure he wasn't baiting her.

"Listen again. Close your eyes. Shut out the music and the voices, and listen out toward the bluff. It isn't the wind."

She did as he said, closing her eyes, tuning her ears for any sound in the trees. A hoot owl called. "I hear an owl."

"Are you sure?" he whispered.

"Yes."

"Are you sure it's an owl?"

"A hoot owl."

Again the bird called mournfully from the timber. She listened with her eyes still closed, and then Sam Houston spoke in a low, mystical monotone, "The Cherokees call him U'guku'—a human ghost who cries out into the night. He's grieved through so many nights there's no flesh on any part of his body except his head." As softly as the bird in the distance, he called, "U'-gu-ku'! hu! hu!" his rhythm matching the bird's. The owl answered.

She opened her eyes and said mockingly, "Why does the owl grieve?"

"His wife has turned him out. He is not a great hunter and has not brought her what she wants."

"And what is it she wants?"

He smiled, and answered, "Who knows what a female wants?" and lifted his hand, touching her eyelids down. "Keep them closed. Keep listening."

A breeze passed over. "There's something walking," she said. "Out in front of us."

"A doe," he answered. "With fawn."

Again she looked at him. "How do you know?"

"Their step. The doe is cautious and hesitant. She stamped her hoof once, in warning. The fawn follows the mother, more skittish. No other animal is so careful, or so curious." He paused. The music had stopped, leaving only the whisper of wind. "The doe is something like you," he said, his face close to Eliza's. "She wants to step out into the open and have a look around." She met his eyes, her expression questioning. "Shall we go see?" he asked. "They're in the brush about fifteen yards out and to the left."

Half Indian, Balie had said. "But no real spirits," she retorted in a normal voice, wanting to break his spell. "Only the owl."

He leaned closer, his breath and the breeze on her face. "Eliza. I find you very stimulating. In a number of ways. I wanted to tell you before Mr. Tyree gets here, because if I'm not mistaken, he's about twenty yards in back of us near the pavilion and walking this way. Unless it's someone else, which I doubt. I'll excuse myself now. Good night." As he took up his cape and stood to go, the doe and fawn darted from the foliage in front of them and out into the shadows.

When Eliza looked, she saw Sam Houston and Will Tyree passing each other beneath a low-hanging limb. Their paces slowed; Sam gave a slight nod of his head, and Will stopped walking. She thought Will would speak, but he did not. They both moved on. Will came and stood in front of her. The swing was not moving at all. She sat still, looking up at him, feeling sorrow and affection, but no desire.

"Did you ask me here to see that? Him?" His voice was quiet.

"No. Of course not."

"But you knew he would be here?"

"I had no idea he would be here. When he came into the dance, I left, and he came out."

"Did he know you were waiting for someone?"

"I told him I was waiting for you."

"But he stayed anyway."

"I thought you weren't coming."

"How could you think that?"

"I waited."

"Not very long." He put his hands in his pockets and looked up through the leaves. "My mother's sick," he said. "I couldn't get away until late."

How could she desert a man like Will? She resented that he told her, as if using his mother's illness and his own loyalty to win her. And yet it was no more than the simple truth. "Is she all right?"

"I think so." Still he was looking up. "Take a look at those stars," he said, his tone seeming flat, but to Eliza, who knew him so well, full of meaning. She thought it so typical of Will to be standing there with his hands in his pockets, looking up with awe and admiration of all that was grand and eternal, and with resignation to the idea that he would never be. And did not really want to be. "They make me feel," he said, "like nothing down here matters."

"I'm sorry about your mother."

He looked at her. "I've been here an hour or so. I saw you in there dancing. You were lovely. It's odd to think I've never seen you dance before." She felt the contrast of it, Sam Houston telling her she danced like fairies, an enchanting myth, and Will saying simply, You were lovely.

"Why didn't you find me when I first came out?"

"Because he did."

"But not for a while."

"I watched him. He saw you go out. I guessed he would follow."

"I don't understand you, Will. Why did you wait for him to?"

"You wanted him to, didn't you? I didn't want to interfere."

Her response was instant. "You just wanted to confront me here with him, to put me on the defensive, after what you said to my father. It's a way to turn the judgment around, isn't it?"

His voice hardened with his first show of provocation. "What happened with your father has nothing to do with any of this. If it weren't for Sam Houston, what happened between your father and me wouldn't matter to you. You just want rid of me, that's all. And now you've found a way. And best of all, your father will approve of it." She could barely see the birthmark on his jaw. "Do you know how much you've changed?" he added in a softer voice.

She wanted to deny it, and everything he said, but knew the truth of it. She wanted him to hold her. "Please hold me," she said.

He stared at her. With composure, he answered, "No, Eliza. There's no use to it. I've never really had you; I won't go on pretending. I was useful to you, that's all."

It was too final, too sudden a severance of the only true intimacy she had ever known. She was about to make some move, to stand and reach for him, when he said passionately, shoving his hands out toward her with the palms up, "What do you want from me?"

"I don't know. I don't want to lose you."

"But you want more than I can give you." It was true. She did not answer. "Decide," he added. "I won't wait around to see how things go with the congressman. Decide now if you want to keep on seeing me."

"Will?"

"Yes." His voice was softer, his face confronting her with a hurt, boyish look, beautiful, the tall trees behind him.

"I . . ." She searched for words, for clear feelings, but found nothing. Only a stillness in the night. She shook her head.

"It isn't your father," he said, wanting her to say it was.

"No."

"Then it's Houston."

"I don't know."

Without saying anything, he turned and left her.

CHAPTER
10

The congressman had gotten drunk. "I've had it up to here with Tyree Springs," he grumbled with a sloppy gesture at his throat. "I'm going on back to Nashville."

"It's a long ride, with no moon," Willoughby answered, meeting his wife's eyes with a sidelong glance.

"I've done plenty politicking for one night," Houston whispered loudly, glancing around at the blur of faces. "I've got to get back." Willoughby eyed him reproachfully, which was irritating, so he said again, louder, "I've done plenty enough politicking for one night."

"You've drank enough for six," the deputy rebuked him. Sam had promised Jackson he would curb his public drinking during the campaign.

Houston drew himself up and grinned, a trace of saliva on his chin. "Call me Governor," he said, "for practice."

Outside, Houston wanted to take just one more look. Just to see if she was still there. Just one glance through the trees from a distance, a turn of his eyes on his way to the stable to fetch his horse. His legs were heavy but he managed to walk straight, just in case she was looking. Perhaps she had already gone. He hoped she was still in the swing, and alone. Maybe she was waiting for him to come back. "You never know," he said aloud.

He had to squint to see out that far; everything seemed in motion, sliding away. He had actually to walk a few steps in that direction to see for sure, but it was just a few steps, and the swing faced out into the woods; likely she was not looking and would never know. "You never know," he said again. And what if she did see him? For a moment, in his drunken mind, he wanted her to see him. To see him and to come to him, all that yellow hair blowing around her oval face, those eyes—one eyebrow arched, one straight, an exquisite imperfection—but he was getting too close. He had come too close when he was sitting in that swing. He had come far too close that morning in the old church. He should not get any closer than this—it was something to be avoided at this time in his life, with the world open and nothing to hold him back . . . or could a woman, possibly, help him move forward, as the General had said? At any rate, just now was not a time to think about it; tomorrow he would consider it, when his mind was clear and her presence not so close and provocative. Better to move on. Just one more step in her direction, and . . .

She was gone. There was only the back of the swing, moving slightly in the breeze. She must have taken a room. Or started home. Or—and then the thought of it—or gone somewhere with that Tyree fellow. Damn him. Certainly she wasn't the type to be off in the woods with him. But . . . "You never know," he said, his irritation rising, turning to anger at himself for leaving her there with Tyree. He should have stayed. But he had to be so goddamn decent. A gallant fool. Brainless.

He veered to go, then looked back once more. Maybe she was lying down in the swing. Maybe she was lying down with him. Tyree. But no, of course she wasn't. She wouldn't do that in public. She wouldn't do it at all. But then, women in love did things. Risky things. But she couldn't be in love with this—boy. Who in the hell was he, anyway? Tyree, like this place. Must be wealthy, reputable, have all those qualities the General said that he, Sam Houston, lacked. Stability. Respectability. Goddamn him to hell. Goddamn them all.

He wheeled and made his way around toward the stable. As he passed by the back entrance of the pavilion, he saw a dark-haired woman standing just outside, her skirt blowing against her thighs, revealing the curves of her body. She had come out to catch her breath. Her hand was holding lightly to the netting; she seemed to be leaning out toward him. "Congressman," she said in a mellow voice, lifting her free hand slightly.

He had met her before, with her husband. She was more lovely than he remembered. He called out, "Mrs. James," and went unsteadily toward her, thinking suddenly of the blue ribbon in his pocket and Eliza, who was with another man. "I have something for you." He stopped a few paces from her and pulled out the tiny slip of satin. "It's a little worn," he said, looking at it, and then at her. "I just found it, but I think the color would be very beautiful on you. It would be"—he belched, then grinned with a look intended to be magnanimous, but appearing instead (and he knew it) ridiculous— "well, it would be lovely in your hair." He made a bow, sweeping the ribbon out toward her, then wished he hadn't. Being drunk was one thing, displaying it in public was quite another. And he was a congressman—a governor-to-be.

She came toward him, not at all hesitant, her body swaying. She seemed very beautiful to him, very soft, her face smiling, her eyes dark and misty. For a moment his vision blurred, and when it cleared again she was almost up against him, her round, compliant face looking up, her hands reaching up and pulling the combs from her hair. "Perhaps you would tie it in for me," she said sweetly, but did not turn or gather her hair together for him.

Her meaning was plain. He felt a heavy pulse in his groin and reached around her neck, collecting the wild strands in his hands, feeling clumsy, frustrated with his clumsiness—he who could move with such grace and speak with such articulate precision—groping, and at a sudden loss for words, or perhaps it was for need of them, for his eyes spoke boldly.

His behavior was insane; he knew it. Whiskey took all caution from a man, all poise and subtlety—the things that made a man great—and left him groping. And yet it did feel good abandoning the rules, or at least thinking about abandoning them, and giving in to this instinctive courting in the night. He touched her hair and moved his fingers around to the back of her neck, just barely caressing her. And then, instead of tying the ribbon, he pulled her forward with it, slowly, and leaned and kissed her mouth. She responded. He tied the ribbon around her hair, looked long into her upturned face, then took her by the hand and led her toward the stable.

The place was dark, quiet but for the occasional movement of horses. Her hand was warm and willing in his, and he turned just inside, pulling her to him. For an instant she was coy, turning her back to him as if to go, but she did not struggle when he reached for her. She leaned back against him, discarding all pretense of retreat or shame.

"I've been watching you dance all evening," he said, which was not true, but sounded as if it might be, his voice quiet and sincere, and only slightly thick. "You move very nicely." Then, as if there were no hurry at all and no chance of being discovered, as if his actions were as innocent as a turn once around the dance floor, he moved his hands down her sides, no longer graceless, but with the ease of instinct, feeling the curves, then up again to the bodice with tiny buttons, which he unfastened, feeling her breasts separate and sag restfully as if they had been waiting for this liberation all night. She leaned into him, the pressure of his groin in the small of her back.

He glanced once at the barn door, aware his position was vulnerable, that anyone stepping in with a light would see them there, the woman's bare breasts, her head tossed back into his shoulder. But he would hear them coming. Unless he lost his senses altogether, which he sometimes did when so aroused—and he was completely aroused, the feeling of risk adding to his excitement.

"You also move very nicely," she murmured. He answered with his hands, sliding them down, loosening the fastening of her skirt and searching beneath the undergarments, over the smooth skin and down into the nest of hair. She shifted her legs apart in a small, cursory movement, lifted one and set it on the low rung of a stall, opening herself to his hands, to the dark stall and smell of horse, as if she were going to make love with the beast in the stall. He pressed against her and began to rock slowly, then with more urgency, thinking of Eliza and how she rode with her legs spread wide over the animal's back. The woman turned to face him in the dark, gliding her hands over his groin and reaching for the button of his trousers. For a brief moment, all of his feeling was centered there. He had no thought of being discovered, or of the campaign, or of Eliza Allen; there were only these hands on him with their tantalizing pressure. . . . And then there was light, the yellow light of a tin lantern shining in the doorway. He squinted and put his hand to his eyes; the woman turned quickly away, the light on her back, pulling her blouse together and working to secure her skirt.

It was Willoughby. He said nothing, just stood there in the doorway with the lantern in his hand, the flame's light glowing on his red beard.

She spoke first, her voice tense and angry, and ashamed. "Pardon," she said, and turned, feigning a proud look, her chin high. She stepped out toward the door, fully dressed now, but her hand pressed fastidiously over her bodice as if she were naked and shy. She did not look at the deputy or at Sam Houston but skirted around them both and out the door, the yellow light catching the folds of her skirt as she passed through.

Willoughby, embarrassed for the woman, and offended, kept

his eyes on Houston. After a moment he lowered the tin lantern to his side.

At last Sam said, "What in the hell do you think you're doing? Damn it, Willoughby, who in the hell do you think you are?"

"That gal's married!" Willoughby declared. "And you knowed it, Sam!"

"Yeah," Houston answered forcefully. "And I bet she 'knowed' it too." He stressed the poor grammar, which rankled Willoughby, but he was accustomed to Sam's sarcasm.

"Well, she don't happen to be running for governor. What in the world has got into you tonight? A married woman, Sam? Have you lost your mind?"

Sam leaned back against the stall railings, staring up into the rafters. "I think I might have, Willoughby," he said quietly.

"What?"

"I think I might have lost my mind. Or lost something, God knows what." He closed his eyes and drifted, then added, as if the thought had just come to him, "God, Willoughby, I must have lost my mind." He looked at his friend again and grinned. "But Deputy Willoughby Williams comes to extricate me, again, just in time. Right? The ubiquitous Willoughby Williams!" He shoved his face toward Willoughby and the lantern. "Right, Willoughby?"

"What's the matter with you, Sam?"

His expression fell; he felt a sinking inside, a dull, slow falling into confusion, all the old unanswered questions. He shook his head. The horse in the stall behind him grunted and pushed its dark head over the planks. "God knows," Houston sighed, and then, trying to make light of it all, "Misery is the lot of man, and miserably do I realize it."

"What for were you running off to Nashville in the first place? And then for goodness' sake, how'd you get sidetracked into something shameful like—"

"Running?" Houston's voice came at him, hard and fierce. "Sam Houston running? Houston has never run from anything in his life."

They stared at each other. Willoughby set the light on the ground, crossed his arms over his chest, took in a breath and let it out slowly. Then, his voice deliberate, he said, "Yeah, you have, Sam. You run away from home more than once. You run away from your mother."

It seemed Houston would attack him physically; his whole drunken body tensed. Then, still glowering, he said, "The devil himself would run from my mother." He sighed and added, "She was a tyrant, you know. Sovereign of the tyrants. She allowed my brothers to drive me like a slave."

"Sam, I know your mother. She's a hard woman. But she ain't a tyrant. She had to support the family, that's all. It took strength to pack up everything and the nine of you kids and move to Tennessee when your pa died."

"Support the family?" His voice was hushed. "No, friend, you're less perceptive than I thought. Her need was not to support us. It was to own us. To own me." He looked at the ground, a pile of fresh horse dung, then back up. "But you are right about one thing," he said bitterly. "My mother never has run short of fortitude. It makes up the balance of her character. And that doesn't mean I owe her a damn thing. You know what Gulliver's Lilliputians say about that? They say men and women are joined together like any other animals, by motives of concupiscence—they don't have babies for the babies' benefit, but to satisfy their own carnal cravings. So a person's not under any obligation to his parents—not to his father for begetting him, nor to his mother for giving him birth."

This was too philosophical for the deputy. He said, "Why don't you stay tonight?"

"No."

"Then I'm gonna ride back with you."

"Don't be such a bullheaded, intractable son of a bitch," Houston said with more force, and no slur at all. "I'm going now, alone. Do you comprehend?"

"All right," Willoughby said, wondering what "intractable" meant. "Go on."

When the deputy was gone, Sam Houston stumbled outside and sat on the ground with his back against the side of the stable. He spat in the dirt, ran his hand down over his face, and closed his eyes. "Now why'd you do that, Houston?" he muttered. "That man's the best friend you have. Fact is, Houston, you push your friends to the limit. Fact is, Houston, they like you anyway—despicable as you are."

He listened to the stableboy come and go with a few horses. The music had stopped. A group of women were walking to the hotel just up the road. He could not see them from where he sat, but their laughter carried in the clear night. Two men came for their mounts; they were discussing property for sale along the Cumberland. He recognized the voices—William Trousdale and Thomas Boyers. Gallatin men, friends of John Allen. Eliza must know them. Eliza. The moments in the swing seemed long ago, the evening a smudge of faces and music and stars in a black sky; the only distinct image was her profile, the chin a little too strong, the one straight eyebrow. And her voice, so low, soft as the night air, "I thought you would write. . . . I hear the wind, and the music. . . . But no real spirits."

He dozed off, and was awakened by a long, low, cry far off over the Highland Rim. He listened, and it came again, a timber wolf howling up to the sky, the noise carrying for miles in every direction. "Every direction," he thought, and then, more specifically, "west." The wild beckoning of the West. "You're a goddamn fool, Congressman," he said aloud, and then, for the hell of it, "You're a goddamn fool, Governor." He smiled. Governor. It did sound good.

For now.

After Will left her, Eliza remained in the swing. She wanted to see Sam Houston, just to look at him. At last she went around the pavilion and stood in back outside the netting. She watched him dance one reel, then speak with Deputy Williams and, alone, step outside through the front entrance. She lost sight of him then. She thought he would walk up the road toward the hotel, where most guests were staying the night, and waited to see.

He did not go to the hotel but after a moment came around toward the stable. Eliza crouched back in shadow near the hedge alongside the pavilion as a woman stepped out through the opening in the netting a few yards away; he greeted the woman and offered her the ribbon. To Eliza the gesture seemed ridiculous, a stupid offering—this man in a black cape, against a dark sky, barren land behind him, two outhouses and the stable, his hand flinging out the tiny ribbon with such ostentation, as if it were some valuable prize. Then the woman went to him, and he kissed her and tied the ribbon in her hair. They went off together to the stable.

Eliza remained in the bushes with the music drumming close beside her. More than ever, more than anything, she wished Will were there to comfort her. Will would never hurt her as this man did.

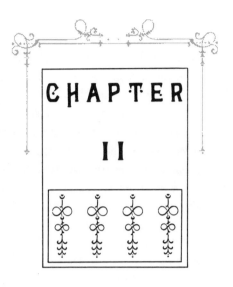

CHAPTER

II

October 1827

Governor Houston sat with his legs
stretched out, his boots propped on his desk and crossed at the
ankles, a book of George Gordon, Lord Byron's poetry open on his
thighs. His correspondence was pushed aside; he was taking a break.
He looked up from his reading and paused, staring at the paint
peeling off the far wall. Then he turned in his creaking spindle-back
chair to look down from the open window of his office onto the
square. It was autumn, and market day, and the streets were full—
not a time to be confined to a rotting old office in a condemned
courthouse. The square was muddy with the night's rain, but this
morning the sun was out. It was high time, Houston mused, setting
aside thoughts brought on by the poem, that the streets of Nashville
were paved.

The stocks and whipping post were vacant; Houston could not

abide whippings and would not allow them on market days. Billy Carroll, the previous governor, had introduced a bill for revision of the penal code, calling for a penitentiary to be built and for the whipping post to be removed. Houston was doing his best to press the bill through, but many legislators believed it was too lenient and wanted to amend the stipulation that the death penalty should be applied only in instances of first-degree murder. Horse thieves, they said, should also be hanged.

Most white men looked on Indians as bloodthirsty savages, Houston thought bitterly. He had never known a Cherokee to steal from his own tribe, let alone to be killed for it. There were so many backward laws and archaic thinkers in this town, so few men of vision. County courts still fixed rates for tavern food, drink and lodging, and on market day it was illegal for establishments to buy and sell produce—a law to which Houston's older brother James, who owned a store just down from the post office, had bowed, renting a market stall himself. But then, thought Sam, James had always adapted to the system and authority. Sam had a sudden image of his mother in her Maryville home at that moment, a large woman with sparse gray hair pulled into a tight knot and her mouth set. She would be alone but for the few slaves she had bought through the years with income from the farm and her interest in the local store. The family was scattered, the three living brothers doing well for themselves, and Eliza Ann, the youngest of the nine, married now. Paxton had been dead for many years from consumption, Isabelle was dead, William was dead from his own hand—a bullet through his head because his heart had been broken—and Mary . . . beautiful Mary. He could not help but blame himself about Mary. He had always been the one she confided in, and he had let her down— had gone off first with his red brothers and then with the army, and then never really home to stay. He should have found a way to be with her at home more, or to take her away from her mother, who was hard on her. But it was done now. Mary had been wed and widowed and wed again, last to an older widower with a large family. He abused her fragile emotions, but she wanted children of her own and would not leave him. Sam had urged her to leave, fearing she would not survive, but she would not hear of it and was slipping, already, into a fanciful world. Mary's instability was not their mother's fault, and Sam knew it; Mrs. Houston had tried and at least had not abandoned the girl as he had. Off chasing his own dreams, escaping the drudgery of home and the farm. It was not leaving home that had been wrong; it was leaving Mary.

He had been through the town campaigning, but his mother had not come out to hear him speak. He had hoped she would, so he could prove some things to her: that his years with the Indians had served him better than farming and keeping the store books, that he wasn't worthless. He had amounted to something. But she took no notice.

He frowned, and sighed. It wasn't such an honor, anyway, being governor of a state without even a capitol building (without even a permanent decision on where the capitol of Tennessee should be), sharing a shabby courthouse with federal and state courts and local officials. His position lacked both grandeur and greatness; the first he desired, the second he craved.

And here was another of his failings: always wanting something grander. Perhaps he was still trying to prove himself to his mother and to win her, trying to make up for all his father's failings. Major Samuel Houston had never been home much; he was a professional soldier in a time of peace, devoted as much to the image as to the occupation, which took more heart and effort than one would have expected. But Sam remembered him well, his look and his voice, if not much of what he said—which, Sam now suspected, was probably not worth remembering. But for one thing, this: that Sam was his namesake. The major always put great emphasis on that, as if it were an honor Sam somehow had to live up to. The fifth son, named for him, a distinction Sam had not asked for and was not sure he wanted but took seriously. He never saw much in his father to admire, and so transposed the responsibility to one of atoning for the man's failings, a charge that at times hindered his endeavor to be his own man and feel good about it. He wanted freedom to blaze his own trails; he was Sam, never Samuel.

But a man could grow bitter dwelling on the past. Better to think on the future and the progress in this state of his. And there was progress. The Nashville Inn across the street, still his home, had grown to a hostelry of considerable pretensions, with two additional wings accommodating several offices for the twenty-four stage lines that came and went at all hours of day and night.

Nashville had a new theater in addition to the one in the old frame salt warehouse on Market Street. Sam enjoyed theater; when he was studying law he had tried his hand at acting in the Dramatic Club of Nashville. He played Glenalvon in *Douglas,* a tragedy by John Home, and Chevalier St. Franc in *Point of Honor.* He reached the height of his career cast as a drunken porter in *Fly by Night;* the audience loved him in this role, and the newspapers lauded him. The owner of the theater claimed he had "never met a man who had a keener sense of the ridiculous, nor one who could more readily assume the ludicrous or the sublime." It was a description Houston cherished, though his acting talent was not as great as his drinking talent; he had soused himself before each performance and managed to keep anyone from knowing it. The real acting was backstage—feigning sobriety.

And there were water pipes to the public square. A few years back, an individual had begun the job, using pipes made from black locust logs drilled through the center. He got the water as far as the reservoir on the north side of Church Street and then ran out of contract money. Two local businessmen took over and extended the pipes to a pump house on the square.

There was reason to be proud of this town. Doc Shelby's covered bridge that spanned the Cumberland from the northeast corner of the public square to the Gallatin turnpike had a fresh coat of yellow paint and could carry twenty animals at a time, and heavy wagons also, provided they were adequately spaced.

And the steamboats! Too many were lost on the Harpeth or Muscle Shoals, and others exploded and burned, with heavy loss of life and property. But most made their journeys intact, carrying sugar and coffee, china, plows, clothing and people—a stream of people—from New Orleans and Pittsburgh and Philadelphia. The boats stayed a few days and then churned off again, taking back with them cotton, hides, tobacco, meat and whiskey. From his window on the third floor Sam could almost see the wharf, now being graduated and expanded. Cranes had been erected so cotton bales could be lifted onto the boats instead of deposited by drays and rolled through the mud, a laborious practice that soiled the cotton and decreased its value. He could see a steamboat leaving, heading downstream toward the Ohio; with the recent rains and water rising, it would reach New Orleans in eight days. He watched the boat maneuver its way through the traffic of frontier craft pulling in and out of dock—flatboats, keelboats, barges and bateaux laden with goods and animals—and had an urge to be going. Anywhere.

The rivers were all heavily traveled these days—the Cumberland, Tennessee and Hiwassee. He had prompted a study of how the waters of the Hiwassee, known to the Cherokees as "Long Man," could be connected with the Coosa, a project that could open intercourse between east Tennessee and south Alabama. Also, engineers employed by the U.S. Government were deciding on the practicality of a canal on the north bank of the Tennessee, whereby the obstructions of Muscle Shoals could be surmounted. The Big Suck on the Tennessee was still a danger, but boaters were mastering it.

But the streets. The streets had to be paved. Mongrels and pigs roamed at leisure in the mud, and . . . horses? There was something going on down there, some unusual commotion.

Houston turned toward his office door. "Dobbs!" he called, and the secretary appeared instantly, closing the door behind him and standing beside it with a military decorum that irritated Houston. His official secretary was out sick, and Willoughby had found Dobbs to stand in. "What in hell is going on down there?" he demanded.

"It's Deputy Williams, sir: he's turnin' them horses loose."

"He's doing what?"

"Turnin' them horses loose, sir, the ones hitched to the side of the courthouse."

"Turning them loose?"

"Yes sir, like he said he would in the papers. 'Cause on market day the hitchin' rails is full and folks hitch all them horses to the courthouse, and they make quite a mess, sir, with all their horseshit, and the deputy's tired of walkin' in it. Plus, some of them horses pull them boards clean away—seein' as they're rotten it ain't hard. Would you like me to get the paper for you, where the deputy said he would do it?"

"Oh for God's sake." He was disgusted with triviality and wished if he had to deal with it he could at least be with Willoughby turning the horses loose.

"Sorry, sir. But if you ask me, sir, it's no real answer to the problem. You see, knowin' Deputy Williams, he'll spend all afternoon helpin' folks get them horses back, and he could shovel a whole lot of horseshit in less time than it's gonna take him to reunite all them folks with all them rovin' horses."

Kirby Dobbs was such a meager man, and with no sense of humor. Houston tried to hide his annoyance and think of an appropriate response that would not demean the fellow completely. He came up with nothing and said, "Thank you. You may go."

Dobbs saluted, an affectation the governor hated, and left the room. Houston sighed, still looking at the door, at the hat rack beside it, his beaver hat. He wished he were at the Hermitage, where important campaign decisions were being made. The governorship seemed so insipid in the larger picture, and Houston preferred the larger picture. But Jackson wanted him here, holding the state together. So here he was. Propping his feet back on his desk, he lowered his eyes again to the open book in his lap and read the same words over:

For as on thee my memory ponders
Perchance to me thine also wanders.

Suddenly he leaned forward and reached for his pen with the eagle quill, one of his own affectations. He despised a goose quill; the goose was a foolheaded bird, the eagle a bird of destiny. He dipped the quill and underlined the words. Then again he took to staring at the wall opposite.

Where had he gone wrong? He had been so decent to her that night. She had not been around when he got himself drunk. He had questioned Willoughby, just to be sure, and Willoughby said she had not come back to the pavilion after Houston did. It was possible she was in love with this Tyree fellow and seeing him privately, though it would have to be privately, for he had asked Doc about Tyree—the boy was poor, and further, he and John Allen had some business conflict which had turned to personal animosity. This was easy to believe, for John Allen was a boor. And Will was bright, Doc had said: young, not particularly enterprising, but honest. And that night Eliza had said she valued honesty.

Houston had called on her twice since then, only to find she was "out riding." She had disappointed and embarrassed him by returning, unopened, the letter he sent with Peyton asking to call on her. Of course, he was far from giving up. Why was she avoiding him, if not because of Tyree? He had never had trouble attracting a woman. And she had missed him when he was in Washington; she had waited for a letter. It could not possibly be that she had seen him with that woman, in the stable—that would be too completely damning. But the thought concerned him. She did like stables, and went to them when she wanted to be alone. Like the day of the races. He had been careless that night, with the woman, but the Conducting Providence could not be so vindictive as to have arranged for Eliza to watch. But then, he had given that ribbon away in broad sight of anyone who happened to be standing in the area. It was a dark night, but there was light enough from the pavilion . . .

Again he tried to remember precisely what he had said to the James woman about the ribbon, how well he had checked to see that no one was watching when he took her to the stable. It was all a blur. A stupid blur. A goddamn stupid blur.

A knock sounded on the door, and Houston called out for the person to come in. He welcomed this interruption.

A young man stepped in; he was small in stature, his unshaven face dirty and pleased. Sweat stains ran from his armpits down to his waist, his fringed buckskin shirt fitting close around him as if molded to his body. His brown hair was shoulder-length and oily, combed back from his forehead. At first glance Houston did not recognize him. "I'm here with western dust still on my clothes!" the man said.

"Wharton!" Houston exclaimed, setting the book aside and standing. "William Wharton!" He crossed the room in three strides and took Wharton's hand in a vigorous shake, his other hand gripping the man's shoulder. "God, look at you!"

"Excuse the appearance, sir," Wharton said, pushing his grimy fingers through his hair. "I rode directly into town to see my brother John. I couldn't wait to see him. He's taking my wife on to Uncle Jesse's. I'm married, sir!"

"Well, congratulations." Houston looked at him and shook his head. "Open spaces agree with you. Sit down, here," he said, indicating one of three chairs. "Tell me about the lady, tell me about Texas."

Houston himself remained standing and untied the silk cravat at his neck.

"They take a man's breath, Governor, the lady and Texas. Her name's Sarah Ann." He smiled. "She loves Texas, too. We're going back, I guarantee that. We've got land in Austin's colony. And"—he paused for emphasis—"we got a baby in the shuck for spring."

Houston suffered a prick of envy. It seemed everyone had children, except him. He kept his smile. "Do you mean to tell me you made the journey with your wife in a family way?"

"Yes sir, there was a group leaving to come this way, and I wanted to see my brother."

Houston said, "He's building up quite a practice in town, quite a reputation," and loosened his cravat again, then jerked it off and tossed it onto the desk behind him. "Here you are," he added, as if joking, but feeling every word, "at least a decade my junior, with a

wife, and a baby on the way, and already been to Texas and back."
He felt the usual sense of urgency that pressed on him these days, an
agitated feeling that he should be somewhere else. Thirty-five years
old, and stalled. Already the General was talking of his running for a
second term as governor, with this one just started. And the old man
made no more mention of Texas, at least no more specific mention
of it, only that abstruse talk of brave men who would one day win the
West—but never how they should win it, or when, or what on God's
earth they should wait for. Repeatedly Houston had tried to pin
Jackson down to names and dates and strategies, until finally the
sinuous old bastard had said, "You worry about Tennessee for a few
years, son; then we'll talk plans." He had heard that line before.
Why did the General tantalize him so? Was he wanting him to take
action on his own? It was possible. But not probable: Jackson liked to
be in the saddle of command himself. Whatever was being conquered, Andrew Jackson wanted full control and full credit and was
apt to ruin any man who tried to take it from him. "Texas," he said,
almost without knowing he had spoken.

Wharton's scrubby face was instantly serious, and he leaned
forward in his chair. "Is it true, sir, that you plan to go there?"

Houston walked back around his desk, around the dusty United
States flag to his chair, stopping for a moment to glance out the
window. The commotion was still raging outside.

Evidently, from Wharton's question, he had heard something
from his brother. News was out that Houston had his eye on Texas.
Where the rumor had started was a mystery; Houston did talk about
Texas, and the West in general, but so did everyone. He was always
careful not to say too much, and he never repeated anything the
General said to him on the topic: such cabalistic, conjectural talk as
Jackson's could easily be misinterpreted and misrepresented. It had
occurred to him that the General might have started the bruit that
Sam Houston was interested in Texas's future. Jackson did tend to
approach things in mysterious ways, and from several directions at
once. It could be he was baiting Houston's interest in Texas with
those talks of his and also slyly planting the idea around Nashville

that Sam Houston was the man for such a job as taking Texas—if Texas were ever taken. Sam would, after all, need followers if he undertook such an endeavor, and what better way for the General to be sure Houston had support than to recommend him for the job?

At any rate, John Wharton had been listening to someone— and talking. But you couldn't expect brothers like these to keep secrets from each other. "Someday," Houston said to William, as if he had not worried the idea much. "I do hope to go there someday."

Wharton glanced at the boarded-up door leading into the court chambers, leaned forward and said in a whisper, "I know nothing of what you have in mind, Governor, but I will tell you this. There will be fighting in Texas. It's inevitable. There's already unrest and skirmishes, and there will be fighting. I believe the Mexican government suspects an Anglo-American conspiracy; they're tightening security and strengthening forces."

"Have they knowledge of a conspiracy, or just suspicions?" Houston asked quietly, suppressing his alarm. What if someone beat him to it? To Texas? Damn the old General for his procrastinating and his ambiguous talk. Damn the governorship of Tennessee. He should be in Texas.

There was a forceful knock at the door. "I'm sorry, sir," Dobbs's muffled voice called through, "but you said to check your schedule, and while I was at it I saw you have a Masonic committee meeting in a hour." He waited, and when the governor did not respond, he said, "I thought you might like to know it, sir."

Wharton said, "They say Santa Anna is a Mason."

"Santa Anna? A Mason?" Houston queried, and then called out, "All right, Dobbs, close the office and go for an early lunch."

The door from the outer office to the hall closed shut. Houston went to his own door, opened it, and checked to be sure the secretary was gone. "That idiot has big ears," he said. He returned to his seat and propped his feet up on the desk. "So. You were going to tell me if the Mexicans know of a conspiracy on Texas or if they just fear one."

"I think it's only a widening of the general distrust," Wharton said, pulling a black twist of tobacco from his trouser pocket and holding it out to the governor, who shook his head. Wharton bit off a chunk and continued talking with his mouth full. "What with Adams and Clay offering to buy Texas, the Mexican government has reason to be nervous. Like a virgin in enemy camp: they don't know what the next approach will be, or where it'll come from, but they intend to keep what they've got."

"And the settlers?"

"We intend to keep what we've got too. We've made more progress in just ten years than the Spanish did in three hundred. We've brought more people in and settled more towns and put more land to farming in a single decade. On last count, Anglos in Texas outnumbered the Mexicans five to one. It's the Mexican government that wants the place, not the people. The Mexican people aren't interested in building homes in the wilderness and fighting off Indians. And we are. And we're doing it." He paused, chewing. "I figure we've paid for our Texas land. And now the Mexicans are cracking down."

"And Texans won't be cracked down on?"

"I don't think so, sir. At least, not this one." Suddenly his temper flashed. "Since Mexico got her independence from Spain, not one Mexican dollar or piece of eight has been spent for Texas, not one Mexican soldier has ever fought with the settlers against the Indians. Mexico has given us no protection at all. And yet they expect us to abide by all their stinking laws and turn Papist." He paused, obviously trying to curb his anger. "Mind if I spit on the floor here?" he asked forcefully.

"Go ahead," the governor answered in a mild tone, hiding his real excitement. He was delighted the settlers were getting fed up with Mexican fetters. He picked up a whittling knife, tapped it aimlessly on his desk, and fed Wharton's passion. "I don't know of one spot on earth where Catholic power and influence prevails in which trial by jury, the right of habeas corpus, or the Magna Carta exists." He kept his voice placid. "So is it independence you're talking, William?"

Wharton hesitated. It was plain to Houston that the man had come to hear what Sam Houston had to say about Texas, not to spill his own resentment, but was caught up. "The Mexicans are clever people," he said, pacing himself, "but Spanish oppression has beat them down. They have no notion how to govern themselves. They can't even decide if they want to be federalized or centralized. It's a regular fandango the way their leaders and policies come and go." He paused and then said, "Yes. I am talking independence. Sooner or later, Texas must be independent."

It made his blood surge, listening to this young man. "You say they're tightening security and strengthening forces," Houston said dispassionately. "Specifically, how?"

"First, they've passed a new law forbidding settlement of Anglo-Americans anywhere near the eastern border, and there's serious talk that within a year Mexico will abolish slavery throughout their republic. Of course, it's a direct effort to deter U.S. immigrants, since slavery doesn't really exist anywhere but in the state of Coahuila and Texas. My guess is they think we won't come without our slaves. And they could be right. I know my father-in-law would not have done it." In a subdued voice he said, "And to top it, Santa Anna's emerging from the woodwork. He's been biding his time lately, with all the conflicts. Eating his opium—that's his way. He just rolls with the punches, then sides with the winners and comes out looking right. Mark me, that man aspires to the purple. And when he gets it, his tactics won't be entirely defensive." The final sentence was barely a whisper—"He's calling himself 'the Napoleon of the West.'"

Houston was totally aroused. Things were moving in Texas. Conflict might come sooner than he had anticipated. And here I sit, he thought, with a sudden rise of anger, in a rat-infested edifice with the goddamn paint peeling off the walls. "Napoleon of the West," he mused. "Ten years ago the Spanish named Andrew Jackson 'Caudillo' and 'the Napoleon of the Woods.'" He took a whetstone from his top drawer, contemplating an encounter of two Napoleons. Sharpening his whittling knife to release tension and disguise his fascination, he asked, "How much control does he really have, this Napoleon of the West?"

"No one knows. One thing I'm certain of: nobody's controlling Texas. That's why there'll be fighting. Mexico's problem is the size of that place. It is vast, I assure you. You can ride for miles and miles and never see a living soul. Some might disagree, but I just don't believe Mexico can dictate to a territory that far from the government, that's bigger than France, England, Scotland and Ireland united. There's no way to enforce laws and press religion and language on a population that remote and scattered."

"And uncooperative," Houston added. "What about Mexico's army?"

"We hear rumors of its strength. But of course it's so far from our settlements that it hardly matters."

"And how are the settlements doing?" Houston asked idly, feigning concentration on his knife.

"Quite a few are failing. Green Dewitt pushed too far west; his settlers are being butchered by the Indians. There's a real shortage of supplies, especially salt, so food can't be cured." He dug a finger in his ear and wiped it on his blue canvas trousers. "For most, money's as scarce as bread. I'd say only about one out of ten transactions involves specie. The rest is barter, and what a man can shoot or dig out of the ground. And living off the land, like most of them are—I mean really living off it—with no spinning wheels, no poultry, just a few tools, well, it's damned hard. Of course, if you marry a wealthy lady like Sarah Ann Groce, it's different, but it's still not what I'd call leisure." He paused and grinned, but the governor was not looking at him.

"What precisely is the Indian situation?" Houston queried, touching the tip of the blade to test its point.

The young man hesitated, and Houston read his thoughts—a man should tread carefully when he spoke to Sam Houston of Indians. "Well," Wharton answered, plunging in, "we have the Karankawas along the coast attacking and eating folks who come by sea—"

"Eating them? I've heard that. Is it true?"

"Yes sir, it is. Alive. They stake their captives down and carve them up. A bite at a time."

Houston set down the knife, then the stone, and looked at Wharton. "Good God," he said. "That's a tall tale if ever I heard one."

Wharton took offense. "Well I, for one, believe it," he said, but refrained from stressing that his opinion was more informed than Houston's. "Anyway," he continued, "in the interior there are the Tonkawas, and on the Brazos there are Tawakonis, Wacos and Comanches. So far, they aren't quite as bad. The Comanches stay busy fighting the Mexicans. The Wacos are a different story; they get along with the Mexicans but aren't too crazy for us. And the Tonkawas just hang about the settlements and beg and cause trouble, and the Wacos and Tawakonis and Comanches come into our settlements to war with them and end up killing a few settlers for good measure. Then we go for revenge. As far as Indians are concerned east Texas is the safest place to be." Wharton stopped talking. Houston declined to fill the silence and again took up his knife and stone. At last Wharton leaned forward and said in a whisper, "I'll tell you something, Governor. Nobody in Coahuila and Texas is in control. Nobody's whipped yet—not the Mexicans or the Indians or us—and nobody intends to be."

So here it was. What Sam Houston had been waiting to hear. He stopped sharpening.

"There will be fighting, sir," Wharton said. "If I have to start it myself. It's a vast place for enterprise and fame, some of it dry, but most of what I've seen is as wet and lush as a happy whore."

Houston scrutinized him. For a full minute, he did not take his eyes from Wharton's. Then he said, his voice low and quick, "In your opinion, what would it take to get control?"

"Someone like you," Wharton answered.

"And do you feel there is urgency?"

"Some. But for now, the time is waiting for the man."

Houston leaned back in his chair, gripped his fingers behind his head and looked up at the ceiling. He knew Wharton was flattering him, but that was beside the point. With or without Jackson's guidance, he would go to Texas. He did not know when or how or with what support or opposition, but he would go. He would finish this term as governor, perhaps serve a second one. And then move on. The populace was fond of saying he would follow in Andrew Jackson's footsteps—maybe even to the presidency. That could be. The presidency would be a good place from which to conquer the West. Buy it. Or bargain for it. Or fight if need be. But one way or the other, as President or private individual, he would take Texas. Still looking up, he said, "I think, William, that the timing is not yet. I will say no more than that, except to assure you that the time will come, and when it does, I will turn my full attentions west. Until then, you and your brother John should rest quiet." He lowered his head slightly, his heavy brow pressed low over his eyes, which fixed on the young man. "Very quiet. Rest with the assurance that when the time arrives for any plan to be effected, you will both figure in it." He paused. Wharton said nothing. "William, John is very young —about twenty?"

"Twenty-one, sir."

"I consider him an able lawyer and a man of intelligence. And, like yourself, capable of keeping his own counsel. In other words: his mouth shut. Neither he nor you should forget that I am governor of Tennessee. As long as I remain governor, the West, for me, is a long way off, and my attentions are given to my constituents. Do you understand?"

"Yes sir."

"Then restrain his tongue."

"He will not discuss any of it. You have my word."

The governor's face softened. "Now that I have your word, tell me exactly what it was John said to you when you saw him this morning."

Wharton hesitated, then answered, "He said I should go to see you, sir, with Texas dust still in my clothes."

Houston threw his head back and laughed. "Did he now! How insightful! What else did he say?"

"Just that he thought you had a grand scheme up your sleeve."

Houston smiled, turned slowly and looked out the window. He watched a woman at a vegetable stand, a man with a quarter of beef over his shoulders, two children in the mud. He watched old man Brooks, with one short leg, auctioning off a dapple horse. But what he saw was an empire. A chimerical, boundless expanse of land and sky. "Your brother chooses words well," he said, and then, quietly, to himself, "a grand scheme in the making."

When he turned back to his desk, the book of Byron's poetry caught his eye. It lay open, two lines marked. Suddenly he slammed the book shut, stood, went to the door and snatched his beaver hat from the stand. He opened the door and turned back to William, who was twisted around in his chair looking at him. The young man stood up. "To hell with the Masonic meeting," Houston said forcefully. "Let's go for a drink."

CHAPTER 12

December 1827

Christmas was three days off. The house smelled of spice and evergreen, all but Laetitia's room, forever permeated with the sour fume of medicines. With a small gesture of her hand, Laetitia said, "Eliza, come sit here on the bed."

"What is it, Mama? Are you cold? It's cold in here. Do you want more wood?"

"No. Come over here."

"What is it? You look as if—"

It was bleak, the cold, bitter room, the dying fire, the dying woman, the gray day through the window. "Eliza, I am going to have a baby."

She looked away so Laetitia could not see her eyes.

"Listen to me, child," her soft voice was pleading. "It is all right."

Eliza shook her head and stared down at the woolen blanket, red checks, the only color in the room. "No, it is not all right. You've been ill and the cough is worse. I cannot believe he—"

"He is my husband."

"And my father. And he's wrong."

"That is not for you to say." Laetitia coughed and turned her eyes to the window beside the bed.

"Then you say it, Mama. Say he is wrong."

"If loving someone is wrong. And if it is, then I'm to blame too. Because I love him."

Searching, she watched her mother's profile. She found no comfort there and went to the window. The trees were bare. "Then God help you, Mama," she said, and then, more gently, turning to her, "I just . . . I'm afraid."

"I know," Laetitia whispered. "I know."

He was in the library, reading beside the fire. When Eliza entered he looked up and closed the book, his finger still marking the page. It was a gesture she knew, meaning she was not to stay long.

She closed the door behind her. "Mama told me."

He knew her feelings. There was nothing to be said, and yet he must respond.

The children were with Dilsey and Martha Ann in the parlor, tapping at the piano. Random notes came through the closed door, an occasional banging on the low keys and Martha Ann's voice saying something, perhaps she was cautioning to be gentle with the piano, it was not a toy. The colonel looked to the fire, then back at Eliza. "She will be fine," he said. "She's had seven children and been fine."

"She almost died with Benjamin."

"But didn't." And then he added quietly, "Why do you despise me, Eliza?" She was silent, thinking he didn't really care why, didn't care that she did. Why did he ask? "Why?" he repeated, echoing his question, and hers.

She could not say it: because you never loved me. She answered, "She's too weak to carry it. Dr. Douglass said so with Benjamin, and she's weaker now. Dr. Shelby said it years ago, even before the consumption."

"And she has lived through two babies since then."

He was too calm and sure; he drove her mad and then came on with his rational voice, subtly suggesting she was losing her mind but that he would help her find it. She matched his voice, low and even. "I could give you all the reasons I despise you, but you wouldn't listen. Or change. You wouldn't even care."

"I'm asking."

"You're killing my mother."

"That is not true. And what transpires between my wife and me is not your concern."

"Then why am I the one who has to deal with it? And sit with her all day. She puts on a show for you and says she's better, but you know it isn't true. You just want to believe it for your own sake, so you can take your liberties." She paused and then said, "I would never marry someone like you. If I marry anyone, it will be a man like Will Tyree."

He looked at her. He was about to order her from the room, to say that the name she had just spoken was forbidden in this house. But he saw something in her eyes that stopped him, and instead, with a slight, slow shake of his head, he smiled and said, "That is not true. You will never marry someone like that. You're too selfish to settle for so little."

For a moment she wavered. A name hung in the air between them, unspoken: Sam Houston. The colonel was thinking: She will marry a man like Sam Houston. With all her silly games—refusing to receive him, avoiding him when he calls, pretending she will have nothing to do with him—despite it all, she will marry a man like Sam Houston.

A log in the fire fell, startling her. "Will Tyree is a better man than you will ever be," she said.

"I have never understood you, Eliza," he answered, "but I know this: if you were determined to marry Tyree, you would do it. Despite me or your mother or anyone else. You would abandon us all, your mother too, if you wanted him." He saw she was shaken. "And if you're looking for someone to blame for your mother's illness, then look to him." From the parlor came a few scattered piano notes and James's laughter, high and long.

"You know that isn't true. You know she was getting sick long before Will . . ." But the conviction in her voice was small.

"No. She was fine before then."

She stared at him. His saying it made it less possible—even made it a lie. "You don't believe that. You want to believe it but you can't. It's too ridiculous."

"I know what happened, Eliza. And when it happened. He wished it on all of us. You also." He leaned back, clasping his hands behind his head. "You are excused," he said without warning, his voice normal again, louder, decisive. He turned his gaze to the fire. One of the boys cried out from the parlor in a sudden temper, banging his hands on the keys, but he was hushed by Dilsey and his cry dropped to a whimper.

A mile upstream from the house, on the riverbank, was an oak tree she went to when she wanted solitude. The river was more narrow there than at the wide bend near the house, about sixty yards across, and the water swifter. Few craft ever came so far upstream from Nashville, only occasional flatboats and keelboats hauling goods down from Carthage. Low-hanging branches added to the privacy, especially in leafy seasons. The roots were as big around as the branches, and on the side near the water were completely exposed, the soil having washed away in heavy rains. There were patches of grass in warmer months, but in December only dirt and rock and a forsaken feeling, the oak like an upright carcass.

It was there that she went that day, to think. She missed Will. She was sitting with her back against the trunk, in a crevice between two massive roots stretching for the water, her knees pulled up against her for warmth, her arms wrapped around them. In her anger she had come out without coat or gloves; she unbraided her hair and let it fall over her for a little more warmth. The leaves had all fallen; gray water merged with gray trees in a dismal sky. She sat watching the far bank through the branches. When at last the cold became severe and she stood to go, she saw him, Governor Sam Houston, sitting with his back against a tree not ten feet from her, watching her. She stood looking at him. He stood up, removed his hat, broad-brimmed with fur nap half an inch long, and held it at his side with one hand, gripping his Indian blanket together at his chest with the other. She thought he would make some move but underestimated his patience; he was comfortable with silences. He just held her gaze and said nothing. At last she turned to go. She thought he would follow, or speak, but he did neither, so she turned back and said accusingly, "Why did you follow me here?"

He answered with a lift of his eyebrows, "How else was I to see you?"

"What is it you want?"

"I want to know why you returned my letter. And declined to see me."

"I'm sure you have other women who would welcome your calls."

"I'm sure I do. But that isn't an answer."

"You're very certain of yourself."

"You said you value honesty."

"And integrity. Does she wear the ribbon often?"

He managed to keep his stare. "I don't know. I haven't seen her since that night," he answered without apology. "You must be freezing." He went to her, loosened his hold where he gripped the blanket together and allowed it to fall open, revealing beaded buckskins. She took a step back, but he was tossing the blanket around her. It hung from her shoulders to the ground. "There," he said, holding it at her neck. "That should help."

"It isn't so easy," she said, pushing his hand away and securing the blanket with her own, "to make me forget."

"Forget?"

"The woman. As I've said before, I don't have any hold on you, but I did feel—"

He reached out and touched her mouth. "No," he said quietly, the word misting on cold air. "You do have a hold on me."

"Then, why?"

"I wasn't aware of any commitment, Eliza. You were with someone else that night also."

"But not in such a way."

"And was I supposed to know that? To know in precisely what way you were with him? You would not dance even one dance with me. You would not agree to receive me if I called. And was I to assume, by your insistence that you were waiting for someone else, and so could not dance with me, or even tolerate my company for more than a few minutes, that we were in some way committed to each other? I don't think so, Eliza. That's a little unfair of you."

"You're distorting it. Something passed between us that had nothing to do with dancing. Or calling on me. It was something . . . else."

"But not a commitment. Unless you made one I wasn't aware of."

It was true she had given him no way to know her feelings that night, how completely he enchanted her. She said, "I wish you would leave and not come back here."

"Do you wish it, really, Eliza?"

She did not want him to go. With sudden bewilderment she stepped forward into his arms, saying in almost a sob, but without tears, that it was not what she wished or wanted. The gesture was not completely spontaneous; she knew what its effect would be. And yet it fulfilled an honest need; he was, at that moment, the father she wanted.

"What is it, Eliza?"

"My mother is with child again," she answered, not looking up at him, her voice calmer now and muted in the blanket and buckskin jacket, smooth and worn. She felt it as his skin, naked against her face.

"And is that so terrible?"

She spoke against his chest, feeling him pull closer. "She's too ill to carry it. She has consumption and arthritis too. My father won't admit she's dying, and it's almost like he's killing her, and the stupid thing is she loves him."

"If she loves him, then why are you so distressed? Eliza, it might be he gives her the only joy she has."

"It isn't like that. It's like he's killing her."

He tightened his hold and moved a hand down over her hair, smoothing it. He felt she was a child; he wanted to protect her. And Eliza was playing into the role. "Perhaps she chooses to live a full life for a shorter time, instead of an empty one prolonged," he said.

She looked up at him, the stubble of his beard, the creases and heavy brow. She did not like for him to placate her as if she were a child, but with some perversity she had invited him to. Perhaps because it was the way into his arms. She wanted him to touch her in a seductive way. "My mother isn't choosing at all," she said. "She's just trying to please him." Fingering the fringe of his jacket, she pressed her face in closer. She could feel his voice when he spoke, not just the breath on her hair, but a vibration inside. Again he ran his hand over her hair, gently pulling it from beneath the blanket, lifting his other hand to her chin and tipping her head back, looking down at her.

"So she chooses to please him," he said. "That's a choice, Eliza. And one you have no right to interfere in."

It was his use of her father's words "You have no right" that caused her to pull away and toss the blanket at his feet. "I have no right? You have no right to tell me that, to come here with your worldly wisdom. I'm not a child. You have no concept at all of what my life is, trapped here, or what it would be if my mother died with this child and left me to raise her other children. I've heard how you ran off with the Cherokees and left your mother and your family. Well I can't do that."

The cold was bitter. His hard face revealed nothing. "I would charge you with egotism, Eliza, were I not so guilty of it myself."

"Perhaps you're right," she said flatly. "About both of us."

"And no remorse?"

"Any remorse I have is private."

"The same as any compassion, or tenderness? Is that all private? Not that I don't believe you feel it, just that I wonder why you fight it. Now your anger—that you share. I'm going to tell you something, and you can be angry if you want: you are a sensual woman, with a beauty and intelligence and a rare charm that fascinates me. But you also have some . . . stubbornness. I don't know what it is or why you take it out on me. Don't go. Listen to me. I didn't make your mother ill. Or your father hard." He paused and in a lower voice said, "What is the matter? Is it Tyree?"

"He has nothing to do with it."

"Eliza. I know something of what you feel about your mother. My brother died of consumption when I was your age."

She turned on him and said with composure, "I don't want your reprimands; I get enough of those at home. And I don't want your sympathy."

"You don't have my sympathy. I'm only saying I understand."

"You don't understand." And then she said it, "Please don't call on me again." She was breaking her own heart. She did not like his gallant, condescending manner, and yet she was drawn to him, drawn to the stress and chaos they shared and to the power he withheld from her, as if he were rationing himself, sprinkling himself down on her like a fine mist when the earth craved rain. In her fantasies of him there was none of this self-conscious expression of sympathy or pomposity, there was honesty and passion and nakedness.

He kept his eyes on her. "I don't take rejections lightly. Is it a sincere one?" She nodded. She almost yielded and asked him not to go but at that instant saw in his eyes not a reflection of the somber day, but what she wanted, an open, simple longing. He was in love with her. And that look and that realization gave her a strength she had never known. She could let her pride prevail and would not stop him from going, but somehow she would have him back. It was not a conscious thought, but an intuition, and one that allowed her to let him go. "I won't come again," he said, but she believed he would. "I wish your mother improved health." He leaned and retrieved the blanket, lifted himself, flung it around him and put on his hat. "My horse is in the woods toward Gallatin. I'll keep to the canebrake so you can take the road." Then he turned away and left her watching after him: a tall man in a dark, woolen blanket against gray trees. Passing the oak where she had first seen him, he glanced back and gestured toward it. "There's something there for you. If you don't want it, have Mr. Peyton return it to me."

She kept the gift, a leather-bound book of Lord Byron's poetry. The title page was pressed with the governor's seal and inscribed:

To Eliza Allen
From Sam Houston
December, 1827

On page seventy-three two lines were marked:

For as on thee my memory ponders
Perchance to me thine also wanders.

CHAPTER 13

April 1828

Polly and Eliza arrived at the Hermitage in midafternoon, on a warm day for April, with sun and scattered clouds. Hannah showed them to the parlor, a small room with papered walls, the woodwork painted a dull gray-green, almost celadon, a black pianoforte taking up a quarter of the room. Floral carpet with huge blossoms in golds and greens stretched from wall to wall. Rachel reclined on a Grecian couch that was upholstered in gold velvet, her dress a drab brown and almost threadbare, tied loosely with a bow beneath her bosom. The couch was the newest thing in furniture. Rachel had the best of furnishings and the worst of clothes, and the effect was what she wanted: a grandiose look of too much heavy furniture, too many patterns and oversize flowers on the carpet and walls and curtains, and herself, plain, like a sparrow hiding in the lush of a spring garden, content with concealment, and safe.

Polly was holding a baby, her twelfth child, in a cotton blanket. Hannah served tea and then propped Rachel's feet on the pillows. Rachel asked pardon—her ankles were blue and puffed with water and aching. She pursed her mouth, and the skin around her lips puckered white. Her voice was tired, her words distant and drifting on the warm spring air from the open window in back of Eliza. She held a worn Bible against her with one arm and with the other hand waved a fan languidly, creating almost no breeze at all, only the hairs which strayed from the frill of her lace bonnet moving in the air. Eliza was sorry for her but wanted to be rid of the room, too much like her mother's room, too tedious and timeless. Rachel talked of the past.

Polly leaned forward from the high-backed chair beside Eliza, baby Margaret suckling at her breast, shielded by the cotton blanket. Polly's eyes, set deep in a square face, had a look of worry incongruous with the child's careless feeding. She had known Rachel since childhood. "Are you all right?" she asked.

One swollen hand moving the fan, the other curled around her Bible, Rachel said, "You seen what they write about me. The General can't hardly take it."

"And you?"

Rachel tapped two fingers on the Bible she held against her breast. "I'm on the Rock of Ages. But the General—" she broke off without finishing, her eyes drifting to the china tea service and the tea caddy and to the clock on the mantel, but she was not reading the time. Time just passed for her these days, and that was all it held for her, a sense of going by. Each day she prayed for her husband's success in the campaign, though his gaining of all he had worked to win would mean the losing of all she had ever wanted: privacy, and family close by.

From a cedar tree near the window a cardinal trilled, three long notes and a series of shorter ones. A breeze moved in. Baby Margaret stopped her suckling and whimpered. Polly fastened the buttons of her bodice and lifted the baby to her shoulder, and Eliza remembered the day in the meetinghouse when she had worn Polly's dress and unbuttoned the bodice to feel her breasts. And Sam Houston had come. With a breath Rachel said, "Did you see it, Polly, the handbill with coffins on it—stories of American boys shot dead at his orders—"

"Rachel, it's nothing but lies. Those were not innocent American boys; they were insubordinate soldiers."

Rachel looked to Eliza with watery eyes and a timid smile. "I should talk of brighter things. Tell me now, how old are you now?"

"Eighteen," Eliza answered, uncomfortable with the maudlin talk. The room darkened as a cloud passed over.

"Eighteen. A woman. Have you ever been in love?"

"Maybe, once. Not now."

"Ah," Rachel said, "I wish it for you."

Outside there was the sound of shod hooves on the gravel, another in the Jacksons' stream of visitors. Hannah stepped in with Rachel's pipe, presented it and left the room as Rachel took a long pull and exhaled slowly. "I tried hard to give it up, you know," she said, lifting the pipe toward Polly, "for the public eye. But the General, he won't let me." She smiled then. "He says it's my only vice and that he can't hardly bear me without a vice." Beyond the window, clouds ran shadows across the lawn among scattered oaks and cedars.

Then the knocker sounded on the front door, followed by commotion in the hall, a man's voice and Hannah's in response, spirited and warm. Rachel looked toward the parlor door, listening with her head cocked to one side, then Hannah looked in. "Governor's here," she said, and Sam Houston appeared in the doorway behind her. Hannah moved away and he stepped in, holding a newspaper. Eliza stared at him, knowing she should lower her eyes, feeling Rachel glance at her and yet not looking down.

This day he was carrying the governorship with him. He was dusty from the ride and looked older. His shirt was open at the throat; the folksy smile he had had at the dance at Tyree Springs was gone, and his demeanor was intense. But around his neck were the Indian beads, a token defiance of it all. They pleased Eliza. He took in the room with a glance, which rested on her for only a second and then passed on to Rachel. "Hello, Aunt Rachel," he said, his face easing, and he went to her, setting the newspaper aside and kneeling beside her couch. She gave him her free hand, the pipe idle in the other, her face smiling like a child's but showing yellowed teeth. Still holding her hand, he turned and greeted Polly, then said to Eliza, in a tone without inflection, "Good day, Miss Allen." He patted Rachel's hand. Baby Margaret, hearing the new voice, stirred, and he went to look at her. Rachel watched him with a bright expression, sparrow's eyes. "Our governor loves children," she said.

"A mutual love," Polly answered. "I can't keep mine off him when he comes to visit Dry." She looked up at him. "Her name is Margaret."

"May I hold her?"

Polly lifted the bundle away from her, and Sam leaned and took it up. Margaret made a small noise, a tiny coo.

"So you and Eliza have met before?" Rachel asked.

"Yes," he answered, still looking at the child. "Eliza and I have met several times."

Eliza wanted him to look at her, but he looked only at the child, cradling her in his arms and cooing to her, a reverent, gentle noise. She envied the child, so comfortable in his arms.

He spoke with Polly and Rachel and asked about Dry Saunders. Occasionally he gave Eliza a glance. Margaret stretched her small fist up from the blanket, and he put out a finger and let her grab hold of it. "Margaret," he said softly, "I am going to give you to Eliza." He said her name with some care and then came and bent down over her, saying, "It seems you will have to pry my finger loose, Eliza." She did not look at him, but at his hand and the small fist clinging to it. She worked the tiny fingers loose, and he placed Margaret in her arms. As he straightened, he met Eliza's eyes, then turned away and put his attention on Rachel, asking where the General could be found.

"In the study, with Judge Overton," Rachel answered. "Sam, say a calming word to him please. He's in a awful temper."

"I will. For you." The governor took up the newspaper again, excused himself, his glance just barely brushing over Eliza, and was gone.

"Now there is a man I love," Rachel said, still looking toward the door. "He's got what makes a man whole—courage, strength, intelligence. And something else, too, that makes a man great. Compassion. He's a passionate, compassionate man."

Eliza wanted to follow. She did not want to lose him. Stroking Margaret's hair, she held out her finger to the child.

"Do you know what I think?" Polly said after a while. "I think that you and I, Rachel, have had greater loves than most women ever find. Myself with Samuel, and my sons, and now Dry, and you with the General, and all the young men who love you so much—my sons included. And Sam Houston. How do you think we found such love?"

"I think, could be, it found us," Rachel answered, and then added, to Eliza, "You said you've been in love, once?"

There was a silence—uncertainty and fallen hopes and the cardinal singing.

Polly answered for her. "Perhaps he failed to completely win her heart."

Rachel looked only at Eliza. She recognized desire when she saw it. She understood little of the world her husband dominated so forcefully; she was uneducated, confused by power, ignorant of military stratagems and political policies, afraid to face people or places unfamiliar to her. But Rachel Jackson knew a great deal about love. "Could be her heart was already won," she said, "by somebody else."

CHAPTER

14

The General was raging. Houston knew it even before he heard him, because no one was in the hall. An entire section of the Hermitage could go completely still when Andrew Jackson was in a rage, and lately he had been in one almost constantly. His old wounds and worsening ailments kept him from sleep; at times he would go three nights without closing his eyes. The pain was worse at night, and his mind was always active when the pain was bad. He wrote letters by candlelight at all hours of darkness, and his eyesight was diminishing. Houston suspected that the sugar of lead he drank and bathed in and dropped into his eyes and the massive doses of calomel he consumed were poisoning rather than healing him. But the old General would not hear of it. "Sam Houston," he told his doctor, "would have savages dancing around my bed with their gruesome chanting if I gave him half a chance."

He did not suffer silently. His rancid temper intensified with the pain. He became irascible, his tirades further debilitating him. He sustained a persistent cough, which he believed was consumption, severe constrictions in his chest, rheumatism, pulmonary hemorrhaging, bouts of fever, abscessed old wounds that he lanced himself, headaches and regular attacks of dysentery.

And—what Jackson considered the curse above all others—he had finally had his teeth pulled and wooden dentures made. Now his gums were constantly irritated, so public speaking was impossible. Not that he had ever done much public speaking—he wasn't good at it and knew it—but he was annoyed at being restricted from anything, whether inclined to it or not. John Overton had persuaded him to get the dentures, though he himself, also toothless, had none. "But I am not the voice of the nation," Overton had said.

The door to the library was cracked open, and Houston could hear the General's strident voice blasting forth, "George Washington also shot deserters!" Houston pictured him in the room, his white hair standing at attention, his lean, slope-shouldered body in motion, crossing the frayed Turkey carpet again and again, tails of an oversized coat flapping against his long thighs, fists clenched together behind him, occasionally separating for his good arm to rise and pound the air. The governor gathered strength to face the blast. Once or twice he heard Judge Overton's voice, placid and distant, but the words, rolling from his toothless mouth, were impossible to understand. "And was George Washington persecuted for it?" Jackson demanded. "No, by God! Because America had not yet seen the likes of Henry Clay! I tell you I would shoot every one of those scoundrels again. George Washington would do it too. Our Secretary of State condemns me for assassinating traitors while in the same breath he assassinates the character of an innocent female! My God, but that man is a swine! He calls me a gambler, as if he's never fingered a dice! He calls me a cockfighter, like he's never done it! He calls me a horse racer, an immoral, irreligious Sabbath breaker!"

There was no breeze in the hall, and Houston's sweat started to run. He was not in a mood to confront the old warrior, for his own

mind was feeling mellow at the moment, turning on Eliza, her delicate hands tenderly working the child's fingers from his own. Her
eyes, her skin, the pale, loose hairs about her face, the subtle widow's
peak. He had a mind to take a walk in Rachel's garden and think
about those eyes—and especially those hands, what else they might
do tenderly. They were sensual, stimulating hands. He was also
tempted to return to the parlor on some pretense or another but
resisted. It was not the thing to do. And there was the General, and
duty to be faced. He knocked and stepped into the room. Jackson
was just as he had suspected, his face contorted with pain and fury
and his white hair at war, his left arm stiff at his side. The other arm
flashed about, frenzied, as if in compensation. Houston guessed the
old Benton ball was festering again.

Judge John Overton, sixty-two, one year older than the General,
sat in a chair by the window to the front lawn, catching the small
cross breeze from the window onto Rachel's garden. His features
were sharp but wore an amiable expression, a hooked nose and dag-
ger of a chin, the usual red bandanna handkerchief draped jauntily
over his bald head, his small eyes bright, face hairless, toothless,
homely, wise. Tolerant and patient without condescension. His eb-
ony walking cane with an ivory handle was propped against the sill
beside him. He sat hunched and shriveled, but somehow not old,
almost timeless. He smiled at Sam, his former law partner, if you
could call taking in a green lawyer in his twenties and sharing your
office with him a partnership. And the judge had called it a partnership—for Sam's sake. He adored the young man, saw himself in him,
actually, as did the General and a number of other prominent men—
Doc Shelby, former Governor McMinn, Isaac Galladay of Lebanon
in east Tennessee. They all identified with different of Sam Houston's traits; he was something of a mixed bag. But a captivating man,
Overton had said to Jackson the night before—with perception and
courage. A good man, all around. But for the drinking . . . and of
course the women.

Overton smiled. He enjoyed a man's weaknesses as much as his
strengths; that was why he loved Andrew so—the volatile temper,

the humanness. He suspected these were traits the populace also liked: Jackson's personal, emotional appeal. Overton lacked the endearing fallibility, and knew it. His own gifts were cerebral. Well, they all had their gifts—and made use of them. And in Overton's eyes, that was all God required.

Houston returned the smile and gave a cursory bow. Judge Overton was a man he respected above all others, save Jackson. He had sometimes pondered what Andrew Jackson would have been had he never met John Overton. He surmised this: Overton's plan for Jackson to be chief magistrate of the United States began long before the General had any such ambitions for himself.

It was Overton who had introduced Andrew Jackson to the ideals of Jeffersonian democracy, and to Rachel Donelson Robards, who was at the time married but separated from her husband. As young men, two of seven licensed lawyers in Tennessee, Overton and Jackson shared a cabin and rode the circuits together. They played the Indian treaties, sometimes taking payment in land guaranteed to the Indians, knowing the treaty would be broken eventually and title cleared. Sometimes they received cash payment and invested it in land, staying one jump ahead of the land-grabbers, and prospering. Together they founded Memphis. They grew in wealth and prestige, together. And Andrew married Rachel.

Now here was General Jackson, raving, and Judge Overton, munching on his gums. Quite a sight, Houston thought, quite a pair. Yet despite the General's ranting and that ridiculous bandanna on the judge's bald head, these men were still the power of Tennessee.

"Sam! Come in!" Jackson thundered, catching sight of him and slackening pace. "Have you heard it: Clay is denying any association with the spy Mr. Day! That dog lies—a shabby English bill collector doesn't go roaming about the country looking for evidence to ruin a virtuous woman just because he finds the task amusing! Day was paid, I tell you. Most likely with government monies. Paid to destroy my wife!"

"I have heard it, sir," Houston said, attempting graveness but vexed that Jackson was so riled about Clay's denial—as if the Secretary of State would admit to setting spies on a woman. "I've brought you a newspaper," he said, holding it out. Jackson did not reach for it, so Houston laid it on top of the correspondence that littered the General's writing desk. He moved a chair from the center of the room to the window, set it down beside Overton, shook hands and seated himself.

"Full of lies and slanders, I suppose," Jackson remarked in a subdued tone, stopping near the desk and eyeing the paper.

"Not this one," Houston answered. "It's Duff Green's."

At that Jackson reached with his agile hand for the smudged spectacles on the desk, the other arm still rigid, as if strapped to his side. He rubbed them on his coat, then awkwardly put them on, took up the paper and began to scan it, muttering, "Adams calls me incompetent, illiterate, immoral—immoral, mind you—while he is using federal funds to buy foreign articles, to buy playing cards, federal funds from some poor widow in Kentucky to furnish the East Room of the White House with a billiard table."

"Andrew," Overton said, "President Adams has proven he paid for the billiard table out of his own pocket."

Jackson ignored the interruption. "We have rats marauding on our treasury," he said and went on talking to himself.

The judge turned to Houston and whispered, "It's Benton's ball."

Houston understood. He knew how a festering wound could foul a man's mood; just last week the musket ball hole in his own shoulder had abscessed. And his thigh was usually irritated or swollen with pus. "I've got two jokes for you, General," he said.

Jackson loved jokes. He usually laughed the longest and the loudest. But today his umbrage was high, and Houston doubted he would laugh at all. It was the General's way; if he did not like it, he did not laugh. But it was worth a try. "Let's hear," Jackson said, setting the paper down and going to the black horsehair couch that faced the empty fireplace. He folded his arm against his body as he sat down onto the couch, stretching out so only his slippered feet, hanging over the scrolled arm, were visible. Slippers and his pipe were the only luxuries he allowed himself.

"All right," Houston said, settling into the wing chair and lifting his arms out slightly for the sweat to dry. It was too hot for spring. Summer would be unbearable. "Why is Adams on ticklish grounds?"

"Because he's a goddamned scoundrel and God himself will condemn him to hell," Jackson answered, it being against his nature to say he did not know.

"That's not it," Houston said. "It's because he stands on slippery Clay."

Overton grinned, brushing a fly from his forehead. The General flapped his feet, bellowing, "That's ingenious! Why is the President on ticklish grounds? Because he stands on slippery Clay!" He lifted his head up over the back of the couch, his dentures showing white in his sallow face, like a snarling dog, and cackled, repeating, "Because he stands on slippery Clay. That's damn near sagacious!" Then his merriment stopped suddenly. "Tell me the other one."

"Two men were walking down a Washington street," Houston said. " 'Hurrah for Jackson,' said one man. 'You mean hurrah for the devil,' said the Federalist. 'Very well,' the Democrat answered, 'you stick to your candidate, and I'll stick to mine.' "

Jackson, still peering over the back of the couch, looked puzzled and then laughed so forcefully that his dentures fell out over the back of the couch. Overton smiled benignly, smacking his gums. When the General's mirth waned, silence followed.

"And by God Adams is the devil!" Jackson said, rising with new energy, retrieving his dentures and shoving them in and setting his step to the worn carpet. "Permitting his Secretary of State to slander a woman as pure as Rachel . . . permitting him to slander a woman at all! I should fight on their terms—an eye for an eye—let my papers print how Adams pimped for the czar of Russia when he was minister there, and print that Mrs. Adams is illegitimate, and that the two of them had premarital relations. I should allow it! Give Duff his hand. But only the base and cowardly war against women and resort to lies. I won't do it. Yet I must bear their base calumnies! They dramatize my fights—a barroom brawler, they call me. As if I am to blame for everything! Even that goddamn murdered Freemason in the Niagara River! Just because I'm a Mason and the Masons drowned him! The best men I know are members of the order. Everybody worth his salt's a Mason. Yet I get the full blame for the bloody deeds in New York. One ex-member threatens to publish a book with the secrets of the first three degrees of Freemasonry and is drowned for it—and deserves to be—and somehow I get the blame! Because I'm a Mason! And I never met the man—never even been to New York! It's frightening as hell. Repeatedly they slander me; they report his body washing ashore on the banks of the Niagara, not once, but six different times! If you ask me, they're tossing it back in so it can wash ashore again and be in the Federalist papers again that the Masons committed murder and that Andrew Jackson is a Mason!"

"Sir," Houston injected, "you have not heard the good news?"

Jackson stopped in midstep. "They've finally buried that rotted corpse?"

"No sir. It's been discovered Clay's a Freemason of rank. I thought you would have heard."

"He can't be."

"He is. Proven."

"Where did you learn it?"

"It's in Duff's paper there. It's been around town."

"Good God." Jackson stood staring at Houston in disbelief. Then a slow pleasure crept over his face. "Is Duff lying?"

"No. The evidence is firm. Clay's registered. Not active, but still a member."

"Duff lied about Adams. Saying he was a Mason."

"This time it's no lie."

Jackson moved his gaze to Overton, then clapped his hands together, a sudden grimace at the pain in his stiff arm. "I never thought," he said, shaking his head and grinning, "that I'd ever be pleased to call Henry Clay my brother. But this, this is good news. I thought he was being unusually mum about the whole affair. The damned old sinner. A Mason himself. Well, I'll be goddamned over that. He is vile, to let me take that heat and the blame for some hotheads in New York, while he sits at his desk gloating and setting spies on Rachel."

Again he paced, somewhat subdued, more the old step of the General—in charge, a skirmish won, a victory in sight, the strategy needing to be pondered. Houston glanced at Overton, who asked him to get the paper so he could read the proof about Clay's Freemasonry.

Retrieving the paper from Jackson's desk, Houston brought it to Overton, who settled in to read while the General beat his path and pronounced on the evils of Secretary Clay. Houston's thoughts returned to Eliza in the parlor. He could not get her out of his mind. She was not beautiful, exactly. But she moved him. Her voice was erotic—unconsciously so—like her hands. She had taken his breath and elicited an emotion he had seldom known before, perhaps what the Cherokees called *uhi'sodi*, "a longing or loneliness for another." Not just for any other, but for her.

If he moved his chair closer to the window he might see her when she left through the front door, if she had not gone already. He pushed his chair back, as if to get more air, and cut his eyes toward the path she would leave by. Flies droned in the heat. He remembered a summer day a decade ago when an old Indian woman had taught him a formula for winning a maiden's heart. The words would cast a spell and make her fall in love. He could recall only pieces and tried to remember it all. *Ku! Sge!* You are most beautiful. Let her put her soul in the very center of my soul, never to turn away. Grant that in the midst of men, she shall never think of them. I take your soul —*Sge*—

"That man is from hell!" the General yelled, a pitch higher than his rantings, and Houston and Overton looked up to see Old Hickory staring down on them, his eyes burning fury. "The whole object of the coalition has become to savage me. Cartloads of coffin handbills, forgeries and pamphlets of the most base calumnies are circulated by the franking privilege of Congress. Even my mother, nearly fifty years in the tomb, who from her cradle to her grave had not a speck upon her character, has been dragged forth by Clay and held to public scorn as a prostitute who intermarried with a Negro! A whore—my mother! My eldest brother sold as a slave in Carolina! Such filthy lies! God send them all to hell!" His face contorted; he turned, pressing his hand to his forehead. "And Rachel . . . Rachel—" A fit of coughing gripped him. He went to the side window, leaned out and spit mucus and blood. "Goddamn lungs," he sputtered, thumping his chest through the oversize suit coat.

When he returned to his track and was going strong again, Overton leaned toward Sam Houston, holding the paper out and pointing to a passage. Houston leaned forward and read the lines: "General Jackson does not at any time play cards; neither does General Jackson swear." He tried to stifle a smile, failed, then was aware of silence and looked up to see Old Hickory watching him. He was an old man, ill. It occurred to Houston with sudden apprehension that the General might die before the election. For the first time, he wondered if Jackson was in fact capable, both physically and emotionally, of being President. All of the ranting, the pacing—the man was ravaged by illness. Still strong, but very ill. Percipient, shrewd, determined, but querulous, excitable. And certainly very ill. And if anything should happen to Rachel—

"Can't you rid yourself of those bloody savage beads around your neck?" It was the voice of the General, the voice of a man who had once called for the impeachment of George Washington for regal behavior and catering to the British. And it was hearty.

"I can," Houston answered. "But I'm not inclined to do it."

Jackson frowned. Houston knew what the old gentleman was thinking: there was a day when Sam Houston would have removed the beads. It seemed a long time ago.

Then without speaking, the General turned ponderously and went to his desk, sat, and buried his face in the bent elbow of his good arm. When he spoke his voice was calm, little more than a muted moan. "I am old and ill, and the vultures are closing in. I pray only that I live to see my enemies prostrate." A breath of air came in the window. Old Hickory lifted his head and said with slow cadence, "God help the nation, men. The Administration has run mad. The patronage of the government for the last three years has been wielded to corrupt everything that comes within its influence. Our national character has been stained with lies and scandal. It rests with the people to work it out." He faltered, his breath coming with difficulty. "The present is a contest between the virtue of the people and the influence of patronage. Should patronage prevail over virtue, should the coalition prevail over us, gentlemen, then the people may prepare themselves to become hewers of wood and drawers of water for the tyrants." Again he stopped, then said with a note of deep sadness, "I am afraid I, too, have run mad; forgive me. But I am faced with a terrible choice. For the country, my country, and its people, I must sit here, and read lies about my wife, and stay quiet, and say nothing. My hands are bound. I cannot defend her. All these letters"—he passed his hand, weathered skin and brown nails, over the correspondence that covered his desk—"from all my friends, Lewis, Coffee, Grundy, Eaton, from you, John—from all my friends, they all say one thing: Let nothing draw you out. Your course should be retirement and silence." He took up a page at random and squinted down at it, not bothering with his spectacles, reading aloud, his voice rasping and spent, " 'Be cautious, be still, be quiet. . . . Weigh and bale your cotton and sell it, and if you see anything about yourself or dear Mrs. Jackson in the papers, just throw the paper in the fire and go on to weigh the cotton.' " Dropping the page from his hand, he lifted tired eyes. "Am I to sacrifice my wife's welfare for the good of the nation? I ask you, gentlemen, you, who love this country as I do; you Sam Houston, who have spilled your blood for it as I have; both of you, who love Rachel Jackson, and love these free United States of America—I ask you, what am I to do? Is there no way I can have them both, save them both?"

Houston felt the April warmth, heard the birds calling and the General's words lingering in the air. Slowly, gradually, like the shadows stretching out over the Hermitage lawn, he came to understand.

The voice he had heard was not that of an old man suffering from old wounds; it was the voice of a man in the agony of a new wound, a man pierced through. A man choosing between two loves: his country and his wife. The three men looked at each other in silence, each knowing what the choice would be, then each knowing it had just been made, and grieving for it.

After a long while the governor turned and looked out the window onto the Hermitage lawn. Oaks were vivid green in late afternoon sun.

Judge Overton leaned back in his chair and closed his eyes.

The General, his mind still turning on Rachel and loyalties and love, at last spoke into the still room. "Sam," he said, with an odd serenity, "when are you going to find yourself a wife?"

Houston continued to gaze from the window; it seemed he had not heard. He felt as if an era of his life was going, sliding off to somewhere; he did not know where.

CHAPTER

15

She would not let him go. His gesture, in giving her the child, held provocative insinuations. Despite her aversion to the idea of having children of her own, and so ensnaring herself in a life of domestic tedium, his tenderness had moved her. And his ease intrigued her. He was not, when he placed the baby in her arms, trying to win her with his strength or fashion. He was appealing to her better self, and her better self responded. And her other self, the one that feared manipulation to the point of craving control, the uncomfortable child, was also impassioned by the momentary situation. Previously, she had dismissed Sam Houston's affections; now she would retrieve them. She felt it was in her power to do so, and she desired it. From the wellspring of all her complicated motivations one abiding current was beginning to flow, clear and without hindrance: she wanted him. That he had now approached her not as a man to a child or a chivalric suitor to a coveted maiden, but with an honest gesture, winsome in its simplicity but mysterious with hidden meaning, touched her. That he had done it as the governor of Tennessee, in the home of Andrew Jackson, won her. She would not cater to power, as she thought her father did; she would capture it. The endeavor was not calculated or cerebral, but emotional; simply, she was drawn to this man, the governor, with a newspaper curled in his hand and his string of Indian beads.

When he left through the front door, Eliza was waiting on the veranda. Polly and Rachel were still in the parlor, Jackson had retired upstairs and John Overton was napping in the study. "I'd like to talk with you," she said.

He offered his arm, and they walked past the General's study at the end of the house, through the picket gate into Rachel's garden. The sun was hanging low over the Hermitage, shadowing the gate and most of the garden but catching the tips of hemlock and shagbark hickory at the east end. Sam was the first to speak. "So," he said, giving her a side glance, "we meet on neutral ground." It was an apology for both of them.

"Enough said," she answered.

They began walking the dirt path because it seemed the thing to do, a logical course laid out before them in the predictable, geometric design of a square cut into quarters, without puzzling junctures. As if by agreement, they moved toward the center beds, where rosemary and lavender were in bloom. He said, "Everything is budding but the tuberose," and added after a pause, "How is your mother?"

"The baby's due end of next month. She's fine."

"And how is Tyree?"

She answered directly, "I don't know. I don't see him anymore."

"I'm glad."

She glanced up to see his expression, but could not read it. He gestured toward the white blossoms of a mandrake flower, and said,

"The Cherokees call this *'u'niskwetu'gi'*, which means, 'it wears a hat.' You see, it looks like that, doesn't it."

She looked at him instead of at the flower. "I can't tell when you're baiting me and when you're serious," she said.

"Baiting? Let's say, I'm serious, very serious, when I'm baiting you." Again he took her arm. His sweaty smell mixed with the magnolia, and she did not find it offensive. "The Cherokees," he said, "are my family. I was adopted by Chief Oo-loo-te-ka when I was fifteen. A few years later I joined the army and helped transport his people—my Indian family—to Arkansas. To see they weren't abused en route. It's a burden, you know," he said casually, looking at the flowers as he walked. "I blame myself. We put them on Osage land, and the Osage are killing them. And whites are also settling that area. There isn't a solution, really." He was winning her. He felt her compliance as unequivocally as if she had looked up into his eyes and said yes, she would be his lover. He imagined himself penetrating her fragile, virgin body, there under the weeping willows with their caressing branches.

"Unless they went farther west," she said, aware of how small she was next to him. This gave her a feeling of importance because he would lean closer or dip his head when she spoke, showing his interest. He was listening. "Surely there's land enough on the continent for everyone. Like in Texas."

Her comment seemed innocent enough but made him wary. There was too much speculation about the governor's interest in Texas. Doc Shelby had confronted him with it just yesterday, saying there were rumors that Houston intended to raise an army somehow, defeat the Napoleon of the West, and take the whole territory of Texas and Coahuila combined. Houston had pretended to scoff at the idea, and Doc had said, "Don't insult my intelligence, Sam. You've got designs, I know. Just be careful, because rumor is rampant."

"If I ever venture farther west than the Red River," Houston told him, as if an afterthought, "it won't be in search of empire, but of fortune. There's money to be made there, in land. I could be worth two millions in two years." It was a lie, and Doc had known. Sam liked money, but it was not his inspiration. Conquest was; he had a passion for conquest. But all Shelby said was, "The eternal optimist. The eternal egotist," and let the topic close.

And now Eliza, giving Sam an enticing look that had little to do with what she was saying, had brought forth Texas like a vixen innocently drags its mangled prey from the undergrowth. Her next offering truly startled him. "I've heard it said that if the General were President he would even bribe for Texas."

"It would take an act of God to get Texas from Mexico," he answered. "And speaking of land, I hear your father made a fine new purchase last week."

"Yes, he did," she said and then returned to the subject of Texas—that wild land where forces of diverse races and cultures and mysterious religions mingled in an attempt to claim the earth. It interested her. "But I hear that the Mexican government is unstable. Their people can only withstand so much poverty. And Anglo settlers are fed up. I hear you plan to go there someday. I even heard you're planning some sort of an enterprise." The idea, though she did not really believe it, tantalized her; perhaps she would go with him.

"I would like to visit Texas," he said. "But doubt I ever will." He had become so accustomed to lying about his ambitions that he did so now instinctively. Yet even had he given thought to it, still he would not have confided in this woman. He was courting her, not recruiting her. It would be stimulating to tell her his dreams and witness her response to their intricacy and gravity, but the risk was too great. Every person to whom he spoke of Texas was a potential hazard to his plans; his only confidences were allotted like playing cards to men who could be essential to the budding scheme. No one but he himself could know where the cards were dealt. Even Jackson, as omnipotent as he was in the thrust toward Texas, did not ask to know Houston's specific thoughts or with whom he was planting his cards. Jackson inspired the movement and the ideas in rambling conversations; Houston discerned the conversations as he pleased and kept his own counsel.

Eliza was not someone he needed in his grand scheme. And he was not inclined to trust a woman anyway.

A hummingbird flew backward from the honeysuckle, remained suspended in the timid breeze as if taking a final, lingering look at his beloved nourishment, then turned and darted out over the fields of sprouting oats and hemp toward the trees lining the river to the west. Sam leaned and picked a mint leaf and chewed it for a moment as they walked on, pausing to admire the flowers. Then he took Eliza's hand and faced her, looking steadily into her eyes. "I know the rumors you've heard," he said, "about my designs on Texas. I haven't any idea how they were started. Likely by my opponents. You see, my constituents would not want their governor plotting revolutions in a foreign country. It's a ludicrous idea, actually. You may tell anyone who asks, that Sam Houston believes the West will someday fall to Anglo rule, but it won't be through his efforts." He smiled down at her and dipped his head to one side. "May I kiss you?"

She was facing him straight on, and something in the evening, the breeze blowing in, the garden smells of soil and lilac and the lowing of cattle in the pasture near the water, infected her with a mellow feeling, almost a sensation of surrender. All his past show of pretentious urbanity seemed no longer annoying or deceitful, but endearing, for it revealed how much he wanted to impress her. She was, in this moment, vulnerable and young, and unthreatened by being so, or by this man looking down at her. The feeling brought to mind two lines from Lord Byron; they were written as comic, and they were comic, but also gently perceptive and lovely. She met Sam Houston's eyes, then looked away and repeated the lines, looking down at the path, a patch of primroses, and then back up, his eyes, the beads at his neck, the hint of stubble on his face and the clouds drifting in a rosy sky,

"A little still she strove, and much repented,
And whispering 'I will ne'er consent'—consented."

CHAPTER
16

She had always dreaded the weaning of foals in October; the separation seemed an act of violence. Brood mares gave birth in March and at nine months would have kicked the fillies and colts away from their udders, but the colonel weaned them at eight months to prevent the foals from being damaged in this natural weaning process. On a bright day when the leaves were falling, the hands would turn the mares and their young into a new pasture. Enamored with the new place and the feel of autumn, the fillies and colts would romp away from their mothers, nosing the smells and testing fence lines. Each day a different mare was taken from the field to a stable in the far paddock where her young one could not hear her frantic calling. And the foal would look up and find her gone.

Since childhood Eliza used to stay up late at night with the squealing foals, a new one each night. Some years there were as many as ten. She would go out after supper, while it was still light, and sit on the boards of the stall and talk to the foal, gradually moving into the stall and reaching out, and after a while it would calm some. Late at night she would go to bed, and in the morning it would be over.

Late in the month she was keeping wake with a blue roan filly. Sam was coming this evening to dine with the family; she would have to leave soon to dress. The sun was lowering, and cool air drifted in the stable door; the night would be cold. The foal was terrified and slow to calm and paced from corner to corner. Pulling her woolen shawl close around herself, Eliza leaned toward her from the top slat of the stall. "Airy," she said softly. "Be still now. I won't hurt you." The filly whinnied and flailed her legs at the slats, and Eliza went on speaking to her.

Sam Houston arrived early, and found her there. He lifted her down. "Let's walk outside," he said and asked if she was cold.

"No, but I think a front's coming in. A rainy front—I can smell it."

They walked through the pasture of sheep and the canebrake down to the bank of the Cumberland and upstream to Eliza's oak. His mood was strange and solemn. At last she asked, "Is something wrong?"

He spread his blanket under the tree and motioned for her to sit. Then he seated himself, cross-legged, facing her. The leaves of low-hanging branches surrounded them like a scarlet curtain; a few drifted down onto the blanket, which was also the colors of autumn. The sun had almost set. Eliza looked over her shoulder at the bloody glow on the cloudless horizon beyond the canebrake and a rise and the cornfields. A row of trees were silhouetted black against the sun. When she looked again at Sam, the eastern sky behind him seemed vapid with its line of pink clouds, only a mild reflection of the sanguine western sky. "Eliza," he said, "what is it you want from life?"

She sat as he did, her skirt spread over her knees, and wondered at his intensity. His eyes were green this evening, with no hint of blue. There were deep grooves on his brow. He was dressed plainly, no cravat, no beads. "I don't know," she said. "I've been told I want too much." A leaf had fallen on the blanket between them; she picked it up and traced its brown veins with her finger, and with delicate movements began tearing it into tiny bits and feeding them to the breeze. It was, in its way, a brutal gesture, but she did not perceive it as such; she seemed oddly removed from the silken manipulation of her hands.

A sparrow chirped repeatedly from the branches. Sam did not look at Eliza but stared off westward, past her. "Do you want to be with me?" he asked.

"Yes."

"And what if I turn out to be someone different from who you think. Does that frighten you?"

"Tell me what you mean."

"Just that we haven't spent much time together. There are things we don't know."

His bearing frustrated her; she wished he would tell her his thoughts. Occasionally he was this way, speaking only in subtleties, even his inflections imperceptible. "When you talk like this, I feel I don't know you at all," she answered with an edge in her voice.

He looked at her. "You're cold," he said, and leaned and pulled her to him. She moved in, nestling her back against his chest. He sniffed her hair and said in a lighter tone, "You smell like the stable."

She saw now what he saw—the last of the sun, the reds through red leaves, radiant, beautiful—and felt his warmth and his hold on her. "That sunset enchants me," he said, "disappearing off there in the west. It gives me a mind to follow." He paused. "These days in particular I'm feeling a need to travel."

"Like Byron's Childe Harold," she said, wanting to maintain this lighter mood.

He pulled her closer, and his voice sank to a whisper. "No. Not in such a way, a drunken exile with a broken heart. I would go under very different circumstances."

She twisted around to look at him. Their faces were close together. She felt he was telling her something of importance, but not in a way that she could understand. It was as if he was pointing at something, some danger, warning her of it but unwilling to tell her what it was. He seemed to be fulfilling some obligation but not actually protecting her. "What circumstances?" she asked.

Moving his face closer he kissed her cheek, then her mouth. She allowed it but detached her emotions from it, knowing there was something she must find out and that she would not get it by resisting him. "Tell me what you're talking about," she said when he stopped kissing her, willing her body not to respond to him, her tone suggesting neither demand nor entreaty, but a simple request.

He tightened his hold and whispered, his hand caressing hers and then lifting to gesture toward the western light, "There's a legend, Eliza, about seven Cherokees who went to find the place where the sun lives, where the sky reaches down to the ground. They traveled for years before they found it. The sky was an arch of rock that hung over the earth; it would swing open to let the sun in, and then swing shut again." Taking one arm from around her, he moved it in a slow fornix before her face, the fingers spread wide in imitation of the sun's movement. "The Indians waited, and the sun came out again to begin its travel along the vaulted rock, but it was so bright they could not look at it and so hot they could not get close to it." He paused. The sparrow had ceased chirping. "So they hid their faces from it. After the sun had moved along, they took their hands from their faces and saw the opening it had come through. One of the seven tried to climb through it, but just then the rock swung shut and crushed him." He wrapped both arms around her. The sun's glow was fading to a pale wash. "The others turned and started back again," he said. "But they had traveled so far they were old men when they reached home."

She was very still. She would have to commune on his terms, in his manner. "And so they spent their whole lives searching for the sun, and where he lives, and nothing came of it?"

"The Cherokees would tell you that just finding it was something. That some people look and never find it, and just finding it is something." An oak leaf circled down. Sam became very still, hardly breathing. "But I think," he said, "they were searching for the wrong thing. What does it matter where the sun lives, if you can find the sun? They should not have shielded their faces from it. They should have stood the heat and the light, and taken possession of the sun." He took his arms from around her, reached back, into his pocket, then took her left hand in his and slipped a ring onto her finger. She looked down: a simple band, her hand in his. "Eliza, marry me."

She saw only their hands. His hands. The ring his mother had given him on his fourth finger and the gold band on her third. The wind was gusting; she turned and met his eyes. The last color caught the clouds in the east: the front was blowing in. There would be no reckoning now. The ring spoke plainly enough, and the question was direct, and the rest was of little consequence.

A few weeks later, Eliza received a letter from Missouri. It said only this:

My Dear Eliza.

I am away from home on some business. I dont know the extent of my stay. I write to say I have heard that the governor calls on you. Whatever comes, I wish you happiness. I have found a girl of my own.

Will.

It was not total absolution, but she could live with her regret. She had Sam Houston.

And Andrew Jackson was elected President of the United States. Tennessee was brash with victory. There was the night of the illumination, when every home in Gallatin and every house in Nashville but two was lit through the night with tapers and oil. The dark houses were mobbed, their inhabitants forced to hide in their cellars while the Democrats raged and the band, directed by a man waving a hickory baton, played "The year of Jubilee is come, return ye ransomed people home." In Madisonville two brave citizens prevented the town from casting a unanimous ticket for the General; they were pursued by Democrats with tar and feathers and hid in the woods until the mayor sent word to the governor and Sam called off the search, threatening to send in the militia.

And it was not in Tennessee only that Democrats were riotous with victory. In Philadelphia drunken Jacksonians stole an empty coffin and went searching for the author of the coffin handbill, intending to bind him and carry him through the streets in it. They smashed his windows and looted his home as he escaped through the back entrance, disguised in his wife's clothes.

In Washington the people of the passing administration locked their doors and were not seen in the streets.

But in December, two days before Christmas, the rejoicing in Tennessee turned to mourning.

CHAPTER

17

December 1828

He let himself in, pulling his Indian blanket around him. Hannah was standing in the hall.

"Hannah."

Her old, swollen eyes lifted to him, her head still low, like a broken tree whose weight eventually uproots itself. "Governor Sam," she said.

"Where is he, Hannah?" He was not sure how to face him. Nothing, Houston knew, could ruin Andrew Jackson but this. He had been Rachel's protector, her strength. But she had been more to him: she had been his cause. He had championed her with the same sustaining venom with which he fought for his country. With this cause lost, the old General could plummet like a bird shot from the sky.

"He's upstairs with Mistus," she said, shifting her eyes toward the stairway. "And he don't want nobody with him. Won't have nobody with him. But her." She took a step forward; he reached for her as she fell against him with a long, high wail. Emily Donelson glided toward them like an ethereal creature given weight only by the coffee service she carried, her attention seemingly fixed on mounting the stairs without dropping it or sloshing the dark liquid from the silver pot, as if that loss would be as tragic as the other loss in the home. She gave Sam a nod of recognition but did not greet him and moved on up the stairs. The governor and Hannah clung silently together in the hall, swaying slightly. "Let me take it for her," he whispered, but Hannah said, "No, he won't see nobody."

So Houston was there in the hall holding Hannah and holding back his sorrow, his body bent over against her, his chin lowered over her head. They moved together to Jackson's library, Houston saying, almost crying, "How did it happen, Hannah; dear God can the General survive it? I know he can, Hannah, but how can he?"

The horsehair couch was before the fireplace. No fire was lit; the room was cold. The wail of mourning slaves penetrated the window out over the lawn. Houston crossed to the window, lifting his hand and touching the lights. The oak leaves had fallen and all was bare but the cedars. A mulatto slave passed by just the other side of the window; far off by the cabins and in the fields other slaves crouched keening, the noise high and grieving, their arms thrown before them on the ground or raised, swaying. "They're cold," he said quietly. "They must be so cold."

"And her too," Hannah said beneath her breath, "cold as the river frozen over." She paused; he did not turn to look at her. And then her voice came at him again, slow and lyrical, "I can just hardly believe it, and the General, he can't believe it at all. He been sayin' over and over it ain't so, she can't be dead. When we laid her on the table she'd been cold for some hours, and he says, 'Put four blankets on that table, case she come around,' he says, 'so she won't lay so hard on that table.' And there weren't no hope then of her comin' around, but he just won't see it. Still he won't see it, won't leave her case she does."

He turned to her, a constriction in his throat. "What happened, Hannah, tell me how . . ."

She eased herself into the chair near the couch. He recalled Aunt Rachel bringing him to this room before the duel, standing childlike beside him, her cherubic face glancing up at him while she listened to her husband snore, her voice so full of pride, "I didn't know he was so asleep." As if even his snoring was cherishable.

Hannah's body filled the chair. She pulled her knitted shawl around her and tucked her hands together deep between her thighs for warmth. "Ain't nobody made a fire in here today," she said. "Major Lewis, he upstairs alone and that room is mighty cold and drafty, and ain't nobody made a fire there neither."

"When did he come?"

"Dawn," she said. " 'Fore dawn. Lots of people's come and gone away. Lots is waitin', too, over at Mr. A.J.'s to see the General, neighbors mostly. Mr. A.J., he been here, but the General won't see him, neither. Won't see nobody. Maybe Colonel Coffee, but he'll be a while. I sent Joey for him. Course I figure the only one in this world might could of helped the General right now is hurtin' too bad hisself to do it. He's taken real sick."

"The judge is ill? Does the General know?" He spoke rapidly, fearing that if John Overton could not come—

"I expect, what he's sick with's the same thing we all got. Too much hurt to take." She paused, looking keenly at Houston. "He loved Mistus same as the General done."

The words were candid, direct, but the phrasing was odd. Doubtless it expressed exactly what she meant. Images flickered through Houston's mind like random lightning—John Overton unmarried until past fifty, his energies used up promoting Jackson, instructing him, defending him and defending Rachel; Overton was the mastermind of the vindication reports: his dwarfish face, his active mind, considering, writing, worrying how each sentence would affect Rachel. Rachel—even the way he spoke her name was reverent. So. But it was too late to matter now.

Houston crossed the room to the couch and sat on the end near

Hannah. He leaned back, looking up at the high ceiling. "How could this happen now?" he murmured.

"How?" she said with a lifting in her voice, a small, bitter note that made him look at her. "She been sick for some time, sir."

He watched her with a puzzled expression, but he knew her meaning. The clock on the mantel ticked steadily.

"I catched her," she said. "The General, he was out in the fields —it was a week ago this happened—and Mistus just fell and I catched her. When they gone for the General I was rubbin' her side and in some time she come round and the General come in and says 'Rub harder,' and I done it till she's all blue and hurtin' and still he's sayin' 'Rub harder.' She was hurtin' bad, twistin' and cryin'; it was her arm and her chest hurtin'. And the General he keeps sayin' 'Rub her more,' and I done it. Miss Emily come, then the doctor, and for two days the General just never would leave her and wouldn't eat nothin'. Just took some coffee. He wouldn't sleep neither. He said, 'Don't send for nobody.' Then come Friday night and she's better, sleepin' some. But she wouldn't talk none, 'cept to say, so we could just hardly hear it, that General should go to bed so's to be rested for that big celebratin' party they givin' for him in Nashville. But he just won't go. Said, 'Goddamn that party in Nashville,' and then was sorry for sayin' it."

Her voice was in soft rhythm with the distant keening of slaves, and her tumid eyes were fixed on Houston's. "I could see real plain he was sorry for alots of things," she said and left another silence. "Six days he stayed in that room, and for that I was thankful to God Almighty, 'cause the General he owed her that. He been leavin' her all the time since they was first married, goin' off and doin' his duty." Her sarcasm burdened the last word, and she lowered her eyelids, as if waiting to be told she was overstepping her bounds. Houston said nothing, which gave her courage. "He weren't so fine a husband," she said and lifted her gaze. "In the end he left her like he always done. She was feelin' better, askin' to sit by the fire, and I helped her there and brought her tobacco pipe. We was alone. And you know what she says to me? She says she'd be more happy to die than to live in Washington City. I'd heard her sayin' it before, sayin' she'd rather be a doorkeeper in the house of God than to live in that palace in Washington. But to me she just said it right out, that she'd just like to die. And real soon she just went forward and I catched her. When the General and them doctors come in, she was dead, already dead. 'Bleed her,' the General starts yellin', sayin' 'For God's sake bleed her,' and they tried, cuttin' her arm right here. But there weren't no blood, not any."

Her staid voice and her eyes accused him. He made no movement, no sound.

" 'Try the temple,' he was yellin' at the doctors, cussin' like I never heard, almost made me sick the way he was actin', 'Try the temple, bring her around, Doctor, rub her, Hannah, rub her,' and I done it, knowin' she was dead and feelin' it in my hands. And he felt her, and I knowed he felt she's dead, but he just won't say it." Her voice faltered, then resumed with new force. "That man, all his life's been wantin' things a man just can't have together. He been wantin' peace and quiet and Mistus at home, and he been wantin'—no, not to be here with her, but to be out makin' everybody in this world outside home to love him and want him and call on him to lead 'em. He been wantin' to be a chosen man. And don't you say no, Hannah, it ain't so. You, you know it's so. Maybe he done told you that stuff he told everybody, how he's just wantin' to be a farmer, to live and die right here weighin' on his cotton. And he do want that. But I known him a long time, sir. And he been wantin' the other real bad too. Always tellin' us and tellin' Mistus it weren't what he wanted but if all them people out there called him he'd go. Well I say he been wantin' to be a chosen man more'n a farmin' man. He been workin' at it, and a man just don't work at what he don't want less he's made to, and I ain't never seen nobody make Master do nothin'. Now. He gone and risked his life to stop them folks from sayin' lies about Mistus, like when he gone and shot that Mr. Dickenson. But I ain't seen him riskin' his chances for bein' a chosen man. He just let them keep stabbin' her. He done tried to fight 'em off, but he don't take her off the sacrificin' altar. And you come in here askin' how can this happen, Hannah, how? Well I done just told you. But you ought to have knowed, 'cause you's just like him. And you been askin' how can he take it. Well he just can, that's all. He done lost somethin' he wanted real bad and loved a awful lot, but he done just got what he wanted more. And he can just take it." Her eyes squinted at him. "It be a real shame if it just ain't worth it to him without her."

For a moment there was only the tick of the clock, and the cold. Then she bent forward, tucking her head into her lap and wailing out her grief, heedless of the hollow, gutted old man in the room up above touching, feeling the cold forehead and still not believing.

Sam Houston stood, and moving to the window turned his eyes out on the winter day, recalling an April afternoon when tree shadows were lengthening across the Hermitage lawn, an afternoon when Andrew Jackson had made a choice. And he, Houston, had made the choice with him. What was the choice between, really? A wife and a nation, or a wife and a man's unmitigated ambition? Destiny demanded its price. He had felt, that April day, that an era of his life was slipping by. He knew, now, that it was already gone. The loss, for one brief moment, was almost too great. Then he turned and said, "Hannah, you must be quiet now. We have too much to do. You must see to the food; I will see to everything else." He went to her and put his hand on her shoulder, realizing suddenly that her sorrow, her loss, was more than his own, perhaps as hard as the General's. "Hannah," he said softly, "we must hold together."

The old woman pulled her shawl to her face and rubbed her eyes dry, but would not look at him. "He had a nigger-woman from the fields one time whipped for showin no respect to Mistus," she said at last. "Might be he should of taken that hide to his own back." A winter wren chirped outside the window, a distant sound through the panes.

CHAPTER

18

By daybreak of the twenty-third, handbills were circulating through the towns and countryside. Editors of the Nashville newspapers had time only to scrawl in the margins of the day's issue: "Mrs. Jackson Has Just Expired."

Balie Peyton brought the news. Eliza was stitching the hem of her dress for the ball in honor of the President-elect and Mrs. Jackson, which had been planned for that night. Balie came riding in from his office in Nashville, his face chapped with cold, his hat pulled down low and collar turned up, the black-bordered handbill that proclaimed her death tucked inside his coat. John Allen met him at the door, as Eliza came down the stairs with Dilsey. Balie pulled his hat off, leaned his head back, pushed his hands through his black hair and said Rachel Jackson had died in the night, the governor had sent him with the news, and the funeral would be the following day, Christmas Eve.

Eliza wore her mother's mourning dress; Laetitia was too ill to go. The family rode together, all but Laetitia and the babies. Roads converging on the Hermitage were crowded; from dark on the twenty-third to the morning of the twenty-fourth, ten thousand persons, twice as many as lived in Nashville, made their way through the countryside. The Allens set out in the night, traveled through the dark hours of dawn on the morning of the twenty-fourth, through the freezing hours of the dim morning that would not give way to light, through crowds of people.

It was Sam Houston she thought of, more than Rachel Jackson. From her first knowledge of Rachel's death, Eliza was hurt and annoyed with her because of it. She had died with a pathetic composure, like defeat. If she had always been a woman with such sad composure, Eliza would not have taken offense at her resignation to death. What confounded Eliza was that Rachel Jackson had once had the reputation of a spirited woman. This, for Eliza, was the tragedy: not that she had died, but that she had forsaken herself and yielded. Eliza took it to heart. She compared herself to Rachel as a young woman, but she resisted taking the comparison further— though it had taken root. She was uncomfortable with it and with herself. And she was uncomfortable with these people who feigned bereavement for a woman whom they hardly knew. Theirs was a token grief, offered up to death in abstract, offered up to a man who had enough grief of his own.

But Sam Houston's grief was real—and seemed more so, to Eliza, because he kept it private. Despite his usually conspicuous and elaborate style, he did not make a show of sorrow.

She was proud of him. He had taken control and created some semblance of order from the disarray. As the people straggled in with their offerings—roasted geese, whole haunches of venison, yams and sweets—he orchestrated in a quiet, forceful manner, effective for the living and respectful for the dead. He had never deferred to convention but had an innate sense of propriety of a more meaningful kind.

And he was, when necessity required, a pragmatist; something had to be done with the food. Under his instruction, makeshift tables were scattered over the front lawn and laden with these festive foods prepared in homes throughout Tennessee for Christmas Day. It was a bright feast for an occasion of mourning on a dismal day, but Sam was touched by the generosity. These were his constituents, his people, paying tribute to a woman he loved.

To the left, flanking the Hermitage, he had ordered a line of latrines dug and screened with brush. The barn of winter fodder was emptied to feed the horses, piles of it scattered under the trees in a field near the stream. In another area carriages and buggies were parked, and scattered throughout were fires with people gathered around. Groups of boys trod off into the woods and returned with more wood and brush for the flames. A wet snow began to fall. The grave was dug in Rachel's garden, a deep wound in the earth where the tuberose had grown.

He did not at first see Eliza. Doc Shelby pressed in through the crowd and said, "Sam, John Coffee's here."

"Thank God," he answered with a long breath that frosted on the air. "Get him in to the General. Is there still no word from Overton?"

"Not a word. Nothing."

"Check on Willoughby, if you would. He's outside the General's door, trying to keep everyone out. I don't want anyone in that room but Coffee, and Overton if he comes. Thanks, Doc." He added as the doctor turned away, "And for God's sake, let's keep the press out of the house."

When he noticed Eliza, he went to her and said without formality, "I'm glad you're here. He's asked me to lead the pallbearers, but I want you to stand with me at the grave."

She nodded. "Tell me how to help."

He smiled briefly and turned up the collar of his coat. "See to the children; they're everywhere. Then, if you want, pay your respects to Rachel and come back to me." He added, "I need you with me."

Impulsively she cupped her hand to his cheek in a tender, maternal fashion and responded to his sorrow. Their alliance was unspoken; he would mourn later, holding her.

Hannah was already seeing to the children; she had no patience with irreverence now and was marching through the grounds ordering every raffish child back to his parents' guardianship. They were making a celebration of Rachel's death, and she would not suffer it. There was no one to check her authority; the governor himself had empowered her.

Inside, the Hermitage was thronged with people. Floors were slick with mud and carpets were ruined. Eliza went up to see the body, more from a need for quiet than from morbid compulsion. Visitors were allowed in one at a time, and Emily Donelson stood watch, greeting each with a piteous cordiality. The draperies were drawn and the room lit with tapers; the ritualistic ambience seemed, to Eliza, an unfortunate and disturbing affectation. She did not stay long. Rachel's body lay on a table at the foot of the bed, dressed in white satin with rouge and ringlets, which Eliza felt was a mockery. Her eyes were shut and covered over with coins, and her bodice was draped with pearls. Around her neck was a gold chain and a locket opened to a miniature of General Jackson—the only piece of her attire that seemed appropriate. White kid gloves had been forced onto her hands, and her swollen feet pressed into white slippers; it was style imposed on an unstylish form. The effect was absurd, almost obscene, and Eliza was offended that this woman, whose most admirable quality had been her lack of pretense, should be buried encumbered with petty trappings. She said to Emily, "Do you like the way her hair looks?"

"Not really, I don't. She never wore it that way. But her cousin dressed her."

Eliza shrugged. "It makes her look silly. And she wasn't, I don't think. I'll help you change it, if you want."

They brushed out the curls, and when Eliza turned to leave, she saw that Hannah had come in and was standing near the door. Hannah nearly spit her words out, "All painted up like the red devil hisself. All these years I been dressin' her, and now they shut me out. That cousin of hers. What you just done, helped."

Eliza looked at Hannah and said, with more feeling than she had yet expressed for Rachel Jackson, "I'm sorry. It is regrettable. I'm really sorry."

She wanted something to take hold of, something to believe in. Everything around her seemed a sham, and Hannah's honesty gave her hope. Sam's anguish would do the same. She wanted to be alone with him. She wished the place could be stripped of all pretense. She could witness misery or bitterness more easily than she could deal with trivialities. Maybe then she would feel something more than she now felt; maybe she would be more sorry for Rachel. As it was, her keenest sensation was that of distress with herself; she felt somehow she had fallen into disfavor and been banned not only from emotion but also from expression of emotion, or pretense of it, or participation in the litany. She felt completely separate and yet disdained to join.

Sam would be a link. Sam provided proximity to optimism and despair and the entire scale between; he was a way for her to get close to it all, without committing to it. Or surrendering to it. She needed to be with him and started down the stairs. The stairway was crowded. She edged to the rail and saw that he was coming up toward her. He was looking at her. It seemed to her, suddenly, for just that moment, that nothing mattered but that he reach her. She held to the rail, pressed by people, and waited. Feeling a light touch on her arm, she turned; a young officer in dress uniform smiled brashly and said, "Pardon me, I'm looking for—" but did not finish, for Sam was instantly between them, demanding, "Do you have a question, Lieutenant?" His tone was acerbic. The lieutenant was at a loss, and stammered out his request—he had been instructed to inquire about a military escort for General Jackson. Sam answered sharply that the General's friends would escort him and dismissed the officer, who turned and started back down the stairs.

So easily it was dislodged, her pervasive desire for Sam to hold her. Now she did not even want for him to touch her. There had been something sinister in his voice, something she did not recognize but feared, and she drew away from it so completely that she found herself stepping back one step higher. "The lieutenant meant no harm," she said.

"There are more likely people he could have asked," he answered. "I doubt his interest was in the General."

"But he chose to ask me." Her voice was only a whisper.

Sam tossed it aside. "Which he now probably regrets." And then, "Have you seen Willoughby Williams?"

The stress was familiar, more familiar than that impulsive flight toward intimacy. She recoiled. She regained her sense of self and reestablished her boundaries. She resorted, as was her custom, to composure. "No," she said indifferently, "I don't know where he is."

And she would not let go of it. Composure, in the end, was what she held on to that day. She stood with Sam throughout the service and hardly listened to the words. Her father and her brother George were nearby, their heads bowed and hands folded modestly behind them. She noted how tall George was getting and wondered briefly why she should notice it at such a time: the cold, a drizzling snow, the sound of stifled crying, and George getting taller. His face was like her father's. The Reverend Mr. Hume's deep Scottish brogue was lost in the feeble snowfall. "The righteous shall be in everlasting remembrance." Cotton bolls spread to cover the muddy path were sunk into it, trod upon, conquered. When he finished speaking, the Donelsons and household servants began to turn and make their way back to the house. General Jackson stood, silent and stoic, supported by his friend John Coffee. Hannah watched him through still eyes; she crossed her arms and tucked her hands in close against her body. Once she gave a slight shrug, as if none of it mattered anymore; once she reached her hand out toward the casket, the brown palm up and rigid with the snow drifting down. Several black men started to lift the casket and place it in the earth. As they leaned the General turned his eyes on Sam Houston; it seemed that for the first time that day he realized what was happening. Sam went to him and wrapped his arm around him. At that moment Hannah flung herself onto the casket, her cries sounding, to Eliza, pitifully insignificant and muted by the snow closing in. The black men stepped away, and Major Rutledge leaned to lift her up and called for someone to take her away. But General Jackson, in the only words Eliza heard him speak that day, said not to touch her. He said to let her cry. Hannah wailed in lamentation, then moaned fitfully, her body heaving across the casket, her black dress trailing in the mud.

Eliza thought of April and the beads that Sam had worn and his voice saying everything was blooming but the tuberose.

CHAPTER
19

January 1829

"That must be her," Willoughby said, pushing his gloved hands deep into his coat pockets.

The governor strained his eyes from under the beaver brim, squinting up river. After a moment he said, "It's her. I see *Pennsylvania* on her side."

"Your sight's like an eagle's," Doc Shelby remarked, and Houston felt a stirring inside—the eagle, his Indian symbol for destiny. Even the word could lift his spirits.

From above them, along the sunny bluff, a cheer began to rise from the people. They had been waiting all afternoon to see the steamboat *Pennsylvania* pass by, coming downriver from the Hermitage, carrying their General along the Cumberland toward the Ohio River to Pittsburgh, where he would take the overland route on to Washington City. He had requested no crowd; he was deep in mourning and said it would be difficult to face the populace without what he termed an "unmanly show of emotion." Now that Rachel was gone, the nation's people were his sole purpose. They had given him victory over those who had slandered his wife.

But there had been no way to keep the people from coming. They had learned the name of the steamboat that would carry him; they had seen it pass up the Cumberland toward the Hermitage landing at the mouth of the Stones River where the General had loaded his cotton through the years, and they had waited for it to come back down. The small crowd of officials and leading citizens who came to bid Old Hickory farewell had made their way to the wharf through a shoving, shouting mob of thousands. There was nothing to do but let them cheer.

Some of the ministers in town had expressed their disapproval with the General for traveling on a Sunday, but since he was going by water, and not by land, and since he was determined to do it, they pardoned the offense. And so the clergy also had come to see him go.

Sam Houston was standing between Deputy Williams and Doc Shelby. Nearby were Mayor Robertson, Congressman James K. Polk, Eliza's uncle Congressman Robert Allen, and Houston's cousins Robert and John McEwen. The McEwens were big men with heavy features that resembled Sam Houston's, the wide nose and square chin. It was Robert McEwen who had gone with Willoughby to meet the stretcher bearing Ensign Houston home after the battle of the Horseshoe. He and his brother John were prominent citizens of Nashville, elders in the Presbyterian church and intimate with the governor, though outspokenly opposed to his consumption of alcohol. Even in public they reprehended him.

Also on the dock were Judge Grundy, former governor William Carroll, House Speaker William Hall, Sheriff Horton, the Reverend Mr. Hume, and Robert Martin, a friend of Houston whose home was on the Gallatin Pike, the frequent stopping place for the governor as he traveled the road between Nashville and Allendale.

Judge John Overton was not present. He had parted with the President-elect at the Hermitage landing earlier that day.

The *Pennsylvania* moved slowly in the low water. It was too large for the crew to hog through the shoals farther along the route, which in dry seasons were up to five miles long and only three feet deep. The Cumberland was low this winter but still moving freely. Houston hoped there would not be severe problems, though even with the best of luck and a river rise, it would be over three weeks before the General reached Washington to take the oath of office. Houston wished he were going with him; a steamboat with its nose downstream had so many possibilities. But for now, his life was rooted, the wedding just four days off. And Eliza was worth staying for.

As the boat neared, the volume on the cliff swelled to a steady roar. Women waved handkerchiefs. Sam Houston could hear a parrot in the crowd not far behind him, shouting, "Jackson, Jackson, hurrah!" its tutored, nasal tone more dubious than enthusiastic. Sam had to smile, knowing that despite the old General's request for a simple farewell, he would be pleased with it all—the crowd, the sun shining for the first time since Rachel's death, even the riotous bird.

Houston had seen Andrew Jackson only once since the funeral. The General had been subdued and somber, but his anger kept him occupied. Many had speculated he would never go to Washington. Yet he was going, an older, sadder man, more determined than ever to sweep the Augean stables clean and start the government anew.

Suddenly Willoughby laughed, pulling one hand from his pocket and pointing to the steamboat's bow. "Look there," he said. "It's two hickory brooms!"

"Looks as if he still intends to clean up Washington!" Robert Allen called out over his shoulder, and the people chanted, "Old Hickory! Old Hickory!" Robert stepped up behind Sam, putting a hand on his shoulder. Sam liked the man. They had shared more than a few bottles and women and long nights in Washington, had traveled together to and from Washington with Congressman Polk. Making love with a woman whom another man had penetrated was an odd but authentic connection to that man, and camping under the stars together also had a way of bonding.

Robert Allen was taller than his brother John, stouter, two years younger. His eyes were thick-lidded like his brother's, but his mouth was broader and less laconic. They would have favored each other more if not for a complete disparity in their natures. Robert laughed more, drank more, and cared less. He was not as wealthy as his brother but lived well enough. Sam had wondered what Eliza would be like if she had been born to Robert instead of John. Perhaps less willful and intense. But therein lay so much of her charm.

Houston lifted his face to the sun to catch its mild warmth. The wind quickened, ruffling the water into sparkles in the white light of winter sun. Turning, he looked behind him at the people lining the rocky cliff, the buildings of Nashville, the tin roof of the old courthouse, the edge to the balcony railing of his room at the Nashville Inn. He felt a rising inside him, a joyous lifting: this was his town, his state; these were his people. And they were good people. With all his plans for the future, his hopes and ambitions, his impatience to get on with life—move on to Texas where revolutions were brewing—the present was still good. Secure. He had so many friends. And Eliza. He had done without a woman for six weeks and intended to hold out the four days. She was worth waiting for: he thought of holding her precise and delicate body naked against his own. It was a familiar fantasy, one that had provided him with quite a lot of enjoyment. Withholding himself from her was tantalizing enough, but the prospect of shucking that restraint had become a constant and pleasurable obsession. Only two things marred the obsession slightly: the apprehension that he might unintentionally hurt her when he pressed inside and the puzzling and persistent intuition that if he had not disciplined himself to maintain her virginity, she would not have required him to. They had been alone a few times, and not once had she resisted his cautious advances. At times he felt she was emotionally removed from him, but she never rejected his touch. He assured himself that this was because she trusted him, but still he was perplexed. It didn't seem quite right.

He pulled his greatcoat closer around him as if wrapping her inside. The *Pennsylvania* was nosing in. General Jackson had not come out on deck. The cheering waned, then trailed off to a waiting, questioning murmur. "What if he doesn't come out?" Willoughby asked.

"He'll come out," Houston answered, his eyes on the deck.

"They're determined to see him off," Willoughby observed, glancing behind him at the citizens.

"He'll come out," Houston repeated.

A score of people stood on the boat deck, leaning against the railing. A. J. Donelson, who had not left the General's side since Rachel's burial, and his wife, Emily, stood side by side, waving. Their young son had gone to the bow. Unknown to his parents he was swinging one of the hickory brooms above his head, stirring the crowd to laughter. Mary Eastin, Rachel's charge who had determined to go to Washington despite Mrs. Jackson's death, leaned against the railing in the bright sunshine of the second deck, smiling a melancholy smile. Major William Lewis, Andrew Jackson, Jr., and Henry Lee, the son of Light-Horse Harry, stood together on the deck directly below her, conversing, occasionally lifting their hands or nodding toward the people on the ridge.

The *Pennsylvania* slowed and settled, her trail of steam puffing white and then diminishing, drifting off downstream in the winter wind as she eased into dock. The churn of her paddle wheel slowed inside its wooden drum as the captain set its pace to match the river's current, and the crew went into action, throwing heavy lines to cleats on shore.

When the boat was secured, Andrew Jackson stepped out into the sunlight on the lower deck. A band blasted "Hail to the Chief" and the crowd cheered. Governor Houston listened, recognized the tune, and laughed out loud, knowing that very few listening had ever heard it, and those who had would be hard put to identify it.

President-elect Jackson was dressed in a black suit, a plain white shirt and a black tie. A mourning band circled his hat and hung to his sloping shoulders in a weeper. Another black band was tied around his sleeve. He stood apart, somber, and for a moment made no gesture at all. Cheers subsided to an expectant silence. Then, without any change in expression, Jackson touched the brim of his hat and lifted it, the weeper flapping in the wind. People cried and laughed together, but no one moved to rush the boat. For this Sam Houston was grateful; there would have been no way to stop them. It seemed the people's decorum resulted from the General's solitary, fragile appearance—a figure monastic in mourning.

Old Hickory replaced his hat and Andrew Jackson Donelson left Emily and stepped to his side. Houston wished it could be him, there beside Jackson; secretary or what have you, it was a great honor to be so close to and so trusted by the General. He felt a surge of his old envy for A.J. but suppressed it; he, Sam Houston, was, after all, governor of a fine and loyal state, and Donelson was still only a secretary. But to a great man.

Jackson gave some instruction, and Donelson nodded and made his way directly to Sam Houston on the dock.

"He wants to see you," he said with formal decorum, "but he asks that no one else come aboard. He doesn't want to stop here more than a few minutes."

Houston nodded, turned to the other officials and relayed the request. Then he removed his greatcoat and handed it to Willoughby; he would not stand in full view of his constituents wearing a coat when Jackson was without his. Donelson escorted him on board and to the General, then left them alone, two tall figures in black. Houston bowed slightly, lifting his hat with a solemn, graceful movement. The gathering on the bluff applauded. He straightened and replaced his hat; the President-elect reached out and clasped his hand, let it go, then turned and moved toward the bow of the boat, out of hearing range from anyone but still under the eyes on the bluff. The governor followed, and they faced each other. The onlookers went silent. Houston waited for Jackson to speak, feeling a sudden distance from him, a broadening chasm, as if the boat were already moving off downstream and leaving him behind. This man, General Andrew Jackson, was now the chief magistrate of the United States, and whatever their relationship had been, whatever it would be in the future, there was a gap between them now: the governor of a backwoods state, and the president of a republic. The old man said nothing.

Sam began, "On behalf of the citizens of Tennessee—"

"You see we put the brooms out," Jackson interrupted quietly, waving the speech aside.

"Yes sir."

"Shovels would have served me better," the General added with a wan smile. "The muck in Washington is waist deep by now."

Houston returned the smile, intimacy restored.

Jackson's face was half in shadow, half in afternoon sunlight. He closed his eyes, then opened them, their yellowed, blood-shot gaze on Houston. When he spoke his voice was low. "May God Almighty forgive her murderers as I know she forgave them. I never can." He turned and stared out over the water. "The last time we left from this dock, Sam, just a year ago, on a day like this, with these same people aboard, and you and Overton and Coffee and Carroll, and with Rachel . . ." he paused and swallowed, "with the sun out and the same Democrats seeing us off, we were headed for New Orleans, to celebrate my victory there." Again he was silent. Turning his gaunt body, he looked up the bluff toward the road that led westward to the Natchez Trace, his weathered hands holding to the rail. "Sometimes I've wondered," he said quietly, "if I shouldn't have gathered my army together after that battle on the Mississippi and marched them west to the Rio Grande. Mexico was a rotten and unstable empire then, as it is now. The back door to our nation stands open and vulnerable. The United States should never have surrendered its claims on Texas and should regain those claims." He looked at Houston. "The only way to get a territory, Sam, is to take it."

The governor felt an instant surge; he searched the eyes, the lined and homely face. Was this the word, finally? After years of meandering intimations, at last, in the bright sunlight of a clear day, under thousands of eyes, the word? Or—a more cautious thought— was this merely an old man in mourning, considering what could have been. No, it was not that. These were not the words of a man spent and bitter and thinking back, but of a statesman mapping the future. Houston only nodded, waiting, hardly breathing.

The Old Hero looked out over the water. "Under my general-ship, Sam, the United States has driven the Spanish, British and Indians from the Southwest. I have taken Florida, twice, and secured our southern boundary. I should have moved my armies on to Cuba from Florida, but that is not my greatest concern now. What is most necessary now is to extend our western boundary past the Sabine, as far south and west as the Great Desert. If Mexico must neighbor us, we need a natural boundary, such as the Rio Grande." He set his gaze on Houston and left a silence. Then he said, "I want Texas for my country. I want you to get it for me, Sam. I don't want to know how you go about doing it, or when. The President of the United States is not an aggressor; he doesn't send men out to win nations, or even territories. I intend to negotiate on the purchase of Texas, but I don't expect the Mexicans to sell. Meanwhile, you make your plans and effect them. You will be on your own. If you fail, you may be hanged as a traitor. If you succeed, the nation will remember you."

He felt the cold wind, the warm sun, the conflict of it all. This he had not anticipated: a total severance of ties, a complete handing over of command. He, Houston, was to conquer Texas, without funds, without guidance, and without support. But under presiden-tial order. At first there was the apprehension of it. And then, the power of it. He was on his own.

He met the General's discerning eyes, and, in answer, offered his hand. Jackson took it. "One more thing, Sam. Whatever I write to you, whatever I say in public, remember this one thing: I have put my trust in you, and I intend to keep it there. Don't let me down."

He felt tears well and did not speak. Jackson tightened his grip. "I wish you a good marriage, son. She's a beautiful young lady, of accomplished manners and respectable connections." Loosing his hand, the General cast him an amused expression; he had not lost his wit. "And of your own selection. It seems you have it all. I'm proud of you."

"Thank you, sir."

"Take care of Tennessee, Sam. Don't leave it in Billy Carroll's hands. I don't trust him anymore."

"I understand."

They fastened their eyes on one another for a long moment, a sober look. Then Sam Houston turned and went ashore, where he stood on the dock, apart from the others.

A shout went up as Andrew Jackson, still standing at the bow between two hickory brooms, lifted his hat again to his people. The *Pennsylvania* turned her nose out and downstream.

Deputy Willoughby Williams took Dr. Shelby's arm and leaned close, saying, "Would you look there at our governor. Here we've got all these hundreds of folks, come to see the General off, and Sam's standing over there by hisself, lookin' off in the wrong direction at God knows what."

He was motionless in the wind, hat in hand, his face lifted to the bluff, his eyes westward toward the Natchez Trace.

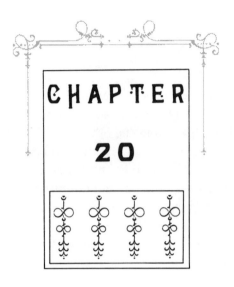

CHAPTER

20

The Reverend Mr. Hume leaned forward, setting his Bible aside, and looked at Eliza. He was Scottish, long-faced and brown-eyed, his forehead high with gray hair fringed down over it scarcely an inch. She disliked his certitude, for she was her father's daughter and had seen how a person could deceive himself by deceiving others. She knew how a man riddled with misgivings—gutted by them—could appear so sure. The Reverend Mr. Hume appeared too sure, and therefore she was cautious. "And so you understand," he said, "that it is not a thing to be entered into lightly, but reverently, advisedly, and in the fear of God."

She said only, "Yes." Beek came into the parlor with dry wood; the last was damp and would not catch. Eliza poured tea from the china service General Jackson had sent as a wedding gift before leaving for Washington City.

"Have you any questions?" the minister asked, lifting the cup to his mouth, his eyes on her and his high brow lifted. He was a descendant of Norman nobles of William the Conquerer.

"No," she said.

He set the cup down. "Then I have something to say, Eliza. To my knowledge, your fiancé gives no evidence of being a religious man. If he adheres to any religion I suppose it would be that of the Cherokee heathen. Do you know anything of the Cherokee religion?"

"I know some of the legends. Certainly I don't perceive them as sinister."

"I'd like to speak to you as if you were my daughter. May I do that, Eliza?"

She wanted him to leave but did not care sufficiently to say so, and nodded impatiently.

"It's a complex religion; the Cherokees are neither simple nor ignorant. But they are heathen. They do not embrace the Lord God as their Savior. Neither, as far as I know, has Sam Houston embraced Him, or ever shown any sign of faith in Him."

He paused, and she spoke into the silence. "I am, of course, aware of his association with the Indians. But I wouldn't say he believes in their religion. He respects it." It was more than she had meant to say.

"Respects it? Do you know they indulge in shameful practices, such as couples dancing around a fire and feeling each other's bodies in sight of others? I won't make unfounded accusations of the governor, because I don't know that he has ever participated in those rituals, and it seems clear he's chosen to adopt the white way of life and the white practice of monogamy. But my conscience compels me to make certain you are aware that your betrothed is well acquainted with another way of life. He was adopted into the Cherokee tribe and has been heard to say he considers the half-breed Rogers brothers as much his kin as his own brothers by birth."

"I'm aware of that," she said, thinking of the passion she had shared with Will Tyree, and how it would disturb the Reverend Mr.

Hume if he knew. The secret gave her an illusion of omnipotence over this boorish, intolerant, silly man. She wanted to demean him and added, "And it doesn't make a difference to me. I didn't choose the governor for his orthodox behavior; surely that's apparent. He is not orthodox. Directly, sir, are you saying I should not marry him because he likes Indians?"

"My dear, I am not trying to discourage your marriage or to censure the governor, but I do feel it my duty, as the one you have asked to join the two of you in marriage, to be certain you have ventured a look down the road you are choosing. If you request me to hold my peace I will do so—at the price of my conscience."

The fire still had not caught. The room was cold. Nothing the man said would make a difference; she would marry Sam Houston. She had her questions, but she wanted him enough to dismiss them. Certainly they were not the same questions that the Reverend Mr. Hume was asking; they had more to do with why she wanted Sam Houston than with who he was or the state of his soul. She answered with a caustic note, "God forbid that I should rob you of your conscience. Please do go on."

He was quiet and she thought perhaps he would not continue, but he was not so easily daunted. He made his decisions after long deliberations and then did not readily reconsider; he would say what he had come to say. "I have said, Eliza, that I cannot believe your betrothed is a man of Christian faith. I pray you are not approaching marriage with the notion you will convert him. Most people never change; they become more like themselves as the years pass. If you marry Sam Houston, and through your influence or someone else's, he becomes a Christian believer, then that is good, and as God wills it." He lifted a finger. "But you must marry the man knowing he may never come to God. And that you cannot force him to God. You must be sure you can live with him, for the rest of your life, just as he is."

Meeting his look, she said, "I don't have any desire to convert him. If you don't want to do the ceremony, I understand." After a pause she added, "I will have him as he is."

"Do you know how he is, Eliza? Do you know he drinks excessively?"

She stood and went to the window and stared out over the fields at the poplars under a winter sky. Her scorn for the Reverend Hume was complete; it gave her strength. "Yes."

"And that his temper is volatile?"

"So I have heard."

"And that he has many eccentricities?"

"Yes," she said again, turning to face him. "I don't know what all of his eccentricities are, but I know it's his nature to be excessive."

"Are you aware of his plans for Texas?"

"He has no such plans. He told me so. There's no truth to those rumors. I'm surprised you believe them."

He considered this child, with her solemn eyes and soft lips and her posture of defiance, one hand on the sill and the other perched on her slender hip. She had turned only halfway around when she looked at him; with just one gentle swivel of her waist she would again be looking out the window with her back to him. He did not like her much. Either she was lying or she had been cunningly deceived; he knew from reliable sources that Sam Houston had a hankering for empire. Yet he was not at liberty to say so. "Perhaps you should ask him again," he offered.

She stared at him. "He has not lied to me. Nothing you say can enlighten me. I know his habits and everything else you've mentioned."

So. He was absolved of responsibility. Arguing would be futile. "And you can live with it all?"

"Yes I can."

"Till death parts you?" he added in a whisper.

"Yes." She held his gaze. A shiver of cold took hold of her; she wanted to go to the fire, which finally, in a single plume of flame, had begun to burn. Instead she turned away again, and looked out at the heavy clouds, and wondered briefly if it would snow, and wished the Reverend Mr. Hume would stand to go.

They were married on the night of January 22 in the parlor of her home. Pocket doors dividing the hallway from the library and the parlor were opened to make a single large candlelit room, smelling of longleaf pine. It was an affair worthy of the governor; John Allen saw to that. The only disappointment was that Sam's mother did not come. She sent a note saying she was ill. One of his brothers came, the grocer from Nashville. He seemed ill at ease with the governor, who paid him scant attention. Sam told Eliza that they had never had much to say to each other.

Their vows were exchanged before the parlor fire, Willoughby standing with Sam, Martha Ann with Eliza. A fire screen shielded them from the heat. The mantel was decorated with evergreen branches and berries; when Eliza was not looking up at Sam, she looked at the berries. Throughout, she avoided the eyes of the Reverend Mr. Hume and chose not to dwell on his words, or on the uncomfortable feel of her hand in the crook of her father's arm. The ritual itself was not essential to her, nor were the toasts and dancing that followed. She observed it all through taper smoke, apparitions moving in a soundless performance. It seemed even the musicians were merely going through the motions, with no notes coming forth. What mattered was that she was now married to Sam Houston. She was not giddy with joy, but she was satisfied. What she wanted now was to be alone with him. For her, the vows themselves—words recited as placidly as children in school recite their lessons—did not wholly confirm the covenant; she needed his body inside of her. Then she could feel the bond and believe in it. A mystical union was not enough; nothing was real without sensation—and some amount of pain. If he drove his body hard enough inside, then perhaps she would feel enough to make it all seem valid; he would purge her, somehow, of her doubts and confusions and the familiar frustrations of childhood. He would need her and fill her emptiness and be her saving grace; in return she would harbor his dreams and his seed and nurture them to maturity—a fair exchange for salvation.

They danced together with exquisite perfection. The rooms became too warm; during a waltz Sam suddenly led her from the dance floor and said he needed to go outside for air.

"I'll go with you," she said, taking his arm and turning toward the door.

But he did not move. "Eliza, dear, we can't both disappear at once."

"Why not? We're married."

"But these are our guests. One of us has to stay here."

"We won't be out long."

His frown was almost imperceptible, but Eliza noted it. "Well," he said, "you go out first, if you want, and I'll stay."

He did not want her with him; she understood that, but her pride kept her from probing it further. She would not go where she was not wanted. "No. You go on."

But he did not go alone. Eliza, as she turned to talk with a young woman wearing a garish yellow dress, watched him. His timing was so precise, so well orchestrated, that all but a wary observer would have missed the gesture completely. His eyes found their mark without having to seek it out; he knew exactly where William Wharton was standing in the room. The motion Sam gave him was less than a nod, just a simple, indistinct lift of his chin and movement of his eyes toward the front door. Gradually Sam made his way through the crowd, pausing to talk and receive congratulations, and at last disappeared through the door. William was only a moment behind him.

And following William was Eliza. She saw them together rounding the corner of the house toward the smokehouse and paced her steps around the other way. The night was dry and cold, with a bright moon casting shadows of winter trees across the back lawn and down by the river. Wind skittered, sparkling moonlight on the water. A servant was coming from the outside kitchen with a steaming dish of food. He said, "What you doin' out here? It's cold."

She brushed her hand through the air. "Just catching my breath."

He smiled like a conspirator and continued toward the house.

Sam and William were not in sight. She perceived they must be in the smokehouse and walked quietly, smelling the stale hickory smoke of cured meat, glancing toward the river and the bare trees lining it, the silver light over everything and naked soil underfoot. Her slippers were satin. She was almost to the building when she heard their voices, and stopped. They spoke in low tones. She drew nearer, close up against the white stone of the smokehouse. The voices paused. Sam said, "I thought I heard something."

They listened. William replied, "It's nothing, sir. The wind." They were not inside, but just around the corner. With only a step, they would see her. She moved up against the stone wall, one breast pressing against it, both palms flat on it as if to support it. The limb of a nearby hackberry moved in a winter gust of air, its shadow scraping the ground.

"And the General knows nothing about any of this?" Wharton asked.

"The General is President of the United States," Sam answered. "He can't afford to know."

"But are your plans under his direction?" Houston was silent and Wharton added, "Pardon my hesitation, Governor. You know I'll do whatever I can to get Texas out of Mexican hands. I intend to live my life there and don't hanker to learn Spanish or turn Papist. But an undertaking of this kind, without government support, wouldn't that be treason? I'm sure you've thought it all out, but an independent citizen planning this kind of thing without official backing—if you failed and never had the chance to prove your intentions by presenting the territory to the Union—not that I think you're capable of treason, but there are those who would like to hang you for it."

There was a long, very long silence in the cold air. "William. I'm going to confide in you because I trust you. Were you watching when I met the General on the *Pennsylvania*?"

"Of course."

"Things transpired. Do you understand?"

"I'm beginning to."

"If I fail, I could very well be tried as a traitor—along with everyone involved. If I'm successful, I, and the men who help me, are in exceedingly agreeable, and visible, positions. I intend to make my fortune in Texas. I intend to win Texas, maybe even further west, for the Union. I know the risks involved. You know them. Great endeavors require great risks." He was quiet, then added in a low voice, "Are you in, or not?"

A small wisp of cloud from nowhere passed over the moon. Eliza smelled the faint odor of cigar smoke and pictured the two men, each standing with one hand in his trouser pocket and the other hand holding a cigar, bringing it to his lips, inhaling and exhaling with a foul, smoky breath, the cigar tip surging red. "I need to know more," Wharton said.

"You will. When you assure me you're in."

"What force are you intending to use? Texan settlers aren't exactly West Point trained."

"That's not your dilemma. Until you say you're in."

The wind gusted. "You have my hand, sir."

"The Cherokees," Sam said.

"The what?"

"The Cherokees. They're in a perfect position, on the border of Texas." He spoke rapidly, excitedly. "They need land, and they know the West is the only place they can get it. With very little persuasion they will join me against the Mexicans. I can command, arm and train seven thousand Indians from here westward to the Great Plains."

She smelled another waft of cigar smoke. She could not still her heart. Shadows of the hackberry branches moved in the wind, creeping up the lace of her gown. "My God," William said and then, softer, "that's the most ingenious thing I ever heard. Killing two birds with one stone, is that it, Governor? You get land for the nation and a home for your Indians."

"I think you understand," Sam answered in a lofty fashion. She pictured him taking a puff on the cigar. He had lied to her. He had mocked her.

Wharton asked more cautiously, "And what would the General say about your using savages to pull this thing off?"

"The General used Cherokees against the Creeks. And he's not your concern."

"He's cut the strings completely?"

"There are no strings."

"And so what is my part?"

"An important one. I need you as my agent. I want you to return to Texas, find out everything you can about the situation there, the Mexican troops and so forth, which Indians might be sympathetic to our cause. Get your father-in-law involved. Do everything you can to prepare the minds of leading Texans for a fight. For independence. And keep me notified. It won't take me long to get the Cherokees ready."

"You're going to do this from the governor's office? You still intend to run?"

"Of course."

"But you'll be stuck here for two more years."

"When Texas is ready, I'll be there. Trust me."

Another moment followed, then Wharton said, with new enthusiasm, "My God, sir, but this is great!" Eliza heard a clap of his hands, then more seriously he added, "Stephen Austin will never go along with us. He's too friendly with the Mexicans."

"Then we'll do it without him."

"That won't be easy."

"I'm not counting on easy."

"But what if the time isn't right?"

"You told me a year ago it was. That the timing would wait for the man. Now the man is ready. Your job is to see that Texans are."

"I'll need help."

"Take your brother."

"I'm not sure he'll go just yet, but I'll try. I have some others in mind too. George Hockley for one. He'd follow you anywhere. And George Childress, he's already high on Texas, and—"

"Enlist anyone you can trust," Sam interrupted. "My father-in-law has agreed to give some funds. Let him know your travel expenses, and he'll pay them."

Eliza was numb with cold, bewildered. Wharton said, "Allen's in on this?"

"He's avid for it. Intends to make a fortune. Land is his passion, and of course there's plenty of it in Texas."

For Eliza, that complicity—her father and her husband—was the hardest betrayal of all. She turned her cheek against the cold, white purity of stone and shut her eyes.

"I'll say one thing," Wharton mused, "I won't take Sarah Ann and the baby back with me until this is over. What will you do about Eliza?"

The air grew still; she heard Sam's voice as from a great distance, low and musical, and pictured him posturing with his Byronic air. "Ah, William, a woman is one thing, an empire is another. It is a grand scheme, such a grand scheme, isn't it, Wharton."

When he came back in, Eliza was dancing. This, she could still control; her moves, her voice, the entire embodiment of Eliza was within her own power. Nothing could violate that. She would not allow intrusion. Her tempo was perfect; she laughed aloud with her partner. She did not even know his name. She did not care. Nothing seemed of consequence in this moment but that she retain some sense of herself—apart from Sam Houston and his schemes, or her father and his deceit, or this crowd of people and the joy they took in their delusions.

He interrupted with a broad gesture of his arm and his usual elegance, "May I retrieve my wife, sir?"

Her partner made no objection, and in the next instant Sam was taking her in his arms.

She allowed it. They moved into the steps together, and as they danced she looked up at him and said in her soft and lyrical voice, "It will be a shame, Sam, if they hang you as a traitor."

His eyes had been scanning the room but now came to bear directly on her. "What do you mean?"

She kept her pleasant smile, "Texas, of course," and tossed his own words back at him, "But then, great endeavors require great risk."

He did not attempt to hide his alarm, but stopped dancing and led her aside, brushing against several couples and not bothering to apologize. He took her to a corner of the room. "What have you heard?"

"Everything."

"Tell me what you've heard."

"I heard you. Talking with William Wharton. Behind the smokehouse." She set forth the sentences like separate gifts, cordial presentations.

His response was quick and anxious. "Have you told anyone?"

"Is that what worries you? That I might tell?" He did not respond, only waited for an answer. "No, I haven't told anyone." A part of her still wanted to please him, to win his trust.

"Thank God," he whispered, with a glance to see that no one was near enough to hear. "Thank God."

"You lied to me," she said, no longer smiling.

"Eliza, we have to talk."

"Tell me why you lied."

"Not here. Can't you understand? I was not at liberty to confide."

"Of course I understand." She laid out her most precious card: "You were honor-bound to the President."

He drew back. The music had stopped; he bent low over her. "I never said that."

"No, not to me."

"I never said it to anyone. You misunderstood. The President has nothing to do with my plans." Still he would lie. His breath smelled of her father's cigars. "We have to talk, Eliza. Alone."

"You trusted my father, but not me. I will never forgive you. There is nothing you can say to make it right." She managed a lilt in her voice as she turned away, saying with her face tilted back over her shoulder to look at him, the fragile lace veil falling over her pale hair to the floor, "If you'll excuse me now, I have guests to entertain. The First Lady has duties, you see."

He carried himself through the rest of the evening like a walking shade. His stupidity appalled him. Seldom had his sense of discretion fallen short, but tonight, of all nights, it had failed him totally and left him vulnerable to miserable ramifications. Everything was in Eliza's hands—not only the power to break his heart but the power to ruin his plans. He had not even a remote idea what she would do. Intuition told him she would not tell his secret; she was, by nature, private. But then, she was so angry. And women, in his estimation, were unpredictable: you never quite knew. If she talked and word got out on a wide scale, Jackson would never again trust him, and constituents would have good reason to reject him. He could still go to Texas, but with damn little support, damn few friends, and a damn sight slimmer chance of success.

And he had been just a few hours away from having her next to him in bed. His life had taken a galling turn for the worse.

They were to stay the night and start for Nashville in the morning; Martha Ann had moved to Laetitia's room to sleep, and Eliza had been closeted in her room alone for some time when Sam finally climbed the stairs. He was sufficiently drunk. When she had first confronted him, he had been eager to be alone with her and try to explain himself and gain forgiveness, but he realized as the night wore on and Eliza flitted about, more gregarious than usual, without so much as a look into his eyes, that pardon would not be soon forthcoming. He thought of begging but rejected the idea on pragmatic grounds: Eliza would not respond to begging. He thought, briefly, of telling her the entire truth but could not bring himself to that. He began to think defensively—why was she so angry, anyway?

Why had she not allowed him to explain himself? Too readily she had assumed her position of defiance. It was almost as if she wanted an excuse to reject him . . . an excuse not to receive him tonight. She had always seemed somewhat distant emotionally; what if, now that he had made her First Lady of the state, she had what she wanted from him, and she wanted no more? But that was too abhorrent. He could not believe that of his wife. His wife. God, she was his wife. And she awaited him behind that door, in some state of unreasonable furor.

He knocked and entered with a sloppy attempt at reverence, dipping his head as if in tribute to her. She was seated at her dressing table, still in her wedding dress, watching the reflection of the fireplace in full flame; their eyes met in the mirror. He waited for her to speak first, but she declined. He said, "I should not have lied to you. I apologize. But I did intend to tell you everything after we were married."

"All right," she said caustically, not taken in, "we're married. Tell me."

He experienced a moment of hope. If he could devise a satisfying lie, she would accept it. But that would take time and clear thinking. He said, "Not tonight, Eliza. Tonight is our wedding night; it isn't the time for business." Even as he said it, he knew how unconvincing it was. He loosed his cravat in a gesture intended to seem casual, as if they had often undressed together, then crossed the room to her and bent to kiss her. It was a bold move.

She ignored it completely, neither lifting her face nor turning away. He planted his lips on the top of her head; she had removed the veil but had not brushed her hair, and it was tangled where pins had anchored the lace. Her quiescence frustrated him, and on besotted impulse he attempted to make light of the entire affair, gathering her hair in his hands and chuckling with an ironic smile into the mirror, from habit looking into his own eyes instead of hers. Then he gently pulled her head back and kissed her mouth.

She pushed him away. "You can't win a woman like you win a country," she said. "—by force."

He let go of her hair and stepped back. "All right," he said. "What do you want?"

"It's too late for what I want. I wanted us to trust each other." That was not all. She had wanted some sense of belonging and importance. And now she saw she had none. Not only was she unnecessary to his schemes, she had no place in them at all. Nothing she could do, as a woman, would gain that place. She had the trappings of influence, the title of it—First Lady of Tennessee—but nothing of its essence. "I wanted to be trusted," she repeated.

He stepped farther back, sat down on the bed, reclined against the pillows and stretched his legs out, crossed at the ankles with his boots on the white cover. "You're making this thing bigger than it is."

"No. I'm not." She was, in fact, making it smaller than it was— addressing only a portion of the conflict, unable to know the breadth of it, and how deeply it affected her.

Twining his fingers behind his head, he looked up at the ceiling, then back at her with a perplexed, boyish mannerism. Spontaneously he said, "I think you're looking for a reason to be angry. And I was careless enough to give you one. But the truth of it is you just don't want me." And suddenly that did seem to be the truth of it. He sat up. "It's Tyree, isn't it? It always has been."

"Don't be stupid."

"I'm getting less so. Admit it; I want to hear it: my wife is in love with another man. . . . God, woman, why did you marry me?" His last words were plaintive, almost a cry, and she did not know if the hurt they suggested was real or dramatized; she had never been able to distinguish the man from his theatrics. She felt he was sincere, but could not reconcile blatant, wounded emotions with the man who two hours before had been planning revolutions, the man who had said a woman was one thing, and an empire another. She wanted to believe he was hurting. She wanted him to hurt. And she did not comfort him. In a hard and steady voice, he said, "I am not so desperate, Eliza, as to take a woman who does not want me." He turned, running his hands through his hair, then took off his coat and threw it on the floor beside the fire. "I'll sleep *there,*" he said, thrusting his hand toward it.

"Fine," she answered.

They stared at each other. At last he flung himself onto his coat, turning his face to the fire.

She did not sleep, but lay on the bed in her wedding dress, watching the flames throw shadows about the walls and listening to her husband snore. His sleep provoked her—a drunken sleep, his arm over his face. He stirred and murmured occasionally, but she could not understand the words.

Before daylight he suddenly started and jumped to his feet, grabbing at his shirt, loosening the buttons at his wrists and pulling it off. She watched him cross the room to the window, tear back the curtains and shove the window open. Cold air blew in with moonlight; Sam leaned out, laboring for breath, his hands on the sill, his face in the light. He muttered in another language (Cherokee, she thought) and seemed to calm some, his face turned up to the moon. She felt she was seeing him for the first time. His profile was hard, his chest covered with dark hair and breathing deeply. She did not understand him, with his presage and his wild eyes, but she saw him lit by the moon as a man with fear. He struggled for air.

She lifted onto her elbow. "Sam?"

"Go back to sleep," he answered hoarsely, pulling the window shut and the curtains together, closing out all but a sliver of light.

"Are you cold?" she asked indifferently.

There was more wood beside the hearth, but he did not use it. "Cold seems to go with sleeping on the floor in January," he said.

By dawn, clouds had pressed in from the north. The governor and his bride were to ride to Nashville alone. Dilsey would come later with Eliza's belongings.

Family and servants waved them off as snow began to fall. Laetitia watched from her window, her breath misting on the window lights, her small face pressed close like a child's.

Sam rode his dapple gray and Eliza a bay mare, a wedding gift from her father. They spoke little, moving through the day in the silence of snowfall, the steady pace of the horses' hooves muffled in flakes that blanketed the ground. Eliza was fatigued with cold and the sleepless night, but anxiety kept her strong. Sam was without contrition; they each had their pride. Her anger grew to fill the silence. They moved through the morning and into the afternoon, scarves tied over their faces, all but their eyes, to keep from breathing the snow in. Occasionally Sam commented on the size of the flakes and how fast they were coming down, his voice through the scarf as stifled as the horses' tread and the cushioned fall of dead limbs breaking under the weight of snow.

Early in the afternoon, Sam said he would not take her any farther into it, as dark would settle before they reached town. He suggested they stop at the Martins' home on the Gallatin Pike, and she agreed, eager to be rid of his quiet intrusion, his unspoken need to be forgiven and desired and reassured.

They dined with the Martins as if all was well, and Eliza retired early. Late in the night she awakened from deep sleep in the Martins' guest room. The fire was crackling. She opened her eyes to the canopy above her head, washed in the yellow movement of firelight. Heat rolled at her from the brick hearth where Sam had lain down to sleep some hours before. Wondering at the roar of the blaze, she looked to see.

He was standing naked before the fire, his hands lifted, the palms raised toward the warmth and level with his head. At first she could see only his shape against the flames. Then he turned slowly as if to warm himself all the way around, and she saw his skin was wet, drops glistening in the hairs on his body. The light played over him, the front of his body burning Indian-red in its glow. His boots and riding trousers and his blanket were on the floor beside him. They were damp also, the toe of one boot mounded with melting snow. His hair was dripping. For a moment she was bewildered, but then it came to her that he had been in the river. He had walked to the water in the middle of the night, the snow still falling and the banks freezing, stripped off his clothes and gone down into it. He had come back and built up the fire and now was standing before it, turning, his eyes not even passing over her, but moving around the room as in a trance.

She studied his body, the deep scars in his shoulder where the musket ball had entered, the purple gash in his groin where the barbed arrow had been pulled free, genitals full, almost erect. He turned in a full circle and stood with his back to her until his skin was dry, then turned in profile, brought his hands down before his face and spat on them, moving them together in a circular motion, spreading spittle to the ends of his fingers.

Watching, she withdrew within herself and encountered there a mystery more puzzling than any of his behavior: she wanted him. Beneath her anger, encased like fragile marrow in her bones, was the desire for alliance. He did not belong to her. He did not even trust her. There was nothing in his soul, not a single essential motive, that she could share. His emotions she could sway, but emotions were fleeting. They were not his driving force. Something less transient than emotions guided this man—something innate and immutable. She wanted just to touch it.

He came to the bed and gently pulled the covers away, easing her flannel gown up and moving onto the bed, straddling but not touching her. He looked at her body, but not into her eyes. She wanted him to see her face and said his name, impulsively lifting her body to touch against his. But he seemed not to hear. Again he spat on his hands and took and rubbed them over her breasts, moving from the Cherokee tongue to English, his voice one she did not recognize, deep and slow and full of sadness, all the while his hands, the fingertips and then the palms, rubbing the spittle into her breasts, water dripping from his hair onto her face. *"Tsa'watsi'lu tsiki' tsiku' aya.* I take your body. I take your flesh. Your heart. Now the souls have come together." It was a pagan ritual; this she understood. He had worked himself into a hypnotic frame. The pace of his voice intensified like an animal that stalks its prey and then pursues it full speed; he felt across her belly, then lifted her hips and pushed himself inside with an urgent, brutal force. "Don't," she said plaintively, pushing against his chest. "You're hurting me." He did not seem to know her, but responded to the pressure and slowed, then pulled from her, and tenderly kissing her breast, murmured against it, "Now the souls have met, never to part. Your soul is wrapped in the web, and you are covered over with loneliness. Your eyes have faded. They had come to fasten themselves on one alone. You will be sorrowing. You will become an aimless wanderer whose trail can never be followed. Your soul can never get through the meshes, for it is bound by the threads."

She was afraid. She was more afraid than she had ever been. If she had railed against him with spiteful words she might have penetrated his trance. But confronting her was the sudden knowledge that she did not know this man at all, and she feared him. She feared breaking through. His tongue tantalized her breast; he was gentle. Without the force, the violation was more frightening. He was infiltrating the marrow, that awesome, haunted part of her to which no one had yet been privy. And he was giving nothing in return; he would not look at her or say her name; it seemed he would invade her most delicate self and then remember nothing of it. She whispered, "Please stop," and then ventured, "Talk to me. Please stop and talk to me. You're frightening me."

But he did not stop. He moved his mouth to hers, smothering her words, and again pressed inside of her. She struggled but without effect. He pinned her arms and continued to kiss her mouth. In panic, knowing she could not win against his strength, she took control in a different way, thrusting herself up against him, eliciting his force and becoming part of it, pulling him inside her body in a perverse and frantic attempt to shun him from her heart. There was no forgiveness here, for either of them, and no understanding. The union was of their bodies only; pain was the validation of their bond. For her, at least the pain was tangible. It would give her something to believe in—to covet and despise.

And for him, there was a temporary loss of self. He transcended, and bore down on her mercilessly with all his weight.

It was late morning when she left the room. On the first landing of the stairs was an arched window with a view over the Martins' lawn. She could hear laughter outside, children playing, and thought of home and the boys, so many miles away. She stopped to look out. The snow was still falling. And running through it, laughing, pursued by the two Martin girls, was her husband. He dived into the snow. The smallest girl fell onto him and they rolled together as the other pounded him with snowballs and then scooped up loose handfuls and showered snow down on him.

"It looks as if the governor is getting the worst of the snowballing," Mrs. Martin said from behind her. "You'd better go out and help him."

The voice startled Eliza. She did not turn to look but kept her gaze on the three figures in the snow. "I wish they would kill him," she said placidly.

"Child," she responded, "you don't mean that."

Eliza turned her face full on the woman who waited with a questioning look. "Yes, I do mean it. I wish to God, from the bottom of my heart, they would kill him."

Sam let out an Indian whoop. The girls screamed with laughter. "If I were you," Mrs. Martin said, "I would keep my wishes to myself."

CHAPTER

21

February

"**A**nd Erwin calls this paper nonpartisan!" Governor Houston declared, holding the newspaper out with one hand and slapping it with the back of the other. "Ha!" Pulling it before him he read, "We are authorized to announce General William Carroll as a candidate for the office of Governor of Tennessee, at the ensuing election." He walked to the Pembroke, threw the paper down and picked up another *Nashville Banner and Whig*, of the present day's date, reading, " 'We are requested to announce the present Governor of Tennessee, Honorable Samuel Houston, as a candidate for re-election.' An honor to announce his candidacy, a goddamn duty to announce mine!"

"You can hardly call that partisan," Doc Shelby said, scooting his chair back from the blazing fire. These February nights were the coldest Nashville had known in years, and with his wife, Anna, in

Philadelphia for the winter, visiting her family, the doctor had taken to sitting through most of the nights by the fire in his study. Often Houston joined him, and they sat in silence, watching the flames. Tonight was not as peaceful, with Jack McGregor yapping louder than the wind and the roar of the fire combined and Willoughby Williams throwing in a word now and then, trying to quiet McGregor before Houston sank into one of his black moods. "Billy Carroll is as much a Jackson man as you are," Shelby added.

"But the President supports *me*," Houston answered.

"Does he now," McGregor drawled sarcastically, taking another chestnut from the wooden bowl on the hearth and tossing it into the flames. "I sure ain't heard him say so." His limp slouch hat lay on the floor beside him like a sleeping dog, and his bald spot shone when he dipped his head toward the fire.

"It's a fact he does," Willoughby said, leaning forward in his chair and stretching, pretending boredom. He could feel conflict coming and was bent on avoiding it. "Maybe we should let you be, Doc. It's getting late."

"No, stay a while," Shelby said, seeing that neither McGregor nor Sam made a move to go; if Willoughby left, there would be no one to curb McGregor's talk. Except Sam, who had tossed the papers in the fire and slumped morosely into his chair to watch them burn—and Sam restraining Jack could mean trouble.

McGregor, squatting on his haunches, dug with brass tongs among the embers for a chestnut. He had lost several nuts in there. "Don't worry about it, Sam," he said. "Talk is, if he beats you for governor, folks just might elect you senator."

"Muzzle it, Jack," Houston retorted, his voice tight as a drawn bowstring, his eyes on the fire. "I'm not running for the Senate."

"Well, is that so," McGregor answered amiably. "I wouldn't be so dern sure if I was you. Billy Carroll's been around a long time. And folks like him." He found a chestnut, pushed it out onto the hearth and cracked it with a blow of the tongs, scattering shell fragments onto the reds and blues of the Turkey carpet.

"Of course it's so, Jack," Willoughby said. "Carroll's got him a good-sized following. But the fact is, Sam's got a bigger one."

"Yep," McGregor affirmed, popping the hot nut in his mouth and spitting it out again when it burned his tongue. "A great big followin'—a mile wide and a inch deep. One day in the heat can dry up a puddle like that." He set his eyes on each of the three men in turn. "All I'm sayin' is, Billy Carroll's been around a lot, since he come to Nashville as a boy sellin' hardware, and that was a good time back, and he's been makin' friends every day ever since. His handshake's well acquainted with the folks that count. In fact, irregardless of the fact Jesse Benton shot his thumb off, Billy Carroll's right good at shakin' hands. What I'm sayin' is, our governor here"—he spoke to Shelby, shoving his thumb at Houston—"needs to hit that campaign trail and run his horse gaunt 'fore he slows up. 'Cause if Carroll ain't in front of him, he for sure ain't far behind."

Willoughby saw Sam's jaw muscle bulge and said, "The best thing, Jack, would be for the President to put Carroll in the army spot Winfield Scott's just left. I heard some talk about that."

"Hell," McGregor said, munching on the nut. "Talk's free."

Houston cut his eyes at McGregor and demanded, "What is that supposed to mean?" He had no patience these days with asinine remarks.

"I'm just havin' me a genial conversation," McGregor announced, glancing sidelong at Houston and throwing another chestnut in the fire. "Want a nut?"

Willoughby and Doc Shelby looked at each other, knowing it was time to end the evening. Houston's temper was hair-triggered these days and fired off at any provocation. Jack McGregor was enough to drive a man to loading and firing a rusty musket; certainly he was unsafe around hair triggers. Especially Sam's. Since his wedding the governor had been touchy, even irascible, some days throwing himself into the campaign as if he had nothing else to live for, some days talking Texas, and at nights drinking until he could hardly stand. More than once Shelby had put him to bed on the sofa, thankful that Anna was out of town. Sam had always been a hard drinker, but this was overmuch. Trouble hung in the air like a thunderous cloud ready to spark lightning. It took no genius to link Sam's dark moods to Eliza. Doc Shelby and the deputy shared unspoken apprehension.

"Well I'm callin' it a night," Willoughby announced, standing up.

McGregor, fishing for the nut he had just thrown in, said, "I got a story for you first."

Houston said coldly, "That nut can't even be warm yet."

"Then I'll eat it raw," McGregor retorted testily. He turned to look at the governor. "Any objections?" They glared at each other. "Anyway, it's my nut, and it's my gut, so keep your mouth shut," Jack said, then smiled at the rhyme he had made. Houston stared at him.

"Tell your story, 'cause I'm ready to go," Willoughby said.

"Well, I've got this cousin in New York," McGregor began, sucking on the raw nut. "And his wife teaches school. Well, about the time Jackson's campaign was real hot and that coffin handbill was circulatin' around, she was teachin' about Cain and Abel. And she asks this one boy who it was slew Abel. And he thinks real hard, and then his face lights up and he says, proud as can be, 'General Andrew Jackson done it, ma'am.' "

Houston did not laugh.

McGregor did. Then he stood, shook out his legs, and spit the nut into the fire with a stream of spittle.

"Don't spit in the fire," the governor admonished.

McGregor scowled. "Why?"

"Just don't do it."

"Why?"

Willoughby intervened, trying to sound indifferent, looking around for his coat. "It's a old Indian notion: it's a insult to the fire. If you spit in it, your teeth rot out. If you piss in it, worms get your bladder. It's for your own good not to do it." He paused. "Where'd I put my coat? There it is. Ready to go, Sam?"

Houston sat rooted in the chair. "He oughta be," McGregor cut in, his voice mean and slow. Then he spat in the fire.

"For God's sake, Jack," Willoughby said.

Shelby stood up.

"I been wonderin'," McGregor continued, spitting again, his eyes on Houston's, "why a randy fellow like our governor stays out with the boys all night when he's got him a new bride waitin' back at the inn. If I had me a woman like that I'd be home pumpin' on her right now."

Houston was on him before the last word was out. He hit McGregor square in the face, knocking him to the floor, then fell on him, pinning him down on the Turkey rug and pummeling his face. His own countenance was without expression; he did not swear, but went at the beating with a sinister calm. McGregor yelled, and Willoughby and Doc Shelby stepped in. Willoughby slung his arms around Sam's neck and pulled back, cutting off his breath, while Shelby got on his knees, put his own head over McGregor's, and tried to pull him away. Struggling, McGregor punched back at Houston blindly with blood running in his eyes from a cut made by the gold ring on Houston's fourth finger. His efforts had no effect. Houston pushed Shelby aside and continued to hit McGregor about his face and ears. He reared back, and with a final blow, brought his fist down onto McGregor's jaw, raised the man's torso by his shirt collar and shoved his head down onto the floor. Then he let go. "God damn you, Jack," he said.

McGregor lay still, beaten, his bloody gaze on Houston. Shelby and Willoughby stood. Houston leaned back against the sofa and closed his eyes. At last McGregor stood up, wiping blood from his eyes and mustache onto his sleeve. Doc Shelby fetched him a rag but did not tend to him. "I'm gonna tell you somethin'," McGregor said, breathing hard, holding out his hand with the rag in it, his finger pointed at the governor, who did not open his eyes. "Ever since you been governor, you ain't been worth a shit to your friends. A couple years back, you needed somebody to do your dirty work, to stand by you at the risk of their life. And Doc here, and the deputy, they wouldn't have nothin' to do with it. But Jack McGregor, stupid pissant Jack McGregor, fell for it and stood with you. You needed me then. But now you're too cocky to need anybody, since you're governor and you got you a fine, wealthy woman. You treat me like dog shit, somethin' to walk around and turn your nose up at. Let me tell you somethin'—there's gonna come a time when you'll need me again." He tossed the rag to the floor. "I'm givin' you fair warning, Governor: I ain't gonna be around."

Houston slit his eyes open and stared at McGregor. "You talk about my wife like that again, and I promise you will not be around."

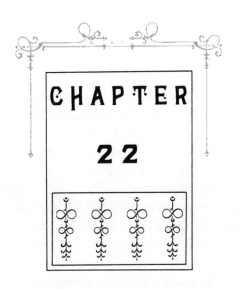

CHAPTER

2 2

For Eliza it was a winter of death: dying
fires, dying hopes, her baby brother Charles dying of consumption,
her mother only lingering. But Sam Houston defied it all, striding
through winter with his singular determination. He dreamed night-
mares and empires; he was despair itself, and then optimism. He
drank and plotted with William Wharton and others, low voices in
the room adjoining hers, and went on striving against the odds,
flourishing, pushing on, the crippled horse determined not only to
finish the race but to win it, to break the records and win it all. His
signature acquired new lavishness. He attired himself in buckskins
and silk and velvet baroque, sometimes wrapping a Cherokee turban
about his head—bright colors at a jaunty angle. He reveled in flam-
boyance and drank himself unconscious. He held his temper, then
lost it in public and warned his critics he would cut off their ears and

nail them to a post. He was desperate, fighting odds, fighting despair, searching for a way out of it all—a way west, to Texas. And he was breaking. General White published his account of the duel, how Sam Houston evoked the challenge from him to avoid fighting the marksman Smith T. White said he awaited the time when the governor would be stripped of his little, brief authority and neither the President's influence nor the misdirected sympathies of a deluded public would protect him. The governor dismissed it all and laughed in the face of it, but at night he woke in a frenzy and rushed to the balcony for air. It was all building, and he was breaking, and Eliza stayed in her room listening in the cold and waiting for the breaking. She did not think of Rachel's garden in April, or Sam chasing lightning bugs with her brothers, or rides along the Cumberland and red sunset through falling oak leaves. She thought of moon shadows of winter limbs scraping the ground, reaching for the lace of her wedding dress. . . . "Ah, William, a woman is one thing, an empire is another." She felt him pressing down on her, into her, his mouth smothering hers. And she could not forgive. She did not want to forgive, but cherished her anger and kept it close, private, all hers and not to be taken. She, too, was breaking. His would be an explosion, a violent cracking and outburst; hers was a slow inward crumpling of sanity into fallen ruins of what might have been, and was not.

Late in March her younger brother Charles died of consumption. Balie brought the news to Sam, who went to her room and took her hand and told her. She did not cry. Sam took her home for the funeral. They stayed the night in her room at Allendale. Before snuffing out the candles, Sam said, "Eliza, I'm sorry. I loved that little boy."

She was standing near the window. She wanted to cry. But then she cast her eyes out and saw the smokehouse shape in darkness, a monument to Sam Houston's deceit. "Charles was never strong," she said.

They returned to the Nashville Inn the following day and she went directly to her room, had the fire lit, and lay on her bed looking up at the ceiling and around the dismal walls: one window with heavy draperies pulled, pegged floorboards, a Scotch ingrain carpet of drab wool with a tobacco stain near the door into Sam's room. It had come down to this: this one room. He had offered to take this room and allow her the larger, brighter one, but the darkness suited her. Here she had spent most of eight weeks in dim firelight with the draperies pulled and meals brought up. Dilsey came up twice a day from her room below to brush Eliza's hair. During the first days, Eliza had looked down from her window at the public square and across at the courthouse. But one morning she saw Sam looking back at her from his office window; she let the curtain fall closed and did not open it again. They never discussed their single intimate encounter. Twice Sam came to her room at night and was shunned; he did not try again.

In her solitude, Eliza began to doubt that she had ever loved him. Late in the night after their return from Allendale, she dressed in her flannel gown and retired. Sam was out. Toward midnight she heard his heavy steps in the hall and guessed by their awkward weight he had been drinking. He stopped at his door, went in, and came to the door adjoining their rooms. She feigned sleep. He opened the door, and she thought he would enter, but then heard him retreat to his room and throw himself on the bed. Turning, she saw he had left the door open. She wanted to shut it, feeling unprotected without that barrier between them, but feared rousing him. Eventually she drifted off.

The fire in her room burned down to embers. She was awakened by a crashing noise from Sam's room, a series of blows, hard and deliberate, and went to the door to shut him away with whatever madness possessed him. But the sight of him held her: the room was dark, but she could see his shape near the foot of his bed, a heavy iron poker from the fireplace held high in both hands then brought down in a wide arch into the massive bedpost, smashing into it as if slicing his sword into an enemy in the heat of battle. His fury was reckless but his movements graceful, each blow striking the post at precisely the same place in a mutilating frenzy, the violence made almost beautiful. His breath came fast and frantic. With a final trenchant blow, the post split in two and hung splintered. Sam turned and saw her watching him through the doorway, framed by the red glow in her room. He lowered the poker to his side, dropped it, put his hands to his chest and choked out, "I couldn't breathe; it was falling in on me."

He was like a child: her brother Benjamin, frightened. She almost stepped forward. It was a full moment; so much hung in the balance like the ravaged bedpost, jagged, damaged, but not yet past mending. Too long she hesitated, and the moment passed. She turned to go back into her room.

"Damn you, Eliza! You walk in here with your hair loose and drive me mad and then walk out again."

She stopped and turned back to look at him. "You were mad before I came in," she said. She could not stop punishing him.

He said, "Since the day we married, you have been driving me mad. You weren't a virgin when I married you, were you? There was no sign of purity because you had none. There was no blood because you have none of that either; your heart pumps cold water if it pumps at all."

"And you. Were you pure?"

"You don't deny it?" he demanded.

She did not. It was too powerful a weapon against him. She answered steadily, "You came to me on our wedding night smelling of the last squaw you'd been with, and now you accuse me of indiscretion. You never wanted a wife; you wanted an ornament, an image to sit on your hearth and raise your children and 'grace your home,' as you so aptly put it."

He stared at her. "If it's an image I wanted, I chose well. I found a cold, hard semblance of a woman, not flesh with love and passion."

"I have passion," she said, standing there in white flannel, pitiless, goading him, "but I've never been partial to cowards." Scornful, she laughed aloud. "Imagine, a grown man afraid of the dark! Perhaps you married me so you wouldn't have to sleep alone at night, with the spirits and ghosts that haunt you; did you want me to protect you? Is that what you wanted?" In a biting whisper, she added, "I'm sorry. I would not defend you from your demons. You're a desperate man—grasping at dreams. How do you expect to win a country when you can't even win a woman and hold on to her?" It was not true. He had won her, and in some way still held her.

He stood there and said nothing. She heard herself saying, in a voice that seemed to speak with a will of its own, "No, I was no more a virgin than you were. I made love with Will Tyree many times." Then she turned and retreated to her room, shutting herself in with her anger and self-loathing.

What frightened her most was that she could not fend off her own demons.

An hour later, dressed in a loose frock with her hair tucked under a wool cap, she left through the door into the hall, down the hallway and stairs and out into the alley. Old Tom Pierce, who earned his food by playing a fiddle and bottoming chairs, was asleep on the ground outside. The streets were quiet, shops and houses dark. A drizzle hung in the air, but the cold was not bitter. She passed the vacant lot used for cockfighting on Saturdays, the office where Sam had practiced as a trial lawyer, the courthouse. No stages were due at this hour. A dog was barking from down Market Street. The deep bay of a hunting hound responded.

Doc Shelby's home was on the corner of Cherry and Cedar streets, one block from the square. The house was brick, with a stone walkway and pecan trees in the garden. He answered her knock as if he had been waiting for it, as if this night had been rehearsed, his cue just given. He took her in and fumbled on the hall table for a box of Congreve lights. Striking one, he set it to a taper. "I need you to come back with me," she said.

Her hair was falling from underneath one side of the wool cap, but she did not bother with it. She seemed, to Doc Shelby, more of a truant child than a woman. "Are you all right?" he asked.

"I don't know. I don't know what I've done," she said directly, and Shelby heard, beneath her serene voice, the child's plea for help.

"What has happened?"

She shook her head, unable to say exactly what it was.

"He loves you, Eliza."

Again she shook her head, and her poise broke into a small, quivering whisper, "Then he should not. He should not love me. I'm not worth loving." He waited for her to say more, but she did not. In those simple sentences, she had come to that place, the marrow, and her terror defied explanation. There was nothing more to say.

Doc Shelby put a hand on her shoulder, then took his coat from beside the door and snuffed the taper, and together they stepped out into the damp air.

She could not face Sam now, when she was confronting her own interior self. She asked the doctor to speak to him alone, and they parted in the hallway outside Sam's door. Returning to her room, she listened at the door between them and heard Shelby's knock. Sam made no response and the doctor let himself in. "Doc?" His voice was sullen and drunk. "Is that you? What brings you here at this regrettable hour?"

He was sitting in the chair near the fireplace, which was not lit. The room was dark; Shelby could just make out the battered bedpost. Sam said, "Sorry, the show's over. You missed it. We had an interesting scene here, dialogue that would curl even your hair." He paused. "What are you doing here?"

Shelby crossed his arms over his chest. "Eliza asked me to come."

"Well," Sam answered, "she went to get you? Isn't that brave. I suppose I should worry about a woman wandering around the streets at night, but not that woman. That woman could stop a grizzly dead in his tracks and back him down with nothing but words." He took a drink, sloshing the bottle, and called out, "Did you hear that, Eliza?"

She heard but did not answer.

"Is she in there?"

"Yes," Shelby replied.

"Then she's listening, count on it. She's sly as a vixen."

"What happened here tonight?"

"Tonight? Not a goddamn thing." He belched. "Except that I learned my wife has been whoring with another man. Actually, I think I already knew. There was no blood the night I had her—the one goddamn single night I had her—not a goddamn drop of it."

"There doesn't have to be, Sam. That doesn't mean anything."

"Go home Doc."

"You're wrong, Sam."

"No." His voice was low, but distinct enough for Eliza to hear. She wondered if he wanted her to listen or if he simply did not care. He put forth each phrase awkwardly, haltingly as a child learning to walk, "You don't know, Doc. She told me. Tonight she told me. Said she'd 'made love' with somebody else. Now isn't that charming. How delightful—my wife making love with another man. 'Many times,' she said. That was her only elaboration—many times. Many goddamn times. She didn't inform me if these many times took place before we married, or after, and I've been sitting here deciding that I really don't give a damn when it was. A strumpet is a strumpet; the timing isn't essential."

There was a moment in which Eliza waited for Doc Shelby's response like a word from God—a denunciation or a quietus. He said nothing at all, and Houston asked, "Cat got your tongue?"

"It doesn't mean she doesn't love you, Sam."

Eliza heard Sam get to his feet, his voice now forceful, "Does a woman who loves you turn you out of her bed? Does a woman who loves you refuse you on your wedding night? You tell me, Doc, did you sleep on the floor the night you were married? Did your wife request a separate room before a week had passed? You know nothing of the hell I've been living in. She never loved me," he said, and then his voice broke and he cried, "She never loved me, and my mother never loved me, she never approved of me and she never will! I wear this goddamn ring," he shouted; she heard him throw it across the room. "Pick it up, light a candle, read it, read what's engraved inside. 'Honor,' it says. It was my father's, and my mother gave it to me when I joined the army, because my father's name was Samuel and he was a soldier too. And when she gave it to me she said not to disgrace it, that she would rather have all her sons buried in a single grave than one of them turn his back to save his life. And here's an interesting fact: my brother also fought in that war, and she never told him anything like that. She wanted him to come home. But from me she wanted honor. And I wanted to give it to her. I determined to make her proud or die in that war, and I slaughtered men with a passion from the devil—not for principle, not for my country, but for my mother, my goddamn mother! And when they brought me home on a horse litter she said nothing at all. She nursed me, but she never said one word. She never said she was proud. She never said she cared. She never said a goddamn thing." There was silence, the last words hanging hard and bitter in the air, and he seemed to get control. "I detest self-pity," he said. "I would go completely mad before I would pity myself or solicit sympathy from others. But I cannot abide your standing there and telling me I do not recognize the absence of love when I encounter it. I'm well acquainted with the feel of it."

So quietly Eliza could hardly hear, the doctor said, "The woman in that room, Sam, is not your mother."

"She might as well be, for all the affection she's given."

"I think she has tried."

"Maybe. If that's the case, I'd prefer she didn't. I'd rather find love in the streets than be married to a woman who has to work at it."

"Everyone has to work at love, Sam."

"Do you believe that? Do you really believe it? Because I don't. I fell in love with that girl without any effort at all."

"I believe," he answered, "that she also fell in love with you. And is still in love with you."

Eliza heard Sam say something else, low and indistinct. The doctor answered. Then there was quiet and Shelby left the room. It seemed to Eliza then, standing pressed against the door to her husband's room, her own room glowing a dim red from the embers, a chill creeping under the draperies, her wool cap lying on the bed, that this moment held the most important revelation of her life. It came to her in the way light creeps over the horizon before the sun comes up, gradual and not yet warm, but with the promise of warmth. She thought: I am not alone. Then she said the words in a whisper that held more conviction than all her adamant declarations, "I am not alone."

And she opened the door and went to him. He was still seated before the unlit fireplace; she stood before him and said, "It was before we married. I never really loved him. And the rest of what I said—none of it was true."

"Yes," he answered slowly, looking at her, his hand tightening around the bottle but his voice tender and without resentment, almost without hope. "Some of it was true."

"But not all of it. Not the worst of it."

"No. Not the worst of it."

They were quiet. She had not completely relinquished her anger, but for the first time she was wanting to. She ventured, "I know what you feel about your mother. I think for a long time I tried to win my father. And failed. The only time he ever took me seriously, and was proud of me, was when I married you."

He did not seem to care and lowered his gaze to the floor and twirled the bottle with a slow rotation of his wrist. "So. We solve the mystery at last. You married me to please your father."

"That isn't true." At least, it was not wholly so. She wanted to comfort him and reached out, but he lifted his forearm before his face, as if to protect himself from a blow, and said, "Don't touch me. Don't ever touch me again."

She waited. He lowered his arm and took a drink and stared at the floor. "Go away," he said at last, and she turned and left him.

CHAPTER 23

April 3, 1829

The desk clerk at the Nashville Inn handed Houston an envelope and informed him "some Indian" had left it. Houston knew the writing before he read the signature; he had, in fact, instructed that hand in the art of penmanship.

Governor Sam Houston

We ask to see you, as men you have called brother.
We will camp for three nights where Pond Creek meets
the Cumberland.

John Rogers
James Rogers

Houston, known to the Cherokees as Ka'lanu, the Raven, "he who leads war parties," reined his mount and watched from beside the road as the new moon rose in a darkening sky. In Cherokee custom one must not look at a new moon for the first time through trees, or the next month would bring illness. When the sliver was in full sight Houston turned his gray gelding north into the woods and made his way along an animal track toward Pond Creek. The air was warm and smelled of spring. A whippoorwill called: someone had died, or soon would. Houston thought of his Cherokee father Chief Oo-loo-te-ka with foreboding. The summoning letter smelled of omen, and his father was an old man now, to be moving farther west before summer, under the terms of last year's treaty. Perhaps Oo-loo-te-ka, called John Jolly by whites, had no heart for another removal. Perhaps it was this the brothers had come to say: that he was dying.

Twilight moved into dusk and darkness, and a breeze touched the treetops. Animals retreated into undergrowth, as if a myriad of Little People moved about in the brush with a language of their own, the break of twigs and rustle of ground cover warning of an approaching stranger.

And he felt like a stranger to the woods. He wore a flannel hunting-shirt, buckskin trousers, moccasins and a turban tied over his hair—the garments of a forest people. Twenty years ago he had learned to belong in the woods, with their awesome integrity. Two decades was a long time. He was thirty-seven now and had forgotten. He reined his horse in, listening, and heard a flutter of wings and the throb of crickets and cicadas. He tuned his ears to the whippoorwill. The calls of evening birds all had meaning; the whippoorwill's he remembered: there was grief in the air, dying mixed with April, the month of birth. Again there was the call, low and warning from the trees ahead. Pressing the mount's sides he moved on, a reverence settling over him, as if a shadow of the old sensations of forest life was descending with darkness, a night journey back in time under the new moon.

He wondered how the brothers would greet him. They were mix-breeds of celebrated ancestry, related to prominent Cherokee

families, the Bushyheads, Black Coats, Little Terrapins, Rat-
tlingourds, and even Chief Oo-loo-te-ka. Their father, "Hellfire"
Jack Rogers, was a Scotch trader who had fought in the American
Revolution as a Tory captain and lived with the Cherokees intermit-
tently for four decades. He had two Cherokee wives and several
children by each.

In his years with the Real People (as Cherokees called themselves), Sam had taught the Rogers brothers Greek history from
Pope's translation of Homer's *Iliad*. In turn they had taught him
Cherokee and how to walk quietly on dry leaves. He had taught
them marksmanship; they had instructed him in the arts of the bow
and arrow. They had played together in the woods by Hiwassee
River, fished naked side by side and grown into men, the brothers
goading Sam to embarrassment when his chest began to sprout hair.
They had fought the Creeks together under the generalship of Andrew Jackson.

John Rogers was older than Sam, James a year younger. John
was more reserved and more cautious than his brother. He kept to
the Indian ways and beliefs, though he advocated schools and the
lessons of white missionaries—not their religion, but their instruction in literacy. He recognized that whites had better ways of farming, superior equipment that, incorporated into the Indian life, had
raised their living from subsistence levels to plenty. He understood
the conflict in this—the old ways against more profitable new ones—
and could not reconcile it. His response was an attitude critical of
both ways of life. Even when Sam knew him as a boy, he had begun
to look on life with skepticism and speak with sarcasm and to search
for a method of preserving the old customs while benefiting from the
new.

James was less serious in temperament, and therefore less bitter
—a sportive rogue, adaptable, handsome, Sam's favorite. He had
accompanied Lieutenant Sam Houston as interpreter for Tah-lhon-
tusky's delegation to Washington in the winter of 1818, when Secretary of War John Calhoun reprimanded Houston for dressing as a
savage and received, in reply, the Raven's resignation from the army.

There was a web of memories.

And now they were men, representing governments in opposition: Governor Houston a protégé of the President of the United States, and the Rogers brothers, captains John and James Rogers, emissaries and interpreters for the Cherokee Nation west of the Mississippi. Eleven years had passed since their last meeting, when John had come to Sam in Nashville with a request from Oo-loo-te-ka: the old chief wanted his son to return to him and serve as agent in dealings with the United States, for Arkansas had been flagrantly misrepresented and held nothing but grief; the whites had lied. The West was *Wudeligunyi,* "the land of death."

Sam, then adjutant general of the Tennessee militia, was finding his employment a tedious business. Moreover, he felt some responsibility for the western Cherokees, since he had encouraged them to remove and had organized the process. He wrote General Jackson that he desired the position of agent in Arkansas, and Jackson wrote to Secretary of War Calhoun recommending Houston for the job. "I have done this," Jackson wrote, as Houston later deduced, "more with a view to the interest of the U. States than his own. . . . In the capacity of agent Houston can draw to the Arkansas in a few years the whole strength of the Cherokee Nation now in the East of the Mississippi River." Despite his earlier controversy with young Houston, Calhoun was practical, and wanted the eastern Cherokees out of Georgia. He made the appointment. But Houston saw the hidden intentions and wavered. He believed in voluntary removal, properly executed, as the only remedy for both whites and Indians. But here was the key—voluntary. He would not coerce the Georgian Cherokees to abandon their fathers' lands. Calhoun, likely, would demand coercion. Houston could not give Jackson and Calhoun what they wanted and remain true to his conscience and his adopted people. He could not work wholeheartedly to secure indemnities for Oo-loo-te-ka and his western tribe without incurring wrath from the U.S. Government. And Calhoun, as Houston saw it, was a damnable swindler when it came to Indians; in the end he would not give them justice. So Raven, knowing he must preserve relations with his own race in order to be any future help to the Cherokees, declined the appointment and instead was elected attorney general of the Nashville district. Oo-loo-te-ka bore the disappointment without remark, and the Rogers brothers made no further attempt to gain Sam Houston's aid. He had explained to them his dilemma; they understood but never approved of his ambivalence. What mattered was, their white brother had chosen a path among white men. They were saddened but not offended; they, like their leader, responded with silence.

Until now. Now they called on him, not in the name of Oo-loo-te-ka, but in their own names—as men he had called brother. The call, coming at this time when Eliza had wounded him so deeply, touched his heart with old memories of intimacy. He was needed. This time he would not disappoint them. This time he had a plan, a way to please both of his fathers, President Andrew Jackson and Chief Oo-loo-te-ka. Texas: security and land for the United States and a home for the Indians. It was an answer to everything—except Eliza.

Damn her. He recalled her in the swing that night at Tyree Springs, the April air moving her hair about her face. It was an evening like this, the same stars through leafy branches, the same spring breeze, cool and clean. And now, like then, a hoot owl was calling mournfully from a limb high above him. He reined his horse and listened, searching the branches of the black walnut, and at last saw the yellow eyes blinking down on him. He shifted weight, the saddle creaked, but all else had gone silent. A breeze touched the highest leaves to movement. He remembered Eliza's voice as it had been that night, so low and full of mystery, asking, "Why does the owl grieve?" And he had answered, "His wife has turned him out. He is not a great hunter and has not brought her what she wants."

"And what in the hell does she want?" he said aloud, causing the gelding to start and the owl to fly his roost. "What in the name of God does she want from me?" He listened and waited, hearing only a deeper stillness. Suddenly he needed to cry. Instead he kicked his horse forward toward Pond Creek.

The woods at night give a man single purpose: to find light and warmth. He smelled smoke before he saw it and went toward it like a man starved of life's comforts. He heard no voices, smelled no meat cooking. The smoke was enough. His gelding plunged ahead, as if he, too, felt spirits in the trees about him.

And then they were on him, bodies dropping from trees like mountain cats. The gelding reared; Sam was pulled sideways and wrestled to the ground. He struggled in the brush, instinctively striking out, stimulated like an animal attacked, his latent senses honing and fighting against the unexpected assault. He heard laughter, familiar laughter, and smelled the old smell, the sweat of a man's body against his own, struggling, a man's breath—no, two men. He struck out and laughed aloud, crying, "Goddamn you!" and in return heard his own name spoken into his ear with panting breath, "Sam, brother, I have missed you."

Easing, he lay back in the forest shrubbery. James's face was next to his, misty dark and black-eyed through brimming tears. "James, brother, I've missed you." Their arms went around each other and their faces pressed. John was on top of them. He leaned down, encircling both men with his arms. "Houston," he said, and then again, "Houston." They held each other and then released, and John stood. James gave Sam a warm look and then also stood, crossing his arms and looking down. "My brother Raven has forgotten how to move," he said with a smile, his teeth showing white. "He moves like a buffalo."

Sam rose, brushing soil and damp leaves from his flannel shirt. "He was eager to see you," he said, referring to himself, in Cherokee fashion, as a separate person, a friend. He added with a meaningful squint of his eyes, "He has missed his brothers."

They surveyed each other. James offered his hand and Sam took it. Their handshake moved into another embrace. John stood watching. Sam reached out to him; he accepted the hand. Together, touching, John holding the reins of Sam's mount, the three moved toward the glint of firelight in the clearing ahead.

She was seated cross-legged by the fire, her back straight and her eyes watching for him. When he stepped into the clearing she stood, and cast her eyes down. He did not at first recognize her.

James said, "Our sister Tiana has come with us."

The memories of her tall, lean body came a hundred in a second. She was heavier now, appealingly so. Her hair was as she had always worn it, in a braid over one shoulder and down almost to her knees; her dress was white doeskin without decoration. She stood with her eyes lowered, then cast a furtive look at him. She did not smile. "Tiana," he said, reaching out a hand. She took a step, and stopped. He remembered her body naked, how she had allowed him to move into her twenty years ago, the sun penetrating forest leaves and dappling her skin and the hollows of her cheeks. She was the first woman he had taken in love. "Tiana," he said again, approaching. She held out a hand to him, with a smile, but did not meet his eyes. He took her hand briefly, then James stepped closer to tell his half sister that Raven had forgotten to walk with caution in the woods. "He came like General Jackson's Thirty-ninth Infantry," James said.

To which John, moving from the shadows, added, "Of which we were a part, though Jackson seems to have forgotten."

A moment was filled with the croak of frogs and rush of waters from Pond Creek meeting the Cumberland. Sam turned to James and said, "Tell me of my father Oo-loo-te-ka."

"He's well," James answered, moving to a supply stash and rummaging through it. "He's old and fat."

"And despondent," John added with a note of reproach. "I'll water your horse." As he turned to go, Sam noted how much heavier he was and how much he had changed, though his garb was traditional skins, a turban and a braided queue tied with a thong. He crossed the clearing, about twenty yards distant, and looked back over his shoulder. The fire lit his face—it appeared as an old face, lined and jowled. "Arkansas is not what you promised," he said, and stepped into the woods toward the creek.

Tiana spoke. "Oo-loo-te-ka sent gifts to his son. . . . James, they are here; I have made them ready."

James stopped searching through supplies and crouched back, looking at his sister, who moved to a knotty oak log near the fire on which were spread an array of objects. She reached toward them, turning her face to Sam but avoiding his eyes. "For you," she said.

Sam moved beside her and looked down at the gifts. Tiana knelt and lifted them to him, one by one, looking at the objects in her hands but not at the man receiving them. He wanted her to look at him. The tail of her braid swept the ground. Her hands were graceful, her color golden against the doeskin; she was lovely with a woman's beauty, no longer a happy child. She named each gift as she gave it, and he admired each in turn: maple syrup, two jars from trees beside Oo-loo-te-ka's wigwam. She explained: his wigwam was on a knoll between the Arkansas and Illinois rivers in a grove of cottonwoods and maples. Next, a woven belt, made by Tiana's mother. A scarf. Houston removed his turban and replaced it with the bright flowered scarf. He tied the belt around his waist, asking Tiana how he looked. She gave him a glance and smiled, but not into his eyes.

"And how is Tiana's mother?" he queried.

Looking down, she answered, "She is well."

"And her father?"

She tilted her face, again smiling toward the ground. Firelight caught her lashes. "Her father still drinks too much whiskey. As when you knew him."

"More children?"

"No more."

"And your brother Charles?"

She hesitated. James approached and answered, "He has built another still."

Houston eyed him. "He said when he removed he would stop producing whiskey."

With a shrug, his profile against the fire, James said, "A man provides for his family."

"He sells to his people?"

James nodded. His features were more Indian than his brother's, though he wore the fashion of a frontiersman, hair cut short and falling over his forehead, his boots of cowhide.

John stepped into the clearing. "Do not criticize, Governor," he said as he looped the reins, securing the horse to a low branch near the other mounts. "We all compromise duty to self-interest. As you know."

Houston did not answer. Tiana presented another gift, a calico sash. He took it and admired it. She said it was made of fine cloth from New Orleans. Houston tied it around his waist, above the belt, noticing that Tiana bit her lip—an endearing habit he remembered. "And these," she said, reaching behind the log and bringing forth a pair of fringed and beaded moccasins. He took and examined them. The work was elaborate.

"Tiana made them herself," James said, shoving his hands in his trouser pockets and watching Raven's face.

Houston looked at the woman; her gaze remained downcast— not an expression of timidity, but of reverence for his soul. To look a person in the eyes was an invasion. He fingered the beads sewn in patterns across the instep and was touched, wanting to reach out to her, wanting her to acknowledge in some way, even in a look, that she remembered, without regret, making love on the bank of Hiwassee. Perhaps she was still angry. He had not been faithful to her after he took her; there had been many Cherokee girls who would have him, and he was young. He had not been true to her for even one week; she had not expected him to but had wanted it. Now, again, he would disappoint her, for he had brought her no gift. He had not guessed she would be with her brothers, but should have brought the men a gift to take back to her. He had not thought of it. He had not thought of her. He had fine knives for John and James but now was reluctant to present them in front of her. He had gifts for Oo-loo-te-ka's wives, expensive finery, but mere storebought trinkets compared to the moccasins. "Tiana's sure they will fit," she said, not under-standing why he hesitated to try them on, a mild reproach in her tone. "They're made from a pattern of the old ones you left . . . before."

No wonder he had loved her. She was so eager to please. Not as a dog is avid for affection, but with a proud and giving spirit. He touched the top of her head, then sat on the log, removed his own moccasins and put on the new ones. She watched and leaned to tie the single thong that laced them, smiling at the perfect fit. 'These," he said quietly, "are the best gift of all." She gave him a glance. "And you, Tiana? It has been too long since we parted."

The air lifted stray hairs about her face. "Twelve years," she said.

"I have heard you married."

She lowered her head and did not answer.

John seated himself at the fire with his back to the others.

"She was married to a white man, David Gentry," James said in a quiet voice. "A fine blacksmith, who is now dead."

"He is dead," John added abruptly, without turning, "at the hand of Osage. As are Tiana's children."

Houston felt a shock, a blush of heat. Tiana's husband and children were dead because of the removal he had advocated—still advocated, believing it the only alternative if Cherokees wished to remain a united people with their own customs. But the United States had not paid the Cherokees for their land or run boundaries and defended them from the Osage as promised. "I am sorry," he said to Tiana, watching light flicker on her bowed head and knowing the inadequacy of his words.

"He is sorry," John echoed dispassionately, still without turning to look at him. "He is sorry, but when he could have helped us, when his father requested help, he did not come."

Tiana did not lift her face. Houston went to the fire and seated himself opposite John, studying him through the smoke. James sat beside Houston and stared into the fire. Tiana rose to tend the flames; she resembled her brother James in supple movement. She had her father's blue eyes; Houston wanted them to look at him. He knew the custom of avoiding another's direct gaze, but it seemed that this woman's refusal to look at him was a subtle condemnation for his part in her family's fate. She was not a woman to judge or place blame; Houston knew this and knew it was he who judged himself and read his self-reproach into her averted eyes. Still, a look from her would feel like forgiveness. . . . For what? He was innocent; he had obeyed his conscience in dealing with her people. But these facts remained: he had led them to remove, had then refused their call for help, and Tiana's husband and children were dead. "Your father, and you also, agreed with removal," he said quietly to John. "You were among the first to take your family into Arkansas."

"I did not know what awaited us there."

"Nor did I," Houston responded.

"But I did not profess to know," John said, and Houston left a silence.

Tiana stood and walked to a red cedar on the edge of the clearing, untied three small carcasses from a branch and carried them back. "Two rabbits and a squirrel," she said gently, holding them up by a thong that bound their legs. She laid the gutted creatures on a flat rock, took up a knife and began cutting away the skin as Houston asked the brothers about their families. While they talked, she kept to her work.

"And you," James remarked, "have taken a wife. We hear of her beauty."

Sam flashed his eyes to Tiana. She set the skins and meat aside, cleansed her hands with water from a flask, and rose and moved to the edge of the clearing, where she cut thin hickory branches to use as skewers. Light from the new moon shimmered on her hair, casting silver on it; the braid swayed in movement with her body as she reached for and cut three branches. Diana, her father had named her —the Greek moon goddess. But her mother pronounced it with a *T*. The doeskin dress hung to her knees. She wore fringed leggings and moccasins; Tiana, like her uncle Oo-loo-te-ka and her brother John, preferred traditional raiment. Houston knew from experience she was naked beneath the dress. "It is true, she is beautiful," he said without passion, returning his stare to the fire. "Her name is Eliza."

James looked to John and their eyes held. Even John had abandoned the taboo of direct gaze and was not averse to meeting eyes in order to convey a message.

"Your father is confounded," John remarked to Houston. "Often I have heard him say you would never marry a white woman."

"No." James laughed loudly, the sudden noise cutting into night air; he pointed a finger at John. "You know that is not what he said. He said a white woman would not marry the Raven, for he has too many of the red ways and needs more than one wife. Our brother Raven has eager *wa'toli!*"

"Very eager *wa'toli*," John smiled, nodding and looking at Sam.

Houston glanced to see if Tiana had heard. She had known his eager *wa'toli*. If she heard, she pretended not to. She returned, worked the carcasses onto the skewers and rested the ends on rocks placed at opposite sides of the fire, the meat over the flames. Then she sat, her elbows resting lightly on her knees, her breasts shadowed from the firelight as if cradled against her.

"We have come to you with a purpose," James said in a lower tone, leaning back on his elbows and stretching his boots to the fire. "Oo-loo-te-ka sent us. We have been to Georgia, where I met with Chief John Ross. He denounces Oo-loo-te-ka as a deserter of his fatherland and the graves of his ancestors. He says the eastern Cherokees will not move to Arkansas. They will not cede one foot more of land. They wish to remain on the land of their fathers. He says that by birthright and by United States laws and treaties, they are entitled to stay. He says the Cherokee are called a poor, ignorant and degraded people, but there is not a man among them so ignorant as not to know he has a right to live on the land of his fathers, and that this right has been acknowledged and guaranteed by the United States. Nor is there a man so degraded as not to feel a keen injury on being deprived of his right and driven into exile. He says Oo-loo-te-ka, the Rogers brothers and the rest who have gone willingly into exile are traitors to their country and their people." Tiana leaned and swiveled the meat to roast evenly. James spoke on, watching her. "In saying so, he condemns more than one fourth of the Cherokee Nation. Four thousand are now living with us west of the Mississippi on the Arkansas."

Houston answered, "John Ross will die proud, but destitute, if he does not remove."

"So says Oo-loo-te-ka." James sat up, wrapping his arms around his knees. He did not sit in Indian fashion as his brother did, but his movements were more Indian. The Rogers were more than half white. It seemed to Houston that John felt more Indian, but James looked it, with the stealth and grace of a nomadic hunter. "Your father still believes you were right to advise us to remove," James added.

Houston turned from James, leaned forward and looked at the older brother. A breeze shifted smoke toward Tiana; Houston could see John's eyes, and met them. "And you say I was wrong?" he asked.

"No. Your government is wrong. Oo-loo-te-ka is right that Cherokees must remove and become a single nation again, with the old ways. But John Ross will not treat with Jackson. He does not trust him; he's seen him at his cheating. When Chief Ross was Jackson's adjutant in the Creek war he saw Jackson dishonor his promises. In the peace treaty ending that war Jackson took as part of the Creek indemnity four million acres of Cherokee land."

"That was by mistake," Houston said.

"You are deceived," John replied.

"The mistake was rectified."

"Yes—when we petitioned the United States War Department."

"It was done by mistake," Houston said forcefully. "Jackson makes a hard bargain, but he does not steal."

"You are deceived," John repeated, his voice lifting, "as we were deceived. As we have been deceived too many times. We removed one decade ago and are still unpaid. Many of us live in poverty. Many of us have perished at the hand of the Osage and savage Quapaw. Our hunting grounds to the westward are inhabited by fierce Pawnees and Comanches. Your government treated that they would run lines to settle these questions, and they have not even attempted. The agents grow rich at our expense. The fur traders interpret bounds as they please and pester us. And now by last year's treaty we must again remove west."

"Why has Oo-loo-te-ka agreed to such a treaty?" Houston demanded.

"Because we need land—good land. Arkansas belongs to the Osage. How can we ask our eastern brothers to join us if we have no land to give them when they come? How can Chief Ross take seriously our cries for a united nation in the West when there is no home for it?"

"I don't argue, brother," Houston said. "But I suspect the new treaty does not provide for enough land, or good land."

"True, it is not enough," John answered. "It has never been enough, since the first treaty."

Houston answered sharply, leaning forward with the fire hot on his face. "My government has dealt in bad faith. But Houston has never dealt with you in bad faith. I will not suffer your blame."

"You could have helped us."

"That's why I'm here. Tonight." He took in a breath. "What are the treaty terms?"

James answered. "The treaty promises sixty-five thousand dollars cash now and two thousand each year for ten years. It promises a permanent home for the Cherokees, never to be made a territory or state. Seven million acres."

"And does Oo-loo-te-ka believe this will be honored?"

James shook his head. John crossed his arms and said nothing. "He is without choice," Tiana answered, not lifting her gaze from the skewers.

"He would do as Chief Ross does," John finally said: "refuse to remove. But he knows the Arkansas land he inhabits will never be his, as the eastern Cherokee Nation will never survive within Georgia's boundaries. Already whites are on our Arkansas land, selling whiskey and stealing livestock."

Houston knew it all too well. He had heard his own constituents laughing over a Georgian ditty:

All I ask in this creation
Is a pretty little wife and a big plantation
Way up yonder in the Cherokee Nation.

The smell of hickory and roasting rabbit drifted up with smoke; meat juices fell and sizzled in hot ashes. Tiana turned the skewers again, then lifted them from the fire, examined the meat and found it almost ready. She dug the ends of the hickory into the ground, the meat suspended upward in smoke, and then poured water from a flask over the stone on which she had skinned the carcasses, cleansing it. She poured a wallet of white cornmeal onto the stone, mixed the cornmeal with water and pressed it into cakes, then grilled them in a skillet over the fire.

They ate without ceremony or talk. Tiana did not take meat for herself, as there was not enough, but the men sliced bites from theirs and passed them to her. Houston felt the injustice of it but did not interfere; it was their custom. He gave her the choicest pieces. When she had eaten enough, she took the empty flask and went into the trees and down to the creek for water and came back with a basket of berries she had picked earlier and cooled in the creek. She offered them first to Raven, who thanked her and took his share. He felt her eyes on him while he ate them, but when he glanced she was intent over the fire, boiling water for tea. She shaved powder from a tea brick into hollowed gourds, then poured in boiling water. Houston allowed his hands to touch hers as he took the gourd from her, but still she would not meet his eyes. The men drank tea and reminisced of the ball games and fishing on Hiwassee River, known to them as Long Man. More serious talk remained unsaid, with the understanding that the old intimacy must be restored before confidence could be given. James brought out a clay pipe and pouch of dry tobacco leaves, and they smoked together. Houston got his whittling knife from his saddlebags and carved on a chunk of hickory he cut from the tree where Tiana had taken branches. A silence fell.

"Why do you carve from hickory?" John asked in a voice turned suddenly harsh.

"Because it's a hardwood with a rich color."

"There are many such woods."

"The tree was close by," Houston answered defensively.

"There are many trees here. I believe it's because Jackson is called Old Hickory, and you are tied to him."

Houston stopped whittling and looked at him.

"That's a stupid thing to say," James said.

"President Jackson is a man of honor," Houston responded harshly. "He is not the one to blame for your troubles. He has only just been elected."

John stared at the fire and took a draw from the pipe.

James laughed, but without mirth, his face dark in the dimming firelight. "Come now, brother Raven, do you suggest that Jackson will now make all the past treaties good? Do you say he will treat with us in good faith? No. We have been told, 'As long as the water flows from the mountains, the Cherokee people will have this land.' And then we are removed. 'As long as the grass grows upon the earth, this land shall be yours.' And then we are again removed." His voice was harsh against night sounds, his face heavy through the smoke. He held the pipe idle. "We are spoken to as children, treated with as men and nations, talked of as bloodthirsty tyrants and driven from our land as slaves. I know your Jackson. I fought under him in battle. I have seen his eyes when he looks at us. He acts with bad faith."

Houston leaned forward, his whittling knife in one hand and the hickory chunk in the other, and spoke quietly, his eyes moving from John to James and back, once casting a glance at Tiana. "All of this I know," he said. "None of it do I deny. Except this: Jackson does not act in bad faith."

A horned owl called from the woods. Tiana, staring down at her hands in her lap, said softly, "Raven speaks as if he believes himself. But I think he's not sure." He stared at her. She stood to put more wood on the coals. Her heavy braid swung low, almost into the embers, and Sam instinctively leaned to push it back. Before he touched it, she lifted, saying with a cautious smile, "Tiana has spent many years over a fire and has not yet let it catch her hair." Then, for an instant, her eyes were on his. "Though she thanks Ka'lanu for his concern," she said.

Her eyes. Not her words, but her eyes: blue eyes in a dark face, a wounded look. Her voice was soft, neither taunting nor reproachful as the words might have seemed, but sincere. Her meanings were many, and Houston understood them. For years she had toiled and survived. She was a woman, alone, accepting of her lot without complaint, though she was grateful for Raven's concern. Ka'lanu, she had called him. Raven. In her own language. As she used to, in her gentle way. His heart reached out to her; he felt, meeting her eyes for the first time in over a decade, that she had stripped naked before him, revealing herself and her sorrows. She was not angry with him. She trusted him.

"Oo-loo-te-ka has a plan," James said.

Tiana took her eyes from Ka'lanu's and stirred the fire with a stick.

"Houston also has a plan," Sam said. "First tell me my father's."

Standing, James pulled from his shirt a small, flat canvas case. From it he took a parchment, unfolded it and held it up in the firelight. "Your father's own words, in my writing. I will translate so you can understand completely. The words are written to our brothers in the eastern Cherokee Nation, John Ross and his people. Oo-loo-te-ka says this"—holding the creased parchment before him he read haltingly, translating—"'I am now advanced in years and . . . have studied a great deal to find out a plan to save our people from . . . wasting and destruction. . . . We are now to be settled beyond all the settlements of white people, and there is no reason to fear that the whites will ever penetrate beyond us . . . in consequence of the grand prairie, unless they go beyond the Rocky Mountains. My plan is to have our brothers of the old nation remove to this country. If they wish to become independent, now is the time, and the only time. Let us unite and be one people and make a wall to the east which shall be no more trodden down or ever passed by whites. . . . Thus may we plan for our posterity for ages to come and for the scattered . . . remnants of other tribes. Instead of being remnants and scattered, we should become the United Tribes of America and preserve the sinking race of native Americans from extinction.' " James lowered the document to his side. "These are my uncle's words."

Houston said, "With whom does he propose this confederation?"

"With all native American tribes," James answered. "He is distressed that some among us want to make allies with Osage and then, aided by Creeks, Choctaws, Delawares and Shawnees, attack the Comanches and Pawnees and all the Indians westward to the plains. They would do this to get hunting grounds your government promised but did not give. Oo-loo-te-ka proposes peace among all natives, and unity, to make a home westward where whites cannot penetrate."

"Therefore," Houston said, "the treaty giving away your Arkansas land is of little consequence to Oo-loo-te-ka."

James nodded.

"And for what reason did he send you to me?"

"You can gain a hearing with Jackson. Jackson is the only man who can make good the broken promises. If he decides to. If he will assign us more land in the West, as he has said, good land, and pay the money owed to us, then it's possible Chief Ross will believe that Jackson treats in honest faith, and will remove. Our nation will be united. Other nations will follow."

And so. Sam Houston was not the only one planning empires and a home for the Cherokees in the West. He glanced at Tiana. Her face was in shadow. He looked to John, who sat cross-legged. James seated himself. Houston felt the time had come; the conversation had been leading to this as fruit ripening on the tree. There would be dissension, argument, as with any new proposal, but it must be put forth. "Houston says this," he pronounced slowly. "Texas is the place. It is fertile. It is vast. Oo-loo-te-ka should consider it the place."

Neither John nor James changed expression. A varmint moved in the brush, and Tiana turned her head toward the sound. Houston saw her profile, dark and Indian, the full lips parted as in surprise, her neck slightly thicker than in her youth. "The Mexicans will not give us land," John said at last. "Chief Bowl and his followers left Arkansas and crossed Red River into Tejas ten years ago, and still the Mexican government won't give title to his land."

Houston took up his knife again and resumed carving. "There are other ways to get title," he said.

John and James exchanged a look. "We don't want war," John said with a squint of his eyes.

"But you want land," Houston responded, not looking up. The breeze gusted; he saw from the corner of his eye how it moved across Tiana's hair. Hina, he used to call her. It was not a word or a name, only an endearment. "When a people fight for land, and so secure it, then it is more rightfully theirs than if it is given, or simply inhabited. It becomes theirs by blood right."

John stood up, shoving his hand toward the ground. "*This* land was ours by blood right. Tennessee. Georgia. Carolina. From the eastern slopes of Blue Ridge to the Mississippi River and from the Ohio south to Georgia. It is where our fathers lived and are buried. It is rightfully ours."

Raven gave him only a glance and continued to carve. At last he lifted his eyes and stilled his hands, saying, "Your land was taken. No matter how, it is no longer yours. Oo-loo-te-ka is right, you must secure a home out of reach of white men. He's right about this also: Ka'lanu will help you do it. He will speak with Jackson in your behalf and try to get your indemnities paid. He will meet with John Ross and attempt to win his trust and encourage removal. But also he has another plan. This." He stuck his knife in the dirt before him and set his eyes on it. "If there were a government established in the area of Texas and Coahuila, under influence of a man friendly to your cause, then . . ." He stopped and lifted his eyes. "Do you understand?"

"Explain," John said.

"With help from the Cherokees I can take Texas," Houston answered. "Already Chief Bowl has allied himself with the Shawano, Delaware, Kickapoo, Quapaw, Choctaw, Biloxi and remnants of other tribes wandered West. Chief Bowl won't get his land by applying to the Mexican government. And even if he did, that government is too unstable to guarantee it. He must fight. I will fight with him. And with you. The United States must secure a natural boundary—the Rio Grande. And the Indians must have a home. The answer to all is Texas—taken." He looked to James. "There is land enough in Texas for your Cherokee Nation, and for the United States."

John scrutinized him. James looked to John. "And what does Raven gain?" John asked in a whisper. "A country?" Houston did not answer, for here was a question with a thousand answers. "It cannot work," John added. "We would be no different from the Cherokees in Georgia. If Tejas is joined to the United States we would again be in her bounds."

Houston left a silence and then said, "You can move your people past the Rocky Mountains. You can move as far west as the Pacific Ocean, but still, some day, the United States will overtake you. Somewhere you must make a stand and fight. If you fight with Houston, he will be in a position to secure your rights. To set your boundaries and give title to your land—legal title—with his signature, written in perfect faith by a man who calls you brother."

John seated himself. "A sovereign nation within a sovereign nation?"

"Brother," Houston said, "I do not have every answer. But I do say, if you fight beside me for Texas and prove loyal to the United States, then it is more likely the United States would see you as allies, not as a threat to national security. There would, of course, be snags. But as men with true intentions, working for one cause, we could succeed."

"One cause?" John queried, blowing out smoke.

Houston was silent. At last he said, "Perhaps our causes are different. I suppose even my own causes are diverse, and I have varied intentions. But the solution for all is single: Texas."

"Too many times the whites have used us to fight their battles," John said. "And for this we have received no credit and no trust."

Houston stood, saying curtly, "It's not only the white man's battle, this struggle for land. It's not I who is without a home. And I don't ask you to go and fight for me. I ask you to fight with me. With the whites who will follow me. With Chief Bowl and his people who have no title to the land they cultivate. This is a cause in which red and white can fight together, under leadership of a man who has lived among both peoples and understands the needs of both."

John rose. "We are not an army," he said. "We are poor. We have no guns."

"Doesn't your new treaty provide for guns?"

James said, "It provides a rifle for every man residing now in Georgia who will remove to the new place."

"I can see they get them. I can see you get your seventy-five thousand dollars. Don't misunderstand; I'm not here to make a bargain. I could make better bargains with white men who have more to bargain with. I will speak to Jackson in your behalf no matter what your course in this. And likely I could defeat the Mexicans without your aid. But if you are amenable to help, even if you do no more than stand ready on the border and are never called upon, then I would have more support from whites in allotting you land. If I take the country, I won't govern alone. I won't dictate. I would need to convince the people that you deserved land, and this would be difficult if you had not fought for it." He paused. "Again, I may call on you for no more than to stand ready. But the people must feel you are on our side, or they will not perceive any justice in rewarding you with land."

John gave a slow blink. "Yes, justice," he said, *"Duyukduh.* It is something white men have heard of?" Houston met the sarcasm with a stare. "When do you plan this—fighting?" John asked in a lower voice.

"Soon."

"And what does your Jackson say?"

"He's not involved."

"Ah." John leaned his head back. "What do you say to this, brother James?" he asked, his eyes still on Raven's.

"I don't care for Jackson's involvement," James answered.

"And you, Tiana?" John asked.

She met Houston's eyes above the sinking flames. "Tiana trusts Ka'lanu. But not his people. Can he make promises?"

"No," Houston answered her. "I can promise nothing but to act in good faith toward you."

She smiled an ironic, almost imperceptible smile; he had betrayed her before, in more subtle ways. Then she lowered her head and did not speak. Raven's gelding snorted and shifted weight.

"We can talk more tomorrow," John said, and they sat in silence. Then Tiana rose, and moving to the supplies lifted blankets and began to lay them out.

Raven went to his saddlebags and with stealth took out his bottle of whiskey. He would never drink with an Indian, even a mixbreed, for he felt whiskey was a ruin to the race. He went into the woods to relieve himself, opened the bottle and took a drink, corked it, then turned to look through the trees at Tiana. She moved about the campfire, stooping to arrange blankets, lifting a stick to stir the embers, pausing a moment to watch the dying flames. What was she thinking? Of her husband? Her children? She cocked her head to the sound of a night bird and lifted her face to the new moon. She was beautiful. Restful. He felt a heat in his groin, and then a hand on his shoulder. He turned with a start. James was grinning in his old boyish way. "You scared the devil out of me," Raven said, furtively dropping the bottle in the undergrowth.

"You're watching my sister," James answered, his grin sliding to a smile. "She hasn't had a man since Gentry."

"You forget, brother; I'm married."

"I think you forget it," James answered with a glance at Houston's loins. "And I remember that my brother Raven has eager *wa'toli.*"

Houston gave him a playful smile, saying his *wa'toli* was not so eager as when he was a boy, and one woman was enough to satisfy it.

Again James cast a discerning look downward, amused. Then he lifted his eyes to Houston's and said seriously, "There is something I should tell you. I'm being paid to encourage John Ross to join us in the West. My family doesn't know. They would not approve. My feeling is if your government will pay me for what I would do without pay, and with good conscience, then I'm glad to dupe them. They have duped my people often enough. So I take their money, but I work for my people, not theirs."

Houston steadied his eyes on him. "I was also paid by the government for encouraging removal, and my reason in accepting pay was the same as yours." Their eyes held. "As were my reasons for urging removal."

James eyed him, then smiled. "It's good to have you back, brother," he said. "Tonight John spoke bitterly. But he doesn't blame you for our fate. When he speaks of you, he calls you Brother Raven."

"That pleases me," Houston said.

James answered, "Sleep well, my friend." He gestured toward the ground. "And you should leave the bottle where it is." With a warm look, after placing a hand momentarily on Houston's shoulder, he returned to the clearing and settled into the pallet Tiana had prepared.

Houston started to retrieve the bottle, decided not to, and walked down to Pond Creek, where he stood watching the water in moonlight, the turbulent junction of creek and river a few yards upstream. He took from his pocket a small heart he had carved from the hickory wood, fingered it, then removed the moccasins Tiana had made and studied them in a patch of light, the perfect seams and patterned red and yellow beads. Setting the moccasins aside, he untied his head scarf and draped it over a spicewood shrub. Then he stripped naked and sank his body into the cold waters, still holding the wooden heart. The moon was high and reflected on the water. It lit the treetops; the banks were dense with vegetation and shadowed. Frogs and insects sounded in rhythm, a steady pulse and throb, like the movement of making love. He wanted Tiana. He thought of Eliza and felt the old desire, but it seemed almost that the longing was for a person deceased. He wanted her, desperately, yet believed he would never have her and that in the end this would not change his fate. He would do what he intended to do, regardless. He would go to Texas. But then, there was the thought of leaving her, the hurt of it. Why could he not have her?

He lay his head back against the bank, his body underwater, and closed his eyes, trying to decide if he would go to Tiana. He recalled their erotic moments together, and decided not to resist her now. As he stood from the water, he saw her standing on the bank a few yards downstream, watching him. She did not move but studied his body in the shadows and at last spoke. "Tiana has taken no man since her husband," she said.

"Why does Tiana watch me?" he asked, feeling in his pulse how he wanted her.

She did not answer, but turned to a red cedar and began pulling away slender strands of shaggy bark.

He sat on a flat stone near his clothes in a spot of moonlight and wondered if her brothers had brought her for his sake—a temptress who could lure him back to them, capture his heart and his loyalty, or at the very least reestablish the old affinity. He did not care much. Betrayal and ambivalence were pervasive in life, and if he could gain a moment's comfort in this woman's arms, he would find it satisfying. "Tiana gathers cedar bark to burn and keep away spirits," he said.

She looked at him. "Yes, *anisgina*," she said. "Ghosts. Ka'lanu has not forgotten." Oddly, their addressing each other in the third tense did not make him feel removed from her, as if they spoke of other people, but instead stimulated the intimacy. It gave them a dignity and omnipotence that allowed them to explore their desire without hazard.

"There are many things he has not forgotten," he answered.

She was quiet, then said, "James says it's stupid to fear *anis-gina.*"

"I fear them," Raven said, and then, softly, "Hina?"

She let the cedar strips fall from her hands and turned and met his eyes. "Tiana also remembers many things." Lowering her eyelids she recited in slow but almost perfect diction,

> *"The Prince replies: 'Ah cease, divinely fair,*
> *Nor add reproaches to the wounds I bear*
> *There are not gods to favor us above;*
> *But let the business of our life be love.' "*

He smiled. " 'Want not'; it is 'There want not gods to favor us above.' "

Her brows lifted in a pleased expression. "Yes? True? And always Tiana has thought it was 'There are not gods'—it is something she learns tonight: the gods favor us." Softly she queried, "If you have me, again you will leave?"

He wanted her more, at that precarious instant, than any woman in the world. The sensation was liberating. "I would still have to go," he answered and stood, moving to her and holding out the wooden heart. She took it, examined it and smiled, the breeze casting leafy moon shadows over her face. "For Hina," he said and gently touched her hands, her arms, her breasts through doeskin.

Later, when he moved into her, he thought of Eliza, but only for a moment, and as of a person dead. The woman he made love with was Tiana, Hina, Diana—the goddess of the moon.

At daylight he woke to the sight of her, naked in Pond Creek, knee-deep, her wet hair loose and just reaching the water, her arms lifted in greetings to Grandmother Sun.

CHAPTER 24

April 7, 1829

He disliked what his wife had reduced him to, a sentinel of some base kind, like a vigilant animal protecting its kill. It would not have mattered now had she begged forgiveness and sworn that she loved him; he could not have believed her. She had never made him feel wanted.

And so, when he overheard the young messenger standing at the front desk in his worn, fawn-colored vest and muddy trousers, asking for Mrs. Houston "specifically," he believed the worst. His blood quickened. He no longer heard the genial talk of his friend John Anderson about the price of imported silk and the steady rain. His senses bore down on the young man with the voracity and distress of a soldier long awaiting a despised enemy and finally sighting him. He watched as the clerk, a balding gentleman by the name of Carter, offered to deliver the message to Mrs. Houston himself and then said, "But right there is the governor. Perhaps he can take it to her."

The young man turned toward him, clearly disconcerted. Houston refrained from reaching for the message; it would seem too eager. He could not allow himself this degrading, watchful posture, and willed his heart to slow. His introduction was cordial, "Sam Houston. You've a message for my wife?"

"Yes, sir. But . . ."

"I'll be happy to give it to her."

The man was at a loss. "No, well, I don't suppose it matters, but I was told to deliver it to her myself."

"Certainly. If that's the case, Mr. Carter can show you the way." He managed a casual nod and with effort resumed his conversation with Anderson. They had arranged to walk together to the courthouse for a meeting with General William Hall, Speaker of the House. He goaded himself to walk outside, into the rain and the muddy streets, before his determination began wearing at the edges and dissolving like the earthen streets in the onslaught of water, fallen in turbid pools around his feet, and he said to Anderson over the noise of the downpour, "I forgot some papers in my room. Tell Hall I'll be over directly," and turned back toward the inn.

He had never entered her room without knocking, but now his suspicion had taken root and flowered into something more than wariness; it had become almost a certainty. His fears would be validated when he opened her door, but there would be some comfort at least in knowing he had not been tricked. The prophecy fulfilled itself; she was seated on the edge of her bed nearest the door, in the dim light filtered through a gap in the draperies at the far side of the room, her mild and lovely face bent over a dampened parchment, the center part of her pale hair slightly jagged toward her forehead, as if she had not taken care with it. She lifted her face when he entered, and clutched the paper against her.

He did not bother with pretense or trivialities; his desire was to get it over with. "You have a message," he said, as if informing her of something she did not know.

Too long she hesitated, then, tucking the letter into her lap, said, "Yes, from my mother. One of the boys is ill." She said it knowing he would not believe it and hearing the contrivance in her voice and phrasing—"one of the boys"—as if Sam did not know their names.

He said, "For God's sake, haven't you deceived me enough without lying outright?"

She stared at him, his wet clothes clinging, his hair dripping, disheveled, thinning at the temples. "I've deceived you no more than you deceived me."

His voice was as passionless as rock. "At least I never pretended affection I didn't feel. You never cared for me. You've accused me of treating you like an image of some sort, and shutting you out of my plans, but the real dilemma was, you never wanted me. What I stood for, maybe, or what I had to offer. But not who I am."

"I don't know who you are," she said, watching him come toward her.

She suffered him to take the letter; it was plain he would take it by force if necessary. She feared he would read it aloud in his accusing voice, but he had the grace not to. He stared at it longer than was necessary, the light, airy hand in ink that had been dampened and smeared slightly from passage in the rain:

I need to see you. Please come to Hadley's boarding house on Water street. I will wait in room #4.

                                                    W.T.

He looked at her. "You won't go," he said, and carrying the letter with him like a laurel of victory, he crossed the room to the door that joined his own room, passed through, and locked it behind him. She did not move, but sat anxious and wondering; he had never locked the door between them. In a moment she heard him again in the hallway, and then at her door; she heard the scraping sound of a key in that lock also.

Composed, quiet, her heart beating fearfully but her hands resting lightly in her lap, she accepted that he had locked her in. She had no key. He must know she would be too proud to call for help. It was manipulation of the most vulgar type, worse than artifice or duplicity. She would rather he had beat her.

When she heard him leave, she tested both locks and found them secure. She tried to manipulate them with a hairpin, but the attempt was worthless, and she returned to sit on the bed.

CHAPTER 25

The hardest thing for Will to accept was not that he was dying, but that he was changed. The idea that he would inherit his father's illness had settled in his mind shortly before his father's death; consumption was a family curse, and Will had never expected privilege.

The change was rapid. Even before he left for Missouri he had identified it by that ironic, half-amusing, half-terrifying, but accurate description, Galloping Consumption. The worst was the wasting to a token of his former self, his skin turning sallow and coarse, his breath sour, his eyes offensively protuberant, as if they wanted to escape his body. He, also, wanted rid of it all, as a reptile needs to shed the faded skin and renew itself. But there could be no renewal. At best, there could be only a sense of completion—which was why he needed to see Eliza.

Originally, he had planned simply to disappear into the West and never again see her. It would be a punishment for both of them. But when his anger dissipated, he had grown homesick and missed her and had written with good intentions, to put her mind at ease. In the letter he had wished her happiness, and pretended to have accomplished it himself.

And then, at last, he had determined to travel the wretched miles and see her. There was barely enough money to get home. He thought of staying in Missouri and merely attempting to express himself in a letter to Eliza, but if it fell into the wrong hands, the scandal would be troublesome for her. Seeing her had even more risk, but he needed to see her. He fantasized that here in the end she might admit her folly and give affection with her genuine heart, but he did not really believe in the fantasy. He hoped for it. The painful journey by passenger coach back to Tennessee was for his sake, not for hers.

The rain was fortunate, serving as a protective cover when he pulled his single, meager bag from the coach; he slung his shabby coat over his head as a further guard from observation and got a room as the wet dawn crept in.

Watching through the spattered window, he waited. His view was of a narrow alleyway and the weather-beaten siding of a tannery; the smell from that place was noisome. But the room itself, though somewhat rank and dirty, was not inappropriate for a secret tryst: it was secluded. He had wanted to take a front room and watch for Eliza through the rain; even with her face hidden by the curve of a cape's hood he would know her singular demeanor, that rare and perfect bearing that suggested eminence. But they needed privacy.

The knock at the door startled him; he had not thought she would come so quickly. He smoothed his hair and looked at himself in the dresser mirror. The birthmark on his jaw seemed a deeper hue in his sullen face. His appearance was a constant and offensive reminder of his misfortune.

Without troubling himself further he opened the door and saw Sam Houston standing there with the collar of his greatcoat pulled up to his ears. Before Will could adjust his thinking, the governor said, "She is not coming," and shoved Will's letter toward him, sodden now with rain.

Sam was moving on impulse, on sheer emotion; he had never felt such hatred. "We'll fight on any terms you choose," he said, knowing what it would mean. If he shot the man, he would have to surrender his career or acknowledge publicly why he had done it: Will Tyree had seduced his wife. Admitting that he, Sam Houston, had played the cuckold would be humiliating. But humiliation was irrelevant, his career was irrelevant, it almost seemed his future was irrelevant. What mattered was revenge. Then through his fury came the sudden, astonishing perception: this man was very ill.

Tyree said, "I'm not interested in fighting. She's your wife. I know that. I wouldn't violate that. I just want to see her once; I have to tell her something."

Houston was at a loss for only an instant, then recovered himself. He could play this game. Perhaps the best revenge had nothing to do with murder. And if Tyree was as sickly as he seemed, murder would have limited satisfactions. He answered, "Even if I allowed it, she wouldn't see you. She showed me this, and asked me to tell you she's not coming." He crumpled the letter and dropped it at Will's feet. "She said she regrets knowing you." He thought as he said the lie, that it would grant him some measure of satisfaction, that to see the look on this man's face when he heard those words would be as gratifying as extracting a wicked thorn—the soreness would remain, but the source of it would be made impotent, a mere sliver that had wedged itself effectively but now could be tossed aside. But he did not feel anything akin to satisfaction. The young man, Will Tyree, was sufficiently hurt—if he was attempting to hide his pain, he was making a bad job of it. His lips parted slightly like a wound gouged deep into the pink and vulnerable parts, a birthmark resembling blood smoothed downward from the wound.

Tyree said, "I don't believe she regrets knowing me."

Houston stared at him without answering.

"What did she tell you?"

They were provoking each other, painfully, and each hurting himself, studying the other with a masochistic fascination. Sam answered, his words coming more easily than he expected, "She told me you took her. Before I married her." He encountered a slight hope that the man, with his pathetic face, would deny it, but Will only nodded, wondering why she had betrayed their intimacy. He had thought their secret was intact, that at least the secret was unviolated.

He asked, "Did you force her to tell you?"

Houston knew the man's agony. It was like his own, sprung from the same roots and nurtured in a despondent mind. He answered with unexpected and unwelcome empathy, "No. She wanted to hurt me." For Houston, it was a concession.

But for Tyree, it was the worst possible answer: Eliza had used his affection simply to antagonize another man. "Ah," he said, his lips turned downward at one corner in a derisive, bitter smile.

That he had known her body was a bludgeon to Houston's pride; that he loved her was a deeper wound. But he accepted it: this man had been intimate with his wife. In a voice that was only a whisper, looking into Will's tired eyes, he asked without planning to, "Do you think she loved you?" and then regretted asking.

Their eyes held on to each other's. "No," Tyree said, "I never felt that," and despised himself for saying it, despised Houston for eliciting it from him. He had admitted it before, had even so accused Eliza on their last parting, but in Missouri he had told himself it wasn't so and developed his last and most coveted delusion: that once, she had truly wanted him. In a single, purging sentence he said, "I never satisfied her." His words were a gift to the living—to Sam Houston—and they were also the completion he was seeking. He had not thought to find it this way. He said, "Still, I would like to see her. Just once."

Houston hesitated, studying him, and Will bore his scrutiny without remark. The man was dying; Houston suspected it but did not ask for confirmation. Despite the meager salve of Will's admission, Sam did not believe she had not loved him. It was easy to see why she had: he was honest and unpretentious and lacked the governor's affectations. "Many times," she had said. "I made love with Will Tyree many times." He looked at Tyree's mouth, the lips that a moment before had appeared like an open wound, and imagined them sucking gently on her tender nipples, furled possessively around them like a suckling babe's.

In a voice as perfectly cadenced as if he were delivering a practiced speech to his constituents, he said, "It is not possible. She will not receive you. If you meet by accident she will likely feign not to know you. You would oblige us all, yourself included, if you would simply stay away." He paused, then added impulsively, "If it's any comfort, she doesn't love me either."

Tyree made no attempt to answer. Someone was coming down the hall. Outside, a wagon clattered through the alleyway, its wheels spattering mud onto the window, then the wind gusted and a sheet of rain washed the panes clean. Houston turned and left Will standing in the doorway.

CHAPTER 26

When Dilsey knocked on Eliza's door, balancing a tray with the noontime meal of cornbread and venison against her hip, Eliza said mildly, "It's locked. I don't have a key." She made no further explanation.

Dilsey set the tray on the floor and went downstairs for an extra key; she returned to find Eliza sitting on the edge of the bed with her hands in her lap, plucking aimlessly at the folds of her gingham skirt. Immediately she stood, and without bothering to knot or braid her hair, she put on her hooded cape and started out the door. Then she turned to Dilsey and said, "It's better if you don't know where I'm going."

She went directly to the boardinghouse. She did not care if she was seen. Nothing mattered but that she get to Will. He seemed her only hope. He had loved her; he still wanted her. At this moment, the reasons why she had let him go were of no consequence; the only essential thing was that with him she had at least retained some comfort with herself, some control and integrity. In too many ways she had not loved him. But she had been loved. That was a start; she could learn the rest. He needed her. What it would lead to, she didn't try to speculate. Mostly, she wanted him to comfort her. For too long she had been harboring herself; she felt unequal to the task. She needed someone.

There was no answer to her knock at his door, and she pushed at the knob, calling his name, not caring if someone overheard her. But there was no answer. At the front desk she asked for a key and was told the room was unoccupied, that Mr. Tyree had left an hour ago. He had not stabled a horse and must have gone by coach.

The stagecoach office adjoined the Nashville Inn; Eliza retraced her steps through the rain. She had abandoned all sense of discretion and made her way as if she felt herself invisible, not speculating where Sam had gone or if she would be recognized. She was greeted once in the street and responded with only a nod. At the office she found that Will had left an hour ago on the northbound coach to Kentucky but had purchased a ticket just as far as Tyree Springs. He was going home. She bought a ticket to the Springs and returned to her room to wait.

She suspected Sam had gone to see him at the boardinghouse. Whatever he had said or done had caused Will to abandon her. Resentment rose with an acrid taste in her mouth. She moved about the room in small jerky movements, touching the dresser, the mirror, the bed, not denying her need to hold on to something, but finding nothing to take hold of. She willed herself to be calm, and failed. She needed Will. She felt, suddenly, after a lifetime of consecutive, re-petitive endeavors toward retribution for, and mere tolerance of, her unhappiness, that Will might be an answer. If Sam returned and tried to prevent her from going, she would resist him, in whatever way was necessary. She would call for help.

The stage was late because of the rain. There were three other passengers, whom Eliza did not know. She took a seat near the window. The woman beside her was reading from a book with gilt-edged pages. A short distance out of Nashville, the woman asked suddenly, "Aren't you the governor's wife?"

Eliza answered, "I do not care to talk," and turned back to the window. The woman stared a moment and then resumed her reading. Across, a couple sat close together. The woman was with child, and the rocking of the stage was uncomfortable. She kept her hands pressed over her swollen belly. The floor of the coach was smeared with mud, and there were gaps between the boards beneath which the road could be seen in passing, a rocky sludge.

It was dusk when the coach neared Tyree Springs and crossed the narrow wooden bridge at the headwaters of Drake's Creek. The pavilion was dark beneath April foliage, but the stage office, a single cabin of notched logs, was lit. Outside at the hitchpost two horses were secured; Eliza recognized one as Willoughby Williams's, a dun gelding with a black back stripe. She had seen the horse often from her window at the inn, tethered at the courthouse hitchrail. She wondered now why Willoughby would be here, but had dismissed any anxiety that had to do with Sam or his discovering her journey. Sooner or later he would know. It made no difference if Willoughby was the one to tell him. She had honed her feelings to one desire: to find Will. With all her confusion and deliberations, she had come down to this one purpose. It was a defiance of Sam Houston, and of her father, and of all the constrictions she had endured, a way to prove she would not be locked in. And it was also a desperate bid for some human connection that would sustain her.

She supposed he had come to see his mother, who lived somewhere nearby, not far from the springs and the property boundary of the resort. He had described the place to her; a few scanty acres of farmed land, a cedar barn, and a frame house with a porch. She even knew the names of the livestock and the dog, but she did not know the direction. There was nothing to do but ask.

She was first out of the stage, and as she stepped into the office, her cape draped over her arm though the rain was still falling— lighter now, but persistent—she saw Willoughby standing in the lamplight near the desk. His back was turned to her, one fist pressed into his hip. The clerk was beside him, a smaller man with a pinched face and eyes with heavy lashes that he turned on her. He said soberly, "Ma'am, you'd better go back out." Behind her, the pregnant woman must also have entered, for he shifted his eyes and said, "And especially you. We got a fellow here who's had a accident. Hank there"—he nodded toward the driver, who had entered wanting respite from the rain—"can take you up to the main building."

It was then that Willoughby turned and saw her. He seemed puzzled and said, "Eliza." The other woman left with the driver. Her husband, who was at the door, turned and went with them. They failed to close the door completely; Eliza moved to shut it and noticed, curiously, that her hands had begun to quiver. She stood looking at Willoughby. He asked, "What are you doing here?"

"I'm looking for a friend. Will Tyree." Her whisper was no more than a breath. She kept her eyes on Willoughby, as if for security.

Looking to the clerk, then at a sheet of paper that lay on the desk beneath the light, he said, "Eliza, I need to take you home."

She shook her head. Only then did she bring herself to take her eyes from him and look directly at the body. It had been there at Willoughby's feet in plain view, lying near the desk of dark-grained wood, the face turned away, but until now she had denied its presence—an intrusion on her mission and her peace like the falling rain that would neither let up nor increase but persisted in its fall. She saw the birthmark. She knew that he was dead. She had known him at once. She thought how odd it was to recognize the dead by a mark given at birth. An imperfection. A blot like an uneradicable taint of sin. She had read that before: "This hard decree / This uneradicable taint of sin." She said, "I know who he is." Willoughby moved toward her, but she lifted a hand to stop him. She said, "Why is he dead."

After a silence the clerk answered, "Shot himself. In the road over by the bluff. Left a note penned on him sayin' to bury him here by his pa. You know his family?"

She had not noticed the blood. She had not allowed herself to. She could know him, and know that he was dead, but she could not permit herself to think how he must have stood in the center of the road so his body would be found, and unbraided his queue of hair, and held the gun with his arm cocked upward, a perfect wound to his temple. She wondered: why had he undone his hair? She felt everything was falling away; she was losing herself. She had been so eager to reach him—for her own sake. She had wanted him to hold her. She had not thought of holding and comforting him, or con- cerned herself with why he needed her. She steadied against the door. He disliked drama; why had he chosen to die this way? For her? She could not believe that. No one could love her enough to die for her. She had never even believed that Christ had done that—and now Will, imperfect with his mark—Will could not have loved her enough for that. What had Sam told him? What had Sam done?

"Do you know his family, ma'am?" the clerk repeated.

Willoughby had come to her and put an arm around her; he was turning her away so she could no longer see the body. He was muddy and smelled dank. There was water in his beard. She whis- pered, "I want to see him."

"No, Eliza. Where is Sam?"

"I want to see him."

"I'll send someone to get him."

"I want to see Will."

"He's dead, Eliza. How do you know him?"

She pulled away; this was Sam's friend, trying to comfort her. She wanted nothing to do with him. For a moment she stood looking at the body like a serene and stoic critic. He had made love with her as if with each thrust inside her, he was producing the tangible substance of it. And she had not received it. She had taken it against her belly and against her throat, between her breasts, but never within. She had been as inept at receiving love as at giving it.

With a sudden cry like a small, tormented animal, she crossed to Will's body and crouched over him on all fours with her head against his chest. He was wet with rain and mud. She felt for the wound; his hair clung damp around it. Willoughby said, "Eliza, no—" The ball had made a perfect mark on entry, but on the other side the skull was ruptured. She pressed her finger further in, feeling the bullet's path, stroking with her other hand the crushed bone where the ball had gone free and crying now without restraint, the noise ugly and foreign, as if someone else were crying. The sound, the finger reaching deeper into the wound, the face she pressed against him seemed detached from her, but the grief was her own. She felt it infiltrating and could not separate from it; she harbored it. When Willoughby pulled her away and cradled her she found no refuge in his arms. She saw the clerk watching her with loathsome eyes, the flame from the oil lamp, and Will beside her with his face turned away. Steadily the rain beat on the tin roof; the noise seemed to be quickening and closing in, as if to mute her cries and diminish their significance. Again she reached for the wound, and Willoughby cupped her bloody hands in his and would not let her touch it.

CHAPTER

27

Dilsey was satisfied with her efforts. Bearing news of such significance had its glory. She had snitched her ticket money from the registration desk at the inn and taken a coach as far as Hendersonville, a post town with one store and a stage office. From there, she went on foot through the rain toward the log home of Colonel Dry Saunders, whistling a tune she had learned at a camp meeting, about an Amazing Grace. It was indeed amazing to stroll down the lane like a free white woman, her shawl and calico dress soaked clear through, the creek running beside her, busy with the rain.

She made Dry wheedle the information out of her, withholding the particulars as long as possible; once she had told all, then Dry would take over, and her importance in the affair would dissipate. There was no telling what he would do. She wanted to play her part well, with an integrity she had never experienced by simply doing as she was told. She was acting on her own judgment and savoring it. And there was revenge in that.

There wasn't much she could tell, but it was enough to get Dry's solid attention. She told that the governor had locked Eliza in her room that morning and that as soon as Dilsey had unlocked the door, Eliza had gone out, without telling where to. She said that previous to this Eliza had seemed unhappy and that the door which adjoined her room to the governor's was always closed. And then she put forth the most heady information of all: on the night after their return from Charles's funeral, the governor had created some ruckus in his room. The room Dilsey shared with various itinerant servants was directly below; she had heard the noise and gone up to check on Eliza. She had overheard Eliza and Sam Houston fighting. He had accused her of being with another man. Dilsey would not have told this had she not been enjoying her role as informant. Yet she drew the line; she did not say that Eliza had admitted her indiscretion. She was, in fact, uncertain that Eliza had admitted it, for she had heard only fragments as the voices rose and fell.

Polly counseled restraint. She wanted to talk with Eliza. But Dry was avid for action. "She's my daughter's daughter," he said, "and that gives me a duty." He saddled up his mount and set out for Allendale with his yellow dog loping behind him, leaving Polly standing in the rain with her jaw clenched and Dilsey wondering if she had been right to come here. Perhaps she should have gone to Colonel Allen, but she had been too afraid. At least Old Dry, with his religious ways, had never owned a slave or ordered one to be whipped. He had a small, homely face under a mound of gray hair, a hooked nose and a discerning, unpleasant expression, yet his looks had a certain hint of kindness, like a house with all the doors shut but the firelight creeping out. And he was known for his omnipotent sense of justice; he grew no cotton, since he owned no slaves, and no tobacco, since it was wicked.

She decided she had done the right thing and accepted Polly's offer of tea, and money for the travel, then started on her journey back to Nashville.

"Thou shalt not," Colonel Dry said, slamming his fist down on John Allen's walnut desktop, "bear false witness against thy neighbor!" He was not getting the response he wanted.

"I would thank you," Allen said between his teeth, "to lower your voice before Laetitia hears you." He frowned at Dry's mangy, wet dog that had come in with his master as if by right and flopped on the rug in a pant. The dog went everywhere with Dry.

"Well maybe Laetitia could make you come to your senses." Dry shot his eyes at young George Allen, who stood with his arms crossed over his chest—a copy of his father, but taller. George was riled, Dry could tell by the way the boy's mouth had gone tight, but that youngster usually followed his father's example, which in the present case was too cryptic to please Dry Saunders. To Dry it seemed that John Allen, sitting there behind his desk, looking through thick lids, was as cool as a salamander in the bog. "If Houston has accused your daughter unjustly," he went on, "—and if he has accused her of indiscretion then it is unjust—then he's borne false witness against her, and against her family, and he must either withdraw the charge publicly or face consequences like any other man."

"As far as I know," Allen said, "the governor hasn't made any accusations publicly."

Dry responded with scorn. "As far as you knew, your daughter was still enjoying her honeymoon bliss! And you don't even know where she is!"

Allen remained still. He respected his father-in-law, but the old man was acting hastily. Eliza wasn't the type for an easy marriage; in fact, he had been glad to see her marry someone as arrogant and hardheaded as herself. With all his bafflement about his daughter— who she was and how on God's earth she got to be that way—John Allen had always understood this one thing: Eliza was devoted to herself, as the governor was to himself. It seemed a fitting match, though destined to the usual clash between self-centered individuals. "Dilsey's always been prone to exaggerate and stir things up," he said. "Eliza likely just went out for a ride, or to visit someone. I'm not worried about where she is at the moment. She can look out for herself until we get to the root of this other thing—these accusations —and see if something needs to be done."

Dry lifted one calloused palm, his voice incredulous. "See if something needs to be done? My good man, your daughter's husband has accused her of infidelity, and you want to sit back and wait and 'see if something needs to be done'? In my time, an insult like this—to the family name—called for something considerably more effective than waiting to see if something needed to be done!"

Saunders's gray eyes, like hard pebbles beneath the matted eyebrows, bore down on his son-in-law. John Allen sat watching the eyes, thinking of another pair of gray eyes that had confronted him over this desk: lovely, angry, feminine eyes. He glanced away, out the window at spring fields; the corn was coming in, just tufts here and there. The rain had stopped completely. Patches of evening sun shone across the new green and the tulip poplars. "Give it some time," he said.

"Time!" Dry spat the word out. "I dare say if your daughter were married to anyone less noted than the governor, you would not need time."

"Now that's going too far," Allen said, standing. He leaned forward, his hands pressing onto the desk, his elbows rigid. "It's true, I think a great deal of Sam Houston. You yourself have been his friend and supported him for years. I don't believe he would make such an accusation without some perceived basis. If he ever did make it. I'm inclined to think the whole thing's just a misunderstanding, or something that nigger Dilsey dreamed up. But if Houston did accuse my daughter, it's because he was mistaken—deceived somehow—and if that's the case, he'll come to his senses, and likely Eliza will forgive him. If you and I step in now, we'll only make things worse. I'm not averse to taking action, and of course I'll clear my daughter's name if it needs clearing. But I intend to move slowly, with a mind to smoothing the whole thing over. I ask you to comply. Sir."

Dry glanced at George; the boy met him face on. The old colonel turned with agility notable for his age, walked the length of the room and back, and said, "All right." He forced a smile and softened his voice. "I suppose I'm too strict a moralist, and you're a realist, John. Not that I think I'm wrong, it's just the old Methodist firebrand in me. I guess a little caution won't make things any worse."

Allen sat down. He was suddenly feeling less cautious. "I'll send George with a letter," he said. "We'll give Houston a chance to clear this up. And that will give Eliza time to come to her senses." He leaned back, then his frustration broke free and he thrust his hand into the air. "Damn that girl! Walking out like that—for whatever reason—without telling where she was going. If he locked her in, he's at fault, but she's taken her sense of righteousness too far—she has a keener sense of it than God Himself!" He tilted his head back, his eyelids closing down on Old Dry and his hand shoved toward him. "She must have got it from you, Colonel; she got it from you."

CHAPTER 28

April 9

Evening spread over the public square. Houston was in his office, leaning back in his spindle-back chair and gazing out the open window. He was drunk. His feet, in the beaded moccasins Tiana had given him, were propped up on the sill. The sun had already gone down, sinking below shingled rooftops on College Street, moving down in the west over the road to the Natchez Trace. And with it, his hopes sank.

"Goddamn it," he said aloud, his voice harsh in descending darkness, and took a pull at his bottle. A dray pulled by mules toiled in the street below; a carriage left from the inn. Eliza's curtains, across the way, were drawn snugly together. The plank floor beneath him eased and settled, as if even the earth were shifting; there was no steadiness in life, nothing solid, no rest, no permanence. Life was all a sort of drifting. And here he was at thirty-six, and he had found no meaning, not even a safe place to go home to. Here he sat in the same office, with the paint still peeling off the walls and the sun sinking into the west, pulling blackness over everything and leaving him alone.

There was nothing for him here but a few good friends. The woman, he had never had. That much was clear. She had wounded him, bound his heart with the spider's web and *uhi'sodi,* "terrible loneliness and desire." He should not have called on the black spider in the Cherokee bonding ritual that night at the Martins' home; an old shaman had warned him long ago that the spider is too powerful a spirit and can turn on a person and bind his heart rather than his beloved's. But he had been desperate to have her.

Turning in his chair, he took a letter from his desk, held it up to the blue evening light and read it once more. The script was a blur; he squinted to make it out.

Dear Sir,

I have been informed by the servant girl that you have ques-tioned my daughter's virtue. I request to know if this is so. If I hear nothing from you I shall assume it is true that you accused Eliza without justification, and I shall come and get her.

John Allen, Esquire

Sam was not surprised to learn that Dilsey had played the stool pigeon. She was smart and no doubt had her motives. He did not particularly care what those motives were, but the consequences were weighty.

It was a feisty letter, he thought, to be composed by a man too craven to face him in person. Allen had sent his son George to deliver the letter to Houston's secretary. John Allen lacked his daughter's courage; whatever her faults, she was not afraid of con-frontation. She had fortitude. He glanced out the window at her drawn curtains. Damn her, she was as hard as his mother. Why did he love her so?

Even now, in her state of despondency, she retained a solemnity he admired. It troubled him. He wished she would resort to accusations or tears. Willoughby had brought her home to the inn in the hours before dawn on the previous day. Sam had been frantic with anxiety, thinking—though he was loathe to admit it now—that she had run off with Will Tyree. That Tyree himself was the one who had prevented that was a bitter piece of news; he had shot himself. And Eliza, no doubt, blamed herself. Or blamed Sam Houston. Whatever emotions she carried, she carried them in silence. He had disclosed to her everything about his encounter with Tyree; he had been honest. He had admitted that his jealousy had caused him to be rash, yet he had not accepted responsibility for Tyree's death. He told her Tyree was ill; he, Sam Houston, had been selfish enough to deny the request of a dying man, but he had not in any way caused the death. If she wanted to assume that burden of sin, she could do so. He would not.

She had sat huddled on the bed wrapped in a blanket, her eyes an unblinking glint in the darkness. Willoughby had stood beside the bed like her protector, and Sam had begged forgiveness. At last she had said quietly, "I believe you. I believe he was dying. His father died of consumption. But I will never forgive you for shutting me away from him." And that was the last she had spoken.

Later, Sam had asked Willoughby outright if Eliza had cried when she saw the body, and Willoughby had said, "Yes, she cried," and left it at that.

He could almost hate her for that. He could almost turn his grief to anger. That she, whom he had never known to weep, had wept for this other man, seemed the last and most brutal perfidy.

Her power was despotic. She had reduced his manhood, and could now destroy his future. If she left him now, no doubt the public would view her as an innocent female, wronged in some way by an ambitious and egocentric husband. She would be mute about the cause of abandonment—that would be inherent to her nature, and to her interest. And he could not defend himself with the truth, for he had his standards. Even if he allowed himself to speak ill of his wife, publicly—as he had never allowed himself to do of his mother —Jackson would damn him for it. In Andrew Jackson's book, the one unpardonable offense was assaulting a woman's virtue. Guilt or innocence on her part was irrelevant. "I never war against women," Jackson had raved when Duff Green printed gossip about Mrs. Adams, "and it is only the base and cowardly who do." Old Hickory was ruthless, even to friends, when it came to defending women. He had honed his skills with Rachel and now championed Peggy O'Neal Timberlake Eaton, War Secretary John Eaton's wife. Houston had taken Peggy to bed more than once when he was in Washington, before she married Eaton. In his estimation she had the morals of an alley cat. She sapped the President's energies by calling on him to defend her name, which she herself had hauled up and down Washington streets in the mud. Emily Donelson was threatening to leave the Presidential Mansion and go home to Tennessee if the President continued to receive Peggy Eaton with other cabinet wives. A.J. said he would go with his wife. The entire Cabinet and Washington society sided against the old man. If Jackson could defend a tramp like Peggy Eaton, he would despise even a friend for turning on his own wife. If Eliza left, Houston had only two choices: to assume blame for the separation or to justify himself by condemning her, which in Jackson's mind would make him a base coward. Cursed alternatives.

Actually, there was a third choice. He could leave now. Just walk out. Take a steamboat west to Cherokee Territory and position himself near Texas. But the President had put his faith in him and left Tennessee under his guidance. "Take care of Tennessee, Sam," he had said. "Don't leave it in Billy Carroll's hands. I don't trust him anymore." Jackson asked a lot. He was a master at seeing a man's qualities and using them, but had no scruples about sacrificing good men who did not measure up. If Houston abandoned his post, Carroll would be elected unopposed and Jackson would lose confidence in Houston. He had to stick out the campaign. Unless . . . unless

Eliza left him before election day. Then, the news would get out, and Billy Carroll would use it to his advantage. Aspersion would follow; Houston might lose the election. And that would be worse: to go West defeated, spurned by his wife and his people. Already his family shunned him. How could he go to Texas as a conqueror if his constituents also turned him out? McGregor had said his support was a mile wide and an inch deep. "One day in the heat can dry up a puddle like that."

He had to go through with it, and win. Then, if he resigned, Speaker of the House William Hall would succeed him as governor. Billy Carroll would be without position. Houston could leave Tennessee and keep Jackson's trust. He would not defend himself against anything Eliza chose to say, but likely she would say nothing. Regardless, scandalmongers would believe the worst.

But . . . if she did not leave him? Then he would leave her after the election. He could not live with a woman who did not love him. He would resign without the slightest noise, leaving the world in darkness as to the cause and all things connected with the whole matter. But first, he must smooth John Allen's blistering ego and convince Eliza to stay until the election was over. Somehow. And he must master his own despondency and put heart into his campaign —a rational plan, he thought, for a man so downhearted and intoxicated he could hardly focus his eyes.

He lit the desk lamp and took up his eagle-quill pen. If John Allen wanted to avoid confrontation, so be it. He would respond in writing and send someone to deliver the letter—whatever the man wanted, anything to pacify him for a time. Houston held the pen poised and thought, smelling the foul stench of whale oil burning in the lamp. The conveyance must be truthful, but only partially so. He would explain why he had questioned her virtue but say he was mistaken. He would make clear the charges had been made privately, in a mood of genuine despair, and were now regretted and withdrawn. He would state that he had made no accusations publicly; Dr. Shelby was the only one to whom he had disclosed his doubts, and that was Eliza's own doing. It was she who had brought Doc into it.

He must keep in mind that John Allen had conflicts of his own with
Eliza, and for that matter with Will Tyree. Allen was an ambitious
man clearly pleased to have married his daughter off to the governor
of Tennessee. He would be eager to dismiss the entire business as a
trifling spat. But he was proud, and if convinced his daughter had
been wronged, he was apt to create a real affair in the name of family
pride. And then, Old Dry was certain to get involved. Pious old son
of a bitch; he had gotten his name from denouncing alcohol. Dry
was a man of honor—family honor most of all—and fond of Eliza.

Houston dipped his quill in the stone inkwell and put it to a
fresh piece of paper.

9 April 1829

*Mr. Allen The most unpleasant & unhappy circumstance
has just taken place in the family, and one that was entirely
unnecessary at this time. Whatever had been my feelings or
opinions in relation to Eliza at one time, I have been satisfied & it is now unfit that anything should be averted to.
Eliza will do me the justice to say that she believes I was
really unhappy That I was satisfied & believed her virtuous,
I had assured her on last night and this morning. This
should have prevented the facts ever coming to your knowledge, & that of Mrs. Allen. I would not for millions it had
ever been known to you.*

Satisfied— it was an odd word, its meaning in this context nebulous,
as he intended. He was, indeed, satisfied in a way—satisfied as to the
course he would pursue: the campaign, the election, a quiet resignation and a steamboat west. He was not satisfied of her purity; she had
admitted her guilt. But let the statement stand. She, too, could make
her accusations. He continued,

*But one human being knew anything of it from me, & that
was by Eliza's consent & wish. I would have perished first,*

& if mortal man had dared to charge my wife or say ought against her virtue I would have slain him. That I have & do love Eliza none can doubt,—that she is the only earthly object dear to me God will witness.

He set down the pen, watching yellow lamplight flicker across the page. Music drifted up from the bar at the inn, a bawdy tune. He did love her. Perhaps things were not past mending. If she could just forgive him for his jealous rage, his denial of Tyree's last request, his . . . But how could she? For that, he could not even forgive himself. He could justify himself: Tyree had no right to call on her. But he could not forgive himself. Again he bent over the paper.

The only way this matter can now be overcome will be for us all to meet as tho it had never occured, & this will keep the world, as it should ever be, ignorant that such thoughts ever were. Eliza stands acquitted by me. I have received her as a virtuous wife, & as such I pray God I may ever regard her, & trust I ever shall.

He leaned back, then forward again and reread his words. They moved seductively on the page, and there was a lack of punctuation, as if he wrote as he would speak, with a slur. But this was petty. There were greater inadequacies. He needed an expiation, a vindication, a reason for his accusations, but not the true reason—not her guilt. He hated this impotent feeling of not defending his honor. He wanted to toss away the pen and shout from the window at her vile curtains in the window across the street.

She was cold to me, and I thought did not love me. She owns that such was one cause of my unhappiness. You can judge how unhappy I was to think I was united to a woman that did not love me. This time is now past . . .

Now there was a lie. But Allen would demand such a declaration. And perhaps Eliza would read it and be swayed. . . . No, Eliza was never swayed.

> . . . *& my future happiness can only exist in the assurance that Eliza and myself can be happy & Mrs. Allen and you can forget the past,—forgive all & find your lost peace & you may rest assured that nothing on my part shall be wanting to restore it. Let me know what is to be done*
>
> Sam Houston

Reading the words once more, he folded the paper, put it into an envelope, then heated sealing wax and dripped it onto the fold. He took up the governor's seal, almost applied it, and set it aside. This was a private matter and should remain so. With a smudge of his thumb he sealed the wax and sat looking down at it, an orange oblong blot on a white envelope. What if she left him? Now? What if this very minute she was packing her things to go? He felt the web tightening its hold and stood to catch his breath. The night air was cool. He could not let her ruin him. A wounded heart was one thing, a broken man was another. He snuffed the lamp and left his office in darkness. Tomorrow he would have the letter delivered. Halfway down the stairs, he remembered the Masons were meeting tonight. A man had to carry on. He turned outside down Union Street, his moccasins padding soundlessly in the street toward the Masonic Lodge.

CHAPTER

29

In the first hours after her return to the inn, Eliza had abandoned herself to an onslaught of emotions so varied that she felt she would never again have any sensation as solid and simple as grief. She dared not speak, for fear some unknown demon would breathe itself from her throat in a voice she did not recognize. There was no solace in familiar surroundings—the crisp sheets of her bed or the washstand in the corner. She refused comfort of any kind. She did not wash and would not allow Dilsey to brush her hair. Dilsey told her she had gone for help, but Eliza did not care: they could come and get her or leave her where she was. She had retreated into herself, and the forces outside had no effect. She felt she could live without food or stimulation of any kind; she could feed off her emotions, sit placidly and consume herself. She tormented herself with memories of Will. When Sam Houston knocked she did not answer. She turned Willoughby away from her door, and she asked Dilsey to leave her alone.

On the second day her feelings wound themselves into a single knot of despair, and she needed someone. She said aloud, "Papa will come for me," and washed herself and waited.

But on the day following, still he did not come, and she resorted to her own strength. Without notifying anyone, she left her room, went down the back way to the stable and requested that her horse be saddled. Then she set out for home.

Mostly, she traveled at a walk, oblivious to spring. It was night when she reached Allendale. Her father's library was lit, and she stood outside looking in at him. He was seated at his desk, neither reading nor writing, but staring across as if someone were sitting opposite speaking to him. Yet there was no one there. She was about to go in to him when suddenly he stood and walked to the front hall and then came outside and turned away from her toward the stables. She said, "Papa."

He turned and saw her there beside the window, the light from inside shining on her. He was quiet, and then said, "I was leaving to get you."

It would be an act of faith to believe him, and Eliza had always thought faith was too tenuous to sustain her. Yet she wanted to believe.

"Are you all right?" he asked.

She said, "I needed you."

He moved a few steps toward her. He was close enough to touch her but did not. There was no breeze, yet the night was cool and full of sound. Fireflies pulsed in the darkness. She thought, he will ask me to explain. And she could not bear the idea of trying to justify herself with details that no longer had relevance. Will was dead, and she had lost all hope for her union with Sam Houston. The only thing on which she could now depend was her chaotic emotion. She might even find some redemption through it. And she would need redemption. But, she thought, she would never find happiness. Perhaps at moments in the future, she would attain joy, but not essential peace. The only way she would ever encounter peace would be to surrender her turmoil, and she had grown dependent on that. She realized, looking at her father standing there, that turmoil was the one abiding force in her life.

And she made a small step toward him. "I won't go back to him," she said.

"Did he abuse you?"

She shook her head. "I don't believe you were coming for me," she said, wanting him to assure her that he was.

He answered, "Believe what you want to. You always have."

She was weary enough that she might have wept and been pitiful, if it would have won him. But she had tried that as a child; she had thrown herself at him in frequent outbursts. Once, when he was going into town, she had wailed fretfully and begged him to take her with him. Her mother had stood by, meek and ineffectual, no doubt wishing her husband would give more attention to the child, and John Allen had said blandly, "When you learn to act like an adult, you can go with me." Eliza had whimpered and thrown her tiny fist up and hit him in the ribs.

But she had put her mind to learning. Before she was six, she had assumed adult airs and stopped crying altogether.

The colonel added, "Anyway, that isn't the issue. The issue here is Sam Houston."

"Yes," she answered. "The issue is Sam Houston. Not Eliza, or Eliza's future, not even Eliza's marriage, but Sam Houston. You would see it that way."

In the window's light she saw him give a slow blink of disgust. He said, "God," closing his lips around the word as if he would not speak again. But then he added, "Does Tyree have anything to do with this? Or did Houston accuse you falsely?"

She wanted to ask him why he would not simply trust her judgment, but felt he would respond with indifference. He would not accept her on her own terms. And even depleted as she was, she would not give in to his. In a voice as firm and sure as if the outcome could not in any way affect her, she answered, "Will Tyree is dead.

He shot himself. You needn't blame yourself. I doubt he did it because of you, or me either. Of course, we will never be sure of that." She paused, adding, "And Sam's accusations don't matter anymore. I won't explain any more than that. If you don't want me here, I'll go to Uncle Robert's. I doubt he would turn me away." With the last statement, she was playing on his weakness, his own sense of inadequacy. Robert had always surpassed him in generosity, and had a fondness for Eliza. She could damage her father this way, as he had damaged her.

But she chose instead, with trepidation, another gesture toward him. "I wanted to please you," she said steadily. "I tried to hate you because I couldn't please you. None of it does any good for either of us. I can't force you to care for me, but I hope you won't turn me out."

For so long he had hated Tyree, and now the boy was dead. He felt it as a gratuitous loss, a deprivation; toward whom would he direct his bitterness now? He responded defensively, "I do care for you," and stared at her, his arms still crossed, the fireflies flashing about him.

His words had come too late, and then too easily to satisfy her, and it was not this vapid declaration that caused her suddenly to step forward and wrap her arms around his neck. She would have done it had he said nothing at all. She moved in against him.

Awkwardly, thinking of Tyree, without spontaneity but with a sense of duty and conviction, he took hold of her. He did not know why he had never loved her enough. Perhaps she was too like him. Perhaps he had somehow made her that way, or she had chosen to fashion herself in his image, too intense when she was young, then, later, perverse and dissatisfied.

So, in spite of everything, there was a bond here. Neither said a word, nor made any sound at all; they just stood there holding each other in the light from the window. He was uncomfortable with the feel of her in his arms, yet he did not let go. She was, after all, his daughter; he should not fail her now. For him, it was no more than that.

CHAPTER

30

During the moment Eliza was in her father's arms for the first time since she could remember, Willoughby was doing his best to lift the governor from a morose temper, and failing. In the darkness he leaned forward in his saddle, running a hand over his mount's neck. He felt a small rise beneath the fur and picked off a blue tick. "What I'd say," he declared, "is that little puddle McGregor talked about just might wash Billy Carroll right out of Tennessee." He liked the metaphor and added, "Maybe flood the whole state. That crowd loved you." Sam did not respond, just rode silently beside him, and Willoughby thought of resorting to poetry, which is what Sam would have done. He didn't know any, so he tried something with a poetic sound to it. "You swayed those people like saplings in a blue norther."

But Houston was not impressed. He was slumped in his saddle, a different man from the one who had spent the day on the stump debating his opponent with wit and energy. For a while, before the cheering crowd, he had dismissed thoughts of Eliza. He no longer could. A response to his letter might have arrived that day during his absence, or John Allen might have come himself, to talk. Houston dreaded an encounter but wanted it over with.

Willoughby decided to shuck his efforts. He disliked trying to play the jovial friend when there were things that should be said. He could resist questioning Sam about Eliza; a man's marriage was private. But there were other matters of importance to the governor these days. Willoughby said directly, "All right, I'll stop trying to cheer you up. But you've got to snap out of this, Sam. You've got the votes if you want them, but you're being careless about some things. Granted, you've got personal problems, but darn it, Sam, you're about to destroy your career. It's this talk about Texas—the wrong people are getting wind of it."

Houston reined in his gray gelding. It sidestepped, wanting to move on. "Who's gotten wind of it?"

Willoughby gave a minor tug on his reins, and the mustang stopped in his tracks. The horse was something of an embarrassment to Willoughby, who was sheriff now and felt keenly the inadequacy of his mount. The creature had been fine enough when it was brought from Texas two years before but had since gotten a hoof disease, which seemed to have slowed it down permanently. It also had an irritating habit of sucking loudly on the bit. "Daniel Donelson, for one," Willoughby answered. "Says you told him yourself. Look, nobody knows what you've got in mind. You've kept that secret good enough. But they know you're planning something, and they know a man can't govern a state and effect some sort of uprising in another country at the same time. If Carroll's people catch on, you're in trouble."

"Donelson, and who else?"

"He's the only one said anything to me. He dragged me aside this afternoon and tried to pump me for more information."

"Damn," Houston said with force. "I would have sworn he was trustworthy."

"He's got him a mouth like the Big Suck, Sam. He takes it in and spits it right back out."

"What did he say, exactly?"

The mustang stretched its skinny neck, maneuvered to the side of the road and began cropping the grass. "That you're intending to conquer Texas or Mexico and be worth two millions in two years. He said you already sent William Wharton to scout out the mood there, and get things ready. Like John the Baptist, he said, preparing for your coming. He said when Wharton sends word, you're gonna leave for Texas and do what he said you call your Grand Scheme, which, he said, amounts to no more than a bootless war. He said there's no way it'll work."

"God," Houston responded. "Has he talked to any Carroll people?"

"I doubt it. It's not to his advantage now, since it's clear you've got more support than Carroll. But who knows? Sam, what exactly is it you have got in mind for Texas?"

"You said you didn't want in on it." Houston loosed his reins and allowed the horse to move on.

Willoughby tugged the ornery mustang from the grass and spurred him forward. "I don't want in on it. But I want to know what you're up to. It makes me mad you don't trust me with the details. You don't trust anyone, do you?"

Not with his plans, he didn't. No one knew the scope of those plans. Houston said sarcastically, "I want you to plead honestly dumb when they try me for treason."

"You'd better be serious about this, Sam. You can bet, with any incentive at all, Donelson will tell his brother A.J., and A.J. will tell the President. Maybe Jackson's put you up to this and already knows everything, but if not, you'd better watch who you talk to." He paused, then ventured, "That's one thing I want to know. Is Jackson behind this?"

Houston gave him a casual glance in the darkness. "Of course not. If Jackson wanted Texas he'd take it himself. He'd send out the army."

So Donelson was talking. Well, there was no helping it. A man couldn't fight the Mexican army on his own. Houston had by necessity confided in a few people. Donelson was a bad choice, but . . . He tried to work it through, yet his thoughts kept returning to Eliza.

A few hours after dark, Houston arrived at the Nashville Inn alone. He woke the stableboy around back, who had fallen asleep in a mound of hay, handed his horse over and went in the back way to avoid the bar. The piano was loud, and he recognized several voices. Jack McGregor was singing at the top of his lungs. Trying to make himself inconspicuous, keeping his back to the bar, Houston went to the desk and asked for messages. There was none from John Allen.

When he opened the door to his room he saw a figure standing in the dark near the balcony doors, and knew by the posture, the long arms hanging idle, that it was Doc Shelby. Houston's pulse quickened, and he looked around the room at the familiar shapes of the bed and table and the broken bedpost, its other half propped in the corner. Everything was as he had left it, but the feeling was different, like a forest gone quiet with malicious spirits. "She's gone," he said.

"Yes, Sam, she is."

He felt a gripping inside, as if something had taken hold with savage claws. "Did Allen come and take her?"

"No. She left alone."

That was worse. At least if her father had come for her, there was a chance she had gone against her will.

Shelby said, "Somebody saw her leaving. The news is already out. And speculation."

Houston closed the door and tried to steady himself. Moving to the table beside his bed, he lit a taper. Shelby watched him carry it to Eliza's door, knock, wait and then go in.

Her room was neat; she had always attempted a sense of order and control in this simple way, by assigning a place for everything and keeping it there, the hairbrush turned a certain way on the dresser, the bedcovers smooth and unobtrusive. Houston went to the wardrobe and opened it. Her clothes were there. "Look here," he said to Doc. "I think she's coming back." He passed his hands over the dresses and held the taper so Shelby could see. "She left everything. Maybe something came up—her mother's ill or something. She must have left a note."

He began to look for it, on the table, in her dresser drawer. He returned to look in his own room but found nothing. Shelby said, "She didn't leave a note, Sam. . . . Sam, listen to me, she didn't leave a note." But he paid no attention. At last Shelby said, "She left this," and held his hand out with Eliza's engagement ring in the palm.

Houston stared at it but did not reach for it. "Where was it?"

"On her bed."

"But not her wedding ring. She didn't leave her wedding ring. That must mean something." He went to open the balcony door, and breathed in the night air. Dissonant music drifted up from the bar. Someone drunk and offensive was singing "Nigger in the Woodpile" with the piano. Shelby came and stood beside Sam with one arm dangling at his side, the other tucked around him, his lanky figure bending slightly forward like an old man.

Turning to him, Houston said, "I have to go after her."

"Not tonight. Give her some time. Don't go tonight."

Houston's voice broke. "Doc? I love her." And he added, "How could she do this to me?"

CHAPTER 31

April 13

"**Y**ou got to give some explanation, Sam," Willoughby said again, for what seemed to Doc Shelby the thirtieth time in two days. "Anything. Listen to them out there."

Houston cast him a drunken, squinting look and leaned his elbows on the table. Then again he lowered his face into his hands, twining his fingers through his oily hair.

Shelby said, "Sam doesn't owe that crowd any explanation."

"They're his constituents," Willoughby retorted.

Doc answered, "They're Carroll's hired boys."

Willoughby shook his head. "Carroll ain't behind that business out there."

"I wouldn't put money on that," Houston said, lifting his face to take a pull at the bottle. "That man's blood would freeze a lizard. Anyway, I don't give a damn if he's behind it or not." He took another drink. "And I don't owe anyone any goddamn explanation about what isn't their business."

A yell went up in the street, "Hey, Governor, where's your wife?" Laughter followed, and "One, two, three," in unison.

> *"The governor's wife wouldn't be no squaw*
> *So the governor's wife went home to Ma!"*

An eruption of guffaws followed. Willoughby went to the balcony doors, and standing so not to be seen, looked out. "Dirty wag," he said under his breath.

"How many?" Houston asked in a disinterested tone.

"Looks like the same dozen as yesterday, plus a few."

"I get the distinct feeling," Houston drawled, wiping his hand across his mouth, "that you're not telling me something, Sheriff."

Willougby turned to look at him.

Shelby sat down on the bed. "People enjoy scuttlebutt, that's all," he remarked.

Houston said flatly, "For the sake of curiosity, what is it they're saying? Not them"—he gestured toward the balcony—"but everyone else."

"You name it," Willoughby answered. "That you acted brutal, forcing her like a squaw in dirty ways. Of course, you could put a stop to it with a statement."

"Forget it, Willoughby." Houston held his bottle up to the light and sloshed it around, studying it. "I won't do that. Now, which one of you gentlemen is going to replace this bottle?"

Willoughby turned his back to Sam and stared down at the crowd.

"You don't need anymore," Shelby said, meeting his look.

In a monotone Houston answered, "Goddamn it I say I do."

"You're killing yourself, Sam."

Houston took the last swallow. "Then it's a job well done."

From below there came a subdued chanting, as if in practice, and then full volume in mock sympathy:

"Poor, poor, Governor Sam,
Can't you tell us where's your ma'am?
Poor, poor, man up there
Could it be he don't know where?"

"I'm going to break this up," Willoughby declared suddenly, crossing to the door.

"They'll just be back," Doc said. "And Sam doesn't need to hide behind you."

Willoughby turned to Sam and said forcefully, "Look, you can't just stay like this forever. Any longer, and you'll lose everything: your friends except us two, the governorship, even your reputation. Make some move to defend yourself!"

Leaning back in the chair, Houston scratched at his three-day growth of beard. "Well, isn't that a turn of events. Willoughby Williams counseling something besides restraint. Just which friends do you happen to be talking about, by the way? The puddle seems to have dried up."

"This ain't a jokin' matter, Sam."

"No? Well, allow me my sense of humor. It may be all I have left."

"If you only knew what they—" Willoughby broke off. Doc shot him a warning look.

From below, another merry outburst:

"The governor can win a battle,
Wear his duds and sit his saddle,
But there's one thing he can't straddle!"

Houston listened, keeping his eyes on Willoughby. "If I only knew what?" he asked when the mirth subsided. "You're itching to tell me. Why don't you just say it?"

Willoughby gave Shelby a look, and said, "They've burned you in effigy, Sam. On the courthouse square in Gallatin."

Wincing, Houston managed a sickly smile. "I guess there was quite a turnout for that?"

"Look, Sam. You can't let them get away with this."

Houston pushed his fingers through his hair. "I guess McGregor's having fun with all this, proving his point about not coming around if I ever needed a friend. That man has all the attributes of a dog, save loyalty." He spat a wad of mucus from his throat and ground it into the floor with the heel of his boot. "Did I tell you, Willoughby, Overton came to see me this morning. To say I still had his support"—he faltered—"his confidence." He put a hand to his eyes, then grabbed the empty whiskey bottle and hurled it at the far wall, where it shattered above the fireplace. "Will one of you get me a goddamn bottle of whiskey?"

"You can't just let them have their way, Sam. If you don't want to talk, all right. But at least show yourself."

"No thanks." Houston focused his bloodshot eyes on the sheriff. "If my character can't survive this thing, then to hell with my character. But I won't sacrifice my principles. This thing is private. I will make no statement." He stood. His voice rose: "Do you understand? I will make no goddamn statement!"

From below:

"The governor had him a little lass
But she just refused to kiss his ass!"

"Listen to me, Sam," Willoughby said.

"Can't you see he's tired of listening to you?" Shelby cut in. "You've said enough."

Willoughby turned on him. "It's fine for you to stand there and say you ain't concerned about that mob outside. But I happen to be in charge of this town, and that crowd out there means business. They get louder and meaner every day. Somebody's gonna chunk a rock at the window and pretty soon we'll have us a big problem on our hands. Sam's my best friend, but he ain't the only one in this hotel. I got a lot of people here to look out for, and from the looks of them in the streets, they're just likely to put a torch to this place when they get enough tipple in their bellies. I won't just wait up here for hell to break loose. Sam's got a right to know the truth." He turned to Houston, adding, "They've posted you as a coward, Sam. All over town. Because you won't show yourself."

Houston met the information with a slow blink of his eyes, and then demanded, *"Who* posted me as a coward?"

"I don't know who—it don't matter who. The fact is they put the placards up faster than I can take 'em down."

Shelby stood, then sat again. "I hope you're satisfied," he said to Willoughby.

Houston queried, "What about Anderson? Is there a placard on his store?"

"Yeah. I doubt he put it there, but it's there."

"And in the newspapers?"

"Yesterday's."

"Oh, for God's sake, Sam," Shelby said, "what difference does it make?"

"And my brother?"

"Your brother's out of town," Willoughby answered.

"Figures. They put one on the courthouse?"

"Several. If you were sober, you could see them from here."

Houston went to the balcony doors and stared over at the courthouse. Shelby and Willoughby exchanged a look, the doctor frowning reprovingly. Sam crossed to the hallway door and opened it.

"Sam. Where are you going?" Shelby asked.

Turning, unsteady on his feet, Houston gave a nod toward the balcony and said quietly, "That, I won't sit for," then went out, and down the hall.

Sheriff Williams started to go with him, and Doc said, "I wouldn't do that if I were you, Willoughby. One man against a crowd is one thing, one man and a sheriff is purely different."

Willoughby hesitated, then turned back in. "How drunk is he, Doc? I mean, medically speaking?"

"Drunk," Shelby answered. "It was sorry judgment, urging him to face that crowd in his condition."

"I didn't mean *now*," Willoughby said and flung his arm up in an angry gesture. "I just can't stand hearing them say those things. It ain't like him to take it. He's been like he's dead. I just don't want him to lose even his own self-respect."

"I think that's what he's maintaining, by keeping silent," Shelby said softly, crossing to the balcony. "To defend himself is to accuse her, and he couldn't respect himself if he did that."

Willoughby moved to stand beside him. For the first time, he broached the topic. "Do you know what happened?"

"Some of it. Not all of it." He paused. "Do you?"

"Not the whole of it. We could piece it together," he ventured, guessing that the doctor would decline. Shelby believed in keeping confidences.

"I'd rather not," Shelby said.

Willoughby accepted that. "What's he got in that little buckskin sack around his neck?"

"Her engagement ring. Shall we step out, Sheriff, and see how this goes?" Willoughby chewed the inside of his cheek, wishing he had not prompted Sam to action. "But take off that pistol. He doesn't need backup from the balcony."

They went out onto the balcony and leaned with their hands on the wooden rail, looking down. The sun was in their eyes, already tipped toward the west. People, mostly men, milled in the streets; a group stood together, composing rhymes and leering.

"If there's fighting I'm going down," Willoughby said. They waited. "What do you figure he'll do?"

"I'm wondering if he's even made it down the stairs," Shelby answered.

Willoughby said, "I wish he'd shaved his face, at least."

Doc eyed the crowd and recognized quite a few faces—not all riffraff and not all Carroll men. Some, standing aside, not joining in but clearly enjoying the jibes, were Sam's former supporters. Willoughby was right about that.

"What's taking him so blame long?" the sheriff mused. "I hope he didn't stop at the bar—" he broke off as Sam appeared below and stepped into the street.

The crowd, not noticing him at first, turned their faces up toward the balcony to begin another chant but saw Sheriff Williams and stalled. One man started out, his solo voice puny, "Governor Sam is—" but then caught sight of Houston standing in the street before him.

"I shouldn't have pushed him," Willoughby said. "I shouldn't have told him about the placards."

Shelby's silence confirmed that he agreed.

There was shuffling as a score of men hurried from the inn to watch.

Houston's gaze was on the man who had spoken out, like a silent mastiff dog who cows a yapping pup. The crowd mumbled, nudging each other and making sly, unintelligible comments. One man stepped forward and spat on the ground at Houston's feet. "It's Old Tom Pierce," Willoughby whispered sourly. "Sam's given that beggar a heap of money too."

Houston looked at Pierce and the other men. "He looks sober," Willoughby observed, watching him step forward. The crowd stilled. A man in canvas pants and a plaid vest called out, "Going to hunt for your wife, Governor?" Several laughed but most kept silent, their eyes on Houston. A woman stepped out of Anderson's grocery and stood to watch. Houston turned to look at the man.

"Here it comes," Willoughby said, but the governor neither spoke nor advanced. The man set his hands on his hips and snickered, then glanced away. Houston moved his stare from man to man; some dared to look him in the eye.

Across the square a crowd filed out of the City Hotel bar, watching their governor. Shopkeepers appeared in the doorways. The streets fell still and silent.

Without pomp Houston began making his way through the crowd and across the street to the courthouse board where notices were posted. He stood before the paper proclaiming him a coward.

Sam Houston
The Hero of the Horseshoe
Is coward as a cur

Houston tore it from the board, and turning his eyes on the gathering held it up, crumpled and dropped it. For a moment he stood there, his face unshaved, his oily hair pushed back; it was a peculiar dignity. Then without a word he walked back across the dusty street to the inn. The men parted for him. He did not give them a look, but set his eyes on the inn. When he was inside, the people fell to murmuring. John G. Anderson moved from the doorway of his establishment on Cedar Street and pulled down another placard. J. Decker followed suit. On the balcony, Doc straightened, raised a long finger to his neck and scratched absently.

Houston returned to the room with a tired countenance and two bottles of whiskey.

April 14

Doc Shelby waited in the hallway, his hands clasped behind his back. He shifted his weight, leaning a shoulder against the wall. A stranger passed and entered a room several doors down. At last the Reverend Mr. Hume emerged from the governor's room. He met Shelby's questioning look with a slight shake of his head and said in his Scottish brogue, "I can't do it, John. I can't justify it."

With an incredulous look, Shelby asked, "You're denying him baptism?"

"I have to, John. I talked it over with the Reverend Jennings this morning, and he agrees."

Doc stepped back a pace. "Don't you see—" he broke off, then continued in a lower voice, "Sam Houston is a devastated man. He requested baptism, and you refuse?"

"On scriptural grounds, John."

Shelby spoke in a whisper, his face horsey and gaunt with the graying hair combed back, "I know what grounds you're talking about. He refused to take communion, didn't he?"

"I'm not at liberty to say."

"Did he say why he refused?" Hume declined to answer and stood examining a loose button on his coat. "When he was a boy, he heard Blackburn speak on the Corinthians scripture about taking communion unworthily," Shelby said. "He's afraid if he takes communion believing he's a Christian and yet not being worthy, then he'll damn his soul. For that reason he's never joined the church. But if you minister to him . . ."

Hume looked at him. "Do you know why he feels he isn't worthy? It's because he doubts his faith."

"And who at times does not?"

"John. He wants the protection and comfort of the Christian community because things have gone badly for him. Yet he shunned the church when his fortunes were rising. That causes me to question his sincerity. If he wants God's comfort, he has to accept the responsibilities that go with it. They include communion and commitment." He paused. "By his own admission he's not worthy of the first. And so by my judgment he's not prepared for the second."

Shelby narrowed his eyes. "You administered marriage vows to Mr. Houston, but you refuse the rites of baptism. Could it be you found performing the marriage ceremony for the governor more uplifting than ministering to a fallen man?"

"I'm going to overlook that insult, John."

"Rather than deny it, I presume."

"I deny it. I'm fallible, like anyone else. But your accusation is unfounded. I did have reservations about that marriage, knowing Houston's past. But I gave him the benefit of doubt." He pursed his mouth. "Now I question if he was sincere when he took those vows. If he even believed in the vows, or the God who stood witness to them. I hope his faith, whatever it is, will sustain him, John, but I can't justify baptizing him in the name of the Holy Trinity when I have no reason to believe he'll honor baptism with any more integrity than he did the marriage covenant."

"You assume he's the one who dishonored the vows. It's my understanding his wife left him."

"With good reason, no doubt," Hume answered.

"No doubt at all?" Shelby queried. "Did he confide in you?"

"No."

"Did she?"

"I haven't spoken with the lady."

"It seems to me that does leave a doubt, doesn't it."

Their eyes held. "I answer to God, not to you," Hume said at last. "I may be wrong, as I was when I performed that marriage. But my conscience won't allow me to baptize Sam Houston at this time." He started to go.

"You realize there may not be another time. He was near broken when he sent me to get you. He came to the church on his knees, and he isn't likely to do it again."

"Then pride will be his downfall," the Reverend Mr. Hume replied, turning to look at the doctor.

"You would damn his soul to save your conscience?"

In a voice low and stern, Hume answered, "I will continue to pray for his soul, Doctor. But if it is damned, it's by his own doing, not mine."

When Shelby entered the room, Sam was combing his hair. "I'm going after her," he said.

"You won't get there until after midnight."

Sam turned his sad and dissipated face on the doctor. "I'm going anyway."

CHAPTER

3 2

He was waiting in the parlor where they were married. The room was lit by moonlight shining through lace curtains and had a dim blue cast that reflected on the glossy surface of the piano. He crossed halfway to meet her. He had not shaved and his hair was damp; she guessed he must have washed it in the river. A breeze drifted in, pushing at the curtains. "I want you to come back," he said quietly.

She shook her head. "I can't." Anger did not guide her; she felt oddly free of agitation.

"Why can't you just forgive me?" His voice was low and plaintive, and he added, "I can forgive you for everything. Why can't you do the same? I was mad with jealousy. It was wrong to lock you in, but—"

"It isn't that. There's just too much between us."

"We can start over."

Again she shook her head. "No."

"We can give it time. Maybe you're just reacting . . . to what you have endured."

She did not answer. There was truth in what he said. She was not acting on hysterical emotions—dullness had set in, and acceptance—but she had not yet begun to heal. She felt she never would.

He added, "I could give you everything."

No, he could not. Here, at least, there was respite from disorder, a sense of place and of belonging. She had not known it before. She had not recognized it. There was refuge, not only within herself but within her family. She answered, "You cannot give me peace."

"You won't find that here, Eliza." His tone was certain.

"My family needs me," she said. "My mother needs me." The words had little relevance; her family had always needed her, and she had wanted only to get away. Perhaps what she meant, but could not yet say, and was only gradually beginning to understand, was that she needed them. She cared about them. There would be no chance here for the provocative life she had coveted, but there was something of importance.

Frustration goaded him. She had made her decision and was not listening to him. He said, "I need you, Eliza. Are you hoping that by leaving me, you can purge yourself somehow of all that's happened— and Eliza, I'm as much to blame as you are."

"I can't go back," she said simply.

"Eliza, please. What is it you want?"

"To be useful here. And to be left alone. I don't feel anything anymore."

He had expected that. This last effort to elicit her emotions had been a desperate performance; he saw now, studying her calm, exquisite face in the blue moonlight, that there was nothing he could do to win her. He accepted it. Already he had known it: she did not love him. He said slowly, "Did you ever feel anything for me? I need to know. I need the truth of it—or if you were simply in love with a dying man, and . . ."

He paused. His question was phrased like a subtle accusation; he might have added, "and saw there was more future in marrying the governor." But that was not his meaning; he did not think her capable of that. He was merely seeking resolution. She understood, and did not take offense. He wanted her, but if he could not have her, he must at least attain some sense of valid memory, unspoiled by deceit. "Yes, I loved you," she answered. "I thought I did. I wonder now if I'm capable of loving, or if I ever have been—but yes, I felt I was in love with you."

He said, "I want you more than I have ever wanted anything."

She had to smile at that, a small tilting of her lips. It was not true. She had read his letter to her father: "That I have & do love Eliza none can doubt,—that she is the only earthly object dear to me God will witness." She was, possibly, the only earthly object dear to him, but his fantasies, his schemes, his destiny, these were more dear to him than Eliza. They would sustain him.

"I wanted so much to please you," he added, and touched her cheek. Outside the crickets were humming.

She answered with a strange and whimsical tone, as if it didn't matter anymore, "But from the beginning you shut me out."

"It isn't too late, Eliza."

She wanted to move into his arms, but something held her back. It was not the demons bending her to their will, flailing their arms at her and frightening her away; it was simply that she had made a decision, and without knowing exactly why, she believed it to be right. She whispered, "It is too late."

He took her hands, and slowly, looking directly into her eyes, he sunk down onto his knees. The gesture was not pageantry; it was not even planned. Simply, it signified his falling, and expressed in a way that words could not, that she had brought him down.

For her, there was no glory in it, rather, a regret, and sorrow. Despite his troubled temperament, he was too great a man for this. "Don't, Sam," she said. "Don't beg me."

"I love you. I swear it. I'll do anything."

He did not understand. He would never understand. He bowed

his head and pressed it against her hands. Moonlight through the lace curtains touched his damp hair. There was the smell of spring; from the night, a breeze pushed in. "But it's too late," she said. "For me, it's too late." It was as simple as that. He lifted his eyes and again searched her face. She took her hand from his and touched his forehead. His lips moved; he was about to speak, but she drew her finger down over his mouth. Nothing he said would matter. His eyes pleaded; she stepped back, away from him.

He stood and said, "I won't come back, Eliza."

"I know."

He left without touching her again.

CHAPTER 33

When he was away from the house he spurred his horse to a canter and did not break stride until he was several miles off the Allen property. Where fields converged on uncultivated land he reeled the dapple-gray into the brush and made his way to the river, allowing the thicket to tear at him. On the Cumberland bank, he dismounted and vomited, then lay sobbing. He dug his fingers into the earth and rubbed soil on his face, wanting, with some primitive instinct, to disguise himself. April air brushed across the river.

At last he lay back, staring into the dark branches and listening to the river and chorus of insects. He thought of riding west from there, then thought of Andrew Jackson and the disgrace of running. Sitting up, he watched the wide bend of the Cumberland curving off downstream. A turtle was resting on a jam of logs along the bank nearby, its shell a dim orb in the moonlight. At last Sam slept. He woke, covered with dew, to a clear dawn and the first tentative notes of a brown thrasher.

When he arrived in Nashville later that morning, he wrote his resignation from the governorship. Willoughby tried to dissuade him, saying that the talk had turned and was against Eliza now, and that he could win the election. Even if Sam had believed him, it would not have changed his course. If he stayed, he would not forget her, and he had to forget her. He reminded Willoughby of the day in January when the two of them, and a few other friends, had ridden to Allendale together for the wedding. There had been a raven, dead, in the rocks beside the road. At the time, he had dismissed the idea that it was an omen of evil, but now he accepted that it had been, and this gave him some comfort. He said to Willoughby, "The marriage was destined to fail. There was nothing I could have done to prevent it."

His letter of resignation, addressed to the House Speaker, was brief and offered no explanation of the personal matters causing him to forfeit his position.

Nashville, Tennessee, 16 April 1829
General William Hall, Speaker of the House

Sir, it has become my duty to resign the office of chief magistrate of the state & to place in your hands the authority & responsibility, which on such an event devolves on you by the provisions of our constitution.

That veneration for public opinion by which I have measured every act of my official life has taught me to hold no delegated power which would not daily be renewed by my constituents, could the choice be daily submitted to a sensible expression of their will. And although shielded by a perfect consciousness of undiminished claim to the confidence and support of my fellow citizens, yet delicately circumstanced as I am, & by my own misfortunes, more than by the fault or contrivance of anyone, overwhelmed by sudden calamities, it is certainly due to myself & more respectful to the world that I should retire from a position, which, in the public judgment, I might seem to occupy by questionable authority.

It yields me no small share of comfort that in resigning my executive charge, I am placing it in the hands of one whose integrity and worth have been long tried, and who understands and will pursue the true interests of the state.

Sam Houston

April 17

On the following day Houston lay resting on the bed while the afternoon sun shone in from the balcony. He was wearing only his trousers; an uncorked whiskey bottle was balanced between his legs. His face was swollen and his stubble lengthening to a full beard. There was a sudden knock at the door. He roused, and thinking it was Doc Shelby said, "Come in."

The door opened, and there stood Congressman David Crockett of east Tennessee in his buckskins. He touched the fur brim of his hat. Houston blinked slowly, drunkenly, and sat up.

"How-do, Governor, sir," Crockett said with a genial nod, holding out a bottle of Madeira wine. Houston did not stand to receive it, thinking the man had come to gloat. "I know we ain't always been on what you might call terms of the most friendly sort," Crockett said, "seeing as how the President feels about me, and as how you feel about the President, but I got some stuff here"—he gave a nod at the bottle—"that's been known to run men together and make 'em forget which is which." Houston did not respond. "Besides," Crockett added, "hard as it may be to believe, David Crockett's bringin' you words from the Old Hero hisself."

At that, Houston corked his bottle, stood unsteadily and went to shake the man's hand. He motioned Crockett to a chair, then returned to the bed and sat again, his bare feet on the floor. Crockett did not sit, but placed the Madeira on the table, propped one boot up on the chair and leaned on his rifle, the finest Houston had ever seen. He was almost as tall as Houston, heavier, a few years older, broad-shouldered and long-haired. His nose was prominent, his eyes close-set.

"So what does he say?" Houston asked, flinching. He had pains behind his eyes from the whiskey.

"Well, as a fact, not much. Just regards. We was in a crowd, you see, his inauguration as a fact, and folks was shovin' in to see him up close and shake his hand, and he caught my eye and said over all the ruckus, 'You going home, Crockett?' I answered affirmative, and he said, "You give my regards to the governor."

"I guess you know you're late for that. I no longer hold that office."

Crockett removed his hat and scratched his head. "So I hear," he said thoughtfully, eyeing Houston, and then, "You do look in a bad way, sir." Houston almost answered with sarcasm but held his tongue. Crockett waited, then said, "Well, I suppose I best be headin' on, now I done my deliverin'." He made a move, then stopped. "But the fact is I'm dry as a powder horn, and it don't look to me like you need that there whole bottle to yourself. If I may say so."

Houston narrowed his eyes. "Spare me your observations, Congressman."

Crockett slapped the hat back on his head with a nod. "Well, I never was big on tact. I speak the plain truth. And the fact is you look bad. Chewed up and spit out. I mean no harm by sayin' it. I ain't one to go rubbin' a man's face in the dirt when he's down. I been jilted once or twice myself, and lost a wife to boot. I'd like to share a drink, but if you ain't for company, I ain't for stayin'."

Oddly, Houston warmed. It was good of the congressman, an old adversary, to stop in, when most of Houston's friends were missing the gall and vinegar of his downfall. He shrugged. "Then wet your whistle," he said, "and tell me about the inauguration."

Crockett tossed his hat on the floor, uncorked the wine with a pocket knife, glanced around for a glass, and seeing none, took a swallow from the bottle. "Notwithstandin' that me and the President ain't on exactly friendly terms, that inauguration was a fine thing for the people. It'd been rainin' cats and dogs for weeks, and that day the sun come out. I never seen so many folks in one place." He shook his head. "I think society buggers was shocked as hell when Jackson let everybody come in the White House—black and white, and the poor to boot. A number of mangy street dogs come in too. And two pigs. I myself saw two pigs rootin' in the dinin' room. I never seen so much mud in all my life as the mud that come in with them folks—enough to bank the whole Cumberland ten miles down." He grinned, took another drink and gave the bottle to Houston, who was leaning forward with an intense expression, even a slight smile. "He shaked hands with everybody," Crockett said. "People was fightin' to get to him and near crushin' him in, and he just stands there firm as you please and shakes hands with 'em all. I had to be admirin' of the man, however damned his politics. But society folks was devilish uneasy. There was these big barrels of orange punch, big around as that door, poured all over the carpet when the crowd rushed on 'em, and glasses smashed everywhere, and china. Folks was crawlin' in and out the windows 'cause the doors was too jammed up to get through. And a whore-lookin' woman"— he lifted a hand—"—I swear it's the truth—was dancin' on old Adams's billiard table. He would of shit if he'd seen it." Crockett sat and settled in with an easy laugh. "I saw one fat black mammy sittin' prim as you please on a satin chair, eatin' jelly with a gold spoon. At the President's house. Now that was a sight to behold." Houston found himself smiling. Life did go on. "I bet that place ain't cleaned up yet. It was damn near destroyed, and I know for sure the furniture was ruint past help. I seen one man spit a wad of tobacco juice big as my fist on one of them chairs. Now, I seen that stuff done many a time at my daddy's tavern, but never on a chair like that. Tobacco juice seepin' into satin is a ominous creature."

Houston took another drink of Madeira. It went down nicely.

Whiskey had been turning his stomach lately, and the wine was a welcome change. It was good of Crockett to bring it. He gave the man a smile and wiped his hand across his mouth. There was a silence between them, the sound of a carriage or cart rolling through the street below. "Good of you to come," Houston said. "You may lose some votes for doing it, you know."

"Aw, hell. Votes. I don't run my life by 'em. And the fact is I owed it to you."

Houston passed the bottle. "You owed it?"

"Yep. You may not recall the reason, but I sure do. Do you happen to recall that fandango just after the election for state legislature, when I first got elected?" Houston gave a single nod. "Well, that night you was standin' with Polk, talkin'. He was just elected to the legislature too, like me. Recall?"

Belching, Houston nodded again.

"Well, you and him was standin' in a group, conversin', and I was wanderin' around feeling mighty uncomfortable in my buckskins, like a old dumb grizzly with nothin' smart to say. And I seed you and recognized you from fightin' Creeks, so I come up and say, 'How-do, I'm Crockett.' You stuck out your hand and was friendly, and Polk, he turns and says, 'Well, Colonel Crockett, I suppose we shall have a radical change in the judiciary at the next session of the legislature.' Well, if I knowed what a judiciary was I wish I may be shot. I had never before heard there was any such thing in all nature, but I weren't too willin' for Polk to know how ignorant I was about it. So I says, 'Very likely, sir,' and made to leave and doin' so caught your eye. And I saw in it that you knowed I don't know what in hell was a judiciary. I took in a big gulp, thinkin' you might say so. And you said, 'Pleased to have met you, Colonel,' like I's as educated as the next man." He nodded. "No matter our differences, for that I owed you. You could have put me real on the spot." With a tip of his head and one eye squinting, he added, "You did know it, didn't you? That I was ignorant about a judiciary."

"I knew it. I also pegged you as a man to find out that very night what a judiciary was."

"That I did. Though it weren't easy, not feelin' free to ask." He eyed Houston for a moment, his mouth pursed thoughtfully to one side. "I always thought, sir, if you and me didn't feel so different about the General, we could of been right amiable." Houston met his look, thinking he could be right, and Crockett added, "You know, Governor, it just don't make good sense, not even good nonsense, for you to be sittin' up here like this with nobody."

Houston glanced instinctively at the door to Eliza's room, which he kept shut. "I still have friends."

"Yep, same number you started out with 'fore all this come up, 'cause a real friend wouldn't stick it to you now, when things is bad." Crockett mused, scratching at his armpit. "The fact is, you been one hell of a governor. Now I got to admit, and you know it, that I'd vote for Carroll. I think the man's good. But you've been good. You speak your mind and hang to your conscience. Nobody, not even that old man in the White House, though he might think different, has got a collar around your neck. That ain't common these days. And now you've had a stroke of bad luck, and it ain't fair for the folks to turn on you like they done. It's bound to be a thorn that rankles a man to no end." He leaned forward with his elbows on his knees. "I see it makes you monstrous solemn."

Houston took a pull at the bottle. "Forget it."

"You know what I'd do? If I'd served good and honest like you done all these years, and the folks of Tennessee treated me like they done to you, I'd recall 'em of my services, pretty straight up and down, for a man may be allowed to speak on such subjects when others are near forgettin' 'em. You can tell me to shut up."

"Go on."

"Well, I'd also tell 'em of the manner in which I'd been knocked down and dragged out, in hardly a fair fight, since you can't exactly defend yourself against a woman." His eyes narrowed on Houston. "I'd put the ingredients in the cup pretty strong, and then I'd tell 'em they could go to hell, but I was goin' to Texas."

He felt it, the old thrill. For the first time since she left. Texas. God bless it—Texas. A place where a man could free himself from a woman. Houston grinned. "Crockett," he said, "we've opposed each other on a lot of issues. But in a few areas we think alike. Such as—" he almost said "Texas" but stopped himself and changed direction. "Such as the Indian situation. I admire the manner in which you've spoken out for the Cherokees. It may lose you your job, you know. Then you may end up in Texas yourself."

"Well, like I always say, a man's honor is worth a damn sight more than his job or what folks have to say about him. So, are you headin' west?"

"West to Arkansas. Chief Jolly's territory."

"And then?"

"Who knows. Maybe the Rocky Mountains."

Crockett smiled. "And maybe Texas," he said. "You can't pull the wool over my eyes. I know what the fightin' fever's like. I get it myself now and then, and there's a job needs doin' in Texas."

"There is at that," Houston said. He passed the bottle, almost empty now, back to Crockett and uncorked the whiskey that lay on his bed. "Could be next time we meet we'll be on the same side." There was a flash in his eyes, only a glint. "Now tell me why you'd vote for Carroll over me, if I were still in."

The congressman understood: Texas talk was over. But only for now. Sam Houston had his eye on that place; and even now, at a low ebb, Houston was clearly the man for the job. "Well, I seen Carroll fight, for one. Though don't many people know it, 'cause Jackson took credit hisself, I swear if it hadn't been for Carroll, we would of all been genteelly licked when we was fightin' the Creeks at Enotachopco, for we was in a devil of a fix. Part of our men on one side of the creek and part on the other, and the Indians all the time pourin' it on us, as hot as fresh mustard to a sore shin." He took up his rifle and laid it across his lap, absently caressing the butt as if it were a woman's, and went on talking. "I won't say exactly that General Jackson was whipped, but I will say that we escaped that one like old Henry Snider goin' to heaven, 'a damn tight squeeze.' I bet Jackson would confess hisself that he was nearer whipped that time than he was at any other, though I know all the world couldn't make him say he was pointedly whipped." He finished off the Madeira. "I know I was mighty glad when it was over and the savages quit us, for I begun to think there was one behind every tree in the woods. You see, what Carroll done was so clever. He . . ." Crockett talked on, stroking his rifle, and Houston drank his whiskey and listened and began forming plans for his departure west. He would go by steamboat. Doc Shelby could make arrangements as soon as possible . . . the first packet coming through . . .

April 22

On the night before departure the dread of it hung heavy. Houston had fallen to morose reverie. Doc was out on a call, and Willoughby was no help; he made attempts at jocularity, but his depression clearly topped Houston's. As Willoughby saw it, Sam, at least, was going off to somewhere new—leaving everything behind, yes, but also gaining adventure and new hope. Willoughby wasn't gaining anything; he was just plain losing a friend.

Music started up in the bar below. A woman's laughter lilted up. "It's a pretty goddamn shameful way to spend my last night here," Sam said.

"I'd hardly recommend a walk through the town," Willoughby answered, trying to sound flippant. "Unless tar and feathers is a new costume you'd like to try."

"So the talk's turned again?"

"Every ten minutes."

"What now?"

"You don't want to hear, Sam," Willoughby said, then added, "Sex, it's all sex."

"Details. I'm up to it. Her sex, or mine?"

"Well, started out yours. With other women. Then they said she did it with another man and you caught 'em at it. In her room." He gave a nod at her door.

"And now?"

"Now, the last I heard, as of this afternoon, you made her do . . . unnatural things."

"Charming," Houston said, and did not pursue a more specific accounting. The details always hurt more than he anticipated. He ventured a question weighing on his mind, "Do you think she's heard it all?"

"I doubt it. The rumor is she still won't see nobody but family —and hardly them. Reverend Hume called on her, and she wouldn't come down."

"Then she's smarter than I was."

They fell silent. A scuffle broke out in the bar below, with a dozen angry voices. Willoughby stepped out to the balcony and listened. The air was still. Someone was calling someone a lizard. "What's the weather like?" Houston asked, staring at the wash of candlelight on the ceiling.

"Still clear."

"Hear anything from McGregor?" Houston inquired.

"Nope. He skirts me. He skirts Doc too."

"Sounds brave."

"Probably just ashamed," Willoughby said. He came back in and stood with his hands behind his back, rocking slightly on his boots. "Well, so daybreak's it."

"Daybreak's it," Houston echoed.

"I still think you should leave in some kind of style, Sam."

"I'm an ordinary citizen taking a steamboat," Houston answered.

"You really don't care what they say?"

"Not a damn's worth."

"You ask a lot of questions for somebody who don't care."

"Curiosity," Houston said and mused, adding, "I do wonder how it's affecting her. And what the General will hear."

"Yeah. He'll hear in a week or so. If I was you, I'd write him a letter now."

"And say what? That she isn't a whore, and I didn't abuse her, and though I won't say what happened, he has my word it wasn't my fault?"

"Yeah."

"Willoughby, you know that's the same as accusing her."

"Well, it was her fault, true?"

Houston shot him a look. "Jackson would despise my even insinuating she was to blame."

"Well, he sure is going to get a kick out of hearing how you took her on the floor like a dog."

Sam winced. Willoughby was no good with secrets. "So that's what they're saying."

The sheriff's voice tightened; he fingered his badge. "They say Indians have sex like that and practice with dogs and that's what you did to her."

"Indians eat dogs, they don't rape them. God."

"Jackson will hear it, Sam. Along with the rest."

They fell silent. "Does anybody actually believe any of it?" Houston asked.

"Who knows."

Houston smiled sadly. Someone was shuffling down the hall, mumbling, and stopped outside the door. In a drunken Irish slur, a voice sang out,

> *"Say what strange motive, Goddess! cou'd compel*
> *A well-bred lord t' assault a gentle belle?*
> *Oh say what stranger cause, yet unexplor'd,*
> *Cou'd make a gentle belle reject a lord?"*

"Who in hell is that?" Houston asked, wondering what drunk in Nashville knew Alexander Pope's poems well enough to quote them. The Irishman knocked.

"Some Irishman that's been downstairs," Willoughby said, moving to the door. "He's been around a week or two. I'll get rid of him."

"See what he wants first."

The sheriff turned and said too loudly, "That's all you need—a drunk Irishman."

"Who knows Pope," Houston said. "See what he wants."

Willoughby opened the door. Houston looked past him from the bed. Standing under the hall lantern was a skinny-limbed man with sparse hair and a rounded paunch, who said loudly, "Be this the room belongin' to Sam Houston, major general, congressman, and ex-governor of this fine state?"

Willoughby crossed his arms at his chest. "Yeah."

"And ye must be the Sheriff Williams?"

"That's right."

"Be it true, sir, that Mr. Houston won't speak of the matter of his wife's leavin'?"

"That's the blame truth, and if it's all you come to—"

"Well thank the good Lord for that, sir! For two full weary weeks I've heard nothin' but about that wee lassie leavin' and who the fault's belongin' to, and I'm weary to me bones of it. Can't even drink me glass of whiskey without hearin' of it, so I brought me glass up here to drink with one who won't be speakin' of it." He held up his hands. Houston saw a glass in one and two bottles, gripped at the neck, in another. He liked the look of it. "Besides," the Irishman concluded, "the news is his excellency's leavin' this town, and leavin' a town with a mouth as big as this one calls for a wee bit of celebratin', for auld lang syne. May I come in?"

Willoughby turned to Sam, who was approaching the door with an outstretched hand. "Sam Houston. Come in."

The Irishman took the hand and caught a potent whiff of whiskey. "Looks like the celebratin's begun without me. H. Haralson's me name." He bowed low, casting a reproachful look at Willoughby. "Seems Mr. Houston's not so choosy with his friends these days; even a drunken Irishman will do." Then he smiled, "No matter, sir, no matter. I don't claim to be no more than that, as long as there's whiskey to drink and places to go, Irish and drunk and on the road is plenty satisfyin'. My, but you've got quite a collection of bottles here, Mr. Houston!"

Propping his feet up on the bedside table, he made himself comfortable in the chair. Sam sat on the bed, and Willoughby pulled up a chair from beside the fireplace. One of the legs was broken off a few inches shorter than the others, so he balanced with his own leg stretched out. When Haralson was settled in and had remarked on the room, the inn and Nashville in general—he found all disagreeable in one way or another, but they suited him fine, as he planned to move on in a day or two anyway—he poured a drink and lifted his glass. "Honored to make the acquaintance," he said, looking at Houston, "and pleased to rest me ears from the mongers of gossip run rampant in this town. And to drink a toast to the man with spunk enough to leave it all behind."

"Well, I'll drink to that myself," Willoughby said, his spirits lifting with Haralson's glass. The vagrant did bring fresh air with him, and a glib, devil-may-care attitude that proved an odd comfort.

Houston was astonished. Willoughby hadn't taken a drink in twenty-five years, since they stole a barrel of corn whiskey from Mrs. Houston's Maryville store and hauled it off to the woods, where they drank until they vomited bile. "You sure, Willoughby? It's been a while."

"I can handle it."

"What have we here?" Haralson exclaimed, "A teetotalin' sheriff drinkin' with a down-and-out governor who's got a likin' for female dogs?" He lifted his glass.

Willoughby expected violence and looked to Sam, whose face went blank. Then, to Willoughby's bafflement, Houston put his head back, laughed and lifted his glass with a toast. "To Nashville—a more interesting place than you thought, Mr. Haralson!" They drank, Haralson with a sudden burst of laughter that sprayed his mouthful, Sam with a bitter smile, and Willoughby with a cautious eye. The Irishman was too crude for his liking.

"So tell me, Haralson," Houston said, "what brought you to Nashville?"

With a somber face, Haralson said, "A steamboat brought me," then burst into a slobbering bout of laughter.

Houston was drunk enough to find this funny. Willoughby just took another swallow.

"And have you ever been west of Tennessee?" Houston asked.

"I aim to." The Irishman nodded. "Anywhere I haven't been has a nice ring to me ear!" He tipped the glass and emptied it in a series of unbroken gulps that Willoughby couldn't help but be impressed at; even Sam couldn't drink like that. Then Haralson took up the bottle. "I've been north, and east too. Here in America for five years. And before that, England, Scotland—you put a name to it, H. Haralson's been there." He belched and slapped his rounded belly. "Your name, sir—Scottish?"

"Scottish," Houston confirmed, scratching absently at his chest. "My great-grandfather brought the family over."

"Same Houston family, descendants of baronets?"

"Same family. What do you know of them?"

"Just that they was clever enough to get out of Scotland. The Scottish are a hard, gruesome lot. Bred in a moorish, cold land. Makes me shiver to me bones to think of it."

"And why did you go there?" Houston asked, wiping his hand across his mouth.

"It's a place, which for me's reason enough." He turned to Willoughby. "Another drink, me good man? For auld lang syne?"

"When I'm ready." The sheriff nursed his glass, for effect, then drained it and offered it to the bottle. He didn't appreciate being called a teetotaler by this shifty Irishman. He was, after all, the law. "No family?" he asked as Haralson poured, by way of reminding the man of his own shortcomings.

"No wee wifie for me," Haralson responded in a genial tone,

"Wi' lightsome heart I pu'd a rose
  Upon its thorny tree;
 But my fause luver staw the rose,
   And left the thorn wi' me."

He finished with a glint in his eye.

"Bobby Burns!" Houston said, delighted to find the man knew Burns as well as Pope.

"A tragedy, his life," Haralson said, shaking his head.

Houston reflected, and said, "He lived it as he chose."

"Aye. Must be he chose a tragic life, which in me own opinion's a more woeful thing than just havin' tragedy come up and grab ye by surprise. Bobby Burns's poetry in me own opinion's the only good thing the Scots brought with 'em to Ireland."

They talked on, about Ireland, England, trade, *Gulliver's Travels* and John C. Calhoun, whom Haralson had met in a Washington bar. Sam said Calhoun was like Swift's Lilliputians, small and deceitful. Haralson declared Swift a misanthrope, and Houston disagreed. They argued. Willoughby drank and listened, wondering what a misanthrope was. The feeling came over him slowly, like the warmth of a spring day: an intoxicated sensation of high bliss. He gave a laugh, for no reason at all, and saw Sam and the Irishman exchange an amused look, which irritated him, and he cut the laugh short.

"Talk is, your honor," Haralson said to Houston, "Indian territory's your destination."

"So it is." Houston drained his glass.

"And these savages, they're right fond of you?"

"And I of them."

"You speak their language?"

"Most of it. It's a damned hard one to learn."

Haralson got another shine in his eye. "Tell me, your honor, do you enjoy dogs?"

Houston was not offended. "Which way do you mean, sir?" he asked.

Haralson's oily features gleamed in the candlelight. "Why, I mean, do they suit your palate, sir?"

"What sort of pallet do you mean, sir?" Houston answered, and both men broke into laughter. Willoughby didn't like it, making light of so ghastly a charge as sodomy, and so horrible a thing as eating dogs. He thought of his own loyal mutt at home, the trusting eyes, and gulped another mouthful of whiskey.

"Tell me, your honor, what be the Indian lasses like?" Haralson inquired.

Houston thought of Tiana, and his heart warmed. He smiled. She would be over a campfire now, serving her brothers, brown skin in the firelight, the braid swinging; they would not yet have reached home. "Bedding down with an Indian woman is the finest pleasure I know," he said, and then thought of Eliza, and felt a sudden gripping inside. "The best thing is, they like it too."

Haralson smacked his mouth. "They clean?"

"Clean enough," Houston answered tersely, thinking it a bigoted question. He recalled the junction of Pond Creek and the Cumberland, the reflection of the new moon, and added with a note of reverence, "Clean as the river, and as wet."

"Ohhhh, that's me own kind of lasses," Haralson said.

At that, Willoughby felt the need of another drink. He stood unsteadily and poured one.

"Pardon me for sayin' it, your honor," Haralson remarked, "but ye got hair on your chest thick as a buffalo mop. Those squaws take a likin' to that?"

Houston squinted. "They're not called squaws," he said. "And anyway, what do you know about buffalo? Ever seen one?"

"It's a sight this Irishman's been lookin' forward to all his born days," Haralson retorted, dismissing the reprimand. "When I go west, me dream's to shoot one."

The thought of this big-mouthed, skinny Irishman with a potbelly bringing down a buffalo was too amusing to Willoughby, and he roared so suddenly and with such force that he spilled his whiskey in his lap. In his humiliation he forgot about the short leg of his chair, and it dumped him on the ground at Haralson's feet, which struck Haralson as funny. Willoughby started to get up but found his legs like water and determined to stay put. "That chair's not worth sittin' in," he said with scorn.

Haralson would not stop laughing. He pointed at the splotch of whiskey on Willoughby's pants. "I've known plenty of men can't hold their whiskey," he blubbered, "but in all me days, I've never met one couldn't hold his whiskey nor his water neither!"

This made Willoughby mad. He had a mind to belt the man one, but his legs were shaky, and crawling over to do violence wouldn't have quite the effect. He glared. Houston said, "Hell, I've fallen out of that chair myself," which helped a little, though Willoughby figured it wasn't true. Even dead drunk, Sam never fell on his face. He did some stupid things, but with such an air—well the fact was, Sam Houston, rejected, despondent, angry, whatever, still had a bravado that made him enviable. He would never slosh whiskey in his lap and fall on his face.

"Pour me another one," Willoughby said, bent on proving he could handle it. No one had ever called him a teetotaler before. Or said he couldn't hold his water.

Sam looked at him curiously, then retrieved his glass, which had rolled off toward the balcony, filled it and handed it over. Willoughby feigned comfort on the floor and put his attention on the whiskey. He felt dizzy, disoriented, and knew better than to drink another drop—and knew that he knew better—but drank it anyway. It lodged in his mouth for a few seconds before his throat would open for it. The floor began to slip away from under him. He focused on one of the pegs to steady his eyes, but the thing seemed to be crawling away from him. Like a bug. It was a bug—a fat, tawny beetle. Sam and the Irishman were discussing what made a man worth something. They were quoting that Scottish poet—money wasn't it. Willoughby thought distantly that whiskey wasn't it either. Houston and the Irishman chanted together, the Irishman stomping his feet:

> *"For a' that, and a' that,*
> *Their tinsel show, and a' that;*
> *The honest man, though e'er sae poor,*
> *Is king o' men for a' that!"*

They sang another verse, and another. Haralson took a harmonica from his pocket and squealed away. The noise grated at Willoughby; he shut it out and sat nursing his whiskey and watching Sam's bearded, laughing face in the candlelight. Willoughby wondered how Sam could be laughing but was glad he was; somehow Sam laughing made things right again. Sam was scratching the hair on his chest—the buffalo mop—singing, pouring another drink and laughing. Willoughby lay back on the floor, closed his eyes and listened. The sound came as if from far away, perhaps from the past. They were laughing in the woods of Maryville; they were playing soldier. Sun filtered through summer leaves. He was slipping away, crawling back in time . . . into the undergrowth . . . crawling off with the tawny beetle . . .

Willoughby awakened on Sam's bed. The fireplace, unlit for weeks, was in full flame. A stench fouled the air. Sam was standing before the fire in his underpants, singing. The Irishman was stark naked in the chair, his penis shriveled like a turtle's head in the firelight. He played his harmonica. No, he was not stark naked; he was wearing socks. With a sudden thought, Willoughby felt his own body: still dressed. He was thirsty. Raising on his elbow, he felt a surge of nausea. "What's going on, Sam?"

Haralson left off playing and wiped saliva from the harmonica onto his thigh. Houston turned full face, gleeful, and lifted his bottle. "A ritual, my friend, to Bacchus!"

Bacchus. Who the heck was Bacchus, Willoughby wondered, but he did not ask. He already felt ignorant enough around these two poetry quoters, especially since Sam didn't have any more schooling than he did, and Haralson was only an Irish sot.

But Sam knew his friend well. "The god of wine!" he said in explanation, with a wink. He was downright triumphant for a broken man, Willoughby thought. No, not broken. Never broken. "We're sacrificing to Bacchus—our clothes, everything! Where I'm going, nature's gifts will supply nature's wants."

The Irishman plunged a knotty fist up, chanting,

"Is there, for honest poverty,
That hangs his head, and a' that!

. . .

The rank is but the guinea's stamp,
The man's the gowd for a' that!"

Willoughby sniffed the air and glanced toward Sam's wardrobe. It was open, and near empty. Sam was burning his clothes. "I feel sick," Willoughby said and lay back.

Sam's face was over him, a quiet voice, "There's only one thing to do for that," he said.

"What?"

"Appease Bacchus," Houston answered.

The sheriff closed his eyes, and then Sam's meaning caught him and he jerked them open. "No, no, it ain't that bad. I'll be all right."

"I've burned my beaver hat, Willoughby. My papers. My patent leather shoes with the buckles. And my silk socks. Damn near everything. Just to appease Bacchus. Don't you go and get him riled again by refusing to give up that one suit." He paused. "An angry god gets mean, my friend."

"Go away." He raised an arm to shove him away, but Houston caught his wrist. "Let go. I don't care if I anger Bacchus; me and him never got along anyway. Go on, Sam, stop it. Leave me alone."

Houston remained firm, smiling, gripping his wrist. "Sorry. I won't let you provoke the gods. If you think you feel sick now, just wait until Bacchus is nettled." His tone hardened, "There's nothing greedier than a god, Willoughby. They want a man stripped naked—clothes, pride, everything." He turned to Haralson. "Come help me divest this man!"

Willoughby swung with his free arm, and suffered again the nausea. Houston, seeing a sudden panicked expression, stepped back. The sheriff writhed, turned and vomited over the side of the bed. Haralson let out a whoop, and a laugh. "Can't hold his stomach neither! Not his liquor nor his water nor his belly! We got us a fine sheriff here! A fine specimen of man, if you ask me!"

"Nobody asked you," Willoughby gasped, managing a fierce sideways look, and heaved again. "I don't know how you do it, Sam. Drinking."

Houston stood watching. "Not quite like you do it, thank God. You have to appease Bacchus; there's no other way. I've done my part. Haralson's done his. Except he's turned sour in the end and won't relinquish his socks."

The stench of vomit mingled with the rank odor of burning patent leather shoes. Willoughby pulled his knees up under him, hung his head over the bed, and closed his eyes. He had a bleary picture of Nancy's face. Smiling. So sweet. He saw himself riding home without clothes. "Please. Sam."

"It's for your own good," Sam responded in a nurturing tone, and Willoughby wondered fleetingly if perhaps Sam actually believed in the god of wine.

Fresh air drifted in the open balcony doors. Willoughby lifted his eyes and caught sight of the tin courthouse roof against a starry sky. He had a moment of relief, and lay back, feeling weighted to the bed. The room was quiet but for the crackle of the fire. It was too warm for a fire. He dozed. Then without warning the two men were on him, laughing. Sam straddled him while Haralson assisted. They began stripping him. Sam tugged at his belt and the button of his pants. He tried to fight but couldn't. His only strategy was to go rigid at the ankles, so they had trouble getting the boots and pants off. Their faces were like two versions of the devil's—Sam's bearded, the Irishman's slick and greasy, sharp-featured, gloating. Sam was no longer gentle. He laughed riotously, the smell of whiskey on his breath, and Willoughby felt the nausea come again. He kept his mouth clenched and fought it down. He thought briefly that it would serve Sam right, and the Irishman too—especially the Irishman—if he heaved in their faces. But he was too proud to do it. He was not so crude as these men. He did not joke about eating dogs. He had his dignity. They might take his clothes but not his sense of decency. "Not my boots, Sam," he said. "Don't burn my boots. I just got 'em wore in right." They got his pants off, and his shirt.

They were taking his underwear too. Sam was saying he had to surrender everything, even his underwear, if he wanted Bacchus to ease up on the emesis. Willoughby wondered what emesis was and where Sam learned such words. How could his best friend be doing this to him? He opened his mouth to plead and then shut it. He would not beg. God. His underwear too? The Irishman pinned his arms down so he could not even cover his groin. Maybe this sot could down a buffalo after all. With his bare arms. Skinny arms with the strength of David . . . David . . . David and Goliath . . . Goliath was on top of him . . . Goliath with chest hair like a buffalo mop. Willoughby closed his eyes, then opened them. Still the mop was there, just inches from his face. He had a sudden thought: what if the rumors were true? What if Sam had done Eliza this way, tearing at her clothes, the buffalo chest pressing down on her, whiskey-fouled breath. . . . But no, Sam would never . . . or would he? Goliath was slinging the underwear above his head crying, "To Bacchus, to Bacchus!" the hairs of his armpit like a nest of daddy longlegs. The man was crazy. With an Indian whoop, he flung the underwear to the fire. Willoughby shut his eyes. He thought of his boots burning. Good boots. Goliath released him, moved to the center of the room and lifted his right arm, the hand spread. A silence fell with sparks from the fire, and then his voice came, powerful and deliberate, without a trace of intoxication:

> *"Self-exiled Harold wanders forth again,*
> *With nought of hope left, but with less of gloom;*
> *The very knowledge that he lived in vain,*
> *That all was over on this side the tomb,*
> *Had made Despair a smilingness assume."*

"Hear, hear!" Haralson cried, holding with one hand to the broken bedpost for balance, lifting his bottle with the other. "Hear, hear! to Lord Byron and Childe Harold and Sam Houston!"

Willoughby tried to tug the blanket over him; he leaned on his elbow and vomited.

"*His breast was arm'd 'gainst fate, his wants were few;*
Peril he sought not, but ne'er shrank to meet:
The scene was savage, but the scene was new—"

"Hear, hear! to travel," Haralson called out, belching. "Hear, hear! to distant lands. I will go with ye, your honor, if ye will have me company!"

Houston bowed low. "We leave at daybreak," he said, "on the packet *Red Rover.*" Then he lifted, his eyes resting on Willoughby, his voice sinking to a lower pitch, now without dramatic cadence— spoken as if he were talking in confidence to his friend of all time, imparting a serious message with his eyes, his words—his huge hand lowered and reaching out slightly toward Willoughby, who sensed the change in mood and lay back, trying to focus.

"*Where rose the mountains, there to him were friends;*
Where roll'd the ocean, thereon was his home;
Where a blue sky, and glowing clime, extends,
He had the passion and the power to roam;
The desert, forest, cavern, breaker's foam;
Were unto him companionship; they spake
Of his land's tongue, which he would oft forsake—"

Houston's voice descended, softened, "For nature's pages glass'd by sunbeams on the lake."

"Hear, hear!" Haralson said. Willoughby was moved; he lifted his hand to toast, but there was no glass in it. He hoped Haralson hadn't noticed the gesture and closed his eyes. His mouth was sour. As he drifted, he heard the Irishman's voice,

"*Here we are met, three merry boys,*
Three merry boys I trow are we;"

and Sam's deep volume, resonant, joining in,

"And mony a night we've merry been,
And mony mae we hope to be!"

When the fire had died down to embers and the drink was almost
gone, Houston spread a blanket on the floor for Haralson and covered Willoughby with a sheet from Eliza's room. He had not been in
her room since the night after she left. He went out onto the balcony
and stood naked in the shadows, staring across the street at the dark
window of his office. No longer his office. Billy Carroll would move
into it in a few weeks. The streets were quiet, the bars had closed.
There was no moon. He leaned against the rail, looking up at a
myriad of stars. *"Tsunkta' tegala'watege'sti,"* he whispered. "Let her
eyes in their sockets be forever watching for me."

A light on Water Street caught his attention, and he leaned to
see. There were three men approaching. The one in the center carried a pine torch. The tallest, on the right, stumbled. They were
obviously drunk, and coming toward the inn. One let out a peal of
laughter in the still street. Not tonight, Houston thought, not tonight. He put a hand to his forehead, then went inside and shut the
doors to a slit, and waited. He heard their low voices in the street
below the balcony. Then, in a burst of song:

"Hey, Mr. Governor, what do you say?
We hear through the vine that you're runnin' away!
Goin' where you'll have plenty squaws to lay!"

They cheered. A dog started barking, and one of the men called out,
"And dogs too!" which brought on laughter. Houston took a breath
and let it out slowly. Behind him the Irishman was snoring. It was
good to be going. But, even with all the ugliness, sad to be leaving.
This had been his town. These had been his people. Well, Billy
Carroll could have them—all of them with their rancorous perfidy.
He started to close the balcony doors completely, and shut it all out.
But a man could only swallow so much. He went to the bed and
shook Willoughby's shoulder. The sheriff groaned and mumbled

something. "Wake up, friend, I need a favor," Houston said. Haralson choked on a snore and sat up coughing. "Willoughby, listen. Willoughby. Wake up, Sheriff. Rouse yourself! I need you." Willoughby opened bloodshot eyes. "It's me, Sam."

"I know," Willoughby answered. "You burn my clothes and need me? Go rot." He turned away and closed his eyes.

"God, you reek," Houston said. "Haralson, come help me."

Outside the wags were at it again. And the dogs. It seemed evey dog in town was barking. "They're calling you!" The men yelled up, "Hey, Governor, these dogs want you to come on down for a little romance!"

Haralson stumbled to his feet, his bony flanks catching the embers' glow. "Help me get him to the balcony," Houston said, and the Irishman rubbed his eyes and came to assist.

"No, Sam, please," Willoughby pleaded. "Don't, Sam, I'm sick. What are you doing to me now, please, Sam. . . . No, not the balcony. I don't got any clothes on. Let go of me, you sotted Irishman. No, Sam, don't throw me over."

"Hang on, friend, I wouldn't do that. Trust me. Look here, we're taking this sheet with you. You aren't naked. . . . Willoughby, it's me, Sam, your old friend—hold him tight, Haralson, just lean him over. Aim him just to the right of that torchlight . . . right there. Good. . . . Good." Houston rubbed a hand on the sheriff's back, coaxing him, "Up with it now, up with it."

The smell of sap wafted up with blue-black smoke. "Sam, don't. I'm sick. . . . I'm gonna be sick. I'm—" He was interrupted by a heave, as the last food and whiskey in his belly tumbled forth. There followed an outraged yelp from below.

"On target!" Houston yelled.

The torchlight was tossed to the ground. The man who had held it fell to his knees, then spread-eagled and retched violently with a gasping, sucking sound like a calf at its mother's teat. Haralson, in the spirit, arched forward and let forth a stream of urine onto the prostrate man, who crawled a foot or two, then rose and made a dash for the pump house, stopping to vomit over the hitching post beside the courthouse. His two companions saw a chance for more fun and beat him to the pump house, where they blocked the door, flapping their arms. Before he reached them, they looked up at the audience on the balcony and waved, calling, "Good shot, Governor. Good shot!" Down Cedar Street a light came aglow in an upstairs window.

Sam and the naked Irishman fell back, slapping each other in congratulations. Willoughby was refreshed. He straightened and pulled the sheet around him. "We got 'em," he said with a slur. "Sam, we finally got 'em."

The three of them clung together on the balcony with a pervasive sensation of camaraderie. Willoughby even warmed to the Irishman. For the first time in weeks, he felt satisfied. He said he wished he could do it again. He said if the wags came back, he would drink a whole bottle just to do it again. But the wags weren't coming back. The stricken man made a dash for the river, and the others followed, their dark silhouettes stumbling, chortling, disappearing around the corner of Market Street.

The dogs quieted. One by one they left off barking and returned to their slumber. One meandered about in the street below, sniffing, then trotted away. A silence fell. Houston threw an arm around Willoughby's shoulder. Haralson went in to fetch his bottle and came back grumbling that it was near empty. He was sure Sam had another stashed away somewhere. He spread out a blanket and sprawled on it to enjoy the last few pulls.

Willoughby and Sam turned their faces up into the clear night, and Houston said, "Have I ever told you the Cherokee tale of how the Milky Way came to be?" Willoughby shook his head, uneasy with Sam's arm around him but liking it too. "There was this dog that stole cornmeal from a miller, and the miller chased him away with the meal spilling from his mouth as he ran across the sky." He took his arm from Willoughby and rested his hands on the rail, still looking up at the stars. Willoughby thought perhaps this was all. Then Houston reached a hand up toward the Milky Way and said in a voice so firm the sheriff wondered if he could be stone sober even after all the whiskey, "I may leave this town with many thinking I'm no better than a thieving dog." He gave Willoughby a keen look, his hand still pointing up. "But I swear by those stars, I'll leave a trail as I go, as wide and far as that one."

For a moment their eyes held. Something passed, some understanding, or hope. And a sadness, too. They would not be so close again. It was almost as if they said so, as if a final farewell was spoken with their eyes. Willoughby looked away and turned sideways so Sam could not see his tears easing out. Houston lowered his hand and returned his gaze to the square below. Haralson belched. "Aye," the Irishman said at last, his voice hushed. "Hear, hear! to clear nights and blazing trails." He took a drink, began to hum, and then sang softly, his voice drifting up into the night,

> *"Should auld acquaintance be forgot*
> *And never brought to min'?*
> *Should auld acquaintance be forgot*
> *And days o' lang syne?"*

As the horizon over the bluff lightened and the stars faded into a rosy wash, four men made their way down toward the steamboat landing, where the packet *Red Rover* stood at harbor. Sam and Doc Shelby walked in front. Sam was recalling a winter day three months before when he had descended this road through a cheering crowd to see General Jackson off. It seemed a different age, a different town; he seemed a different man from the one who had clasped the new President's hand and bowed before the people. Pulling his blanket around him, he shifted his canvas satchel to the other shoulder. The satchel held his only possessions: a few books, a whetstone and whittling knife, and a single change of clothes. He was wearing the moccasins made by Tiana, the flowered scarf, and, beneath a striped blanket, the woven belt her mother had sent.

Willoughby and the Irishman had fallen behind. They did not speak to each other but trod slowly. The sheriff, his head pounding and stomach wrestling with three cups of coffee, occasionally stooped to cuff up the brown velvet pants Sam had saved from the fire. He carried the matching jacket and wore the ruffled linen shirt Sam had worn to the opening of the stump at Cockrill Springs—eleven long days ago. The day Eliza went home. Willoughby had always admired this suit on Sam. It was too big on him, Sam being slightly longer limbed, but he was proud to have it. It was, in fact, the finest suit he had ever owned. Nancy could tailor it; she would be pleased. In the jacket pocket were the charred silver buckles Sam had burned with his patent leather shoes and then fished out of the ashes for Willoughby, and on his feet were his own boots—not incinerated after all. "You're a better friend to me than Bacchus ever was," Sam had said when he pulled them from under the bed and handed them over. Willoughby had almost strangled on a stifled sob.

The dock was beginning to stir. A father and son unloaded fur pelts from a keelboat. They did not recognize their former governor, a tall, bearded half-breed with glassy eyes. Casting him only a look, they kept at their labor. A man with Negro features, possibly half white from the looks of his skin and hair, assisted from the dock, catching and piling the rolls of pelts as they tossed them up. Several yards away a drunk snored against an abandoned cotton bale that had fallen in the mud near the water. The river was rising with winter melts from the mountains and the bale was scattered and soiled past salvaging.

Another man stood beside the *Red Rover* with his arms crossed at his chest. He was small and wiry, with a dirty slouch hat pulled low over his forehead. Houston saw him, approached, and stopped. The man removed his hat. He had a nervous look and twirled a toothpick in his mouth. With a pull at his mustache, he said, "How-do, Sam."

Houston gave a nod. "Jack."

Willoughby and Shelby looked on, hoping McGregor had not come to gloat. Haralson set his trunk down and made himself busy with a broken hinge.

"I, uh, come to see you off," McGregor muttered with a shift of his eyes, then spat the toothpick from his mouth, blurting, "I been a wrathy bastard Sam and I come to say I'm sorry."

Houston studied him in the dawning light. "You weren't far wrong," he said at last. "About that puddle."

Turning a sad smile, McGregor said, "I admire what you done, Sam. Keepin' quiet about what folks got no right to interfere in. It took some guts." Houston's face softened, and Jack reached in his pocket, bringing out a stack of paper tender. "Here. I got somethin' for you," he said with a shove of his hand toward Houston, who did not move to take the money. "Don't say no to it. I know you got your pride, but you'll be needin' this. I know you got nothin' of your own."

Houston guessed it was almost all the man had. He made a motion with his hand to resist but caught Doc Shelby's eye. The doctor nodded, and mouthed the words "Take it." Houston hesitated, and then, his eyes on McGregor's, accepted the money.

"I know I said I wouldn't come around," McGregor said, "but—"

"I'm glad you did," Houston answered.

They stood surveying each other, McGregor jabbing the toe of his boot against the dock planks, then turned their attention to two men boarding the *Red Rover.* The sun tipped the horizon and shone full on McGregor's eyes. He slapped his hat on and said, "Well, I got business to be tendin' to. Guess I better head on back."

"Stay around, if you want to," Houston said.

Uneasy, McGregor glanced at Willoughby and Doc Shelby.

"He'll be boardin' any minute," the sheriff said. "Hang around. Go back up with us."

Jack shrugged. "Well, heck," he said. Then, "Naw, I guess I said all I come to say. Better get on back to the tannin' business and make back some of that wad."

Houston put out his hand. McGregor took it; for only an instant their eyes met, and then McGregor loosed his hold and turned and headed up the bluff. The others watched him go. A minute later he looked back, morning rays catching the brim of his hat. Lifting the hat, the sun on his face, he called out, "If you get in another one of them duels, you know where to find me!"

Houston raised his hand, the fingers spread wide, and held it up as McGregor replaced his hat at a sportive angle and continued up the hill.

"Jack's better angel always did speak last," Shelby said, his words mingling with the captain's strident call that all who were coming aboard should get aboard.

Haralson stepped up and offered his hand to Shelby, then turned to Willoughby. "If you ever be needin' a drinkin' partner, look me up in Indian territory. You was right entertainin' with that bottle and your pantaloons wet clear through. And the vomit, sir, that was the most lovely of all—bloody impressive. I never seen such a sure shot. Ye could down a duelin' man with that ability." Willoughby cut him short with a scowl and a dismissing wave of his hand. The Irishman laughed heartily and went aboard, his scant hair moving in the air like tufts of new corn.

"You're booked under the name Samuelson," Shelby said to Sam. "I hope that's all right. As Houston, you wouldn't get a moment's peace."

Houston nodded.

"The passage is paid."

"How much?"

"Don't worry about it."

"But I do. Did you get sufficient from my horse to pay the inn?"

Shelby nodded. "And the passage." It was a lie.

"But not the bill at Anderson's?"

"He waived the bill."

"I want to pay him anyway. Here, use this." He thumbed out half of McGregor's money. "Pay Anderson, and anyone else I owe."

"You'll need all of that, Sam," Shelby said and refused to take it. He smiled. "If not, then use the balance for passage back." He fixed his good eye on Houston. "We're going to miss you, Sam."

Willoughby's eyes filled; he turned and pretended interest in a couple boarding. Houston made busy tucking the money into his shirt pocket as the captain called out behind him that *Red Rover* was heading out. Then, in a gesture that took them by surprise, Houston reached his arms around both men at once, enclosing them in his blanket, pressing his bearded face between them. He clung to them, and they to him. Willoughby tried to hold back a sob, and knew Sam felt it. Releasing his hold, Houston squared his shoulders beneath the blanket and looked at his friends. Willoughby's face puckered beneath the red beard. Shelby's blind eye shifted. Then Houston turned away and crossed the plank to board the *Red Rover,* where he stood on deck apart from the other passengers, staring into the water. The plank was lifted, and as the paddle wheel began to churn and the broad-beamed little packet boat eased her nose downstream, he lifted his eyes toward the bluff and the town of Nashville, rosy in the morning light. He looked again at the two figures on the landing, and with tears distorting the image, he watched them wave, turn together and make their way back up the slope toward town. Halfway up, Willoughby stooped to cuff his velvet pants, then turned again to the steamboat and raised both arms high in sweeping waves above his head.

CHAPTER

34

Dry was doing the talking, his energy impressive for an old man. He refused to sit. He had brought his black walking cane and was pacing about the room tapping it on various surfaces: the windowsill, the mantel, the back of the sofa. His wild gesturing annoyed John Allen, who said at last, leaning forward over his desk, "I wish you'd put that goddamn thing down or use it properly."

Turning his torso halfway around to stare at his son-in-law, Dry retorted, "I don't need it for walking. And your language offends me."

Congressman Robert Allen shifted in his chair and cleared his throat. He was impatient and annoyed. "Let's get on with it," he said.

John turned on him. "What do you care? She's not your daughter."

"Thank God" was his instant response, and then he added, "No, I didn't mean that, John. She's always been a favorite of mine. I'll do what I can."

"Which is the very dilemma I'm trying to address here, gentlemen," Dry continued, giving John Allen's desk a single whack with his cane. "What should be done? That child has put us in a bind. She—"

"Woman," John Allen corrected him. "She's not a child now. She's a woman."

"You're avoiding the issue, John, and we're out of time," Dry said. He turned to his grandson George, who was standing beside the fireplace, tense and hostile, not leaning against the mantel but resting his elbow lightly on it, as if he were posing for a portrait. "What's your opinion about this mess?" the grandfather asked.

George was taking it to heart. His friends had been harassing him. "I think we should go after him," he said. "The boat can't reach Clarksville much before sunset, and we can be there by then. I think we should shoot the son of a bitch."

Dry remarked, "You're overzealous." John and Robert chose to ignore the boy's sentiment.

"We're not even sure he's on that boat," John said.

"If he's not, we haven't lost anything," Dry answered. "If he is, at least there's some chance he'll cooperate."

"He won't sign that thing," Robert injected, stroking his brow to display boredom. The episode was, for him, bothersome; the more commotion about it, the worse for his career. Not only was he the bride's uncle, he was also a longtime friend and supporter of the disgraced governor. "Read it again," he said with a sigh. "Maybe if we phrase it differently, there'd be a better chance of it."

"There's nothing wrong with the phrasing," Dry said defensively, retrieving the sheet of paper from the desktop. He had authored the statement and read dramatically, holding it at a distance from his face rather than troubling with his spectacles. He did, in fact, almost know the words by heart; he had composed them an hour before, when the household received news that Sam Houston, in disguise, had left Nashville at daybreak.

For the last two days, the men had been together at Allendale (various other relatives had come and gone), mulling over rumors that the governor intended to leave town. They felt the family should make a united stand and were gathered to determine what it should be. And now Sam Houston had gone, slipping out of Nashville in Indian garb, without warning, on an innocuous steamboat called, presumably, and with a distastefully ironic suitability, *Red Rover*. Dry read: "I, Sam Houston, late governor of Tennessee, do hereby absolve my wife, Eliza Allen Houston, of any charges I might, in a deluded frame of mind, have made against her. She is a worthy, chaste woman, and has been a faithful wife. Sam Houston."

"He won't sign it," Robert repeated.

"Unless you convince him to," Dry answered.

"Forget it. You won't find me chasing after a renegade governor on some pissant packet boat."

"*You* introduced him to this family, didn't you."

"That hardly makes me responsible for this drama."

Dry's voice lifted. "That's what's the matter with the entire lot of you: nobody will take any responsibility around here. Not even Eliza, or Houston, with their damnable silence on the subject. But if that girl,"—he glanced at John and corrected himself emphatically —"if that *woman* refuses to clear her own name by giving us some explanation, then it's our duty to clear it for her. I will take responsibility for that, and would track Houston down myself if I were ten years younger. Certainly he shouldn't be averse to clearing her name, if he cares anything about her."

"Maybe he doesn't," George said contentiously. He reached his arm back over his shoulder in a contorted position and squeezed at a pimple on his neck, grimacing.

"Don't be asinine," Dry said. "Of course he cares for her. Why else would he have come here the other night?"

"Politics," Robert answered.

The children were playing outside, just beyond the open window, their voices shrill and intemperate. Four-year-old Benjamin Franklin Allen had climbed too far up in a tree, and Dilsey was trying to coax him down.

"All we're asking," Dry said, "is for him to vindicate her. He's essentially done that in the letter to you, but he ought to do it publicly. It wouldn't be enough for us just to publish that letter. Everyone expects a man to tell his father-in-law his wife is virtuous; it doesn't mean a thing. We need a public vindication. A statement."

And in the final sentences of this diatribe, Eliza opened the door and walked in. She was wearing a dress of simple homespun; her braid hung to her waist. She did not bother to knock, and entered the conversation as if she had been a participant from the beginning. Her tone was slow and secure. "You might need a statement. I don't. I don't need anyone to vindicate me."

There was triumph in that truth, and comfort. She knew the rumors about her, and about Sam. Dilsey had told her. She did not care. She would manage her own vindication, as her husband would manage his: privately, separately, each seeking isolation. And in the effort they might attain an unspoken covenant that was more lasting than all their promises and declarations to each other—a trust kept, when so many others had been broken. They would keep their secret.

Dry stopped in the center of the room with his walking cane lifted a few inches off the floor. John Allen said gently, "Eliza, I think we can manage this better, and you'll be happier, if you don't get involved."

She lifted her chin and answered blithely, but with a hint of indignation, "I don't want to be involved. I don't have any reason to be involved. This isn't about me; it's about family honor. You may all do as you wish, in regard to family honor; I only request that you don't pretend you're doing it for me."

Outside, Benjamin's taunting, boyish voice had suddenly ascended to a wail; he had gone too far up the tree, and his exhilaration had turned, without warning, to fear. He was squealing, and then calling for Eliza. He wanted Eliza. With a quick, commanding gesture of her hand and the single word "George," she motioned her brother to come with her. He responded reluctantly, and together they went out to help the boy down.

When they were gone, Dry said, "That girl's high-minded attitude infuriates me. Here she's created all this chaos, and she's leaving us to deal with it."

Robert said, "My vote is to forget it. But if you want to press it, Dry, and if John agrees"—he looked to his brother—"then I'll do what I can."

John Allen stood and went to the window; he could see Eliza on the lawn, beneath the tree, not far away. She was in a patch of sunlight that shone full on her brown dress, the heavy braid swinging behind her as she tilted her head back, her arms lifted toward Benjamin maneuvering his little body down through the leafy branches. George was climbing up a few limbs to meet him, but as the child made his way down, stretching his legs to the next limb, his bare feet pointed and reaching for purchase, it was to Eliza he looked. He clung, his hands gripping from branch to branch and his anxious face turned downward, seeking Eliza. Dilsey stood by with the other children.

Touching the warmth of the windowsill in the April sun, John turned to his brother. "Then try to meet him at Clarksville," he said quietly. "You have a better chance than anyone of getting him to sign. Take George with you. If he signs the statement agreeably, fine, but if he refuses, don't press him." He paused. "And be sure he knows that Eliza did not ask him to."

She was holding Benjamin now, his smudged face pressed against hers. She felt his arms around her neck like a grip of possession, yet the sensation was more liberating than encumbering. He had the familiar smell of a sweaty child, and bits of bark in his hair. "I have you now," she said, tightening her hold, and in a sudden, intense need to release emotion, she laughed and cried aloud, "I have you now—"

CHAPTER

35

Houston remained on deck, speaking to no one. The half dozen other passengers retired below, where Haralson entertained them with vagabond stories. Whiskey was no comfort; he thought of tossing it to the river, but did not do it; it seemed his only friend. Wooded banks of the Cumberland passed in a monotony of green, each turn of the paddle wheel moving him farther from Eliza. He remembered her picking a thorn from little Joseph's thumb, the fall of leaves behind her. The autumn landscape was clear in his memory, the posture of her bent head as she studied the tiny thumb, the curve of her cheek. But her face was bowed; he could not see her eyes. He struggled to picture her, but somewhere deep he craved forgetfulness and found a degree of it. Whiskey dulled his thinking. By afternoon he was restless with frustration; he could not dismiss her. She inhabited his mind like a featureless apparition. Only her voice was clear to him, but what it said had no meaning, for he could not separate her truth from her lies. She had said she loved him. But there had always been Tyree.

Tyree, who was dead. And what would become of Eliza?

By midmorning the packet passed the junction of Pond Creek. Houston studied the bank where he had loved Tiana, now bright in sunlight, the sugar maple and pawpaw and shagbark hickory that had filtered moonlight onto her body, the cedar tree from which she had pulled sparse strips to burn and keep away the ghosts—*anisgina.* And for a while she had kept them away: Eliza had vanished while Tiana lifted her body to meet his. He would see Tiana in Arkansas. She was a hope.

All day he stood on deck, without a hat, squinting in the sun and feeling his skin sear. It was late afternoon when the boat docked at Clarksville, a post town on the land point at the meeting of the Cumberland and Red rivers, fifty miles downriver from Nashville. A few passengers disembarked, others boarded, and the crew unloaded a score of barrels and crates. Haralson joined Houston on deck and remarked on the size of the town, suggesting they stop off for a day or two. But Houston refused to stop. He was heading due west, and that fact kept him going. Haralson wasn't avid for reaching Indian territory on his own and said he would keep with Houston's schedule.

As the crew prepared to leave, Sam noted two men approaching on horseback from the main road that wound itself from the tree line to the dock; he recognized their mounts and suffered an onslaught of emotion. He would not allow himself to hope that she wanted him back and told himself he would not go even if she did. "Those men are Eliza's kin," he said to Haralson, who stayed beside him, turning an empty bottle in his hands, feeling the smooth glass as he watched the men approach.

They secured their mounts to a post and boarded. Robert said, "Sam, let's talk as men who have been colleagues and friends."

"Let's talk as colleagues and friends," Houston replied. He offered his hand, which the congressman accepted. George, however, refused it, his animosity apparent, and he tightened his mouth into a petulant knot.

Robert dipped his head so the brim of his stylish hat shadowed his eyes from the lowering sun. "Whatever happened, Sam, is between you and Eliza. I'm not asking for explanations or apologies. But you've heard the tales. The most persistent one is that you were goaded to madness and exile by detecting her in crime. We both know that isn't true." He did not pause long enough for Houston to challenge the presumption. "I'm here to ask you to sign a statement to that effect. John would have come but he—"

Houston interrupted, "How is she?"

"Does my answer affect whether you sign?"

"No."

"She's weathering it."

"You know I won't sign anything, Robert."

"Goddamn," Robert responded. "It isn't a confession." He pulled the paper from his coat pocket. It was heavily creased, and unfolding it, he said, "You have nothing to lose by signing it."

"And nothing to gain," Houston countered, refusing to accept it from Robert's offering hand.

Haralson and George were silent; George looked contemptuously at the Irishman, then again at Sam Houston.

Robert said, "Then think of her. You can abandon society and walk away from everything, but she can't. It's bad enough, your leaving her to stand the heat alone. But to leave her without—"

"She left me, Congressman," Houston injected. In saying it, he felt for the first time the extent of his anger. She had done worse than reject him; she had forsaken him. She had not assumed blame or made any public explanations. She had not, as far as he knew, revealed the circumstances of their separation to anyone. He said, "And it seems she knows, as well as I do, the impotence of public statements. She had nothing to say while my effigy was burning on the courthouse square in Gallatin." He stopped. He had touched on something; through his indignation, an idea began to form—a provocative idea that came to him suddenly, with hope. Her silence might not be rooted in a reluctance to forgive him; perhaps it was comparable to his own reticence and was in some way a connection between them. "Does she want me to sign this?" he asked.

Robert looked toward shore, then back to Houston. Despite the conflict, he liked this man. He wished he had not acquiesced to this frivolous mission. "She doesn't seem to care," he said, which was close enough to true.

With that statement a sense of finality settled. As if to confirm it, the captain called out from his perch above, "We're heading out. If you two men are going along, I need payment now." They ignored him. Haralson, to fill the awkward moment, dropped his empty bottle overboard and watched it sink through the debris of trash and riverwash.

But George was unwilling to let the matter close and said to Houston, "We won't leave until you sign it." With a subtle motion, he drew a small pistol from the loose front pocket of his trousers.

The action took Houston off guard, but he met it without changing expression. He found himself oddly separate from the scene, viewing it as a bystander might: a hotheaded youth with a pistol aimed at the belly of a man who, in all actuality, had little reason to want to go on living anyway. For two weeks he had cared nothing for life. But the irony of being shot in the belly by this boy —his wife's brother—would be too damning to his memory. After his bravery at the Horseshoe, his career and his personal integrity, it would seem a silly ending. If he was to die over this thing, it would be by his own hand. "Put that away," he said.

"Not until you sign." With his free hand, George grabbed the paper from his uncle and shoved it out toward Houston.

Robert said, "George, give me that," and reached for the gun, but it was obvious he doubted the boy would obey.

George took a step back, out of reach, cocked the pistol and shouted in a voice loud enough to call attention, "Sign it, or by God I will make you pay!"

The deckhands turned to look. The scene became a still image; no one moved. The captain peered over the rail above, squinting down at them with a monkeyish face and splotched skin. Then a man on the dock, shirtless, muscular, sweating from his labor of loading cords of wood for the boat's furnace, put a hand to his eyes to block the sun and said aloud, "Goddamn, it's Sam Houston."

The recognition was, for Sam, an unexpected blessing. It gave his identity back. He was standing there on this boat, facing a pistol, not as the governor, or the former major general of the Tennessee militia, the advocate of Indian rights, the friend of Andrew Jackson. Not as the husband of an errant woman, or the former congressman —not as a former anything, but as Sam Houston. Intact. It was enough. With his eyes bearing on Robert, dismissing George completely, he lifted his hand and his voice. "I will sign nothing! And in the presence of the captain and these gentlemen I request you, sir, to publish in the Nashville papers that if any wretch dares to utter a word against my wife's purity then I, Sam Houston, will come back and write the libel in his heart's blood!"

Silence returned. A fish flopped in the water. Then Robert said, "I thank you for the statement, but it's not enough. You're crazed, Houston. If that nineteen-year-old girl lives the rest of her life in shame, you can attribute it to your stubborn pride."

Houston said, "I will attribute it to her decision to leave me."

There could be nothing more. George surrendered the gun to his uncle, his countenance still furious. Houston turned his back on them while they went ashore, and Haralson watched after them without comment. The captain yelled to his crew, "Get ready to shove off, men!" Gradually, with side glances, commotion resumed. From above, the captain called, "Mr. Samuelson?" Sam looked up at him, and saw one of the squinting eyes close into a full wink, not of amusement, but of comradeship. "We'll be moving off now, Mr. *Samuelson.*"

As the *Red Rover* joined the current, Houston moved to the bow and watched the sun lower in the sky before him. Haralson brought him hardtack and smoked pork and left him to eat alone. He could hear the Irishman's harmonica down below, the strains of an old Irish love song lilting out over the water:

Will you come to the bower I have shaded for you?
Our bed shall be roses all spangled with dew.
There under the bower on roses you'll lie
With a blush on your cheek but a smile in your eye.

Again despair settled over him, weighing down on him as the sun descended in the west. He thought of Andrew Jackson and the bitter disappointment the General would feel when he heard. He thought of friends and how he had let them down, of Tennessee. Eliza. He fingered the leather pouch at his neck, feeling the delicate ring inside. Below, the water churned with the incessant noise of the paddle wheel. How easy it would be to drown himself, to slip into it as into his own anguish and self-recriminations. There was nothing left to cling to, yet he held on. To a memory? To a dream? Or simply to the wooden railing of a packet steamboat called *Red Rover,* plowing steadily through the water and moving westward toward . . . something, some future. But what future was there for a man such as he, without position, or the woman he loved, with only a scheme, a grand scheme, an intricate web of strategy now mangled, stripped of its connecting threads: the support, the desire, the power—gone.

For an instant, staring down into the muddy water, he remembered her face, clearly. It seemed her gray eyes held a secret. Their secret. However terrible it might be, however infused with folly and regret, it was theirs: a bond of silence, a trust. For a moment he felt it, like her slender arms around him, encircling him. She had also, in her own way, found exile.

Far above the cliff he heard a cry and lifted his eyes to see an eagle glide, then swoop low, beating its wild wings in the April air and then lifting with a scream. Encumbered as it was with the demons that caused it to cry aloud in flight, the eagle rose and labored westward on the wind.

And Sam Houston, watching it, felt the old appreciation stirring. This tragedy, his own personal drama, had its moments of elegance. He accepted this as one of them, and gloried in it: his Conducting Providence had brought the bird.

CHAPTER 36

Three years later
September 1832

The wind was up and autumn blowing in. Dilsey sang softly as she walked from the big house to her cabin, a song about a Rock of Ages, her long legs moving slow and easy so not to wake the baby she carried on her hip.

Dilsey was, in fact, carrying two babies: Laetitia Allen's ninth child, Margaret, asleep against her, and her own child in the womb. The evening wind warned of winter coming on, but Dilsey was looking forward to the cold this year, for just today the fireplace in her cabin was completed.

Wind molded the smock of blue domestic against her rounding belly as she sang and thought about the fireplace. She pictured herself sitting by her own fire, her naked feet stretched out to the warmth, her baby nursing at her breast. The man, the father, was long gone. He was a free black she had known at a camp meeting, drifting, looking for something in this wide world. He would not find it; she was sure of that—white or black, free or slave, folks bent on searching never found what they were looking for. Perhaps he would come back. She hoped so but would not grieve with waiting. She had a baby to tend to.

"Dilsey."

She halted and looked around, cautious, but no one was there. The other slaves were still at supper around the side of the big house. She listened, fallen leaves skittering at the hem of her dress. The child on her hip opened sleepy eyes and seemed to listen too, her blue gaze cast up into the trees. Sometimes devil spirits hung about the woods, and Dilsey knew better than to embolden them by showing fear. "Who's that," she said.

He appeared like a vision, soundless on dry leaves, a blanket of red and brown over his shoulders, the largest Indian Dilsey had ever seen—and she had seen plenty in her youth, moving along the Cumberland in their silent canoes or passing through the woods. But never one like this, with a full beard and eyes so deep and keen and—

"Governor," she said with more breath than voice.

He put a finger to his lips and turned his head toward the house. His auburn hair was long and braided in a queue down his neck.

She spoke in a whisper, "I knowed you was comin' back. I told her so."

He looked at her, his expression hidden in the beard but his eyes pulling at her, hungry, wanting something—as a baby would suck at her breast. He shook his head. "I only came to see her. But she isn't to know."

Dilsey lowered her face but looked at him with bold eyes. "That's mighty cruel."

Suddenly the child she held reached her tiny arms out to the man. He looked at her, and then again at Dilsey, saying, "Whose?"

"Not Eliza's, if that's what you was thinkin'," Dilsey answered, narrowing her gaze with a lift of her chin. "She ain't hardly seen a man that weren't her kin since . . . since you been gone." She waited, then added, "What you really come back for?"

A bobwhite called from near the water. "Just to see her."

"Just look and say nothin'?"

"Yes." He controlled her with his eyes, moved her; she looked away. The baby reached up and pulled at her chin. And then again he spoke, "Have her come out to the cabin. I'll watch from outside. She won't see me."

She defied him with a look of scorn. He had no right to boss her now. "How come you ain't come to get her? She been waitin'. She won't say it, but I know she been hopin' you'd come back. And now here you is—come back, but not to take her, just to look. It seems mighty cruel to me."

Houston studied her, then brought out a small leather wallet, from which he took six silver coins. He held them out to her. Even in his large hand they were not dwarfed, but seemed a fortune, silver pieces glittering there in silver evening light. Dilsey shifted her eyes to the big house; no one was in sight. The money could buy something nice for her baby. Margaret made a small cooing sound and reached for the coins, which Dilsey took as a sign. "I'll get Eliza," she said with feigned reluctance, careful not to eye the money, "if you swear to only look and say nothin', unless you choose to stay for good or take her with you."

"You have my word," he said. "She will not see me."

She took the coins and tucked them into the pocket of her smock. They were heavy, and made the pocket sag; she shifted Margaret so her plump legs hung down over the sag. "Case you forgot, my cabin's that one there. With the chimney. If you get outside the window, I'll fix it so you can see in." She suppressed a coy smile; playing games on a white—any white, even Eliza, as much as she loved her—had its justice. And telling a man like Governor Sam Houston what to do, well, it felt fine. . . . She turned toward the house, saying, "Hide yourself good." The child held to her shoulder, smiling at Sam Houston as she was carried away.

The Raven concealed himself in buckbrush outside the window of Dilsey's cabin. For a moment he crouched, then stood, thinking he should not go through with this. Then he lowered himself again into the brush, his heart beating like the drums in the Green Corn dance, a steady pulse, hard and boding. He would be leaving his home, Wigwam Neosho on the banks of the Neosho River, for Texas in November. Tiana had said she would not go with him—she would stay with her family. Again he would be alone, moving west, following his call. . . . When the gray wolf howled it was from the west; when the eagle and the raven flew it was toward the west, toward Texas, his grand scheme, the web now mended, its strands all back in place. Jackson had furnished the money for him to go—five hundred dollars—and the pretense: to learn the Indian situation there—and had left the rest to Houston. The Cherokees and scattered tribes between Tennessee and Texas were in agreement with Raven's cause. Seeking respite through action, within weeks of his departure from Tennessee in the spring of 1829 he had gained influence over seven thousand Indians—a strand running through the very center of his scheme. And whites, also, were seeking his counsel and aid. "Matters are getting worse in Texas every day," John Wharton had written. "I will visit my brother there in August. . . . When Texans are ready for action I will be with them. . . . You can be of more service to their cause than any other man. . . . They look for you."

All was in place. Still, something of the familiar sadness persisted. He had thought that the sight of Eliza would release him in some way. But now, waiting, he felt instead a tightening of her hold; she was so near. He recalled the autumn evening when he had asked her to marry him, how they had watched the sun set as he told her of the Indians who searched for the place where the sun lives. "But I think," he had said, "they were searching for the wrong thing. What does it matter where the sun lives, if you can find the sun? They should not have shielded their faces from it. They should have stood the heat and the light, and taken possession of the sun." He had been so wrong. The heat could sear a man's heart and soul, and the light could cast shadows, and the sun would not be taken.

Now the light was gone down, only a silver glow still lingering. He kept his eyes turned on the house, waiting. At last Dilsey came out of the back door, then Eliza, walking behind her and holding the baby, Margaret. His heart cramped at the sight of her with the child in her arms; she seemed only a child herself, diminutive next to Dilsey's height, yet she moved with singular grace. She was wearing black, and her hair was cut short. Rising wind whipped her dress against her body, showing the smallness of it. He felt the old longing, and doubted again that she had ever loved him.

The two women walked without speaking. When they entered the cabin Houston rose and moved closer to the window, two solid planks of wood latched shut. In a moment he heard Dilsey flip the latch, and he stepped aside against the cabin as she opened the shutters outward. She glanced for sight of him but did not see him against the wall in dimming light, concealed in his blanket the colors of earth and autumn. She turned and crossed the room, took a taper from a wooden chest near the door and replaced the short tallow stump in the tin holder on a table near the window. Striking a light, she touched it to the wick. The Raven moved to see her face, angular in the flickering glow, keeping his own features shadowed.

"There," she said to Eliza, turning to the far wall. "There. If the mortar was dry we could have us a fire."

Eliza placed the sleepy child on a patchwork quilt that covered one of two beds, her slender body leaning, her arm curved and her hand supporting the baby's head. Then she moved to the center of the room—the ease in movement he remembered—and stood with her back to the window, looking at the stone fireplace set into hewn logs. "I'll miss you coming to sit by mine," she said at last, softly. His heart twisted; he moved in closer. "But I am glad for you." She continued to look at the fireplace. He wanted her to turn; he wanted to see her face in the light. "It will be another hard winter for Mama, with the new baby due so soon after Margaret. And the cold makes her pain so bad." Then she added, "I'm glad you finally have your fire, though I really will miss you."

Dilsey lowered her eyes and ran her large hand across her belly. "Anyways, I just wanted to show you, 'cause I'm happy with it." She smiled. "And 'cause I figure you had somethin' to do with gettin' it built."

Eliza turned—the familiar tilt of her head—and looked at Dilsey. "You've waited a long time," she said.

Her profile was in full light. She seemed so young and vulnerable without her long hair, the gray eyes set deep by the touch of taperlight. She was not yet twenty-three. Yet the youthful, defiant striving was gone.

Dilsey cut her eyes toward the window. "I guess you know about waitin'," she said.

Eliza turned full face to the open window, moved forward and reached her hands out to the sill. For a moment Raven feared she had seen him, almost hoped she had. He saw she was wearing her wedding ring. The close side of her face glowed in the flickering light, pale wisps of hair catching the light as they lifted in the wind gusting in. Oo-loo-te-ka had taught the Raven that movement can be seen even in darkness; he did not step away from the window, but stood motionless, almost close enough to touch his wife. He smelled the tallow and damp mortar, felt surely she had seen him, but saw her eyes were looking a long way off, past him and out into the dark.

She spoke in a whisper. "Yes. I know about waiting." She paused, her eyes steady. "I saw coming out here the red oaks are turning already; the oak upstream where I go sometimes is starting to drop." Again she was quiet. Then, "The leaves were just the same when he asked me to marry him. Papa was weaning the foals."

Dilsey moved closer in apprehension. Could Eliza have seen him? It was dark, there was no moon, but the heart—the heart sees so many things. Perhaps, Dilsey thought, it was the spirits of the woods eating at her soul that made Eliza speak into the black night and reach her hand out against the wind and say again, in a soft animal whimper, "Papa was weaning the foals."

A heavy gust of wind rustled the trees and dry buckbrush. Dilsey spread both hands over her belly and baby Margaret cried out from the bed. Sam Houston reached out and took one step toward Eliza, almost into the light. Then another gust came on with force, and Eliza leaned out and pulled the shutters closed.

AFTERWORD

After leaving Nashville in April of 1829 Sam Houston resigned his United States citizenship and resided with Tiana Rogers Gentry in Arkansas, serving as Cherokee ambassador to Andrew Jackson. Legend says he was known by two Cherokee names, *Ka'lanu*, "the Raven," and *Oo-tse-tee Ar-dee-tah-skee*, translated "Big Drunk." He refused to speak English, and in Cherokee raiment lay about Cantonment Gibson, often too intoxicated to mount his horse and ride home to his wigwam. Christian missionaries found him to be a log in their already thorny path. "We regard the residence of . . . Governor Houston among the Indians as a most injurious circumstance," one missionary noted. "He is vicious to a fearful extent and hostile to Christians and Christianity . . . he has very considerable influence."

In December of 1832, before crossing Red River into Texas, Houston reported his "health and spirits good . . . habits sober, and . . . heart straight." Eight days later he entered Texas.

Sam Houston in Texas is another story. He was commander-in-chief of the army which won Texan independence in 1836. Twice he served as president of the Republic of Texas, and held the offices of senator and governor when Texas joined the United States. He reportedly claimed that Sam Houston "made" Texas, and an adversary commented mournfully that Texas was "very little more than Big Drunk's big ranch." Probably United States history would have been different had he never left there. Certainly Texas history would have been different had he never arrived there.

In 1837 Houston divorced Eliza, and in 1840 married Margaret Temple Lea of Alabama. A friend of Houston's suspected the marriage would fail, writing of Houston that "in all my intercourse with life I have never met with an inidividual more totally disqualified for domestic happiness." Yet the union lasted, and produced eight children. In time Houston renounced the bottle and joined a Baptist church. Upon baptism in a stream near his Huntsville, Texas, home the minister told him his sins had all been washed away. Houston replied, "Lord help the fish down below."

While serving as governor of Texas he spoke out against secession and was deposed because he would not pledge his allegiance to the Confederacy. He honored Jackson's creed—"The Union: it must be preserved." As his name was called repeatedly to come forward and take his oath to the Confederacy, Houston sat whittling. He left the governor's mansion in March 1861, the month Eliza died at her home in Tennessee.

In his last days he suffered from the familiar pains of old war wounds, particularly the "San Jacinto ankle," and from watching the Union he had fought to defend split apart, and the state he had won and nurtured turn away from him. The United States was engaged in a civil war; Texas was sinking with the Confederacy; Sam Houston, Jr., was serving in the Confederate army; and the Cherokee Nation was only a remnant. Houston died July 26, 1863, believing that all he had fought for was lost and his endeavors were in vain. But he kept his convictions. In his personal dictionary, on the page where the word *temporize* is defined "to comply with the time or occasion, to yield . . ." a solid line is marked through the word and definition, and in the margin is Houston's notation, "Out with it!"

After her separation from Sam Houston, Eliza retired from society, reportedly in a mood of "dejection and despondency." One acquaintance wrote that she "lived a life of complete seclusion for a year or two—a picture of perfect woe. She afterwords professed religion and was at times quite cheerful, but the look of sadness never, so long as I knew her, left her face." In 1832 Laetitia Allen died at age forty, after giving birth to her tenth child. The following year Colonel John Allen was kicked in the abdomen by a horse and died a few days later. Eliza then devoted herself to caring for her younger siblings.

In October 1836 John Campbell, a relative of Eliza, wrote to Sam Houston:

Dear Genl.

I have now an opportunity of sending you a letter by a private conveyance . . . and . . . know that the subjects I will touch on will be more than interesting to your feallings.

    I passed through Tennessee on my way to this place; and spent two or three weeks there part of the time at my Brother Davids . . . in Lebanon. Mrs. Houston was there about the time the news that you had gained the victory over Santa Anna . . . reached that place. . . . She showed great pleasure at your success and fairly exulted. . . . No subject . . . was so interesting to her as when you were the subject of conversation; and she shew evident marks of displeasure and mortification if some person was to say anything unfavorable of you. . . . Some of her friends wanted her to git a divorce; and she positively refused; and said she was not displeased with her present name; therefore she would not change it on this earth; but would take it to the grave with her.—she has conducted herself with great surcumspiction and prudence and with great dignity of character so much that she has gained the universal respect of all that knows her. She is certainly a most estimable woman; to have sustained herself as she has under all difficulties she has had to encounter.—I have dwelt on this subject as I believed it to be one that would not try your patience.

If Houston answered Campbell's letter there is no record of his response. Later that month he was sworn in as president of the Republic of Texas. Eliza was legally first lady of a country she would never see. It was in April of the following year that Houston obtained a divorce, resting his application "mainly on the length of time that has elapsed since the separation" and "the impossibility of a reunion."

In November 1840, six months after Houston's marriage to Margaret Lea, Eliza married Dr. Elmore Douglass of Gallatin, a widower with ten children. She bore him four children. The eldest, Martha, lived to age twenty-five; her only child was named Eliza Haggard and died as an infant. Eliza's second daughter died of tuberculosis, "consumption," at age ten, and the third at age thirty-five. A fourth child, William H. Douglass, lived only eight months.

Eliza Allen Houston Douglass died of stomach cancer on March 3, 1861, at age fifty-one. She has no descendants. Tradition holds that before her death she requested all likenesses of herself destroyed, all personal letters and papers burned, and an unmarked grave. She left not even a signature and was buried without a stone in the Gallatin cemetery. A century later a marker was placed on her grave.

ACKNOWLEDGMENTS

For their help in the creation of this novel, I am grateful to these friends:

Neal R. McCrillis, for his search into the society of 1820s Tennessee, and Eva Barnes Denning, a lifetime resident of Gallatin, for her ability to ferret out both facts and fables.

John Jenkins, who shared with me his knowledge of obscure historical records. These forgotten accounts gave breath to pedantic data.

Liz Carpenter, who read the entire first draft one night in a ranch house in the Texas hill country while a storm ripped trees from the bluff, and thereafter lent her singular enthusiasm to the project.

Bill Moyers, for his interest, Richard B. Rice, of the Sam Houston Memorial Museum, for his time, and Dr. Jody Potts, for her insight into nineteenth-century women.

My literary agent, Lisa DiMona, who does not tread with trepidation, for her conviction and her efforts.

Betsy Williams, who gave the manuscript close scrutiny; it is better for it.

Stephen Harrigan, who took time from his own writing. His guidance was gentle and astute. He received an Eliza I had partly discovered, and partly created, and helped me to liberate and discern her. Without a word that sounded anything like criticism, he led me to significant changes.

I am also beholden to Jeff Long, a fine writer, for helping me find and unburden the soul of this novel. And for his friendship.

And to Marshall De Bruhl.

I offer a most special thanks to Lawrence A. Stone.

I am grateful to Bill Lowman, who saw this effort as a book long before I could.

And I offer true gratitude to my editors at Doubleday, Jacqueline Kennedy Onassis and Shaye Areheart, who made the endeavor worthwhile.

My family provided essential support. Charles Butt financed much of the research and was a source of encouragement. Mary Holdsworth Butt read the manuscript with a grandmother's appreciation, accepting the vulgarities with good grace. William Crook, Jr., and Noel Crook Moore devoted hours of listening; I consider each moment a gift. Their comments were always perceptive. Eileen C. Vance blithely picked her way with me through the brambles of Tennessee in search of long-forgotten cemeteries. Eleanor Butt Crook also shared in that probe into the past, and as the story evolved proofed consecutive drafts for nuance and cohesion.

My father, William H. Crook, was truly my touchstone. When, at various stages, I buried myself in tedium and lost all but a worm's-eye perspective, he lifted me to eye level with my characters, and sometimes to the bird's-eye view, with its detachment and peripheral scope.